Dimar: Lost Waters
The first of the Dimar Series

Dimar: Lost Waters
The first of the Dimar Series

Dee Dreslough

greatunpublished.com
Title No. 588
2001

Dimar: Lost Waters
The first of the Dimar Series

CONTENTS

Introduction

Greetings, and Welcome to Dimar.

Dee here. I made this novel public domain so that you can feel free to be inspired by it however you like.

What does public domain mean? It means I will not enforce my copyright over this work, except to the extent that enforcement is necessary to keep Dimar free and available for everyone.

What does this mean for you:

You can draw pictures based on it. You can sell these pictures. They are your property and you will hold copyright over them.

You can write stories based on it, and publish them. Your stories are your own, and you will hold copyright over them.

You can print this book and sell it. Anyone can, in the form it is presented in on my website and in this edition.

You can run games, write games, create anything you want based on Dimar and with no fear of getting sued by me.

It's YOURS as much as it is mine. Public domain is compared to the shared land of parks, government buildings and highways. We all own it. We all benefit from it being free.

Okay...Legal mumbo jumbo out of the way. Whew.

The book's rough, I know. Dozens upon DOZENS of rejections from publishing agents have told me this-you don't need to tell me again. And, the concepts in it are hardly new ground for science fiction.

I love this world and it's characters, and I draw them incessantly. So, if you want to understand my art, it will help you to struggle through my writing. And, I'd like to share this playground I live in with you.

What the heck brought on this massive collection of words?

Dimar is a place where I can just let my imagination and problem solving ability run wild. I find myself thinking "Wouldn't it be cool if there was a world that had...", and then I create a rationale for it to exist. And it gets incorporated into Dimar. If you can think of it, it probably has a way of happening on Dimar. It's more of a fantasy than sci-fi, really, but I like engines and ships and medical technology. The unexplained nature of magic has never sat well with me. So, I tried to emulate effects of magic that I liked with crude psuedo-scientific explanations.

And, I wanted to create a way for the creatures of my dreams to become *real*. I have a friend who's a geneticist who's talked of how eventually, in our distant future, we'll tinker with genetic code to get what we want. I like this idea, but I'm not crazy about the slap-dash way humans have of creating things. So I thought-"Hey...why not just create a race that could engineer anything I wanted and do it with the discipline and knowledge to do it right? And, since they've got to be really smart and really cool, they've got to look like my favorite fantasy creature (dragons)!" The Dimar were born, and my novel long adventure in wish fulfillment began.

There are reasons why Dimar look like our historical dragons-it's not just a coincidence, and this will be covered in short stories to come. You can probably guess where our legends come from... Again, I'm sure my little fantasies are hardly new ground, but it helps me flesh out the world.

I like to share, as if my art copying policy at www.dreslough.com doesn't make this obvious. I welcome you, if you like this world, to write your own stories and draw your own pictures of Dimar and share them with me and others. Thanks to this new and wonderful world of Print-On-Demand publishing, we now have a way to share our visions in print. I plan to compile several anthologies of stories written by readers of Dimar: Lost Waters, so if you have a story, please submit it! You don't need to make your work public domain, either. You're welcome to hold copyright and sell your work.

I also would eventually like to found a permanent MUSH or some kind of interactive game on this world. Stop by Dimar.org to get the latest news on interactive games and new features in the Dimar universe.

And please, realize that this book is only the very first, at the very start of the history of Dimar-Earth contact. I will outline in rough form what evolves on the planet over time. The possibilities are ENDLESS! If you have something you'd like to see happen on Dimar, but aren't sure how it would come about, drop me a line at dee@dreslough.com and I bet together, we can figure a way for it to happen in one of the corners of this very very big world.

I will continue to create my own evolution of Dimar, and you are welcome to create an entirely different alternate Dimar if you want! Take the world in any direction you want. I just want to have like minds to share with, in this new virtual wonderland.

I write for myself. I share because I am proud of what I've done, and I'd like to meet people and share my dreams with them. In turn, I hope they share their dreams with me, and I can help them 'grow' their worlds, through my art, through my stories, and through my support. Perhaps we can build a world together. I'll give you unlimited virtual space if you'll do me the same favor.

-Dee Dreslough
dee@dreslough.com-Please, no flames.

Please visit www.dreslough.com or www.Dimar.org for the very latest on the Dimar Project!

Prologue

The Gate Program

In the year 2072, a military pilot program in conjunction with several major worldwide universities was approved by the United Nations. A select team of scientists was transported by a set of new ion drive ships to Earth's outpost at Pluto. Project Darkstar had permission for a limited testing of a theory involving exotic matter and black holes. If the results were promising, further experimentation in the next decade would be funded and permitted.

Not sure what the team would find, they generated two small black holes at the furthest reachable edge of the solar system, barely within the orbit of our sun. As expected from calculations, the force of these two tiny singularities ripped a hole in the fabric of space. They sent a probe through, receiving a variety of data for a few seconds before the gate closed. The data from the probe was conclusive: it did survive and pass through to the other side. The project was immediately classified.

In secret, several small holes were opened over the course of the two-year experimentation period. The team was able to pop one gate closed and use the force from this operation to open the next. Using exotic matter, they found they could open the gates and keep them stable. By the third year, the gates had graduated to a larger and practical size: the Large Gate.

Although data was collected at a phenomenal rate, no one

knew why the gates worked, and funding was quickly drying up for the project. The possible practical applications of the gates were staggering, but no holes had opened near enough to any system to make them useful.

Arrallin-Human Contact

The fifth Large Gate changed all that. The glimmering hole opened just within ion drive range of a tiny system in a far wing of the galaxy. A flickering candle in space, the gateway beckoned the ships of the nearest inhabited planet to it like moths.

The Arrallins themselves found humanity irresistible. The Arrallins are a hive species, comprised of thousands of Arallakeeni "Beta" individuals all centered on supporting the Arrallin "Alpha" mated pairs. Charismatic and self-serving humans registered quite immediately to the Arrallakeeni as leaders.

Captains and individuals with strong personalities on human fleet ships found themselves mobbed by little furry groupies, long separated from their own true Arrallin Alphas back on their home world.

Much of the Arrallin population had been put to service on their long range fusion drive ships to mine neighboring star systems for valuable materials for more hives. Their dedicated engineers had worked up through numerous designs for engines to create a stable and efficient sub-light vehicle. Plasma weaponry for fighting the occasional hive wars, as well as mining and construction, were also well developed.

Their technology was well beyond Earth in all respects, however their biology had not well adapted to their space-faring lifestyle.

Unsupported by close contact with Alphas, the Arrallakeeni on board these ships lacked the leadership support they needed to keep at peak efficiency. On long voyages of years at a time, Arrallakeeni found themselves in Alpha withdrawal. Armies of Arrallakeeni deserted their home world almost instinctively upon contact with humans, gladly providing them with the keys to fusion drives and plasma tools to bring them up from the dark ages of space exploration, in return for the security of finding strong personalities to trigger some of the necessary chemical reactions for Arallakeeni health.

Back on Earth, humanity was quick to adapt to their new partners as well. Within a generation, they found places for Arallakeeni in all aspects of human life-especially all the humdrum jobs humans were reluctant to continue. Grinding research in all manner of human projects was taken over by dedicated and patient teams of Arallakeeni, while the more intuitive humans were free to lead and guide research and analyze results. This particular pairing was positive. Arallakeeni also made excellent teachers and child care specialists, as on Arralla they would each be paired with an Arallakeeni infant for raising. But, the arrival of the Arallakeeni also completely destroyed humanity's current way of life.

Causes of the Unwilling War

Without a profit motive, Arallakeeni destabilized the entire capitalist system on Earth. They would fix a person's car because it was broken, not because they would be paid. They would do what was asked of them because it was unheard of on Arralla for an Alpha to ask anything of a hive member that was not in the best interest of the Hive. They were, at the start, a willing slave population. In all aspects of society, demand for Arallakeeni rose to a clamorous level, and regard for their individual rights, needs and personalities dropped.

Over the next seventy years, flaws in this situation made themselves evident. Alphas needed their Betas on Arralla to continue parenting the population of their planet. (Betas take guardianship of kits produced by the Alphas of a hive, producing milk to nourish them.) Arallakeeni could not be true parents on Earth—they needed to receive their children from the Alphas on Arralla, and to trigger milk production, they needed to be in contact with an Arrallin Alpha for at least three months. Some Arallakeeni could find satisfaction in raising human infants, but for most, the drive to continue their species the Arrallin way was overwhelming. The life spans of Arrallakeeni on Earth were becoming alarmingly short from stress, as they were refused the right to return to Arralla to start families and receive kits from the Alphas of their Hive.

Physically, exposure to Alphas was essential for Beta health. On Earth, Arrallakeeni were completely removed from exposure to Alphas, and in less than half a normal life span they would sicken, go mad and die. Young betas taken to Earth would grow stunted, and lacked the aptitudes of those whom had spent their entire maturing years in the presence of a true Alpha.

Despite their physical need to spend part of their time in the presence of an Alpha leader, Arrallakeeni as individuals are as diverse as humans themselves and many were great leaders in their own right. Most leader-oriented Arallakeeni betas, a large subset of the beta population, were unable to find comfortable positions on Earth. On Arralla, they generally rose in the ranks to positions of ship captains, diplomatic liaisons, societal leaders and even stewards of entire Hives in situations where the mated pairs were too young or inexperienced to take leadership. Some of these individuals found places on Earth where their ability and status were recognized, but many were cast out as aberrations to the more desirable servile beta norm.

After 70 years (a beta lifetime), the effects of the human/ Arrallin situation were becoming alarmingly clear. Entire hives were on the verge of extinction on Arralla, but shuttle ships from Earth continued to arrive, loaded with their best pitch-people to lure Betas to Earth to work for corporations that had thrived during the early Arrallin contact. Exploitive humans had seen the problem coming and secretly mounted defenses around the tenuous wormhole that linked Arralla to Earth. Trade ships quietly carried armament, and various hive heavy cruisers turned up missing more and more often. Alphas were lavished with the best humanity had to offer to ensure that the situation was still considered mutually beneficial.

Just as human leaders can forget the needs and rights of those under their leadership, some Alphas had grown indolent and spoiled with centuries of comfortable living under the constant care of their Arrallakeeni. The health and fate of the Arallakeeni outside of their immediate court and provinces was of no concern to them. They would now gladly produce and raise more children and send them to Earth, for a price. But for some, the situation was too painful to continue.

The Unwilling War

The Unwilling War, as it was known, was a long and sordid affair. Individual hive leaders began to mount resistance to Earth's advances, ripping through fleets that approached Arralla. However, they were unwilling to crash the gateway between Earth and Arralla as many held the continued hope that they could rescue and return their Arallakeeni to the home world. Shutting the gate would have quickly ended the conflict, but the tactic could never be agreed upon by the strongly individualistic Hives.

For the first four years, it was vicious open war, with successful strikes against many places on Earth by pirate fleets on the earth side of the gate. Attacks on the gate guardians on the Arrallin side were also successful, but they never captured control of the gate. This was in part because of participation of the complacent Hives, who lent their ships to the Arrallin effort, but their people to Earth. The Arrallin fighters had been constantly demoralized by having to fire on their own brethren on board Earth ships, all now unwilling conscripts. Because of this they tended to damage rather than destroy the earth ships sent against them.

Earth-friendly hives would secretly supply these damaged ships with fresh Arallakeeni crews for repairs. This gave Earthers the breathing room they needed to hold out for the first four years and maintain control of the gate.

In the first four years, all older Arrallakeeni on board the ships would refuse to repair them, even fatally sabotage the ships resulting in the death of all on board. The new Arallakeeni were specially groomed for the war and worked willingly, believing the propaganda fed to them by both Earth and their Alphas. By the end of the first four years, all Arallakeeni from the first generation of contact were executed quietly and without trial on the fleet ships and on Earth. Earth's guns blazed on in the silence of space, computer guided and controlled, as Arallakeeni-operated guns and ships faltered and failed with insufficient supplies and support.

Earth never lost control of the wormhole. Hives dedicated to the defeat of Earth made vast concessions to their complacent neighbors to continue their effort. As the war dragged on much longer than the Hives expected, they found their holdings completely absorbed by their neighbors, who in turn used their resources to populate Earth's fleet ships with Arallakeeni.

After fifteen years of fighting, the war reached its inevitable end. Of ten thousand hives on Arralla, each with fifty to one hundred breeding Alphas per hive, one hundred and seventeen still existed in their original form on the home world. All others were believed to have been destroyed; their breeding pairs lost leading fleet ships into battle against Earth. The one hundred and seventeen Hives remained to produce Arrallakeeni to suit the needs of Earth, unwilling to hear the cries of protest from their own populations for freedom. With only 7,020 known Alphas left, and complete removal of the balanced system that had produced the Arallakeeni populations of the first generation of contact, the entire species was dying, but no one seemed willing to face it.

Effects of Human-Arrallin Contact

When Arralla was discovered by humans, there were 2 billion individuals in its population. This was comprised of essentially 4,000 hives, with 250,000 members each, split into provinces that varied based on terrain and resources. Each Hive had between 50-100 mated pairs, each with a breeding life span of 50 years, in which they could produce 100 kits a year in three litters. By the end of the Unwilling War, there were one hundred and seventeen

Hives remaining, with 50 million total individuals on the planet or on Earth. Imagine the current population of Earth reduced to approximately the size of the population of Nigeria. This is what happened to Arralla.

The Gate program had continued over this hundred years unabated, despite having uncovered only two useable systems. The discovery of Arralla had proved so profitable humanity would continue it indefinitely, honing gate-opening skills and profiting from the technological boost from Arralla.

The Insurrection

Humanity's role in Arralla's downfall did not unnoticed, and, typical to our species, the outcry for equal rights for the Arrallins was powerful, but late. The fight to save Arralla on Earth took many forms, but one in particular was separatist movement. This is where the story begins.

Tara Hunt, a retired Lt. Colonel of the United Earth Command (United Earth Confederacy's military branch), now working under the guise of a private trading and colonization company, heads one wing of the separatist resistance. She is leading three mated pairs and two betrothed Alphas hidden among the Arallakeeni on her ships on a search for a colony world or system where they can re-establish a Hive in balance with humanity.

For my dad, who believes in the power of my creations, even though he's not really sure what they are.

Special Thanks:
Clay Dreslough, Ian Smith, Eugene Arenhaus, Paul 'Draco', Meilin Wong, David 'Taemar' Baxter and everyone else who sent in edits and wonderful supportive comments!

Chapter 1

Tara stood stock-still, waiting for the first tiny gleam from the scout craft to appear in the darkness of the wormhole. The gentle constant breeze of recycled air from the vent above blew an annoying hair against her nose, but she ignored it.

A gasp from the psychic broke her silent vigil, and she turned.

"Results, Harmon?" she suppressed the surge of annoyance that ran through her as she contemplated the psi's gift of getting all the hot news first.

Harmon's face slowly animated—joy sweeping in to replace stern concentration. "Tarrin says the planet's a freaking gemstone! Thriving with life, large and small forms, no buildings of any kind, hydrocarbons, metals, and a stable atmosphere. He's not even bringing them back through for a face-to-face briefing. He says we should come through now, immediately, before the probe is reported late."

"Harmon, tell that good for nothing son of a beta to get his hindquarters through the gate and back here NOW, or I'll open fire on him when we come back through." Tara fumed. Of all the impertinence! Tarrin, no doubt with orders from Mason, was questioning her command decisions. *That's what I get for not using mercenaries.*

She returned to her watch, regarding her own reflection in the long window. Mahogany-black curly hair, cut short in the typical military style framed a careworn, dark-skinned face. It was not an attractive face right now; her ebony eyes shadowed by hours on the watch, full lips pursed with frustration. She had the look of every leader she had ever known. At six foot two, she stood a full head taller than even her Arrallin first officer. Her glowering expression completed the imposing effect. She picked imaginary flecks off her stark gray jumpsuit, and snorted. *You look like hell, Tar. Don't blow this. Don't let fatigue get to you.*

She used the discretion of the mirrored window to secretively survey her crew. Harmon was an excellent addition to the bridge team, but was she open minded enough to defy United Earth Command and sever all ties from Earth? She watched the psi bob her head, unaware of the rest of the bridge, shaking blonde curls as she chattered away with the approaching psi relay on Mason's ship. She seemed so depthless—self conscious and shallow on the outside, but having that incredible gift. There had to be more to her.

Well, if she didn't pan out, she'd be terminated. Any crewmember that would jeopardize the project was meat. It would be a shame to lose that talent, though.

Rakal, her first officer, was staring pensively at his panel. He was what this was all about. She watched his graceful fingers ending in thick black claws tap out calculations on the panel. His pointed ears swiveled back and forth, catching every sound from the bridge, while his long tail swished to the rhythm of his thoughts. Only those humans of the Arrallin Insurrection inner team knew he was no common 'beta furry'. His silken fur, which would be tawny golden and striped with jet-black bands, was dyed perfectly to a pure black, and his mane trimmed and thinned as to be indistinguishable from the rest of his coat. His eyes had been treated and darkened to a rich purple to disguise the brilliant golden yellow color that would mark him as an Alpha Arrallin, and leader of his hive. And, humans didn't "see with smell" like Arrallakeeni betas, so that aspect of his leadership was well hidden. The betas all knew, and would die to protect him. But, rather than the dashing leader he would someday be, he looked like an overgrown wolf who'd learned touch-typing.

The scout ship re-emerged from the hole—a brilliant speck

emerging from a sphere of velvety blackness. It's hail crackled across the comm, and Tara spun to retake her seat at the helm. "Launch the second probe. Won't Central be crushed to learn that another gateway has yielded little more than a class F planet and a white dwarf system? Level 1 and 2 staffers should prepare to be briefed and move out. This sounds like it's the one." A distinctive whuffle of pleasure rippled through the betas on the bridge, and Rakal let loose a small growl, as if to caution his charges against false hope. They'd scouted twenty-seven gates so far, and none had turned up anything worth the Insurrection's time. Tara would not let giddy hopes drag them onto a rock that would spell the end for the project, and the Arrallin species.

Chapter 2

Tara waited for the last of the inner circle to file in. Rakal, Tarrin, Mason, Tulera, Kimmer, and finally Marshal.

"Mason, report." Tara barked with irritation.

"It's a one-in-a-million find, sir. Class A, the right mix of nitrogen, oxygen and trace gasses, and a level of life teeming on the surface unlike anything I've had the pleasure of visiting yet. It's vibrant down there, and the plants are a classic carbon based set. Well evolved—possibly far past the level of earth. It's 75% the size of earth, meaning we'll have 75% gravity, but we're not planning on going back to earth after this run anyway." Cy Mason rattled out, getting slightly flushed as he called up chart after chart.

"And, to top it off, despite the age and power on this planet, it has no intelligent life in residence. We went back about 3000 years, and at one point it did indeed have some form of builder, so there are ruins left, but we expect that some form of natural disaster did them in, or they abandoned the planet. They may have been space farers—the ruins show a high level of technology. We'll set the betas loose on it, and they'll go wild. Not only do we have a great place to start Arralla over, we've got new tech to keep the betas from going crazy. They can build all they want." Rakal rumbled with amusement at the comment. "The only problem I can foresee with a settlement is related to these large raptors, and two forms of ground based predators, and the fires that tend to sweep across the land when hydrocarbons release from the planet's crust in the dry season.

The weather is very turbulent, and the ocean currents are strong, and there's no doubt that the indigenous life there may find us a tasty addition to the food chain. And then there's the matter of the bacteria and viral problems, parasites and radiation problems..." Mason stopped to catch his breath, smoothing back his unruly brown hair with one hand as he flipped through page after page of data.

"Radiation? Micro-organisms we can handle, but radiation would render this 'gemstone' of yours completely useless, Cy." Tara called up the radiation scans and started to peruse the data.

"It's not radiation, it's just a strong and erratic magnetic field. This planet has a high iron content, good for building I might add, and the field spectrums that are strongest are, thankfully, harmless to embryo development for humans, and my research tells me also Arrallins. It's no big deal, we just get aurora borealis all over the planet, really. I look forward to lying in the treetops watching it, myself."

Tara cocked an eyebrow at the man. "Okay, Mason...you're obviously moving to this place with or without the rest of us. Let's get an objective review, now, eh? Kimmer, what's your take on Planet Gemstone?" Mason grinned wryly and plucked at his mustache absently, watching Kimmer hopefully. Tara turned to face the calico beta, who swiveled her ears forward and flexed her whiskers nervously.

"Too good to be true, I'd say. Not to say that we shouldn't move in, but we should keep our guard up. I don't like the fact that a planet this far along doesn't already have some form of organized higher life. Something did them in, and it will get us if we dance into this. My recommendation—take the flagship down, and land it for a base camp. Leave the two transports in orbit, and unload one using the scout as a shuttle. We've got hydrocarbons galore down there to work with for refining, and plenty of oxygen ice in the rings around the fourth planet. With the resources down there, we could even go back to gas powered engines if we wanted to for years before we fried ourselves." Tara could see that despite her reservations, Kimmer was still itching to get on this rock and look around.

"Okay... two thumbs up from the experts. Is this it? Votes? Concerns?" Tara surveyed the group.

One by one, the vote counter registered green. "It's ulaminated, sir. We're going!" Kimmer's tail swept along the floor as she tried to keep from yipping with delight.

Tara smiled, "Unanimous, Kim, and yes...we'll go."

Chapter 3

The four ships swung into orbit above the western continent, Tara's Golden Hinde taking the lead ahead of the Dark Hope and Singularity II with the diminutive scout ship Arralla's Pride following behind.

"I'll take the helm, Ir'est. I'd like to land this bird personally." Tara shot a stern glance at the bristling Rakal. She was still reeling from his disobedience. He had no right to risk himself or any other Alphas in this dangerous landing, but refused to transfer to any of the other ships. He argued long for the honor of landing the first ship on the new home world, but she would do the landing. On the new home world, he would far outrank her as a regent of his hive, but for now, she was Captain. If she'd had the time, she would have thrown him in the brig, but they had to start the mission, and she did need him. At least the seven other Alphas remained safe on board the other ships. His ego be damned-he'd have his place in the history of his people. This was her landing.

You'll take a more important place in the songs, my friend—as the head of the first free hive since Gate Five on Earth, she thought to herself, holding back a pang of worry for the Arrallin she had come to respect so much. He was sensitive, and after all he'd been through at the hands of humans, she didn't really want to hurt him now. He took the second seat, and strapped in, slamming the buckle shut with an annoyed clack. Tara allowed not a trace of emotion to flicker across her face, and set her own buckle and adjusted the straps for her larger frame.

The ship reacted sluggishly to her adjustments as she expected. "This is your last flight, you poor old tub—make it a good one." she whispered reverently to the controls. "This will be bumpy... this ship was never designed to make more than an emergency landing in atmosphere. Sound general quarters and get everyone ready for the worst."

The metal screens slowly lowered to cover the windows, shutting out the yellow glow that had begun as the ship dropped lower into the atmosphere. They swept in from over the smaller of the two continents, passing over the wider of the two oceans, dubbed 'Sea of Kayev' by the survey crew. Extending the braking fans, the ship lunged and bucked as it approached the large continent. Her goal was to splash down right near the coast, and pull up to shore to make a base camp, but the ship had other ideas. Tara compensated for the turbulence, pulling up the nose and extending the splashdown pads. "1000, 800, 700, 600, 450 meters". Suddenly, a radiation scale went red as a warning siren sounded.

A ripping blast shook the ship, punctuated by a scream from Harmon. Frantically, Tara tried to keep the nose up as the ship pitched and caught the ground with a wing. The last thing she remembered was Rakal, his fur on end, grabbing her jumpsuit in his teeth, dragging her along with wicked feral strength and muttering "Next time I land..."

Chapter 4

Luuko held his position above the ranks with difficulty. The Wind was extremely unstable this day, which made holding the fire line even more difficult. The last storm had taken out half of the third rank alone, and the worst of the fire season hadn't even begun. Whispering a silent prayer, he stretched his wings out and signaled his partner to rise. Five seasons of experience had taught him that when the leaves of the low lying trees suddenly flipped up, that a fire geyser was about to blow, and this one was dangerously close to the barryd.

The geyser opened with violent force, spewing flames well past the top of the highest trees, which themselves burst out in brilliant yellow green flame. Luuko felt the matriarch's order, and watched five young ones sweep in to douse the trees. *Ah, the bravery of youth. If only I still had that speed and energy,* he commented wryly to his partner. Tewi was struggling to maintain her position in the front line of the rank, to keep those flames from drifting toward the firebreaks around the barryd, but still managed to wiggle her ears with amusement.

Luuko maintained his position with considerably more ease, even though Tewi was five heads taller than he. His knowledge of the Wind, and having to learn to cope with the difficulty of his size had brought him quickly to the top of his flight class. He resisted the urge to whuffle with pride at the thought, for fear that it would distract Tewi. *Pride leads to fireburns* he reminded himself. He'd get a branding from the matriarch if he lorded it over any of his rankmates; that kind of foolishness wasn't tolerated at Telka Barryd, and it was a good thing. The neighboring barryd, Mulkol, was riddled with fire control problems because of the extreme youth of their wings, and the lack of restraint their patriarch had over their carousing. Luuko knew from experience that they were fierce in the territorial dances. He shot a glance at the tear in his right wing, and the long white scar that ran the length of his firescaled side. He'd carry that mark for the rest of the season, thanks to the dancers of Mulkol.

Luuko turned back to his work, eddying the Wind, encouraging it toward the flames to push them back. With the two thousand other Dimar stationed all around the barryd, together they were able to generate a formidable barrier to push the fires away as they started. The younger Dimar flew fire patrols, dousing the brush as it ignited with either foam or The Water.

Luuko watched the five fliers that had been dispatched to save the tree near the fire geyser. Four had foam lita carry bags, and one had a set of three on her back with the Water, and was marked with the banners of the honor guard. He watched as they slowly compressed the lita sacks, dispensing the foam over the seared branches, extinguishing them. The honor guard poured the Water sparingly near the trunk, rejuvenating it somewhat, so that it would not go into shock. *That tree will live to see many more seasons* Luuko rumbled approvingly, broadcasting to the honor guard's distant mind.

As the fire geyser died down, Luuko and his partner dropped back into the tighter formation of his rank, and relaxed, eddied by the strength and support of his rankmates. Three more hours, and he could enjoy a short swim in the Water, and a long sleep on his favorite spire in the barryd. Some Dimar hated this season, but Luuko found it invigorating. He looked forward to taking his shift again in another thirteen hours. *Ah, Wind. You and I are good friends. I enjoy your company, and your support,* he whispered lovingly into the buffeting energy that surrounded him, with respect and reverence. *I'll never find a mate that understands me as well as you do,* he chuckled wryly, careful that Tewi would not hear him. His ramblings about the Wind had brought him trouble as a youth, and he had carefully lead everyone to believe that his worship of the Wind had been just a phase.

As if to answer him, the Wind suddenly changed. Luuko shot a concerned look out across the forest, to see what the problem was. At the same time, he strained to contact the matriarch. *Something's wrong, Great Mother! I'm not sure what it is...* Her answer was troubled. *I felt it too, Child. I have not felt anything like it...LOOK!* She broadcast the image to all the ranks—a flaming star, tumbling down in the far south sky.

With the power that only a matriarch could wield, she summoned all the resting ranks, and they poured forth from every passage in the barryd, filling the sky with the gleaming sinuous bodies of over a hundred thousand Dimar. Quickly, they formed into their respective ranks, taking positions in the Line, awaiting orders. The combined force of all the ranks nearly knocked over the trees around the barryd, and pushed the encroaching fires back four hundred feet.

Luuko listened to the Matriarch organize the ranks absently as he strained to hear a faint cry for help from the south. He hoped the young Ekal Barryd had not been hit by the meteor, but was troubled that the cry he had heard was not familiar to him.

Rank Tinar One—go to investigate with Rank Tinar Four. Luuko wondered why the matriarch would send his firefighting rank, half spent from their watch to go investigate, but was relieved to see that the Fourth rank would be accompanying them. Upon further consideration, he realized that it was wise to keep the freshest wings near the barryd, and to send the more experienced fliers out to Ekal.

Swinging his wings slightly to generate more resistance from the Wind, he rose with his rank to take his place behind the leader. Liur raised his tail in a signal for the assembled Dimar to move out, and in an instant, they were speeding along to the west toward a pillar of white smoke that had begun to billow up from behind the southern mountain range.

They passed low over Ekal, bellowing and broadcasting

greetings to the tiny rank that defended the seedling barryd plant as it grew into a true barryd city like Telka. Luuko saw the pride in their faces as Liur heralded them with the traditional greeting accorded to a full barryd, and felt a momentary pang of remorse for not choosing to follow the new barryd seed when it flew from the blossom spire of Telka four cycles ago. There would be other seeds, and other chances to lead a new barryd to glory, he mused, as they passed over the mountains.

What greeted Luuko's eyes was like nothing he had ever seen before. A typical meteor furrow had cut a swath through the forest jungle below, but where a stone should have been, a twisted boxy metal tree-like structure lay half buried in the rich soil. Trees around the thing burst into flame, parched from the long dry season. Swarming out of it were creatures, the likes of which Luuko had never seen. He recoiled—they were mindless! He felt Liur's horror as he broadcast the images back to the matriarch, and suffused himself in the support of the mind-contact of his rank. They circled the gash in the ground, watching for any form of threatening movement from the creatures that had scattered themselves around the silver tree-thing from which they had come.

With instinctive grace, Luuko followed Liur in close as he gave the order to douse the fires that had started. Bolstered by the support of the Great Mother, and by Rank Four, they made short work of the blazes that were starting all around the twisted metal wreck. The ~~ship~~ had been lucky to crash in a streambed, and the vegetation to either side of it was well fortified against the heat.

Three creatures in particular caught his eye, and the entire rank descended. These creatures had minds! Relief swept through the rank as Liur examined the three, feeling the rich resonation of their thoughts. The matriarch looked on through Liur's eyes, carefully examining the small four legged minds that huddled on the ground. *Greet them, you foolish morraks!* The matriarch commanded, suppressing the fear Liur and Luuko both felt.

Luuko was the first to act, as fear gave way to curiosity. Tentatively, he reached out with his mind, and recoiled as he felt the pain of the golden haired mind. His Dimar sympathy soon took hold of him, and with Liur, they quelled her pain enough for her to speak intelligently. *Her...it is an egg layer, isn't it?* He questioned Liur, who was picking over the memories as the little creature recalled exactly what had just happened to them. Luuko turned his attention to another of the minds, realizing that this one was in much better condition, and had been listening with rapt attention to their exchange with the golden haired mind.

Luuko regarded the healthier creature, noting with approval that this little one was much more like a proper Dimar. Its silky brown fur was flecked with white spots, and it had a long, graceful tail. All in all, it looked very much like a Dimar in the growing season, except that it lacked the strong wings and graceful neck of his kind. Its round face peered up at him, pivoting wide pointed ears in his direction. It held it's narrow muzzle open, displaying rows of white meat-eating teeth.

Carefully, he touched its mind. *...me! Don't eat me! Don't eat me!* It was repeating again and again, and he sensed that it was poised to spring and attack.

I won't eat you, friend. I won't eat you. Luuko flooded his mind with reassurances, showing him that Dimar prefer fish and plants to land-dwellers in a series of visual images. It was a bit of a fib, as Dimar would eat just about anything, but he did prefer fish to land-dwellers himself. He felt the mind relax, and begin to regard him with curiosity and wonder.

What exactly are you? Luuko queried, edging closer to the little one to catch a whiff of him.

I'm an Arrallakeeni—a beta furry to the humans, The mind responded matter-of-factly as it stumbled forward to touch noses with Luuko. Luuko resisted the urge to pull back, realizing that this was a form of greeting for the Arrallakeeni, and that it gave him comfort. The creature smelled musty, like a typical land-dweller, but its command of the talents of mind-speaking were impressive.

Greetings, Arrallakeeni. I am Luuko, of the Dimar of Telka Barryd. I offer friendship. He continued to monitor Liur's progress with the strange looking female mind, learning that these creatures came from beyond the sun seeking refuge from tyrannical forces. To Luuko's surprise, the Arrallakeeni was also listening in on the exchange, and echoed agreement to the statements and images of the female mind, adding his own images of his home, and the human tyrants, and then finally of a larger jet black beast.

With that image, the Arrallakeeni sprang up, and on all fours sprinted off into the crowd of mindless ones amassed behind them, beckoning desperately for Luuko to follow. *We have to find the Arrallin—we have to find Rakal! He is the only hope for the Arrallakeeni—he is our only Hive leader. We must keep him safe!*

Luuko started into the crowd, threading his way past the mindless humans as they tended their wounded, toward a knot of the furry creatures, who, obviously were bent on keeping this Arrallin safe as well. They fluffed out their fur coats and growled, showing sharp fangs. They ranged from speckled ones like the Arrallakeeni mind, to mottled calicos, browns, blacks, stripes, painted patterns, all with swishing angry tails, bright eyes and dangerous looking teeth. They clumped together around an unseen object, blending into one giant knot of fur and fury. Luuko put his ears forward and lowered his head in greeting, hoping that his fire-scales would protect him from any misunderstandings with those sharp fanged ones. The Arrallakeeni barked out some kind of command, and Luuko discreetly listened in on his thoughts to find out just exactly what he was telling them.

To his shock and amazement, the little Arrallakeeni was giving them a clear picture of his barryd, including details that Luuko had not included in his introduction. The little morrak had read into his mind for more details! Luuko swished his tail with aggravation. It was in very poor form to break into someone's thoughts, punishable by a month in the muck-room, but perhaps the little one hadn't known that. Luuko chuckled at his own foolishness. *Of course the little one didn't know that. He's not Dimar. Perhaps where they come from, it's a well-accepted practice to sneak into the minds of others. However, with all these mindless ones, I can't see how he'd manage it. He must be quite a talent to have prying abilities with no one to practice with. Well, I'll return the favor while he's getting those blank-minds to let down their guard.*

Discreetly, Luuko pried further into the memories of the Arrallakeeni, learning that they, a bit like the Dimar, had a patriarchal and matriarchal structure, and that they were protecting their leader, Rakal. He was one of very few patriarchs left, so they needed to protect him. *Why protect him? Why not just choose another from the ranks?* His curiosity led him to delve further, and again, he suffered a shock. *Only the Leaders can breed! How terrible!* He withdrew quietly as he realized that the Arrallakeeni was becoming aware of his indiscretion. He could feel that the Arrallakeeni was not angry at his prying, and he was greatly relieved. He wondered if the humans were also part of the Hive in the Arrallakeeni's pictures. The Arrallakeeni heard his query, and filled his mind with images in explanation, all while encouraging the defensive knot of other Arrallakeeni to let down their guard.

Luuko relayed his findings to the matriarch, who, also in very poor form, had been listening in on his exchange with the little mind without telling him. *These humans seem to be quite a muddled bunch, Great Mother. Here, one group has nearly killed the leaders of the Arrallakeeni hives, and yet this bunch of humans with them fights like fire-born to save them. We'll have to be careful about them, and about this patriarch of which they speak.* The Great Mother was strangely silent for a while, and absently answered him with an affirmative. Luuko wondered how she'd react to these alien visitors.

Slowly, the mindless ones disengaged from one another, melting back into individuals, and moving away from one extremely large member of the knot. Luuko knew immediately that this was the patriarch in the Arrallakeeni's images, and could sense his personal strength, even if his mind lacked the rich color and resonance of a Dimar. His deep violet eyes matched the blooms of the barryd, and with a confident and piercing gaze he sized up Luuko. He rose onto his hind legs, muscles rippling beneath his lustrous jet-black coat, and the Arrallakeeni all had their eyes on him. Truly, this was their great leader, Luuko mused, feeling the pride from the little

Arrallakeeni mind that had guided him here. The Arrallin raised a front leg, extending his clawed fingers, and then retracting them, turning his palm toward the sky. In low, guttural tones, he spoke, but the noise meant nothing to Luuko. Desperately, Luuko tried to get even a glimmer of resonance from the patriarch's mind, but it was flat and toneless. He had no idea what the Leader was saying, and just waited.

The little Arrallakeeni was kind enough to intercede. *I, Tarrin, shall interpret, Luuko. Rakal Arralla, of Hive Yenzenti greets you, Luuko of the Dimar of Telka Barryd. Rakal requests permission to settle on your home world, and to build in peace and communion with your Dimar kindred a new future for his people.*

Luuko, in the Dimar spoken tongue answered with a formal greeting, echoing the meaning to Tarrin, explaining in his best formal speech that his request would be heard by their Leader, the matriarch, and by all the leaders of the barryds and an answer would be forthcoming. In an aside to Tarrin, he apologized for not being able to give an immediate answer on the question of residency, and hoped that this would not be considered an insult. The laughter in Tarrin's thoughts reassured him that his answer had been more than adequate, and that his worries were a bit foolish, but understandable.

It's not often that a completely alien race dumps itself on your back doorstep, Luuko. You're doing quite well in dealing with this, all things considered. Luuko was surprised at how quickly he had become accustomed to Tarrin's voice in his mind. Already, Tarrin felt like an old friend.

The black-coated patriarch spoke again, gesturing to the motionless form of a human on the ground. Her foreleg was bloody, and the covering on her side was rent, exposing deep wounds along her side. Luuko turned back to Tarrin, awaiting the translation.

This is Tara, leader of the humans pledged to help us rebuild our world and our people. She is in dire need of medical help—can you assist us in reviving her? Tarrin's mind was filled with worry for the human, and his fondness for her and her people was genuine.

Luuko mused, regarding the ugly, hairless female with a bit of contempt. He scoffed privately at Tarrin's concern, but consulted the matriarch anyway.

Great Mother, these people have wounded with them. Can we take them to the Water?

The matriarch's rich mind-voice filled his ears. *That is a good question, Child. However, it is risky to expose our treasure to them—we must mislead them at this time, until we know they can be trusted. If only they had more minds among them.* The matriarch's voice was tired, and Luuko realized that she had been both monitoring the fire line and all the minds of the Ranks here during the firestorm. She dispatched the entire honor guard to meet them, and echoed the order to the ranks to keep them informed. She also cautioned all Dimar against allowing the alien minds to learn of the Water, or of the Seeds, until she knew more about these visitors.

Chapter 5

Tara blinked, squinting against the intense light of the sun. She listened for the moans of pain around her, expecting to hear a chorus of trouble. To her surprise, she only heard excited babble, and the distinct and unnerving sound of Arrallins in mourning. There had been fatalities, after all, but what of injuries? Her left arm tingled, as did her side. She shut her eyes and grunted, bracing herself for what she might see.

She opened her eyes again, and looked down at her arm. It was in one piece, but her dark skin was mottled with unnaturally white skin, and her sleeve and uniform side were blood-soaked, although she couldn't see the wound.

"What the..." she uttered, and turned her head to see what could only be described as a massive blue-green dragon walking straight toward her.

Screaming, she leapt up and grabbed a piece of twisted metal from the wreckage, and swung it wildly at the beast as it loomed above her. "RAKAL!! HARMON! GET THE RIFLES!!" She hollered, managing to regain her command voice as the creature stopped and seated itself in front of her. She planted her feet for her best home run swing as the creature lowered its huge scaly head into her striking range.

"I wouldn't do that, Tara! It's not polite to smack the critter that saved your life, you know." Rakal's deep, amused voice boomed out over the crowd. Tara dropped the metal mid-swing, just missing the

creature's head, sending the bar flying into the rubble. She sank
to her knees, thanking the stars that Rakal had made it to the
surface alive. The dragon just cocked its head and continued to watch
her intently. With adrenaline flooding her veins, she instinctively
resumed command, and demanded full status reports.

"Rakal, what the HELL is going on here? What are these
things? New pets? Well, you damned well better keep them off the
furniture—that's for sure. What the hell happened?" Her memories
of the landing flooded back into her mind, and she felt the sweat
break on her neck. Rakal ambled up on all fours, a feral Arrallin
grin on his muzzle, and just chuckled. "Why aren't we dead, Rakal?
Mmmm? Can you tell me that?" She muttered at him through
clenched teeth.

Rakal sat, wrapping his silky tail around his feet in a catlike
manner. Tara knew he was enjoying this situation immensely. "We're
not dead because, despite that magnetic storm that threw the entire
Golden Hinde navigation computer into deep space, you did manage
to land us flatly. We went into a tumble, you know. Do you remember
that much?"

Tara half-smiled back at him, appreciating the supportive words
in the face of the disaster. "I do remember that 'next time, I land'
comment, bub." She tried to hold back a grim expression as she
replayed the landing in her mind.

"We lost four betas—only FOUR...out of three hundred, and
we lost three humans—three out of sixty, and they were expendable
humans, if you get my meaning." Rakal was quick to comfort her. He
shot a furtive glance at the dragon sitting next to him. It seemed to
comprehend nothing, but shot a glance at Tarrin and Harmon from
time to time. As Tarrin walked up, its ears went forward, and it stuck
its nose out to greet the little speckled beta like any beta might.

"Are these dragons psis? What's with Tarrin? And what ARE
these dragons, anyway? Those raptors we saw in the report?" Tara
tried to remember the briefing, but the memories were indistinct.

"These 'dragons' are not dragons, really. They're not evil, they're
Dimar. They do have the ability to communicate with our psis, and

are," he paused, sighing, "intelligent indigenous life, as far as we can tell. They just don't *build* anything, like we do. We had no way of knowing before the landing."

"Shit." Tara slammed a fist into the ground. "Do they mind us dropping in on them like this? I know I'd be a tad upset."

"As far as Tarrin can tell, the verdict's out on whether or not we're welcome here, but they did heal the one-hundred seventeen casualties quicker than anything with this magic fairy water they have." Rakal chuckled, watching Tarrin and the beast. "They're already trying to learn English, and are starting to master Arrallin. Here, I'll show you." He beckoned the dragon over. "Luuko, meet TARA. She's the boss lady of the Golden Hinde." Rakal seemed exceedingly comfortable near the giant monster, but Tara didn't share his enthusiasm.

"Hedoooo, Taaallla, dabosslaaaaddeee Gouwtim Hinde." The dragon dipped his head, and extended a foreleg. His voice was gravelly at first, like a low growl, but cleared to a metallic bell-like tone. "Sake."

"He means 'Shake'." Tarrin added. "They're working on the 'sh' sound, but they're great with the 'rrrr' sound in Arrallin."

She tentatively took hold of the scaly paw, feeling the soft under fur that lined the skin beneath the scales. His paw-pads were rough, but he had four long, graceful fingers with sharp, raptor-like claws, and two opposable thumbs, one on each side of his paw. She shook his paw, and greeted him. "Hello, Luuko. A pleasure to meet you."

"Dapleeesure's minde." he chimed, and wiggled his long, equine ears. Tarrin just laughed, and patted him on the shoulder.

"He's a natural, " Tarrin laughed. "Soon, we'll have him writing speeches for Rakal. He's exceptionally bright, and a real Talent, too. They all seem to be, but this one's not as shy. Harmon is getting along farmerly with Liur, the leader of this expedition."

"Farmerly? Tarrin, you could use a little English refresher course, there. Try famously." Rakal grinned, leaning toward Tarrin, who just shrugged and smiled.

Tara gave the dragon a close look, standing to be eye to eye with the lowered head. Two long, spiraling horns jutted out from next to its ears, which flicked forward and back, very much like a horse or a goat. Its heavy eyebrows were coated in tiny scales that carefully interlocked as it moved them, frowning down at her quizzically. The muzzle seemed to be a cross between a cat and a camel, with a long nose, and nostrils like a camel, but the upper lips and lower jaw meshed in a feline way. Creamy fur tufted out from beneath the heavy scales on his cheeks. It, no, he, had a long neck, more like a heron than a snake, which emerged from a powerful set of withers. His head was swiveling to her right and then left, regarding her as much as she was regarding him. Two golden orbs, like a bald eagle's, drank her in.

She took a step closer, sizing up the beast. His shoulder was a few inches higher than her head-and all muscle. She resisted the urge to pat his side, not knowing how he'd react. His front legs were long, configured like a cat's, ending in clawed fingers. She took a step back, not wanting to dwell on those claws very long.

Luuko ruffled his wings and turned his attention back to Tarrin, undisturbed by her continued examination of him. The creature's wings looked a bit unnatural, emerging just behind the shoulders. He had them neatly tucked onto his back, and they gleamed with an almost metallic shine. The wing spars too were coated in scales, but the scales had a silvery luster that set the wings apart from the rest of the body. His back legs were heavily muscled, ending with an elongated six-toed foot that looked perfect for leaping. Each toe was graced with a formidable hooked claw, and Tara shuddered to think about what the creature might hunt with that arsenal. Like Rakal, he had wrapped his tail around his feet, and twitched it from time to time, the spade-like blade at the end gleaming as it caught the golden light of the setting sun.

Tara looked around at the hundred-odd Dimar dragons that sat, scattered between both the humans and the Arrallins. They ranged in color from earthy reds and browns to greens, yellows and like Luuko, blue-green. A few of the smaller ones had huge leather sacks strapped to their backs and bellies, and held hoses in their forepaws.

Each of these ones wore long, silky flags stretching from their horns down to their wrists. As three betas returned from the woods with two bloodied survivors, these bannered Dimar gave the injured ones water-showers from the sacks. Tara nearly charged them when the first beta they Watered fell to the ground and howled, but Rakal jumped up to block her way.

"Just watch. I'm telling you, it's high magic, this water." He turned, watching the beta on the ground whine with relief as his wounds sealed themselves, white fur and skin growing over exposed muscle and bone. The bannered Dimar repeated the process with the next beta, and again, the same miraculous results. "They say that the water is a rare and precious resource here, and is sacred to the Dimar."

"I can see why! That's incredible." Tara held up her left arm, and pulled apart the rends in her uniform to examine the greenish-white skin on her side. "It doesn't really go with my real skin, but I don't mind being a pinto for a while. Is it permanent?"

Rakal pointed to Luuko's side. "It seems to be permanent for him. We should ask, especially for the sake of you humans." He chuckled, fluffing the fur on his head, mocking Harmon's patented self-aware gesture. He shot a glance toward Harmon, hoping that she didn't catch his joke. She was covered in large swatches of bright white skin herself.

In Arrallin, he asked Tarrin to find out about the permanence of the healing marks. Tara didn't understand much of it, as her Arrallin still needed some serious work, but she did catch a few words. "Hey, cool. I understood some of that, " she smiled at Rakal, who looked surprised.

"Well, this will put a significant dent in our gossiping, now that you're becoming a scholar in our language. Will make playing poker more challenging too." He smiled good-naturedly, a learned expression from his time on Earth, but Tara wondered if he was bothered.

Tarrin's answer brought a sigh of relief from those around them. "He says if the wounds are superficial, nor particularly deep, your

natural skin will replace the green-white skin. It's not permanent."
Tarrin strode over on two legs, and apologetically approached Tara.
"However, your wounds were severe. Your arm will return to it's
natural color, but your side may retain a lighter tinge. I'm sorry."

Tara shrugged. "Hey, since when have I cared about my
looks, eh? I'm just glad to be in one piece! Thanks for letting me
know, Tarrin." She patted his shoulder reassuringly, and he looked
considerably relieved. She wondered if Harmon knew, and felt a
pang of sympathetic pain for her. She was much more appearance
conscious than most of the crew.

"Okay, kids. Break time's over. I want a staff meeting um...over
here by this tree so we can figure out how we're going to set up camp,
now that a significant portion of the ship is a pretzel." Tara waved
over the human and beta officers, and began formulating a plan for a
new base camp.

Chapter 6

Luuko looked on as the tiny mindless ones sprang into a flurry of action. Moving throughout the wreckage of their twisted metal tree-ship, the humans and Arrallins quickly constructed shelters, the likes of which Luuko had only seen in his history books. Perplexed, he quietly reached out to his Leader, and she viewed the scene through his eyes. *Great Mother, should we not offer them the appropriate shelter seedlings, instead of letting them smother the ground beneath them with these shade-covers? These flimsy membranes and branches won't hold up against a serious firestorm.*

Her answer was reserved, and unemotional. *We have to see how they manage on their own. We can learn from them by watching. Study them, and report to me tomorrow. You, and all of the First and Fourth are relieved from fire-duty, and can stay on there to help these newcomers set up their camp.*

Luuko's attention was drawn away from the matriarch, as a wing of familiar and unwelcome forms glided in from the north. *Mulkol First Regiment—fan out!* The order from the flight leader was poorly shielded, and edged with aggression meant to scare the Telka Dimar already stationed around the new encampment. Luuko moved to Liur's side with several others, and in formation, they moved to greet them in the formal style.

The activity of the humans had not changed with the arrival of the Mulkol regiment, and Luuko breathed a sigh of relief. They were not aware of the danger, and for now, that was for the best.

I, Liur of the First Tinar Rank, accord all honor and grace to you, head of Mulkol First. However, you are currently on Telka grounds, and we must ask that you leave. Liur's formal tone was tightly controlled, sounding almost bored, Luuko mused with pride. That would rankle in the Regiment leader's craw, that he had not unsettled them as much as the Mulkol had hoped.

All honor and grace to you, First Tinar, but we must make a full report on this ... event. We cannot return to our barryd until we have made a full investigation and taken the appropriate samples. The Regiment leader was eyeing an injured Arrallin resting nearby with a sadistically curious eye.

Our apologies to you, Regiment leader, but no samples may be taken from this site. Nor are you to cross our borders again without retribution. Your shortcoming on this day shall be forgiven by the Leader, and she forgives your lapse in memory. The Great Mother can forgive one infraction, but further incidents will require correction of you, her erring child. All honor and grace to you, and good day. Liur, with a condescending tone that made Luuko wince to hear it, promptly dismissed the Mukoli. The insult was not lost on the regiment leader.

Growling, his tail snapping back and forth with fury, he sprang into the air, knocking a gust of wind toward the membrane-buildings of the settlement.

Luuko quickly quelled the breeze with a flick of his wing, catching Liur's quiet, satisfied chuckle in his mind.

The Regiment leader bellowed a vocal call to his unit, and in disheveled order they rose into the air, heading northwest, toward Ekal.

Sighing, Liur sent a warning message ahead to Ekal, broadcasting it so that the Mulkol regiment, as well as the First and Fourth Tinar Ranks could listen and enjoy it. *Ekal—a herd of Mulkol are heading your way. Expect little trouble, if any.*

Luuko turned to find Tarrin sitting beside him, listening intently. *Well, my big friend, seems the Dimar have problems of their own. Who were those striplings, if I might ask?*

Luuko felt the Great Mother's encouragement to share the

danger of the Mulkol reaching out to all of the Dimar present at the settlement. Openly, he sent images of the Mulkol—their violent dancers, howling herd-raids in the valley, their fire-burned sub-barryds and decaying vines, and sick children. *They are the shame of Dimar, my friend. The worst organized, most poorly managed barryd on this continent—and our neighbors. Beware of any Dimar bearing their colors— blue, black and red. Their fighters are fierce and fearless, and unpredictable.*

Nerves still a bit jangled, Luuko and the other Dimar around him took up their observation posts again and continued studying the structures as they were erected.

"YAHOO!"

A combat scream from behind Luuko sent him leaping into the air, his tail lashing back and forth in front of him, and all claws bared. Hanging in attack stance, he looked down to see Tara, but she had changed! Luuko could not believe his eyes, and circled in close. *Tarrin, what happened to Tara? She's much larger, and why does she have an extra set of...no, wait...are those her feet there?*

Tarrin's laughter filled his mind. *No, no, Luuko! It's fine...she's riding another 'mindless beast', but one even more mindless than you might think. That's a horse she's on—a sub-intelligent species that humans are quite fond of, used in their ancient days for transport. She's just happy that it survived the crash. Several other horses in that cargo bay, um, weren't so fortunate.* Tarrin, using images of horses without riders in his mind helped Luuko distinguish where Tara ended and the beast began. He helped Rakal and some other betas carve up what was left of a small pinto horse who was lost in the crash. *Horses are also excellent eating, if you'd like to partake in this one with me.*

Thank you, Tarrin...I'd enjoy trying some of your off-Dimar delicacies. Luuko could feel the concern about Tara's horse from other Dimar around him, and broadcast a summary of what he had learned to the others. A rumble of approval issued from the knot of Dimar who had moved off into a tree to observe, and they chattered away about the humans and their resource harvesting. He landed, and nipped a sample off the haunch of the unfortunate beast near where Tarrin had pointed. It tasted like morrak, but with a pungent aftertaste.

These humans are like proper Dimar, in that sense, aren't they, Luuko? However, why would they keep their form and use a subcreant 'HORSE' for transport when they can just engineer extra land running legs? It seems that the subcreant has it's own will, as well, making it difficult to manipulate. Goothib, a member of Rank Tinar First, the highest firefighting flight rank, but also a Telkai sub-creation engineer of the highest class, bombarded him with questions and queries about the genetic design of sub-creation 'HORSE', flashing image after image of chromosomal blueprints, flooding Luuko's mind with what was to him, nonsense.

Goothib, I was never very good at my Telkai studies—I have no idea what you're talking about. From what I can tell, they do not sub-create like we do. They 'borrow' creatures from their surroundings and learn to work with them. The less intelligent the creatures are, like this one, the more luck the humans seem to have with them. Luuko tried to draw a parallel within Dimar culture, *Think back to your history, before the days of sub-creation, before the Flight. When we used morraks, miruls and oolars to pull down the trees, and to bend the branches, or to furrow the ground to sew the vines. That is what they have here. These are slave species, or adopted animals, but not sub-creation.*

Goothib admitted being as bad a student of history as Luuko was of the principles of Telkai genetic engineering, but understood. With a frustrated sigh, he continued watching the progress of the settlement. *Primitives. The Great Mother should station a history rank here, not a rank that has half the Telkai first class aboard, I should think.* He resumed his private discussions with the others near him, nodding to Luuko with thanks.

Luuko studied the carcass in front of him carefully. The long legs seemed frail, lacking muscle or protective scaling, but the musculature on the body was impressive, and even tasty.

These animals are designed to eat and run. That's all. Tarrin had been eavesdropping on his musings again. *They've got a social nature, though, which allows the humans to work with them. That's one thing you've got to understand about humans, Luuko—they'll mother anything. They'll adopt anything, and as long as it will love them, they'll love it.*

Tara honestly thinks she's the mother of that horse, Tarrin giggled.

Luuko's ears flapped back and forth wildly as he howled with laughter. He rolled onto one side, snorting and roaring, barely missing knocking Tarrin into a nearby tree. *Tara hatched that thing? What...what did she mate with to get THAT?*

No no... She didn't hatch it, or birth it. She adopted it when it was born, and raised it as her own kind, really. Humans do this. That's why they've been so successful in dealing with us Arrallakeeni. Tarrin was warbling a high-pitched growling laugh, watching Tara struggle to remain aboard her horse in the presence of the laughing Dimar. *Our matriarch, the Alpha female, is the only one of us who can breed—she is our version of your Great Mother. We are drawn to the mother like the comets are drawn to the gravity of stars, like your Tinar Rank was when the Great Mother called you to help us. Because humans adopt so well, and so freely, the humans began to replace our own Alphas in what seemed quite a natural and harmless process. However, humans as Alphas do not breed more Arrallakeeni, and thus, our numbers are dropping.*

Luuko caught his breath and rolled back onto his haunches to sit. *I understand this adopting. It is common for us to take in the young from friendly barryds that have had their adult population ravaged by a Great Dance or a bad fire season. However, we do not mother the morraks in the fields—they are mindless. How can you love something that has no mind? It is foolishness to try.*

Remember, Luuko—all humans, except for a few, are 'mindless'—and most Arrallakeeni are as well. We learn not to see minds, but to hear speech, and to see movement in their faces and bodies to feel their feelings. Tarrin's mind-voice seemed to be struggling with expressing what he was feeling, and it all made little sense to Luuko. He would watch and learn, and eventually understand the movement of feelings that was so important to Tarrin.

Chapter 7

"It's been a month, Landry. What kind of techs did you bring on that hulk of yours?" Tara masked her annoyance behind a half-smile. The Dark Hope had to be not only ready to make a fast run back toward the jump gate to close it, but also to return and unload the last of the vital supplies to the rapidly evolving human and Arrallin colony. Landry's angular features tensed momentarily, and loosened into a toothy, sly grin. *He's going to ask for something. I know that look.*

"Well, fearless leader, if I could be so bold as to borrow a tech or two from the more spaceworthy Singularity II, I can have this entire problem straightened in a matter of days. The majority of the engineering betas are on the Singularity II, whereas I got the dubious honor of carting the gate crasher. Useful though it will be, that piece of equipment is doing nothing for this aging ship. I need staff, Tara, regardless of the risk."

Landry scratched at his clean-shaven scalp, frowning as the stubble rasped under his roughened fingers. Turning, he tapped on a monitor behind him, outlining the cross section of the engineering bay of the ship. Red indicators showed a plethora of failing systems. "I've been over the engineering roster for the Singularity II. Kiralla, Malry, and Linaro, just those three, should be able to set my beta team straight and get us ready for the gate closing." He held up his hands imploringly.

Tara caught her breath, and scrutinized Landry closely. Kiralla was the best engineer on the Singularity II, that was true, and was a logical choice for this assignment, but she was also the only unmated Alpha Arrallin female in the entire fleet. She was Rakal's only hope for founding a new hive in the next twenty years. On Landry's ship, she'd be dangerously isolated from members of the Arrallin Insurrection on the Singularity II. Landry was an independent operator brought in only because he had a gate crasher. Landry's participation in the mission had been ratified by a vote of five to four when the inner circle of the Insurrection team met to decide on how to deal with the gate, and tensions about him ran high in every meeting.

Emotions struggled inside Tara, but she looked over the data file with a practiced nonchalance. She quelled a spike of fearsome jealousy for the beautiful, intelligent Kiralla, destined to take a place in history beside Rakal, but Tara knew her duty lay far beyond her personal wants and needs. Kiralla and Rakal were both desperately needed to give a wider genetic base to the new Hives. All of the Arrallin species may depend on the decision she made at this moment.

Crushing all her personal feelings, she assessed Landry. He was a known 'furvert', preferring Arrallin furries for his passions over humans. He treated them like animals, or worse. Beta murders, especially ones related to sex, were rarely pursued by Earth authorities, but Landry had been brought to trial twice. To his credit, he was acquitted twice, but his violence was legendary among the Beta brothels.

Kiralla was, despite her beta disguise, a rare beauty. As an Alpha she was naturally strong willed, even when acting her beta part. His purpose in requesting her transfer could be libidinous, as much as a request of necessity. Could he know that she was indeed an Alpha female, close to her season? How far did his obsession go, and how much information did he have? He had accepted a fairly low fee to take on the risky job of jumping through and crashing the gate. Members of the inner circle were wagering that he wouldn't in fact go through the gate, just close it down and return to join the colony as the proud leader of his own personal Arrallin harem, without the rules of earthly propriety to bind him. He had been lead to believe that they were all in this project to dodge criminal problems back on Earth, and as far as she knew, he had no idea that the ships carried three mated pairs, as well as the two unmated Arrallin Alphas, Kiralla and Rakal. They had all been carefully disguised.

Tingles of sweat dripped down Tara's back as she returned Landry's awaiting gaze in the view screen. Consciously, she controlled her tone of voice, maintaining the distracted tone she had had all through their conversation. "Three's fine, Landry. The other ships are operating well—Dark Hope is the biggest system failure risk, and it's just too important to leave to an inexperienced engineering crew. Be sure to get them back aboard the Singularity II as soon as the repairs are done, though. I want as many of the engineers down here to work on the colony, and the Arralla's Pride will be making the second shuttle run in two weeks. The weather down here is going to get really wet soon, and we need the best structures we can manage." She looked down, pretending to scrutinize a colony structure report with frustration.

"Thank you, Tara. I'll have this ship as good as new in no time." His smug smile made a knot form in Tara's belly. "I don't envy you down there. Looks like a real jungle. I thought Gates City was bad." He laughed at his own weak joke, and Tara managed a completely contrived smile. "Landry out."

His face faded away on the screen, a menacing visage as the shadows darkened and grew until the screen was a flat black. The screen faded in an instant, but to Tara, it felt like an hour. A feeling of foreboding, as strong as her combat instincts from Earth Command training, flooded into her, along with a sense of both danger and power, but not from above. It was from the east, where the troubled Mulkol Barryd lay. "Tara, you're getting soft in the head. The Telkans can take care of their own." She muttered, and turned to look to the east, seeing for a fleeting instant a radiant orange glow across the hillside. Looking toward Ekal and Telka, the sky glowed a yellow-green along the tree line, brightest along the mountain pass that lead toward the regions to the north. As soon as the light had appeared, it vanished, leaving her with a momentary longing to head north.

Tarrin, the psi from the Arralla's Pride, and Rakal strode up on their hind legs. "So, Tara, how goes operations up above?" Rakal rumbled in his deep Alpha voice. He made no effort to disguise himself in actions, but maintained the black coat and thinned mane for safety.

"Did you see that light? Did you hear those sounds just now?" Tara looked from Rakal and then to Tarrin and back, leaning against the communications console.

"Um...no, Tara. When was the last time you slept?" Rakal's concern was plainly evident. "You're going to sleep NOW, Tara. You look like one of those floppy eared morraks the Dimar seem so fond of."

Tarrin signaled Mason over, and he instantly surmised the situation. "Don't worry, Tar—I'll wake you if anything interesting happens. I hear that the Dimar are finishing council talks to decide whether or not we will be welcomed here. I'll wake you as soon as the report comes back from the north." Mason picked up the duty roster and leafed through screen after screen. "No problem. This thing's so organized even Tarrin here could run the details, eh Tarrin?" He grinned good-naturedly to the beta Talent, who snorted with mock indignance.

"Mason, Rakal—I'm leaving things in your hands. I do need the rest." Tara shot a worried glance at the duty roster screen on the console, as Kiralla and the other engineers registered as transferred to the Dark Hope. "First, I want to let you all know that Landry requested three engineers to work on the Dark Hope. It's having significant engine problems and we need it ready to go as soon as that Dimar council gets out and decides whether or not we can stay. That gate crasher is key to the success of this operation. We wouldn't survive a day against an Earth Command contingent sent through the jump gate." Nervously she looked up at Rakal, who was already scanning the transfer logs.

"Kiralla's gone over." His voice was monotone, but the fur along his neck rose to its full height. "Was there no way to avoid that?"

"Not without giving Landry a possible hint that he was onto

something. He's been prying around personnel records since the start and I didn't want to give him any sign that we might have Alphas aboard." Tara knew that her decision had been based on rational thought, and probably would have been the decision made by Mason, Tarrin, or any of the other Arrallin Insurrection leaders, but the guilt gnawed at the back of her mind.

Rakal turned toward Tara, his eyes searching her face. Slowly, he nodded with agreement. "It's been fifteen years that we've been in hiding, and not one human, not even members of the Earth Command, have cracked our cover. Landry will not be a problem. You being a walking shadow of yourself—that is a problem." His hackles lowered as he turned to guide Tara toward her tent.

Tara smiled, almost shyly at Rakal as they walked toward her tent away from the crowd. In a hoarse whisper, she tried to explain. "Look, Rakal—I...I didn't want to risk her, but if he suspected that she was...well, from what we know, he probably would have gone aboard and kidnapped her. You know of my species dark affinity for the young Alpha females..."

Rakal interrupted quickly, wincing with pain. "Don't. I know...I know all too well. You would never jeopardize this movement or..."

"Or your happiness, Rakal." Tara uttered with more emotion than she had wanted. She gazed into his face, studying the graceful lines of his muzzle, and the sheen of his jet-black fur. His eyes, violet through the disguise coloring, were clouded with pity for her.

With a flash of indignance, she turned and strode into her tent to get some much-needed rest.

It seemed that she had only just fallen asleep when Mason came charging in. "Word's back from the north, sir! You're not going to believe this."

Chapter 8

"So, give me an example of this sub-creation of yours" Harmon, the human psi from the Golden Hinde both mind spoke and verbalized her curiosity to Luuko and Goothib. Her excitement and anxiety to learn more disturbed Luuko deeply, and he quietly set up walls around his few fleeting memories of Telkai engineering skills. Goothib, being more a pure engineer had no reservations about teaching his craft.

It's all around you, Harmon. You're looking at two products of sub-creation right now, Luuko and myself. See how our wings are of a different coloring and nature from the rest of our bodies? Well, they're a powerful addition, and central to the history and teaching of the Telkai study. Without hesitation, he flashed images to Harmon and Luuko both, of the ancient, wingless Dimar, and the engineering design for the chromosomes that would make the now familiar wing structure a permanent addition to most members of the Dimar species. *During the Flight, a time of great turmoil for our species, it was discovered that through careful study and exploration of the systems in our bodies that generate our forms, alterations could be made to allow us to better survive in even the harshest conditions. Using a cell permeation technique on miruls, we created the ill-fated turraks, that, unfortunately, did not breed and quickly died due to a poor initial design. But, the groundwork was laid for what has become the central art, and the key to success of the Dimar species: the art and study of Telkai, named for the great healer of the barryd at which the first of the experiments were done. Every species has been affected in some way, tested and improved by both selective breeding and by cell permeation Telkai engineering. Even our barryds are engineered for optimum environmental impact, and we're improving the design every day...*

In a panic, Luuko interjected on a private bandwidth. *Goothib, is this wise? Do you not sense her anticipation of your every word? Learn her intent before you tell her of the high arts! What if she comes from the Mulkai culture from Earth, and will make war like the Mulkol at every chance? What if she'll use the gift of the Water to destroy someone, or against us, its true Waters-born children?* Luuko held back on the scalding reprisal, tempering it with a tone of worry, hoping to convince Goothib that what he was doing truly was dangerous for the barryd. He felt Goothib's defensive wall go up in his mind—but not against Harmon, only against him. He had not reached him; he had been too harsh.

Goothib snarled at him, *Fool! She does not have the Water, nor does she yet fully understand any of this. But she'll need to, very soon. Have you not been listening to the council reports? We're going to be taking these people in, as our own kin, to teach them a new way of living, and to learn from them. It's a new age of peace and exploration, and this person deeply wants to be a true child of the Water. It would dishonor my guild and my rank not to teach one so sincere in her curiosity. You may go.* Goothib's indignation was clear, and his tail lashed back and forth during their private exchange. Harmon watched intently, unable to break the walls they had both carefully constructed around the exchange to keep her out. Luuko could feel her prying in, to try to get a glimpse at why they were arguing. He really must explain to the alien Talents that prying is in poor form.

Luuko turned to leave, but paused. He sent a feeler out to the Great Mother, but she was soundly sleeping. Her first acolyte was on watch, maintaining the fire line with two others, but even he was not in a position to make a call on this issue. It was the divine duty of all the Telkai students to increase the knowledge of others who wished to know more of the high art of subcreation. The issue of the student's planet of origin had never arisen before. The newer students of the Telkai were often unaware of the havoc their creations could wreak, and didn't consider consequences carefully in much of their decision-making. If he left now, he'd have no idea what Goothib would teach Harmon. If he stayed, he'd at least have the knowledge of how much she knew. In a way, Goothib was right. If they were to take in the humans and Arrallins, then it would be proper to teach their talents and as much of their culture as possible to start the integration process. Despite the fact that the subject matter desperately bored him, Luuko reached out to Goothib apologetically.

You are right, Goothib. She does need and deserve to learn of the Telkai ways. And I could use some work on my Telkai as well. Do you mind if I remain in the conversation? Luuko managed to feel some measure of true remorse for his distrust of Harmon, and the sentiment rang through his apology to Goothib.

Goothib quickly dropped his mental block and enthusiastically welcomed him back into their three-way mind exchange.

I'm glad to hear you embrace our new barryd mates, Luuko. And I'm excited to have the opportunity to teach not one but two avid pupils. I do so love to teach! Goothib rumbled happily as he continued the conversation with Harmon, quickly updating Luuko on Harmon's questions and his answers.

Luuko reviewed the images, amazed at the turn the conversation had taken. Goothib, true to the Great Mother's request, had not revealed the Water, but Harmon wasn't really curious about how subcreation was done. She wanted to know exactly what subcreation could do. Weird creatures, the likes of which Luuko had never imagined, flickered through Harmon's side of the conversation, and Goothib was joyously eating them up. Harmon had only just heard of subcreation, and already there were things she wanted to make. She settled on an image of a winged human, and began to concentrate.

That design would be more difficult, Harmon. You see, the wings don't fit well with the sides of the body. We ran into a similar problem placing our Wings back before the Flight, but a simple modification of the shoulder structure rectified it. Well, simple, no... It took years of tinkering and modeling to create the perfect match of strength and flexibility for our wings to work as they needed to. But, yes, it can be made. Harmon, how do you think the wings should mesh with the body in that design of yours? Goothib was comparing an image of the winged human along side an image of a Dimar. He was clearly flattered by her desire to become more like a Dimar, and have wings, but her wings were of a different design. He was trying to coax her into the first step of Telkai design, encouraging her to truly understand the form she was trying to create, from the inside and out, and create a solution for the design problems taking factors of blood flow, muscle stress, weight distribution and center of gravity into account. Harmon struggled, slowly, taking pieces of the Dimar shoulder design and altering them to fit in with the human structure. *Very good...now, let's see if it will fly.*

Luuko gasped. He was going to call the design into the simulation system back at the barryd and test it. It would be integrated into the stores of designs. It would be accessed by students of the Telkai for generations. He wondered if Goothib understood just how historic this occasion was, and if it might have negative repercussions with the head of the Telkai. Her design could be fatally flawed, and result in the death of the first human it was tested on...if it was tested on one. Did they understand the fundamental shift the Telkai changes could cause in their people? Could he understand the change it could cause in the Telkai art? Luuko's head spun. He had been trained, as all Dimar were, to consider every ramification of an action. Goothib was just glibly pushing ahead, treating Harmon like any hatchling in the Telkai Seventh Class. Blocking his concerns from Harmon, he channeled his concern, all walls down, to Goothib, hoping to reach him just this one time.

Goothib turned, with a look of concern, his ears forward. *Luuko, perhaps you are right. I will not use the central testing stores, but instead I will use my smaller personal testing bay. It will not be as thorough as the central, but it will do, and it will not release the design to all Telkai stores. I will clean it out after the test, and store it.* He released his block, and reached out to the barryd far to the north, letting both Harmon and Luuko watch the results. *This will take some time. This testing store is not as fast as some others, and this design is completely new for it.*

After fifteen nervous minutes for Harmon, Goothib and Luuko, the image signal returned to Goothib. He broadcast the human figure, wings held outstretched, and they watched as it ran. The wings flapped, generating lift through the Wind—a feature Goothib had added, and the figure lifted off the theoretical ground. Awkwardly, it flew, legs hanging down uselessly below it. The wing joint flashed yellow on the image, an indication from the tester that there was a serious design problem, and red as tendons in the wing snapped under the weight, denoting a critical failure. The figure fell, and as it rushed toward the theoretical ground, faded. Harmon was crestfallen, and did little to hide her disappointment.

It was an excellent first design, Harmon. We can improve it. You will fly someday. If it's possible for a Dimar to add wings and fly, so it will be for humans. The problem really is quite simple. We need to add a system to transfer lift energy near the hips of the human. That avian design you chose lacks the wing membrane connections along the sides the Dimar have. We can hide the membranes beneath the lifting surfaces you chose, and the overall image will remain much the same. Goothib was hacking away on the design in his mind, pulling the connections down, and strengthening the organs that would harness the power of the Wind as it moved by the wings. Remembering his student, he returned the design to Harmon's control, reverting to the older, failed model. *Did you understand those changes? Do they make sense?*

Yes. I know what I did wrong this time. I think moving the membranes too far down might make walking more uncomfortable. Can we put lifting organs in the legs and feet, and pull the membrane up? The legs won't hang that way. With surprising skill, she re-altered the image in the simulation system, copying and pulling the representations of lifting organs down to the calves and arches.

The lifting organs take quite a bit of energy to support. A small frame like this would not survive having more than four. There are ways of augmenting the amount of energy a body can produce, but I do not know enough of human structure to be sure they would survive these changes. We need to do a full permeation study of you and get detailed designs... Goothib mulled the problems out loud, halting at the mention of the study. He connected with Luuko on a private channel to discuss the problem further.

A study would require immersion in the central Waters. We can't do that with her yet. She'd broadcast the Waters to every Talent—including the ones that are starborn currently. Luuko reminded him of what he already knew. *Perhaps Ekal's tiny Water stores would do for the study? If they are moving in, we will have to show them the Waters eventually, and teach them how to use all of the Telkai equipment. I wish the Great Mother would awaken. We do need her advice on this.* Luuko sighed, realizing that everything they did today was truly history making.

Harmon butted in excitedly. *When can we do a study? Do we need an embryo to make these changes on, or can this change be made directly to an existing adult human? Can this work with furries...I mean... Arrallins? They're similar to us in design.* Harmon was hopping up and down, her blond curls falling into her eyes. Her hands flew from some unseen form in front of her up to her face and back, continuing to improve the design image. She filled out the very rough image of the human with proper organs, bones and muscles. Completely engrossed in her work with the simulator, she was unaware of how silly she looked.

Luuko and Goothib exchanged amused, and then worried glances, retracting their minds from the three-way conversation to ponder the situation.

She's got real skill in design, and I can tell that she'll stop at nothing to master this art. I've been there myself. Goothib's mental tone was tinged with pride, and he was obviously impressed with his new student.

You saw all those things she's got running around in that mind of hers. Who knows what they'd do to the environment if she did actually create all of them? We need to teach her balance and care in her creation, or we'll end up with another Deadland. Luuko called up images of the southern desert, created by a set of fast growing plant eaters designed by a well meaning but careless barryd engineer. It had taken the five neighboring barryds four cycles to bring the creatures back under control, and then dispose of them, and the region that had once housed a sprawling, successful barryd was now the slowly recovering Deadland region. *However, you're right. She's very, very good at Telkai. She'll probably win awards at the Mirrai Festival.*

The Mirrai? Yes...yes. She'd take the Seventh Class design competition, no crosswinds to bar her. She's possibly good enough to be in Sixth Class, except that she lacks so much of the fundamentals of Telkai, it wouldn't be fair. I'll continue to work with her. Goothib reached out his mind to rejoin Harmon and the design tester, and reared back as he saw her progress.

Luuko hurriedly resumed his contact, and gave a celebratory roar. She had the human flying, and it was a good solid, level flight. The wing joints, formerly glowing yellow and red with failure warnings, were now a light green, the color for success, and were operating flawlessly. She had restricted the design to four lifting organs, one in each wing, and one dispersed along the calf and toward the ankle of each leg. That, coupled with her wing design, which provided lift in a traditional way, with air pressure differences above and below the wing, was enough to give the human very respectable flight capabilities. Luuko could feel her happiness, and looked at her face. She was bearing all her teeth at them, and wrinkling up her eyes. He made a note to associate this with happiness and success.

Sighing with the effort, Harmon dropped to the ground, retaining a link with the tester to watch the human model fly through virtual space with endless energy. Goothib, the watchful teacher, monitored her exertion level. *Harmon, it takes much energy to generate designs and test them. I think you've made excellent progress this first day, but you should rest now. There is much more to Telkai then visualizing and testing the design, and you need to learn it all before we can proceed to actualize your design.*

Luuko added, *You have laid the groundwork here for the first human Flight. To be successful, we must proceed carefully with your design, and, in all honesty, we must consult the Great Mother, and the Council, before we allow you to sprout your own wings.* Luuko used his gentlest tone, not wanting to disappoint her at her moment of triumph.

He caught a spike of an unexpected emotion from her as she released the image. She didn't want wings, but had another design in mind for herself. She suppressed the thought too quickly for Luuko to get a glimpse at her other design concept. *So, tell me about this Flight of yours, anyway. You keep mentioning it, and it seems important to the art of Telkai.* Harmon discreetly probed Luuko to see if she could tell what he had caught from her, and felt relieved as she realized that he had not seen her other design. Her curiosity for the tale of Flight was genuine, and she pressed them for more information.

Ahh...The Flight. It's been a while since I've had to recite the presentation. You'll have to learn this too, Harmon, to rise to the Sixth Class in Telkai. Let me see... Goothib paused for a moment, scratching his scaled belly absently with one paw.

In the darkness of the War with the Isle, now 1120 cycles ago, in the barryd of Telmirrai, Telkai studied the healing arts to save her kith and kin. Barryds and waters were new in that age, little more than shelters and pools for drinking. Mulkai studies (War studies) were the dominant art of the time, and most engineers worked to develop a more defensible barryd, where the very walls would work to actively repel invaders. The same was wished for the water pools. They would fill with water that could recognize residents from invaders, and act accordingly. Telkai was called in by the Mulkai council to instill in the waters the will to heal. She knew of every creature's internal plan, the genetics by your human term. She created in the water an active cell virus that would find the plan, compare the plan to wherever it was within the magnetic field of the individual in the Water, and, drawing on the energy sugars and proteins in the Water rebuild whatever was missing from the creature.

Goothib carefully illustrated each major point with a carefully rehearsed image. The first scene was of towers, blood red, twisting with what looked like a knotwork of veins, ending in a sparse leafy top—the first war barryds. He began to illustrate the pools of water versus the new Water, but halted. The image he called was not like the first. It was improvised. Luuko hoped Harmon would not realize the deception. They could not learn of the location of the pools until it was time. Goothib chose to show Harmon two vials: one clear, like stream water, and one with a greenish tinge, the Water. Goothib returned to the standard images of the recital, showing the wingless Mulkai leaders—in drab browns and dark greens, with Telkai—a shining white Dimar, her wings outlined as a shimmering blue halo, in the prime of her molt, with flowing white fur tufting out under the last of her molting firescales, standing before them. Luuko secretly wondered just how accurate the image was. Goothib worshipped Telkai as much as he, Luuko, worshipped the Wind.

The Mulkai council saw the genius of her work, and with the darkness in their minds, they wanted to push it further, toward the end of destruction. Telkai was ordered to create a cell, that when given an internal plan would convert the entire being within the particular magnetic field to the form the cell was given. Telkai, working with a host of others, created a system by which genetic code can be examined, tested and released into particular pools of the Water.

Telkai, flanked by her team of eight wingless Dimar, each of a different primary color, stood in a line before the first tester. The scene was pure fantasy—no one, not even the Leaders Council, had records on who had worked on the first Telkai engineering testing system. Luuko wiggled his ears, realizing that Harmon was amused by the scene. Goothib was off in his own world, continuing the story obliviously.

The Mulkai council used this new wonder badly. They turned Great Leaders of other barryds into hideous beasts, or killing them by turning their own cells against them. The deaths were horribly cruel and painful. Lost Waters, wandering through the supply of regular water would kill entire barryds, even friendly ones, seeking out only Dimar code and altering it to die.

Luuko stopped laughing as these scenes played out, and laid his ears back instinctively. These images were based on actual execution recordings, and were painfully real. He thought of Mulkol, one of the last of the war barryds just a half day's flight east of Telka, and wondered just how many captured Telkans had ended up in those pits. Harmon broadcast a clear emotion: horror. The battle scenes had not bothered her, but the scenes of the horribly painful slow deaths didn't sit well with her. Her mouth hung open and she covered it with one hand. Her skin was very pale. Her eyes were wide, and moisture formed at the corners. Luuko made a mental note that this was horror.

Telkai and her rank mates were deeply troubled, and set about a plan to end the War of the Isle while there were still Dimar left to survive. The War had begun because the Mulkai of the Island Continents were swimming through the Great Sea to settle on the shores of Mainland. They were different, and more powerful than the Mulkai Dimar of Mainland and of the southern archipelagos, and because of the differences the fighting had begun. Dimar of Mainland saw the weakening of the western barryds as a great opportunity to take lands from them. Trapped, members of the western barryds could do little but fight to stave off their attacks.

The Island Continent Dimar were perennially in disfavor with the Mainland Dimar, and Goothib was not particularly fond of Dimar of the Isles himself. The images reflected this, showing hulking, gray bodies climbing up on shore on stocky legs. Instead of the graceful heads of Mainland Dimar, Goothib showed the Dimar of the Isles as block headed, with flat, blunt snouts and thick necks. Luuko had seen Dimar of the Isles in his travels, and knew that they were actually just a more sinuous, smaller variety of Dimar. He broadcast a revised image to Harmon, not letting Goothib know that he was correcting him.

Telkai would free them. Telkai would give all Dimar wings, so that they might mingle freely in the air safely, or flee attacks to restart barryds elsewhere when greed takes hold of their neighbors. Telkai allowed Dimar to transcend their war, literally.

Working in secret, Telkai and her team tested and re-tested the design. It had to be perfect, and breed true in all the Dimar subspecies. The cell had to be released somehow into every barryd's water supply, a Lost Water with a benevolent purpose. Every barryd had to be given the secret of Water so that the cell could work. Any time a Dimar was immersed in Water, the cell could act, adding wing structure code to each Dimar little by little.

Telkai betrayed her barryd to save it. She left her Barryd in the West and went to the other side. She seeded the Mainland conquered barryds of the East, and the north and south twin continents, teaching them of the healing powers of Water. Soon, all barryds were producing Water, seeded with his special cell, set not to act until the appointed day. Once all barryd-dwelling Dimar were set, Telkai had to devise a way to infuse the cell in the Dimar from the Isle, who did not have barryd technology.

In what was seen as an act of ultimate betrayal, Telkai taught the Isle Dimar the key to disarming Telmirrai—her own home in the West, and the last outpost of free Mainland Dimar. In the bloodiest of all battles, it fell to the Dimar of the Isles. The surviving Telmirrai leaders regrouped at Iladinal barryd in secret to discuss what had happened, and there, Telkai turned herself in to suffer her fate. The Leaders of Telmirrai immersed her in a pool of flesh-eating cells—the most horrible execution ever devised. It is told that at the moment of her death, a great cry went up all over Dimar. Her wing-making cells awakened, drawing all Dimar inexorably toward the Water to soothe the flaming pains that consumed them. As she slowly decayed in the pool at Iladinal, all of Dimar grew wings.

Luuko chuckled inwardly. Harmon clearly understood that this was a romanticized version of the truth, if near the truth at all, and was amused by the sugary sweet propaganda Goothib was tossing at her.

Goothib emerged from his reverie sighing. *If only I had been around in that time, to live to see the great one give us the power of Flight and subcreation. I, no doubt would have been a key member of her development team.* Goothib chuckled, wiggling his ears and crooning smugly.

You probably would have ended up on the wrong end of a war-oolar's tusks in some battle, Goothib. Most Telkans that were conscripted ended up as fertilizer, Luuko jokingly admonished him. Goothib looked crushed, and looked away. Thinking more positively, he reminded him, *and if you'd been there, then you wouldn't be here to teach Harmon, the first non-Dimar, the art of the Telkai studies. Your place in history is here, Goothib— doing the true work of the true child of the Water.*

Goothib brightened considerably, whuffling toward Harmon. *Shall I teach you the image-ballad so you can work your way toward the Sixth Class?*

Luuko had had all he could stand of Telkai for the day, and excused himself. Learning ballads of Dimar long dead was not his style, and he trundled off on all fours to find something useful to do around the encampment.

Chapter 9

"Sir, they've requested that all high ranking personnel be brought to the Telka Barryd central meeting room for a tour, a meeting and an announcement. It seems that it would be detrimental to some great plan they have for us to continue with our own encampment out here. They're inviting us to become part of their barryd, providing the details can be worked out satisfactorily. Can you believe this? Having three hundred sixty-odd people in a field sixty miles away is going to interrupt their great plan. These guys think ahead—I can't wait to poke around their barryd thing." Mason seemed oblivious to the fact that Tara had just woken up from a sleep that was far too short for her needs.

Tara yawned and stretched, realizing that for the last month, she had been oscillating between two very dirty outfits. Currently, she was wearing the poorly patched uniform she had crashed in. "In other words, we're being worked into their Great Plan. I wonder if their plan will work with ours. This meeting will be interesting, to say the least." She got up, feeling around the nylar mat under her feet for her slippers. "Time to break out the dress grays. Tell everyone from the Arrallin Insurrection team that's down here to get ready for the meeting. If we're going to openly discuss options, we're going to have to consider letting the Dimar know about the hive restructuring, and I'd prefer that certain humans down here didn't know about the Alphas just yet. We still haven't closed the gate, and if Landry got wind of things, we could be leaving the planet open for an invasion force."

She scrunched her feet into the warm fuzzy yellow morrak slippers that Tarrin had made for her as a joke. The Dimar had fallen over in sneezing fits when she made the mistake of wearing them outside for the first time to go to the showers. She looked down at the two pair of beady black eyes, formerly shirt buttons, on each slipper, noting how the rabbit-like ears flopped as she moved her feet. They really did look like morraks. At least, the heads did. True to the real McCoy, the slippers had the distinctive blunt snouts, with a cow-like nose and floppy ears. Morraks themselves resembled a cross between a cow and a flop-eared rabbit, and were proving to be exceptional pack animals.

"Mason, any word on the palatability of local flora and fauna? These slippers are making me hungry, and I'd bet they'd have some kind of food waiting for us when we get there. I'd hate to have to turn them down because we weren't sure we could eat it and risk permanently insulting them."

"From everything we've seen, as long as it's cooked, we can eat it. The animals here are, aside from some structural differences, no different from animals on earth. The basic lines of evolution are the same. They're carbon-based life—they're just evolved about four million years past our animals, plus they've been tinkered with fairly severely to produce more high-grade meat. Feel free to eat hardy. Now lets just hope that they won't be offended if we throw everything they serve us into the fire..." Mason pulled at his mustache, his trademark nervous gesture, as he pondered the possibility of a political incident relating to food. "There are native botulism strains, and other toxin-producing bacteria, but if the kills are fresh, we'll be fine. The fish are especially good eating, I'll wager. I just hope they're not serving sushi."

"What about plants? Do we need to cook them too? What varieties of fruit have you seen the Dimar around here eat, and can we eat them?" Tara slipped out of her casual uniform, fingering the collar on her dress gray jacket.

Mason politely turned away, allowing her privacy while continuing his report. "We've done a full spectrum of plant tests.

Most of the plants are inedible, but the nectar on most flowers is fine, and the fruits on especially the 'potato tree' look like they'll be a native mainstay of our diet. The giant grape-like vines are also fine eating, and I suspect that the betas are already brewing a test vat." Mason caught Tara's angry look, and smiled appeasingly. "Okay...okay...we shouldn't have tried the grapes, and we shouldn't be brewing, but what else is there to do between analysis tests? They're really long, and brewing is a great way to stay practiced in our chem lab skills. Anyway, I'm not dead, and the grapes are some of the best I've tasted. And I hate grapes. Then again, I've been living on C rations for the last three months, and the only fresh meat I had was from that dead pony in cargo bay twelve. Pony jerky just doesn't cut it. The betas are complaining that if they're going to have to keep eating like this, they've got to have booze."

"What else have you and other members of the encampment sampled without ill effect?" Tara buttoned up the front of the starchy white dress shirt, tucking it carefully into the gray suit pants so that no wrinkles would show on the front. Waiting for Mason's reply, she turned toward the mirror and slipped on the close-cut gray jacket. The long wool sleeves were a bit much in the heat of the Dimar dry season, but she'd suffer to make a good impression. The Insurrection had altered the standard Earth Confederacy uniform to create their own look. In the imperial style of the Arrallins, rank was denoted by a set of silver interlocking triangles. Tara wore nine triangles, denoting her as a general in the Arrallin structure, but not an Alpha, who would have ten. Awards for valor were denoted by tiny gems set in each of the silver triangles, and the AI had granted Tara two deep blue sapphires and one emerald for putting together the team that had brought them here. She buckled the wide leather belt, forgoing the traditional saber for this occasion and opting for a sidearm instead. She'd prefer not to try to slay any dragons in the traditional style, and would trust the plasma burst to do the job of a blade for her.

"I've been munching on the potato fruits from that potato tree, and, well, they need bacon bits, but other than that, they're delicious.

Raw, they're a little tough, but if you nuke them for a few minutes, they're good eating. And then there's those blueberry tasting red fruit trees. I couldn't find any problems with the fruit, so I had some of those. They're delicious with cream from our cattle. And morrak itself is great." Mason rattled off the native foods he had sampled, counting off on both fingers.

Tara turned and gaped at him. "MASON! You could have gotten yourself killed! That's not proper procedure...and it explains why you've gained about five kilograms since we landed. What were you thinking?"

"Well, sir, we've had a month to do basic analysis, and with the betas going hog wild on the place, it didn't even take them two weeks to get all the basic safety requirements for foods checked. They're really throwing themselves into the work, because they know that this is their new home. We're ready to start introducing native foods into the current rations, and I felt that as chief of the survey team, I should be the first to take the risk." Mason was deadly serious about his responsibility for the safety of the foods they ate on the new planet. Tara knew he had taken every precaution, it was just that they were at least three weeks ahead of schedule on food if what he said was true, and it was a little hard to believe, even with the propensity for betas to work themselves to death.

"Well, it's a great coincidence that all these foods can be cleared for eating now. I'm glad things turned out this way, but I want you to get a full medical examination before we leave for the northern barryd, okay? I'll need you there to guide me away from the foods that are poisonous, and I can't have you upchucking or passing out right there on the meeting table. I'll bring that report and a reader with me just in case. You should go get dressed so you can head out with Rakal and me in the hovercar." She slipped out of her slippers and into her high black boots, standing to dismiss Mason formally.

He turned and together they headed out into the central clearing to meet Rakal, Kimmer, Mason and Tarrin by the transport. Dust kicked up around her feet in the area where they had cleared the vegetation to prevent more flash-fires from the hovercar engines.

"Is this thing going to work with all that magnetism? I'd prefer that we keep at least one piece of transport equipment intact for use around the encampment." Tara checked the controls, making sure all ailerons and hydraulics were working. This tiny car had been doing a lot of low-altitude short range surveying for them. Losing it would mean that they'd be stuck in the clearing, surrounded by woods with few trails. She tapped the gyroscope and the compass. The gyroscope was fine, but the compass was useless. "Fun...we don't know which way's north."

Luuko, Liur and several other Dimar from Rank 1 swept in from the north, landing in the clearing east of the main encampment. With the ambling gait of the Dimar, they sauntered over on all fours and sat around the hovercar.

"They say they're here to guide us, sir. They understand that the Wind is disrupting our controls." Tarrin relayed to the non-Talented in the car. "When they rise into the air and raise their tails, it's a signal for us to follow. We can take a place in their formation right behind Luuko, and fly in proper Dimar Rank style. That will go over well with the council." Tarrin grinned. "These guys are as into image as any humans."

Tara watched as the seven Dimar dropped from sitting on their haunches to all fours, and gracefully extended their wings. Liur, in the front, was outfitted in what Tara had come to understand was the honor colors of Telka: purple, green and gold. The billowing silky material stretched from each of his spiral horns down to his forelegs, and as he rose into the air, it flowed back along his sides. His tail banner was a new addition to the outfit, and it was marked with the image of some odd beast on a circle of purple, banded by gold on a sparrow-tailed banner of green. She judged by the colors that it was perhaps the particular Rank's insignia.

Two more Dimar she didn't know rose to take positions behind Liur. They seemed unaware of the effortless grace with which they rose. In a half leap, beating their wings hard to get started, they each launched, but once airborne, they had only to move their wings slightly to remain in the air. They looked like seagulls coasting on a strong inshore breeze, but she could tell from the wind speed meter that the air was almost completely still.

Luuko's launch was the smoothest and most understated of all. He hardly used his legs at all as he moved his wings in a figure eight. It was as if some unseen hand was gently placing him in his position with the others. Liur's tail rose, and Tara gently pressed the pedal. With a jerking start, the car rose up to take a place behind Luuko. Checking the rearview, Tara watched the last Dimar take her place behind the car.

Liur raised his tail again, and together they sped off toward the north. Tara worked hard to stay directly behind Luuko, using Tarrin's spoken play-by-play of their conversations to know when they'd be making adjustments or speeding up. The car faltered often, especially when they passed over the tiny Ekal Barryd, but it seemed to be holding out against the magnetic disruptions.

A wall of smoke billowed out ahead from a raging fire below. Through the gray veil, Tara could make out the silhouettes of the twin spires of Telka Barryd, still many miles off.

Passing over the heart of the fire, the hovercar gave out. Tarrin's link with the Dimar was all that stood between them and a fiery death. He was quick to let them know that the hover system was failing.

Tara aimed the car toward a treetop, hoping the gnarled, fire-resistant branches would survive the weight and heat of the hovercar's underside. The engines cut in again, unexpectedly, giving her some extra maneuvering room with which to place them in the tree. As unexpectedly, the engines again gave out.

Out of the corner of her eye, she saw the blue-green scales of Luuko's side, as he tried to slide under the car to help guide them. If the engines cut in while he was under there, he'd be cooked alive. Panicked, she barked out "LUUKO, DON'T!" hoping he'd hear her through the car's plastic canopy. Luuko dropped his wing out from under the car just as the engines cut in again, and fell away from the car down under tree level.

Using the last bit of engine power, she landed the car in

the treetop, and shut the engines down. Prayerfully, they waited a moment to see if the tree would hold the car's weight and not burst into flames. Tara popped the canopy, swearing as it caught on a branch, and slid out onto the wide limb on which the car was partially resting. Luuko rose up from below, voicing his concern with barking cries.

Rakal and Tarrin, then Mason climbed out onto the branch. Both Rakal's and Tarrin's fur was on end, and they stared at Tara with a look of shock.

"What? You Arrallins never made an emergency treetop landing before? Sheesh." She grinned. Arrallins were lousy passengers, even betas. They turned away, conversing in low, guttural growls. Tara could make out the imprecations in the sentences, but not much else.

Mason was still in the car, looking a bit shaken himself.

"It's over Mason, come on out and join the party, " Tara poked her head into the car and offered the scientist a hand. Unsteadily, he climbed out onto the branch.

"I'm not too keen on heights, or fires, or crashing hovercars, sir. Oh, and nice landing." Mason hugged the upright branches of tree, and watched the roaring fires just a hundred meters away with a combination of curiosity and concern. "Actually, fires are quite interesting, providing you can get away." Realizing he was dirtying his uniform, Mason leaned against the hovercar and attempted to dust off the bits of reddish-brown bark all over his gray uniform jacket.

"Tarrin, can you see if the Dimar would be willing to offer us a lift? We can make arrangements later to try and get this car back to the camp. Being late for the meeting could prove disastrous, though, and our first priority should be getting to Telka." Tara was running diagnostics from the side panel of the car, while Luuko looked on over her shoulder with curiosity.

Luuko raised his head and trumpeted a call to the rest of the Rank, who had been circling above the crash site. Carefully, they flew in and took positions in the trees around them.

"Luuko says you can ride with them back to Telka. It would be just as effective for us to glide in on their backs as to come in as a member of the rank formation. Letting the council members see that touching us won't cause disease or death will be a powerful image to soothe their fears about us as alien invaders or monsters." Tarrin translated the message from Luuko, who lowered a shoulder to Tara. "He's the best flier of the group, Liur says, so you or Rakal can fly in on him. Liur is the second best, and will take whichever of you doesn't fly with Luuko." Perplexed, he paused. "Hey, what are Mason and I? Chopped libber? Liver? Whatever..."

Luuko wiggled his ears and sneezed, which Tara knew was laughter. Liur glided in, landed on the branch next to the car, and lowered his shoulder to Rakal, who carefully climbed aboard, grabbing the long hairs that tufted out along the dorsal ridge on Liur's neck. Rakal's dark black fur stood out boldly against Liur's light golden-brown fire scales. He slid back, lying himself against Liur's back, wrapping his paws in the Dimar's long cream-colored mane. His black tail lashed from side to side. Tara could tell he was a bit nervous about the trip. Arrallins did not have a history of riding other creatures like humans did.

Luuko nudged Tara's arm, and dipped his shoulder to her. Much as she would board her horse, she grabbed a handful of mane and jumped up so that her belly was across his neck. Swinging her right leg over, she settled into a sitting position on his mane-covered shoulders. "Is this obstructing his wings at all, Tarrin?" She took up two handfuls of the creamy hairs, but knew that she would be able to stay on using just her legs.

"Nope...he says that will be fine, providing you feel safe and comfortable." Tarrin replied absently, taking his place on another Dimar's back much as Rakal did. His voice was impassive, but his hackles, which were standing completely on end, showed just how nervous he was about the current proposal.

Mason regarded with trepidation the forest green Dimar that dipped her shoulder to him. He opted for the sitting position that Tara had taken, and grabbed a double fistful of the creature's dark brown mane, wrapping it around his hands tightly. "I'm going to hate this. I can tell."

Luuko, not Liur, took the lead, guiding the group out of the treetops in such a way that they could keep their backs relatively level. Once they were in clear sky, Liur took his position at the lead, but Luuko remained at his side. Tarrin and his reddish-brown Dimar friend took a position directly behind them, close enough so that he could yell translations of conversations to them.

"Goothib here says that they've got you both in front so that you both appear as equals and leaders when we arrive. We've really got to be ready to put on a show when we get there. It seems that the leaders, matriarchs and patriarchs from more than three dozen major barryds are at Telka, which is considered a mid-sized barryd. They've got some myth that invaders from the stars will return here to crush the peaceful barryds. Seems they have a history of space travel themselves, and many of the war barryds chose the Path of the Starborn. They don't fear other species as much as they fear the return of these Dimar. Seeing us will soothe fears, and prove that we're not their returning ancestors." Tarrin was howled against the wind as it roared by.

Tara watched in amazement as the ground rushed beneath them. She could tell that Luuko was not using the air currents to fly, but something carried them along with incredible power. She shifted her weight, testing Luuko's balance. He was rock-solid in the air, as if he was a part of it. The entire experience was exhilarating! *This is the right way to travel*, she mused, remembering the feeling of riding her horse over an extra-wide jump. *It's like a jump, but you never get that jarring sensation of hitting the ground.* Instinctively, she shifted her weight to remain over Luuko's center of gravity as he banked to avoid the rising smoke from the fire that raged in the dense forest below. A group of Dimar had formed a small line near the fire, while another group darted in and out between the trees dousing flames and moving away from the heat as fast as possible.

Tara watched them, almost feeling the heat against their fire scales herself. A blast punctuated the scene as a spout of flame shot up from the darkness of the tree cover. A dark blue one reeled back, partially burned, as others rushed in to douse it with foam and Water. Others shot down the fireballs from the geyser with a different kind of lita, as the Dimar called the sacks they wore to fight fires. They looked almost like bagpipes, with two nozzles, one that shot a high-pressure stream of some liquid toward the different masses of flaming material that fell toward the fallen Dimar. The injured dark blue managed a faltering flight, and another of its group swept in to carry the weight of the only half functional wing and side. Together they sped off toward a small spire in the distance—a sub-barryd, as Tara understood. It was not like Ekal, a new young central barryd, but more like a suburb of Telka, called an Abari. As they sped off, she could see the blue and it's companion fly into one of the many shadows in the forest and disappear. She looked forward to seeing what the inside of the barryds were like, and turned to peer off into the distance at the approaching twin spires of Telka.

Even with the center of the barryd kilometers in the distance, Tara noticed a definite pattern in the forest growth around the barryd proper. Rich bands and glades of trees with thick heavy trunks sprang up, interconnected by hedgerows of smaller leafed bushes and shrubs. Fields, each holding herds of morraks and other land-based vegetarians, dotted the landscape in between these massive groups and rows of taller plants. As the spires grew closer, she could make out the multicolored bodies of Dimar, all resting on branches off the central spire. Down below, a thick canopy of leaves and vines blocked her view of internal structure of the barryd. They approached a large clearing near the southernmost of the central spires, and the melodic cries of the Dimar beneath the leaves resounded and echoed in unseen halls. Dimar on the spire launched themselves toward them, and Tara looked to see Rakal bristle, his tail swishing from side to side.

She was a little nervous herself, with so many large animals flying toward them.

The trumpeting subsided, and was replaced by an eerie song, as the mass of Dimar flying toward them assumed a rank formation.

Luuko tried to vocalize an explanation to Tara, "Dey are sayink Heddoo."

The eight members of their group descended toward the clearing, and the singing Dimar settled in the canopies all around them.

Remaining as level as possible, Luuko, Liur and the two others landed on all fours, and gently sat down on their haunches, allowing them to all slide down their backs into the thick grasses and flowering plants in the field.

Mason slid off his Dimar and disappeared into the meter-high grass. "You should check this biodiversity! I could write about seventeen theses on this patch here alone. They've got insects and at least fifteen species of plant right here, along with these small lizardy-looking critters that we recorded before and...OUCH." There was a pause, but he continued. "Some bite. No matter—I'll medic it." The grass rustled as he dug around and hopped up with his medkit, sucking on his left index finger.

"Mason, I know you're a scientist, but we are on a diplomatic mission. Try not to dig up their front yard until after we've met them, eh?" Rakal's ears were back and his tail swished from side to side as he surveyed the thousands of singing Dimar all around them.

The singing rose to a crescendo and abruptly halted as figures appeared in the gaping doorway ahead of them. Liur and Luuko rose up on their haunches and stood attentively as a column of Dimar, each glittering with gold or silver bands around their necks, and silken tapestries of various three-color combinations and stripe-widths hanging from their horns to their wrists, strode on all fours out into the sunlit courtyard.

Tara instantly noticed that in the third row, a murky brown and black striped Dimar was wearing the colors of Mulkol. He looked particularly fearsome, and despite the fact that he was a male, he dwarfed most of the females in the group. Tara had learned that the males had much narrower hips and shorter tails than the females, and were often smaller, as they did not need to carry eggs. Tarrin stood between Rakal and Tara, ready to translate announcements and discussions.

The bannered Dimar filed out, each taking a position to the right or left of the main doorway.

Tarrin whispered, "The great mother of this barryd will be the last to file out. These are all matriarchs or patriarchs of other barryds. Looks like there's 38 barryds represented here. The ones with gold bands on their wrists and horns are Tel barryds, the engineering-focus barryds. The silver colored ones, that's actually platinum I think, mean that those matriarchs and patriarchs are from the Ela barryds, or the food-production and animal breeding focus barryds. Guild-based barryds, which are like trading cities, use stone-types to denote themselves. See the green stone cuffs on that one...ooh...look: That one there, the blue, black and red bannered one with the iron-black wrist and horn cuffs—he's Mulkol. He's got his psi-walls up clear to the moon, and the other 'archs each occasionally try to peer into his thoughts. I'm not even going to try. This guy's a pro."

Luuko rumbled approvingly as a deep purple Dimar appeared in the doorway. Her mane was snowy white, and her muzzle hair was grizzled with age. She was a massive female, and she strode out with a slight limp. The banner colors of Telka swept down around her forelegs, and she dipped her head to them with stately grace. Her banners were decorated with many small golden circles, much like the belt a belly dancer might wear, and they jingled as the wind rustled the silk.

"She's wearing the golden circles to show that she's the discussion leader for this Council Gathering. It's a day of high honor for Telka, being allowed to host this many major barryd dignitaries, as her barryd is only considered a secondary one. Some of these 'archs have come from as far away as the twin continents to the east." Tarrin pointed to one light blue female and a coppery male, each wearing gold bands of a Tel barryd. "The blue, yellow, and green silked female there and the copper one with the red yellow and green are from the twin continents." Tarrin conferred with Luuko again, and returned to explain more. "Check the bracelets of the Dimar you see along the wall. If they're wearing bands of the colors of a particular 'arch, then, you guessed it, they're from that barryd.

Oops... the Leader is getting ready to declare the Great Council open to you guys. Be ready to smile, but with no teeth, and bow, Luuko says."

Tarrin straightened up, and Rakal fluffed out his cropped mane and tail instinctively. Tara shot a glance at Mason, who was discreetly continuing to take readings with his hand-held scanner.

Suddenly, all the 'archs roared out "OOOLLLLAAAAAHM!" and the crowd fell silent.

The great mother first approached Liur, who bowed his head before her. Affectionately, she touched her muzzle to the top of his brow. She repeated this gesture to Luuko, and each member of the rank that had brought them.

"She's welcoming them as her children with a traditional parent-child greeting. It's like a shoulder rub or a playful bat for Arrallakeeni. She won't do that to us, thank Ghu. She looks strong enough to drive us into the ground like tent-spikes." Tarrin watched the careful procession closely. "Okay...now she's going to sit up on two legs and call us over. Luuko says we need to go over and bow to her, and she will declare us welcome to the meeting. Then, we get to go eat!" Tarrin licked his chops enthusiastically, and quickly shut his mouth. "We shouldn't bear our teeth, no matter what happens. That would be a threat. No smiling, you humans."

Mason was recording the whole scene, and surreptitiously turned the camera back to the Great Mother of Telka. She rose onto her hind legs, and slowly warbled a long, singsong message. Then, she lowered her paws, pads out, toward the four of them.

"Okay...now bow, and rise up, and show your paw-pads to them." Tarrin whispered as he started to bow.

Together they all bowed. Mason kept the recorder going but clipped it to his belt. They rose, and as instructed, offered their palms and paws to her.

She rumbled with approval, and with a brassy trumpet, signaled the resumption of the Council talks.

Taking places in the long line of 'archs, they followed the group into the first chamber of the barryd proper. The room glowed with blue fires stationed in cubbyholes all along the walls of the barryd. The floor was even, and inlaid with a pattern of braided wood. The walls, which were twisting knots of rich mahogany, rose up several meters to a balcony, with a railing of a lighter, golden wood. The ceiling rose up, cathedral style for more than thirteen meters, and tiny blue and yellow fires illuminated the scene in the darker back half of the chamber. The front half was awash in hundreds of colors of light, as the sunlight streamed through a brilliant stained-glass window. Instead of lead between the panes of glass, the mahogany wall striations twisted through the panels, holding them in place. It was as if they had grown the branches of a tree around the glass itself. The windows depicted a white Dimar standing on her hind legs in a blood red pool of water with her forepaws raised to the sun, and eight other Dimar standing in deep green pools with their heads bowed. The vibrancy of the color surpassed any stained glass Tara had seen on Earth.

Mason interrupted her reverie, "Sir...you're not going to believe this, but..."

"Hmm? Mason... what is it?" She checked the readings on his scanner.

"The floor's alive, and the walls are moving." Mason stared at one of the rich cords of mahogany, and tentatively reached out to stroke it. "The whole room is a set of cooperative plant species. I've never seen anything like this."

The walls didn't move that Tara could see, so she checked the scanner. Sure enough, he was right. The motion sensor did detect almost imperceptible movement, and there was definitely biological activity in both the floors and the walls. "Incredible! I was just thinking to myself that it looked like they had grown a tree around the stained glass window. I guess they did!" Tara continued to marvel at the stained glass window, noting that the panes were, in fact, glass.

Tara approached the fountain pedestal at the rear of the room where many of the 'archs were drinking and lounging. Two of the 'archs made way for her to see. She turned to smile at them, but remembered the all-important rule about not bearing teeth. She bowed to them instead, and regarded the pool. The wood had grown into a large scallop shape, and the water, which according to the scan was just plain old water with the trace elements they knew were common on Dimar, flowed from a tube of a lighter, golden wood. She cupped her hands and sipped the cool liquid, realizing just how hot she was in her wool jacket and pants. Other 'archs lowered their heads into the fountain and catlike, lapped away. Bowing, she took her leave and headed toward one of the other large pedestals stationed around the room. Mason joined her.

"According to the scanner, these pedestals aren't alive. They look like they were crafted by some Dimar, probably as dinner tables of some kind. They're made of ceramic, and have been fired with a glaze. The cracks of the glaze hold residues of whatever they've put in here, and according to this, this table has held vegetable matter." Mason looked relieved.

"Why the fuss over what they keep in their bowls, Mason?" She fingered the glittering glaze in the bowl shaped top of the pedestal.

"I was worried that they used them as sacrificial altars or something." He shrugged.

Tara resisted the urge to laugh, but realized his concern was logical. They really didn't know enough about Dimar yet to fully trust their hospitality. Tarrin had gotten a fairly complete history on them, and supposedly many of their most warlike ancestors had taken to the stars and been lost, but the fact remained that they had a history of war, torture and sacrifice that rivaled that of earth. The stained glass panel, she knew from her studies, was of Telkai, the great engineer that gave them all wings, but she still wasn't sure exactly how they did their biotechnical alterations, or what experiments the engineers of the Dimar might want to perform on their new neighbors.

Two by two, various Dimar, all wearing the colors of Telka, entered the room bearing trays of steaming fruits and vegetables. They deposited each of the trays into a different, small pedestal-bowl. Two large females brought out half a morrak carcass slung between them, also thoroughly cooked, and hung it on a spit over a larger bowl.

More pairs emerged from the dark corridor and placed raw fruits, vegetables and meats of various animals in other pedestal-bowls around the room. Tarrin hurried over to explain. "These guys did their homework. The cooked food is for us. The raw stuff is really meant for the other Dimar, but we can risk it if we want. They do cook, but not to the extent that we do. They prefer to marinade, and only cook if the food is old. Most of them can survive the various toxins produced by the old foods. It's just a flavor issue. Seems the genetic tinkering they did for their war two thousand years ago left them mostly immune to food poisoning and many forms of disease. That Mulkol guy over there could probably eat just about anything and not mind." Tarrin was staring at the massive half-morrak carcass, barely able to control his drooling.

"Go ahead, Tarrin...I'll join you. Enough of these frigging C rations. Let's eat!" Tara and Tarrin race-walked toward the carcass. Mason and Rakal were already digging in.

Tara reached for her saber, and cursed herself for choosing the sidearm instead. She looked around the pedestal for something to cut with, and found a long, spiked knife on a chain under the lip of the pedestal. It was gray and shiny, but not metal, and cut the meat easily.

"Hey, Tarrin. What's with the chain on the knife? Do they think we're going to steal it like the pens at the banks back on Earth?" She again resisted the urge to grin, noticing that many of the 'archs were watching them intently as they ate. "Mason, didn't you say we could eat the potato fruit and the giant grapes without cooking? Might be a good excuse to break the ice with some of those 'archs over there." Tara loaded a well-seasoned morrak steak onto the wooden plates that were stacked nearby and carved it into bite-sized cubes.

Tarrin explained the chain and knife as he gnawed away on the leg of the carcass hanging from the spit. "According to Luuko, it's a precaution so that if a fight breaks out, no one will be able to use them. The chain is so strong that not even the biggest Dimar can break it. Seems that very early in their history, Dimar stabbing other Dimar was a big problem. That knife is made from a type of tree found in the barryd. It's really a thorn from the tree that has been used as a ceremonial site for eons. The tree is the human equivalent of Edelweiss. Young Dimar, both male and female, try to climb the tree without using their wings to grab a bunch of the blue flowers at the top. Bringing a bunch of those flowers to a love is a sign of true devotion and daring. If they slip, they might impale themselves on the thorns, which happens quite often."

Mason had trundled over to the giant grape table and had one on his plate. The 'archs snuffled around him curiously, but his mind was only on the grape. Again, Tara resisted the urge to grin. On Earth, he had hated grapes with a passion.

Tarrin, looking satisfied, shuffled up next to Tara. "You haven't touched a bite of that steak. You going to eat it?"

She flipped a cube of meat at him, and he snatched it from the air. "You wolf...it's mine. You've got the rest of the carcass. Go carve your own, and tell me what they're all talking about, while you're at it." She took a seat along the wall, using a roughly level shelf as a makeshift table. Using her fingers, she picked up the cubes of steak.

She could tell from the glances being exchanged that there was a discussion being held all around them, that only Tarrin could hope to hear.

"They're all using private bandwidths. I've been told that it's poor form to pry into conversations and thoughts. I figure, with these being 'archs, they'll let us know what we need to know when they're ready."

Rakal dislodged himself from the shoulder of the carcass, in which he had barely made a dent, and slumped against the wall. "I'd like the rest to go, please." He winked at a passing red Dimar, who wiggled his ears as Tarrin translated.

Just as Tara was finishing the last of her steak, the Great Mother, who had been reclining on a Dimar-sized couch in front of the largest fire pit, rose and addressed the crowd in a lilting tuneful voice.

"She's getting the meeting underway. She'll start with a synopsis of the discussion until now, so that we'll know what they're talking about. She's authorized me to translate. Shnu, like she had any choice." Tarrin whuffled with amusement.

"Okay... it seems that they've been studying us through the Dimar that have been stationed around our camp. Because we do not use Telkai, we are smothering the soil beneath our buildings and decreasing the total life that Dimar can hold. She doesn't mean this as an insult, and she understands that our ways are different. There's a sacred plan being realized by all the barryds that will encourage the planet to carry more life than ever before, as well as bringing an end to fires on Mainland. They would prefer that the plan continue, and that we try to adopt the ways of Telkai and live in barryds if this is at all possible. They will teach us what we need to know, and Telka hereby welcomes us into the barryd as residents, if we choose to accept their offer of kinship. If the blending of our colony into Telka is successful, other barryds will allow our people in, and as our population grows, we will take a place in each barryd as an integral part of their social and executive structure." Tarrin struggled to translate the concepts in clear speech.

"She thinks in incredibly vivid pictures. I wish you guys could see what she's envisioning for the future. According to what I can see, she's got entire wings of the barryd that she's ready to dedicate to human and Arrallin habitation, providing we allow one Dimar to reside in each room to see if we can all get along. She knows that humans and Arrallins live side by side with ease, so she doesn't anticipate any major difficulties. She'd also like our help in improving the fire walls and helping to stave off the fires that threaten the barryd every dry season. Boy, does she ever believe in the power of positive thinking." Tarrin regarded the Great Mother with the same look of respect and appreciation he often directed at Rakal.

"Um...hold on, guy. Huddle time." Tara said, waving Mason over. "Mason, leave the grape and get your butt over here." He left his plate by the pedestal almost forlornly and hurried over to where they sat. "This is all going a bit too fast for me. What are we missing here? How will this hurt us, and how will this help us? Why are they being so generous?"

Rakal agreed. "There's no such thing as a free lunch, or are these guys just saints?"

"More importantly, is this an ultimatum, or can we choose to stay at the colony instead? Will they shuffle us back out through the gate?" Mason looked around the room nervously. He wasn't a man who enjoyed not having options.

Tarrin clarified, "We can stay in colony form, providing that we adopt either a subterranean lifestyle, or we can borrow some of their plant-tech and start developing our own living home structures. They really just don't want us using nylar or dead materials over the topsoil. It sours the soil and kills plants that are necessary for balance in the region."

"Oh good. We've got a choice in this, what little choice it is. We've got some mining equipment that can be refitted for use in atmosphere, and our plasma rifles can act as cutters." Mason's gaze drifted as he contemplated the engineering options.

"She's also sent me a message on a very private bandwidth, warning us that the firestorms are moving toward our area. The other 'archs wanted to see how well we deal with the storms without their help, so she was risking some serious loss of face by telling us even that much." Tarrin turned back toward the Great Mother's dais, watching her curiously.

"Like we couldn't tell about the fires. We've been watching them for the last two weeks, and I've noticed that our friends from Ranks One and Four who have been hanging out with us fly over at night and dig firebreaks. We've got at least one ally with Telka." Tara whispered to the four, forgetting that none of the 'archs would understand. "So, what time frame are they giving us? When can we decide?"

Tarrin cocked his head and his eyes grew distant. "Um, the offer stands for the next 2 cycles. Seems they move slowly with these kinds of things."

"Two cycles? That's four years! Cool. I'll revise my timetable accordingly." Mason, looking relieved, trundled off and brought back his grape.

"So, it looks like we can shut the jump gate. We've got a new home." Rakal rumbled, "Give the Great Mother our thanks, and let her know that we'll make a decision on their generous offer of cohabitation within the two cycles allotted. Now, I have a morrak to finish, if you all don't mind..."

With that, he leapt back onto the pedestal and dug back into the massive shoulder.

Chapter 10

The feasting and festivities lasted well into the afternoon. The Dimar performed plays from their history, calling on the powers of their ancestors to sustain them in the time of the fires. They did a small war-dance demonstration, showing how each season, they use this blood sport to help define the boundaries of each barryd each year, trading harvest fields and suburbs between major barryd centers. The war dances were often fixed according to the needs of both barryds, except in the case of Telka and Mulkol. The dances between any barryd and a war barryd were deadly serious, ending in death for an unlucky few. Living next door to one of the last war barryds on Dimar made life difficult for the Telkans.

Tara most enjoyed the barryd tour, and worked to memorize the general structure of most barryds. The hall they had feasted in was much like a great hall in a castle, except that only one-sixth the main population feasted there every night. The barryd had six dining halls stationed throughout, with multiple kitchens and food storage areas off each. Guilds, the economic equivalents of corporations, competed with each other to feed the population and make the most nila, their form of money, creating a restaurant row in each hall. Between the graciously appointed mahogany halls and golden walled kitchens, corridors large enough for even the Great Mother led to various workrooms and crafter's workshops, as well as the rooms for Tinar, Telkai, Ela, Tel, and even Mulkai studies. All passages, each in varying hues of wood-tones depending on the major plant-types that had been used to create each wing, were richly decorated with stained glass panels, paintings, tapestries and sculpture. Each passage also connected to one of the two central spires, which, unlike the residence spires that towered over each of the six dining halls, were hollow, and lead up to the clear sky and straight down into the heart of the barryd, shrouded in darkness. They entered a massive oblong chamber that dwarfed any of the six dining halls, and each end of the room had one huge hole in the floor, surrounded by golden wood railings, large enough to fit four Dimar through. They were not allowed to descend, and the scanner's bioactivity scale nearly broke when they lowered the receiver down into the chasm.

All halls, passages and rooms were well lit by the same blue or yellow flame cubbyholes that dotted the main hall. Tarrin relayed for the tour guide. "The barryd is constantly breaking down impure hydrocarbons in the crust and incorporating them into the structure, but the gas that the barryd can't consume is burned for light, and the waste produced, mostly carbon monoxide is filtered by the leaves higher up and again recycled for use in the barryd. Nothing is lost, nothing wasted. We could learn from these guys — this place is a self contained bio-bubble."

The red Dimar male continued the tour, rumbling in low tones, and Tarrin rushed to keep up, "The rooms along the outside, with window views of places in the distance are highly sought after by most Dimar, especially the visual artists. To avoid distress among members of the barryd, the rooms are assigned in cycles to anyone who applies, allowing all a chance to enjoy the beautiful views where they work. If a Dimar doesn't have a window room for working, he or she is usually stationed in a window room for sleeping. Many prefer to work in the dark, or without a good view — much like our programming teams — and opt to have a window room residence permanently. Refusing to give up a particular chamber at the appointed time is considered a treason against the barryd, and punishable by a week in the muck-room." Tarrin paused, and his speckled ears drooped.

"We're going to visit the muck-rooms next. It's not a pretty sight, but serves an important function for the barryd." Tarrin shuffled a bit, trying to get a spot in the back of the tour group.

They walked down a long, fairly deserted corridor that angled down, and stopped on a circular pad. Behind them, a plant-wall constricted, blocking their way out. Rakal decided to toss the tooth bearing restriction and let loose with a low, spine-tingling growl. The tour guide backed to the wall rearing on two legs, as another similar plant-wall released.

"Rakal! Rakal! It's okay...this is an airlock...ooooh...." Tarrin grabbed his muzzle as a blast of foul air from the room beyond reached him.

Rakal's ears drooped and he howled, grabbing his nose. "That stench! What is this place?"

"The tour guide is explaining that this is the muck room, where all the biological animal waste is recycled into the finest fertilizer ever known to Dimar. The processing secrets were a gift from Elanuru, a farming barryd to the northeast. He forgives your aggressive behavior, and understands that you are in uncertain surroundings. He wishes peace." Tarrin went nose to nose with the tour guide to apologize. "Come on, Rakal. He didn't mean not to tell us about the airlock, and he does understand why the smell bothers us. They're fairly immune to it, but they still dislike the idea of the place. Give him some nose."

Tara wasn't particularly bothered by the stench, being used to her horses, dogs, goats, sheep, llamas and other animals stored in the animal pens on board the Golden Hinde. Mason was a little less enthusiastic.

"They can't smell this? Must be part of that war-engineering they all underwent to be able to eat toxins. Maybe I'll get a Telkai nose job myself." Mason peered in the door to see Dimar, young and old alike, walking along catwalks with paddles to stir and check the consistency of the various filtration pools. "Why do they have the airlocks if they can't smell it?"

"Good question...I'll ask." Tarrin tilted his head toward the tour guide, who was touching noses with Rakal. "Ooooh...uuurk. The system goes through a periodic cleansing. One set of pools is always filled with water, up to the ceiling. During the fire season this water is pumped from cycling room to cycling room to dilute the minerals and refuse and either spread it to the far ends of the barryd lands, or to feed the main barryd itself. The mineral rich water is pumped out of the barryds and is slowly released to the grasses and other non-integrated plant life in each area in such a way that salinization from irrigation never occurs and the plants can resist the fire. However, the distance the system can cover is severely limited."

"I'd hate to get caught in a room when it floods." Mason winced as he tentatively stepped out onto a catwalk and scanned a pool. "Hey...this place is a tiny microcosm of the ecology outside. That far pool there—you could swim in it! They're just speeding up nature's own recycling system in here."

Tarrin relayed Mason's concern, "Our guide, Uurlin, openly admits that leaving a Dimar in a flooding muck-room was a popular form of execution in some of the wars immediately after the war with the Isles, but now, the barryd itself has sensors and will not cleanse a room unless it is completely free of air breathing animal life."

Two surly looking Dimar struggled with paddles to bring raw refuse into the first cycling pool. The tour guide pointed to them, and motioned to Tarrin.

"He says that those two, the green and brown females over there are down here for bullying a smaller male who is not as good at Tinar, the firefighting flight, as they. That particular chore is reserved for Dimar with discipline problems, and to teach them to work together. If they work well together, they can finish their allotment of the shoveling and return to their normal schedules sooner. If they can forge a friendship and maintain it, the Great Mother will reward them both with places of honor at her table for a time." Tarrin looked impressed. "They have a punishment system, but they prefer to focus on rewarding positive behaviors instead of just punishing negatives. It's a reform discipline system, without institutionalized revenge, but they've still got a vengeance problem among their residents. Seems fighting and killing one another off was at one point encouraged by the leaders to control the populations and was a form of entertainment. Bread and circus."

Much to the relief of the Arrallins, they were soon out of the muck-room and into one of the many garden courtyards along the outer wall of the barryd proper.

"Each of these huge hedgerows is actually a sub-dwelling for various families or individuals who choose to live outside of the barryd proper. Usually they maintain the fields or herds, and often work long hours maintaining the fire line, as their houses go first when the heat gets through in the dry season." Tarrin began backing toward the entrance, his tail a bottlebrush, as a herd of large, strange looking animals raced toward them. "Oolars!"

Rakal, Mason and Tara all stood their ground as the vicious ram-horned, warthog tusked canine creatures bounded around them. The tour guide sat back on his hind legs as they tried to climb on him, and he warbled to them joyously. They ranged from tawny gold to pure black, with smooth gray ram horns and claws and white tusks. Their tails were more catlike than dog-like, but in general, they acted more like dogs than anything. Curiously, but not threateningly, they nosed around the feet of the visitors. Tarrin had climbed to the top of a hedgerow to observe and translate.

"These guys are one of their forms of pet species. They are used to patrol perimeters, and have been bred into huge, armored war-beasts in ages previous. The tour guide has let them know that you are not invaders, but advises caution around them anyway. They're used to playing with Dimar, who, even when they shed their firescales have much thicker fur and hide than we do. The females have white tufts behind their ears and on their chin. They're also egg-layers, and the females are larger than the males."

Tara knelt down and reached out a hand to a black and white oolar that had been fascinated by her wool jacket sleeve. She enthusiastically whuffled Tara's palm with a warm, dry nose. She scratched the beast between the horns, and stroked her fuzzy muzzle. "I could get to like these critters. I wonder how Koji and the other dogs will get along with them."

"Dogs, nothing. The cats will be scared silly. Good thing the morraks seem to have a fancy for the felines — they'll need big allies with these guys around. And what will the goats and pigs think?" Mason was sitting on the ground scratching the belly of a tawny, spotted female, while Rakal was on all fours tussling with a buff-colored male.

Tarrin, holding his position in the safety of the hedgerow, continued his translation, "They're good for patrols, herding, hauling, digging, and baby-sitting, and have been Telkai altered to be more tractable and intelligent than their wild siblings who still roam much of Dimar's unsettled regions. Let's get out of here, please."

Tara smiled up at Tarrin. "Come on down and get used to these guys. I'm going to try to get a pup or two for the colony, so you'd better learn to adapt," she chimed teasingly.

Gingerly, he made his way down the side of the 5-meter high wall of shrubs, and landed on all fours in front of Tara's female. They touched noses, and she sat in front of him and lowered her head for a pat. As if expecting an electric shock, he carefully patted her head once. With more confidence, he stroked her broad head, and then sat back on his haunches. "Hey... they're not so bad. They're better than your dogs, I'd say, and they've got a tiny glimmer of awareness in there. Not Talent as I know it, but enough to relay good fast commands."

A wing of Dimar swept in — it was Luuko, Liur and the others.

"Ah, here's our ride to the upper levels. Seems that since all Dimar can fly, and most Oolars are carried by their keepers or use the venting tunnels to move about, we'll need to take another flight to continue the tour." Tarrin trundled toward his red-brown Dimar friend and hopped onto his back, grabbing two fistfuls of his mane. "Not going to drop me, Goothib, right? Mason, Tewi is willing to take you again, providing you don't rip out too much of her mane this time." He whuffled an Arrallin chuckle.

The dark green Dimar wiggled her ears at Mason, who blushed. With considerably more confidence, he climbed aboard her shoulder and sat astride her back. "Yee-haw," he muttered with a half grin.

Rakal was aboard Liur, again choosing the reclined position on his back. Like Tarrin, he was much more comfortable with the idea of riding Dimar-back, but he still wasn't ready to risk sitting up.

Tara bowed to Luuko, and hopped across his neck with the grace of a practiced horseback rider. Her time riding in the minute spaces of the cargo holds of the Golden Hinde had allowed her to keep her skills well honed, but she still took two handfuls of Luuko's mane, just to be safe.

The tour guide led, and gracefully, the five forms rose with cautious speed. Sweeping around the twin central spires of the barryd, Tara was able to get a much closer view of the structures. Layer after layer of canopied tree cover was stacked around the central spires. Flat-topped branches reached from the spires over roof-branches of the residence rooms, serving as perches for the Dimar who were off duty from their various crafts or fire line duty. At the top of each spire, there was a wide platform, and various Dimar, each wearing the honor silks of Telka sat, watching the fire line intently. Above the platforms, large bulbous pods ending in rich violet petals, arrayed like a set of bluebells, hung over providing shade to the Dimar on the platform.

They circled, echoing the greetings from relaxing Dimar on the branches with musical warbling cries, and swept in onto a platform at the end of a long passage on the top level. All the rooms that faced the outer wall had railed balconies, and were wide enough for two or three Dimar to land and sit comfortably. Tara envisioned three Dimar with a pellet-stove having a barbecue, and stifled a giggle as she slid from Luuko's shoulder.

"Oh, the great mother bids us to come and witness a...miracle?" Tarrin looked intrigued and padded down the hall on all fours, forcing the humans to double time it to keep up. His gaze was distant, as if he was guided by a strong scent, and not any visual cue.

They skittered around corners and worked their way through the twisting residence passages coming to a halt before a spacious set of living quarters, huge by human standards, currently packed with Dimar of all colors. The yellow wall fires burned brightly, bathing the room in warmth. Judging from the many beautiful paintings that hung about the place, it was the residence of a more prominent artisan of the barryd, or of a very serious art collector.

"Okay, Mason and I are allowed to enter, but Rakal and Tara must remain in the other room. The Great Mother of the barryd is the only 'arch allowed to be in the same room with a hatchling, to prevent child-stealing." Tarrin slipped through the doorway on two legs and sat slightly behind the deep purple back of the Telka Matriarch. Mason followed, the scanner and recorder buzzing in his hands.

"Oh, great." Rakal muttered, and the Great Mother turned to hiss at him.

Tarrin translated, "They need silence to listen for problems in the eggs."

Tara and Rakal both stood in the doorway, careful not to cross the braided knot of floor that marked the base of the door. Two eggs sat in a large leaf-lined nest, with carefully quilted pads all around them. Their shells were speckled with dark brown blotches and multicolored spots on a variegated tan base, and looked a bit like giant wild chicken eggs, except that they were lightly coated with a chalky powder. Each egg had many holes knocked in it, and fractures along the sides, but neither had opened to reveal enough of the babies to know what they looked like.

In the deathly silence, they could hear the frantic tapping of the young inside.

After what seemed like hours to Tara, a tiny clawed hand emerged, punching it's way through the wall of the more greenish of the two eggs, soon followed by a wet nose with a shiny black egg-tooth and a decidedly grumpy face. The little gray-blue Dimar, wrinkled and scaleless, without even a hint of underfur, fell out of the egg and down the side of the nest onto one of the quilted pads. It's father, a small brown, crooned over it, touching his muzzle to it's forehead, and gently lifted the pad with the exhausted baby toward it's mother, a light green Dimar with an almost white mane, who also greeted it in Dimar style. The baby screeched crossly, but quieted when the father settled it in the thick mane on the mother's back and shoulders. With unusual strength, the baby grabbed onto the mother's fur, wrapping itself deep into the silken mane, and fell into a deep sleep with only the end of it's muzzle and the spade of it's tiny tail showing.

Not to be outdone, the second blue and brown speckled egg shattered with force, popping the pointed end of the egg off and onto one of the pads. The little blue-gray baby inside kicked away at the shell and fell on its belly into the nest. The mother this time lifted the tiny baby, who, unlike it's cross sibling, only warbled. Both parents greeted it warmly. She nestled it in the rich chocolate brown fur on the back of the father, and it too dug in and disappeared, except for a wing tip and the tiny snout, with it's shiny black egg tooth.

Once both children were safely hatched, the noise of half-spoken, half-thought conversations filled every room in the apartment, and the Great Mother sung a long, complex tune in a major key to welcome the new barrydmates.

Mason came out of the room, wiping tears from his eyes, followed by Tarrin.

"Much more dignified than whelping, I'd say." Rakal chuckled, watching the new parents, craning their long necks to watch their sleeping charges.

"So, what's the story? Those wrinkly little guys are male? Female? Will they both be gray-blue? What's their gestation period? What's the hatching period?" Mason bombarded Tarrin with questions faster than he could get answers from the people in the crowd.

"Okay...okay...they'll be whatever color and sex they turn out to be. Oh, there! Look...see that little velvety guy over there—with the deep blue velvet skin. He's an immature Dimar, like a human twelve-year-old. He'll fly by a firestorm and shed that velvet to reveal his first coat of firescales, and he'll probably be blue, judging from the velvet. Sometimes the color of the immature velvet doesn't match their scales and fur, much like all Arrallins are born camouflaged and develop their mature coloring. It will be a cycle before they'll be able to discern visibly what sex the babies are. The Dimar don't differentiate much between egg layers and egg keepers, female and male, so it doesn't affect their schooling or socialization. Their vocal language is gender neutral in most cases." Tarrin kept his eyes on the tiny snouts that poked through the fur on the parents' shoulders.

"Seems the big dark green male and the yellow female in there are the alternates — God-parent equivalents for Dimar, and the Great Mother or one of her acolytes is required to witness the hatchings and help if necessary. Because Telka is a Telkai-focus barryd, the 'archs are taught the healing arts, and this 'arch tries to make every hatching she can." Tarrin continued, bowing his head to the matriarch as she turned to regard them.

Tara felt totally drained, and was glad Mason had brought extra disks for the recorder. She'd need to review all of this to make a final determination on the feasibility of cohabitation with this species. With the Arrallins 30 years ago, the decision had been easy, as the betas naturally flocked to the captains of their alien ships, full of new and interesting human technology to study. The humans couldn't beat the betas off with a plasma cannon. But these Dimar were very individual, and much more advanced than both humans and Arrallins in their knowledge of biotech. The problem would be keeping her people from flocking to the Dimar.

She got that now familiar feeling in the back of her mind, and turned slowly to face the red-brown Dimar that had brought Mason in. She stared at him, seeing a faint blue-green light behind him and an image of Harmon flashed into her mind. Her stomach knotted.

"Tara? You still with us?" Rakal nudged her shoulder.

"Yeah...I'm just completely beat. After that huge red-meat meal, and then all this," she held out her arms, as if to encircle the room, "to deal with. It's given me the stares." Quietly, she asided to Rakal, "I think we're going to have the same trouble keeping our ranks in line as you had when humans dropped in on Arralla."

Rakal nodded somberly, watching the matriarch who had been very pointedly not looking at them, but lavishing attention on Tarrin and Mason. The end of his tail twitched slightly, as if he were stalking something.

Tara had dealt with ornery captains, uppity first mates, generals, prime ministers and dozens of cutthroat politicians. She had even survived working with Rakal, an Arrallin Alpha. She could handle one competitive fuzz-lizard. It would just take time.

Chapter 11

Luuko eyed Tara closely. For a moment, he thought he may have heard her speak, but she was just staring at Goothib, who was babbling away with Harmon, relaying the joyous birth of the new barrydmates to her. They were the first of the season, and very early, as most eggs wouldn't be hatching until the middle of the rainy season.

He turned back to listen to Tarrin and the Great Mother, rapid firing questions back and forth about child rearing in all three species. The humans, it seemed, were more like the Dimar, in that they paired off and each pair would produce an offspring that often would be raised either by a group or by the pair, or by just one individual. They did not often produce two offspring in one hatching, and neither species laid eggs. His mind boggled at the thought. In fact, both Arrallins and humans produced nectar in their chests and abdomens to feed their young directly after they were born! Luuko reared back, a bit disgusted, but Tarrin clearly broadcast that this was considered a wonderful thing by the parents of both human and Arrallins.

The Arrallins were especially puzzling to Luuko. Without eggs, they'd produce sometimes as many as two dozen offspring, each one popping out of the egg-layer one after the other, and then both parents and all the Arrallakeeni would produce nectar to feed all the hungry mouths. It must be a horrible sight—all those squalling youngsters popping out all over the place! Luuko would be as supportive as possible when the Arrallins finally began producing offspring.

Luuko looked back through the doorway at Tara and Rakal, wondering if they were angry that they couldn't enter the room with the Great Mother. Tarrin had expressed a deep concern about this, explaining that it would be considered a personal insult to Rakal and Tara, but the Great Mother had stood firm on the ancient rule that the Leader of the barryd would be the only Leader allowed into a room with hatching eggs. Back during the wars, Leaders and their barryd children, rendered sterile by a particularly virulent strain of the active Telkai cells, took to smuggling away hatchlings from their parents, and since those days, no Leaders other than the properly vested leader of the barryd, or it's acolytes, would be allowed into the chamber until the babies were properly nestled on their parents' backs.

Luuko had argued fervently that although Rakal and Tara were both technically Leaders, that they were not likely to try stuffing the new babies in their clothing and go running off, especially when they had no idea how to leave the upper level of the barryd without some Dimar to fly them to the courtyard level below. Luuko felt another surge of pride, remembering the stunned looks from the various Leaders as he and Liur, side by side, flew the Leaders of the starborn colony to the Council.

Even now, he could hear the paranoid whispers of the visiting Dimar in chambers nearby, wondering if humans and Arrallins were in fact the ancient warriors of the Mulkai returned to Dimar to conquer. He knew, not only from his exchanges with Tarrin, but from his overall experience at the colony, that they were, in fact, just Lost Waters from another world, not quite sure where they are, but following their chosen path regardless of the tide. Luuko rather enjoyed their company.

Do not let yourself be lured off by strange nectars, Luuko. Telka needs you now more than ever. It was the Great Mother speaking to him, spikes of protectiveness flooding the message. Luuko blanched, embarrassed that she had heard his ramblings. *I know where my duty lies, Mother. However, if they choose to accept the honor, Tara, Rakal, Mason, and all the others will be barrydmates. Their ways will become ours as much as ours will be theirs, so I struggle to learn.* He could sense that she was exhausted from the meetings and the constant mental games that the other Leaders played.

That is an excellent endeavor, Luuko. Do charge yourself to learn the vocalization of both of the species if you can, and encourage your siblings at the colony to do likewise. Having only a few Minds among them is making communication and learning very difficult, and there will be crises soon. The fires will hit the dry wells near them and spread at twice the rate. Warn them, if you can. The Great Mother's tone was torn, echoing a friction toward Rakal and Tara, but concern for all their children. *Oh, and watch your tail around the other Leaders. They're a dangerous lot, as I'm sure you've found.* Her tone was suffused in pride for Luuko. He had been quite a sensation among the dignitaries of other barryds.

More than one Leader had approached him about flying the fires and becoming a Tinar instructor at their barryd. They could sense his comfort on the Wind, as well as his comfort with the new, strange starborn visitors. His knowledge of them and his skill with the fires would make him a popular and welcome addition to many of the major barryds on Mainland, as he was well aware. However, as each offer topped the first, it made him realize more and more that making Telka, or a barryd like Telka, the safest, healthiest barryd on Dimar was truly his first goal. He'd be lost on the Twin Continents and in the Southern Archipelago, which had no fires and a weaker Wind at best, and the Isle held no barryds at all, even to this day. The barryds to the east held some attraction, but the easterners were traditionally their major rivals at the Mirrai festival. How could he face his barrydmates in the Wind games, to fly against them?

He followed Tara and Rakal into the hallway, leaving the happy parents and their family to celebrate without the pressure of a full honor guard and three Leaders in their midst. The Great Mother filed out last, following Tarrin and Mason, who continued, even while walking, to bombard her with questions about everything under the sun.

He touched minds with Tarrin. *The Great Mother is quite tired from the day's exertions, Tarrin. Can I help with the questions? I would enjoy helping you learn about our home.* His inflection on the 'our' included Tarrin, Mason and the others affectionately. *Plus, we have been charged with the task of learning your vocal language, so that we can be better 'mates to more than just your Talents. Can you help me?*

Tarrin nearly howled with laughter. *Shnu! I remember how much fun I had learning English when I took my first assignment on a human ship. Where should we start?*

Luuko could sense a mischievous intent in Tarrin's enthusiasm, but he could survive the occasional embarrassment in order to complete his task. *How do you say hatchling in English? And Egg? Nest? We can start with the events at hand.* He sent Tarrin clear pictures of each item, waiting for the verbal equivalents.

Mmmm...hatchling would be 'Baby', egg is 'egg' and nest is 'nest'. Oh, oh oh! Try this...go over to Tara and say 'Hey Baby, nice eggs.' Tarrin was snorting and whuffling, and whispered something to Mason in English.

Luuko managed to understand 'Tara', 'Baby' and 'eggs', but not much else. Gamely, he approached the human Leader, looking back toward Tarrin and Mason, who were both laughing now.

"Heeeeee babeeeee, naaahce eggs." His muzzle mouthed the words with some difficulty, but he could see that she understood, and was covering her mouth in an effort not to expose her teeth as she laughed.

"Thank you," she replied, talking as slowly as possible so he could catch each syllable.

"Taaahnk oooo," Luuko echoed, getting the meaning from Tarrin. *Is this some wonderful compliment for the humans? Should I compliment Mason on his eggs? Neither of them have eggs, which puzzles me.* Before he could catch Tarrin's reply, he barked out the line at Mason, "Haaay babeee, nice eggs!" with better results, who had to lean against a wall to stay standing, he was laughing so hard.

Actually, it's a play on a common human intimidation phrase, often directed from males to females to scare them into thinking that the male might want to mate with them forcibly. They really say 'Hey baby, nice legs!', and often whistle and make strange gestures. Normally, Tara would have probably struck you or stunned you, as is the proper response for human females when the males bother them. Tarrin relayed the information to Luuko very matter-of-factly, still chuckling, but Luuko began to fret.

Does Tara think I want to mate with her?! His tail lashed from side to side as he tried to read some reaction from Tara.

No, no, no... She understands you were just doing what we told you, and she thanked you for talking to her. She's not mad at all...in fact, she's flattered that you want to learn English. That's why she said 'Thank you'. Tarrin soothed Luuko's fears, understanding that if he had made an offer of mating to one of his own kind, it might be considered the same as asking for marriage, and very serious. *You will know when a joke is being said by their faces, and the noises they make. If you say something and she smiles and laughs, it's a funny or good thing you've said. If she frowns...* Tarrin asked Tara to demonstrate an angry frown, *or looks confused then she either doesn't like or understand what you've said. Watch the faces, and listen for the tone people use when talking. Sarcasm is one of the most confusing aspects of human vocalization.*

Luuko nodded, noting that Dimar had a similar tradition of humor in their culture. He practiced more words, with Tarrin and Mason demonstrating each, as well as common facial expressions for humans and Arrallins, and soon, he was feeling quite the scholar.

He reached out across the barryd to where Liur was resting with other rankmates on a ledge still warmed by the setting sun. *Liur! The Great Mother has charged us with quite a task, you know. We're to learn the languages of the humans and Arrallins. I've already begun, here with Tarrin. We should have Goothib work with Harmon.*

Well, it is better than 13 hour shifts in the fire line, Liur echoed back. *We should take them back to their camp and begin our learning with them. Rank 4, the Great Mother tells me, and Rank 5 will come with us to learn too, as well as continue our work on the firebreaks during the night.* The second half of the message came through heavily shielded. Luuko was willing to wager that Liur was being approached by a Leader of another barryd.

I'll meet you on the southern platform with Tewi, Goothib and the others, and we can fly them back. Luuko relayed that message to Tarrin as well, and listened closely as he translated. "Thaaahnk yoou, Tarrin."

Tarrin smiled up at him with surprise.

With the help of Ranks 4 and 5, the group managed to rescue the downed hovercar from the treetop. It took a few minutes to herd out the various birds, lizards and numu, small ferret-like animals, that had started making homes all through the vehicle. Slung between tree branches, the larger members of Rank 4 and 5 were able to carry the ailing machine back to the repair station at the colony.

The language classes began almost immediately, halting work on the buildings for a time and providing a much-needed diversion for the exhausted beta and human laborers. Within two weeks, all the Dimar at the colony understood the basic mechanics of the English language.

Chapter 12

It was late in the day, and Tara felt Luuko was ready to progress to a basic geology lesson.

Luuko watched with fascination as Tara produced detailed maps of her home world, with six continents instead of five, and huge oceans that covered most of the surface. Arralla was even more strange, having only three major landmasses, and slightly less water than the humans' Earth.

"Ooooo-rope. Ooooorope. Eeeeoooorope." He mouthed the strange sounds, letting each consonant drag out so that Tara could make sure he was correct in each. Her smile was wide with the last try, and Luuko wiggled his ears and warbled proudly. A bit shocked, he realized that he no longer felt the spike of fear when the humans and Arrallins bared their teeth at him. In fact, he welcomed the strange expression.

"Norf Eeeeoooorope has Feeeooooords," Luuko strung together the odd sentence carefully, mimicking Tara as closely as possible. She pointed to the northeast portion of the map of his own native Mainland continent, and then to the northwestern portion of Europe on her map of Earth. Luuko liked the word 'Fjord'. It just sounded right. "Feeord! Feeord! Feeord!" He chimed, rumbling as Tara laughed.

Luuko replayed memories from earlier times at the colony, realizing that Tara smiled far too little. He was glad that he could make her burden as Leader of her strange, lost barryd less of a strain.

He looked over to Rakal, who was enjoying his work with Liur, who had also taken to chiming away particular words in Arrallin. Despite the fact that both Rakal and Tara were Leaders of the same barryd, they worked very well together with only occasional arguments. If only the Great Mother would consider such a close kinship with another Leader possible. He sighed inwardly, and continued viewing the map.

The far southern continent looked like the Island Continent to the west of Mainland, except that it wasn't nearly as round. "Auuuu-stray-leeeee-aaaaaaarrr, Auuu-stray-lee-ar" He listened, trying to drop the 'r' at the end. "No good." He furrowed his heavy, scaled brows and looked up at the stars.

"You are doing great, Luuko. They do say Australiar over here." Tara pointed to the northwest corner of the eastern continent on Earth. "In Bah-stahn. Boston to the rest of the world." She patted his arm. "You'll get it. Try again."

"Bah-staaaaahn. Auuuu-straaaay-leeee-ahhhh." He whuffled, relieved to finally get the word. Grateful for her unfailing support, he tried his best to express his feelings. "Thank you."

Liur and Rakal strode up. Liur was the first to speak. "Hello, Tara. Hello, Luuko. I am not an egg."

Luuko rumbled appreciatively! Liur's English was flawless, and he was very confident in his vocalizations. He truly understood what he was saying, and his mind echoed mirth. 'I am not an egg' was one of his first sentences, and had become a greeting between him and Tara. Luuko sighed, comparing his own slow progress to Liur's blinding pace. In a private bandwidth to Luuko, Liur explained, *Because Rakal had to learn English after he learned Arrallin, he understands the difficulties we have with learning their speech. He's an excellent and patient teacher.*

Feeling slightly protective of Tara's teaching ability, Luuko quickly shot back, *Tara, too is an excellent teacher, but I am slow to learn.* It was tradition for the failure of the student to be attributed to the teacher in classes, and Luuko did not want his shortcomings in language attributed to the tiny Leader. *Fjord!*

Fjord? What is fjord? I like it. Liur vocalized it, barking it out. "Fjord!" Luuko sent him images of the tiny inlets all over the northern and western edge of Mainland.

"Um, Tara, what have you gone and taught them?" Rakal looked up at Liur and Luuko, who were nose to nose, rapidly exchanging words above them.

"We were doing geography, learning the continents. I was showing him similarities between their Murrkila, the mainland here, and Europe and Asia." Tara pointed on the map and beamed up at Luuko and Liur, who understood more through context the words 'similarities' and 'geography'.

Luuko stuck out a middle claw and pointed to the Isle. "Like Australiar-lia." Liur pointed to the map of Earth, "Australia."

"Great!" Tara smiled. "You will teach the others?" She looked up at Luuko expectantly.

"Yes, thank you." Luuko purred. *We will confer with all the other ranks during the fire-dig tonight and exchange all our learning. I am especially curious about what Goothib and Harmon have exchanged. They were climbing through the metal tree with many Arrallakeeni betas today.* He and Liur both turned to regard the knot of people and Dimar around the remains of the front half of the ship, which currently served as an animal pen and cover.

"These 38 hour days are killing me. I've got to sleep." Rakal stretched, yawning. "Night shift will take over." Luuko felt a spike of concern for Rakal's health, but remembered that that was just an expression for being very tired.

"Sounds good. Goodnight, Luuko and Liur," Tara bowed, and patted Luuko on the shoulder. Waving to others, many of the tiny colonists wandered off to climb inside parts of the ship, or the membrane coverings all around the building-site. The betas, Dimar and humans with Goothib at the pens did not look tired at all, but chattered back and forth with excited exclamations.

Liur and Luuko together strode over to listen to the language lesson, hailed excitedly by Goothib. *Liur, Luuko! You will not believe what we have learned today. I will try to tell you in English, to practice.*

"Humans fly in spahce. Spahce has nothink, empteeer than a morrakus head. Humans put holes in spahce. Holes lead to Arralla, and Arrallins and humans are friendus. Arrallins fly in spahce. Arrallins do not punch holes in spahce, but have fahst enginus. Humans and Arrallins make good sips together. Sips. Suuuhips. No good." He struggled, as they all did, with the 'sh' sound, his emotions in a frenzy. Luuko couldn't understand why he was so excited, and waited, struggling with the concept of the new word 'spahce.'

Holes in space? Holes in something that has nothing? I can't understand this in the English, Goothib. Luuko struggled, clearly aware that Goothib felt that all of these new concepts were very important.

They can teach us how to be starborn again. They don't know Telkai, but they know how to get their metal trees into space, to make holes, and go through them. This is very, very important, Luuko! We're going to recover the lost art of the Starborn Mul, and can find out what happened to them at long last. Goothib was pulling at the metal sheeting that covered the trunk of the oddly rounded tree, exposing its multicolored metal roots.

Following the path of the starborn is forbidden, Goothib! What if they hear us out in space, and we accidentally guide them back to crush Dimar? Mulkai are starborn—not Tel. Tel make barryds, and guard Dimar as it has always been. Luuko was flabbergasted. What Goothib was suggesting was heresy for a loyal member of any barryd except for Mulkol. The violent ancestors of the war barryds like Mulkol had, using secrets that no living barryds possessed, taken to the stars to find richer worlds to plunder. The truth of the matter was, and all Dimar well knew, that the most ancient race of Mulkai had mostly conquered all of Dimar by the age of Telkai and in doing so had disrupted the planet's ecosystem so badly that it was dying.

Once the leaders had abandoned the surface, the Dimar of the other arts had set about to retake the planet and restore it to balance. Millions of lives were lost to new diseases, famine, pollution and remnant wars with the few remaining Mulkai barryds, but the more peaceful Dimar survivors persevered and the planet was now much closer to its original glory. In fact, with the spread of the new Dimar and the increase in population, the Plan was finally coming together to unite all barryds and end the waves of firestorms that ravaged Mainland and parts of the southern twin continent.

Well, what better way to guard Dimar? By taking to the stars, we can root out the ancient Mulkai and strike at them before they strike at us. Goothib's resolve was only half-hearted. As was his engineering nature, he simply wanted to see Dimar return to the Path of the Starborn to see if they could. His spike of fear made Dimar heads all around turn as he made a second, more frightening realization. Harmon stopped her teaching for a moment, but could not read his private band. *Plus, we have learned that the hole that leads back to the other home worlds is not closed. More humans and Arrallins could flood through and continue their dead-building here if we do not find a way to close it. Harmon wants it closed, but does not know how. She doesn't like Earth. She wants to defend Dimar. We must tell the Great Mother— we've got to close that hole, or expect many more silver trees like this one. Already there are four above, one larger than this one. Earth has thousands!* Goothib's fear was sincere. Much as he was fond of Harmon and even the blank-minds, he knew thousands of ships would spell the end of the Plan, and the barryds would be overrun. It would mean war.

Can we fill the hole? Does Tara know of it? Does she plan to bring many more humans through? Luuko wanted to wake her, to rip open her canopy and find her to ask. How could his smiling, laughing teacher bring about the end of his world? And what of the brave Rakal? Did he intend the same? An unfamiliar sense of betrayal flooded through him, and he quelled it.

Liur was well ahead of him in action, having woken the Great Mother and her acolytes to relay a full report on the hole in space. She would not pass this information on to the other Leaders until she was sure that the colonists were not willing to close the hole, as they all knew the other barryds would sweep in and slaughter them mercilessly. She suggested interrogating Harmon thoroughly, and Tarrin as well. The minds might be willing to share the truth, and if not, they could be made to tell what they know.

Luuko needed no second order. As Liur cut through the crowd

toward Goothib and Harmon, he spun on his haunches and launched himself in the air toward the set of tents that held Tarrin, Tara and Rakal. Both mentally and vocally screaming, he called them, "TARRIN! TARA! RAKAL! MUST SPEAK NOW!" He slammed his tail down into the dusty, grass-free ground, watching as lights flicked on all over the encampment.

Tarrin, his fur on end, galloped out on all fours, skidding to a halt in front of him. He swung his speckled head from side to side. *Fire? Fire? Luuko, what's wrong? What? Tell me!*

THE HOLE! THE HOLE IN SPACE!! You will close it? You will not bring more through? It would be war—you must not. They'll kill you! Struggling with divided loyalty for his home barryd and the tiny struggling colony, he reared on his haunches and lashed his tail from side to side.

Tara burst through the flap of her silvery-gray tent clad only in her robe and the morrak slippers, clutching a plasma rifle. The slippers elicited no whuffling or ear wiggling from Luuko and the crowd of Dimar amassed around the tents tonight. "Um, Tarrin? Report, now."

"They know about the jump gate, and it panics them. We've got to close it immediately or they'll declare war." Tarrin's fur was still on end.

"Oh, is that all? Tell them it will be done, and put them in touch with the psi on the Singularity II so that they can monitor the Dark Hope's progress. Give them a Full report." Tara nodded her head and made a hand gesture Luuko didn't understand.

Immediately, Tarrin began flooding him and Liur with images of the people above that they hadn't met yet. He cautioned them that Harmon, although a psi, was not a member of this group. She must not know what he was about to explain to them, so Goothib was not to know. The four trees they have are all that are to come through the space hole. There would be no more people or Arrallins brought to the world, because they were running from their own Mulkai culture. He showed them the Dark Hope, with it's dented hull and failing engines, and explained that the hole filler was here, but the ship was broken. It would take a while to close the gate, but they too needed it closed immediately, or their Mulkai pursuers would come and destroy both them and Dimar.

Luuko studied the images of the survey team and the meeting on the Golden Hinde, relaying them to the Great Mother with Liur. He cocked his head as a thought struck him. *Great Mother, if these four trees hadn't come through and sent back the misinformed probe, the human Mulkai would already be here flooding us. They have saved us, in truth.*

The Great Mother paused to consider that fact, as the details of the crew and resources of the ship flooded through Liur to her. *You are correct, Luuko. They have accidentally averted an even greater calamity, but the fact remains. They must close that hole, and they cannot guarantee that the Landry of Dark Hope will perform the task, despite Tarrin's confidence.*

Luuko could feel Harmon trying to pry into their exchange, and he pushed her mind away. She was not part of the inner circle of leaders, and she could broadcast dangerous information to the starborn in the ships above, and they might not close the gate.

He watched Tara on the communications panel. "Landry, good, you're awake," she seemed strangely nervous talking to the face in the viewer.

"You forget, we up here are still on a 24 hour day. What's up—looks like you're throwing a party down there with all that hubbub." Landry grinned, and Luuko did get a surge of fear looking at his teeth. He continued to listen and broadcast back to the Great Mother.

"The Dimar have made their final decision—and we're welcome to stay here. You should close that gate immediately, and we'll bring the rest of the crew down separately afterward with the Arralla's Pride." Tara smiled, but Luuko did not sense in her body movement the enthusiasm in her voice. "We've got a bit of a victory party going on down here, and seeing the fireworks as the gate shuts behind you would really finish the effect, not to mention impress the heck out of the Dimar."

"Not an option, fearless leader. Sorry to burst your bubble, but check out this engine display. Kiralla and the other two have been working round the clock, but as soon as they get one system online, another breaks." He shrugged. "We'll be ready to shut the gate for you on schedule, but not before."

"This won't reduce the number of credits that will be transferred to you when you get through to the other side, Landry. We don't work that way. In fact, I'd be willing to wager that you getting us here safely ahead of schedule and sealing off the gate would probably get you a bonus." Tara smiled again. Luuko watched Landry's face, hoping for some nod of agreement, but none came.

"That's not the problem. We're just not able to fly yet. I'm sorry. I'll speed things up as much as I can, but all hands are already pulling double shifts." Landry shook his head.

"Kir? Mm... What's her name? Kirana is leading the engineering team with who else? Have them report—patch them in to me, please." Tara was gripping the sides of the console tightly, but her face looked very calm to Luuko. He was confused by her mixed body language, and watched, trying to learn more.

"Um, Kiralla and Murram and a few others, actually. They're working in the lower hold, and I'm afraid I don't have communications consoles down there. Would you like me to call you back when they come up for lunch?" Landry's face was unreadable to Luuko, but Tara's hands gripped the console tighter. He wondered what she saw.

"Do that. I've got a very bad feeling about the gate, and I want to be safely on this side as soon as possible." Tara dismissed him absently, "Tara out." The screen faded.

"SHIT!!! SHIT!!! SHIT!!!" She was stamping up and down. Luuko had not learned that word yet, and tried the difficult 'sh' sound.

"Seeeehit! Seeeit! Sit!" He mimicked, usually evoking a smile or a laugh. Tara just sank to the ground and groaned.

Rakal had been standing next to the console, and his fur was on end. Something was very, very wrong. Luuko transmitted the scene to the Great Mother, Rakal turned back to Kiralla, his hackles rising puzzling over it as they did so. *I have much to learn about facial expressions and English, I'm afraid. I sense that very much has transpired here, but I'm not sure what.*

Their Landry is disobeying. That much is clear. He will not close the gate yet, but, if what we have heard is true, he will close the gate. Do you, my child, believe that these people will be true to their word? Our barryd—all barryds are at stake now. The Great Mother's voice was firm, and there was no evidence of the fear in her that Luuko felt, just a grim feeling of resolve.

I trust Tara and Rakal. However, it is Landry we must be concerned with. A ship is due to land here tomorrow and Tarrin says they can use it to help fill the hole in space. There are three ships above perhaps they are enough to fill the hole. Luuko felt confident that his new friends would find a way around the problem, and could feel Tarrin's distant call to the other ship above.

The comm crackled to life, and Tara leapt to her feet, fluidly assuming a nonchalant stance in front of it. Luuko snorted with confusion, and a bit of amazement at Tara's actions. *These humans are very good at the art of misrepresentation...but I wonder why she must act so calm before the eyes of the starborn?*

She is a Leader, Luuko. You are seeing a rare aspect of our difficult tasks...a Leader must never show weakness to unruly subordinates, and Tara is preparing herself to command the Landry. The Great Mother's tone belied a minute resonance of respect, although it was clear that she disapproved of Tara's outburst a moment before.

"Mmm, yes?" Tara fiddled with another screen, scrolling wildly past a set of atmosphere reports.

"Kiralla's here for her report to you, sir. Landry transferring," Landry's pale, thin face faded as the communication lines switched.

A black spotted chocolate brown Arrallin face with striking green eyes came into view on the screen, and Luuko studied her features closely. He realized that she wasn't actually spotted, but that the marks were from soiling of some kind. "Kiralla, Ir'mora of the Singularity II reporting, sir. Man...I wish I were back on the II. This tub stinks!" She laid back her ears and turned to snarl at the jumble of wires and tubes behind her.

Tara grinned widely, and Rakal made a show of smoothing his ruffled hackles before he strode around from next to the console to come into the viewer's range.

"Hey there, guy! Nice pets...those iguanas on sterobols, or what?" She pointed a clawed finger at her screen toward Luuko.

"Yes...I tamed them myself with only my claws and fangs. Impressed?" Rakal whuffled, and swept his tail from side to side, moving very close to the view panel. Luuko struggled with the context for the word 'tamed', and finally assumed it meant 'found.' He relayed his best guess to the Great Mother.

"Yeah...right." Kiralla winked. "So, why'd you pull me out of the lower hold for? Lemme guess, the timetable's been moved up?" She slouched a bit as Tara nodded. "When do you need this thing moving, and what are you planning to do with it when it does move? We're not going to be landing this in atmosphere, I hope."

"Nope...you've just got to close that gate. Seems our iguanas here hate the idea of a thousand Earth Command heavy cruisers coming through that hole as much as we do, and we lose our welcome-wagon if it doesn't shut soon." Tara looked up at Luuko, who agreed.

"Yes. Fill the hole, please. Thank you." Luuko bowed to the face in the screen.

Kiralla whuffled, "SHNU! You taught them to speak! Wow!"

Luuko was pleased that he had had such a striking effect on the Arrallin. It was obvious from her demeanor and the actions of Tara and Rakal that she was considered an equal. He rumbled happily.

"Well, this channel is secure—I should know... I rewired it." Kiralla bared her teeth in a vicious Arrallin grin. "I've got to tell you, though. Things around here should not be in the incredible state of disrepair that they are. Someone may be throwing a monkey in the wrench, so to speak, and that makes me plenty nervous. This tub is old, but some of the failures have been on newer systems. Landry is right—the engineering crew here has barely lost it's milk teeth, but I have trouble believing that any full-blooded Arrallakeeni would let things get as fouled as they are here. I'm going to keep my guard up."

"I want you to transfer to the Singularity II as soon as you can. We can't take any more chances—gate or no gate. Leave Malry and

Linaro to finish the job. The Pride will be bringing the next load of colonists and supplies in tomorrow. Can you be on that flight?" Tara cast a glance up at Luuko, who shook his head.

They must fill the hole, Luuko. Even if she is a Leader, any proper Leader knows that losing life to save their children is a high honor. The Great Mother echoed what he already knew with such strength that all Dimar, Harmon and Tarrin instinctively turned toward the north.

An unfamiliar voice answered bitterly, *Children? Easy for your Great Mother to talk of children! If I die on this tub, I will never get a chance to breed, and my people will be left one line shorter of a full blood Arrallin of the second House. I* know *my duty. The gate will close.*

The brown speckled face in the viewer snarled loudly, as Tara and Rakal backed away. Kiralla's indignation at the Great Mother's superlative tone was clear. The fury hit Luuko broadside.

Luuko whipped his head around and nearly smashed the console. He hadn't even bothered to look, but there—clear and true—Kiralla's resonance shone through. She was a Talent, however minor, and had heard the Mother's call! He paused, not sure how to proceed.

"Whoa...Kiralla! Okay...don't transfer." Tara snapped back, holding her fists to her sides. Tara was oblivious to the exchange, Luuko realized.

"She is a Talent. She is mad at us for our talk." Luuko spoke quietly to Tara, hanging his head low, and letting his ears droop. Had he been more cautious, he would have known to block her from his channel with the Great Mother, and they would not have insulted one another. He had caused a political incident for his carelessness. "She would like to transfer, but knows to fill the hole is her honor and duty."

"A Talent, huh? Kiralla...we'll talk later." He turned to Luuko to explain. "There is more than one way to close the hole, Luuko. We can slam the Pride right through and puncture the containment field to close it. There are three hundred plus Arrallakeeni down here who would pay credits to be the one to do it and be sung as martyrs in the Exodus saga. Not to mention Kiralla's engineers with her. They'd love to be the heroes that close the gate. It'll get done, but you need to be patient." Luuko didn't understand much of what Rakal had said, but dutifully committed it to memory. Now was not the time to be demanding word definitions. He turned back to Kiralla, his hackles rising again with frustration and anger. "Transfer on this run or the next, but GET DOWN HERE." Rakal's tone was imperious, and many Arrallakeeni near the console sat down unexpectedly.

Kiralla just laughed. "Don't try that Arrallin command-voice crap on me, Rakal. I know my duty, and I'll get there when I can. Kiralla out." She slapped a soiled paw onto the console and the picture faded.

Luuko reached out to Kiralla, seeking the fiery red resonance of her mind. *We meant not to insult. Please come down for them. We did not know that you were not the only one who could fill the hole. We fully trust that your engineers Malry and Linaro will complete this vital task. We are sorry.* He managed to slip in a deep chord of remorse for the incident, and hoped that she would accept his apology as that of the Great Mother. He walled the Great Mother's own indignant echoes in his mind, making sure they didn't carry through his message.

Fine...now can I get back to work? Make sure that no one starts sending psi-chatter my way, too. You guys are the loudest bunch I've ever orbited above, and it's hard enough blocking you out without having every curious hatchling paging me. Kiralla was straining to reach him, and he could not tell if she truly accepted his attempt at amends. He could only hear the words, not the tone.

You will not be bothered. Good luck in your work. Luuko withdrew from the exchange still worried, and returned to translating Rakal and Tara's excited chatter.

"Ghu, I thought it was all over. When Landry said that she couldn't report, I nearly died." Tara was smiling, leaning against the console.

"You're relieved? Ha! When she snarled after you ordered her back, I was panicked that she'd passed her season and had chosen some other mate. I saw my bloodline flash before my eyes." Rakal was whuffling happily, resting on his haunches.

Luuko struggled to translate the strange expressions. "Bloodline flassss before your eyes? Passed season? Can you explain these, please?"

"Okay...now remember how only Arrallin Alphas mate? Well, when the female has her first season, she will choose a mate for life. If it is not an Arrallin male, she will bond sometimes with a beta, or even a human, of either male or female type." Rakal looked around, careful that there were no humans that were out of the inner circle in earshot.

"So, Kiralla is an Alpha female who has not mated?" Luuko was careful to relay the information clearly to the Great Mother.

"Yes. That's why she's so, well...actually, Kiralla is always that aggressive, angry. We have known each other since we were kits. I like her very much. I want to be her mate, and she would like to be mine." Rakal spoke slowly, using simple words. Luuko understood perfectly.

"I understand. Ssse will wass when ssee comes to Dimar?" Luuko wiggled his ears, thinking of how the Great Mother, who already had made it plain that she did not like the Arrallin female, would react when she arrived covered in soil spots.

Rakal stared at him, and tilted his head to the side with confusion.

"Wass? Oh, wash!" Tara laughed. "Yes, Luuko. She'll be clean when she meets the Great Mother. Don't worry."

Rakal whuffled, and patted Luuko on the leg. "Well, if anyone can fill the hole, Kiralla can. We'll let you know how she does."

Chapter 13

Despite Luuko's best efforts to soothe the nightmarish worries of the other Dimar, tensions ran high around the camp. With the advent of the knowledge of English, the Dimar had become aware of nuances of the colonist situation, details and dangers for which they were not prepared. The firebreaks all along the north and west were failing, despite the nighttime efforts of 3 full ranks — including the currently most skilled rank, Liur's Tinar Rank 1, as well as the exhaustive efforts of the six hundred and seventy new and old colonists. The tiny colony that had imperiled all of Dimar was itself nearing a fire crisis, and loyalties in every rank stationed there were divided. To make matters worse, the stormy Kiralla had not come down with the colony ship the day after the revelation of the hole in space. The Dark Hope had not been operable when the smaller transport shuttle had arrived to collect her. Rakal's usually level temper was becoming increasingly uneven as the time wore on, and with the new colonists arrivals, he and Tara needed to be more Leaders than ever.

If the colony did ignite, would the Great Mother still extend the branches of the Telka Barryd openly to the human and Arrallin people, as agreed at the council? Luuko's slumbers were plagued with images of the charred remains of the tiny creatures, as he struggled alone to halt the fires in his dreams.

Aching from half a night at the firebreaks, he called upon the Wind to gently lift him to his chosen perch next to a nest of tiny numu. Forlorn, he settled on the wide, flat-topped branch, listening to the young numu chattering with annoyance as he settled. Sighing, he let his eyelids droop, shutting out the dim light of Dimar's one waning moon, as the wind, and the Wind lulled him to sleep.

Luuko...

Luuko...

A voice touched his dreams, calling him back to the land of the living. It was Goothib, resting as he always did in the branch near Harmon's tent.

Yes, Goothib? Is there a problem? Luuko flicked an eyelid open to survey his tree, but all was fine.

No...Well, yes, in truth. It's Harmon. His voice had a guilty, pained ring to it.

Is she sick? Did you do something you shouldn't have? Luuko's mind slowly churned over the possibilities, reaching out to probe Goothib mildly.

No, no...It's nothing like that. I haven't taken her to the Water, or done any more than the most basic and important lessons for her Seventh Class studies. Goothib's tail was visible in the dim light, flicking back and forth thoughtfully. *I just...I would not like to lose her. I am considering sun-bonding with her. Is this wise? She is, after all, an important member of another barryd, and would add diversity to Telka, as is preferred.*

Bond? You mean the Sun Ceremony? With a human? I would think it could not be done. She would add much diversity, that is true, but, well, it's never been done, Goothib. It could kill her, or burn her mind. Luuko's thoughts turned grave, imagining the tiny human trying to encompass all that was Goothib with her mind, and him hers, while dancing the whirling, dangerous dance of the sun ceremony. It was not for the faint of heart—a bond more true than even physical mating, and the most complete sharing of souls two individuals could endure. And, it was a luxury lavished on only the most precious of minds in a barryd, as it provided a permanent active record of the experiences of each individual in the other. It would take twenty or more major Talents to oversee the procedure, and could be costly to them too. *I do not think you could get the acolytes to agree to it. From what*

I can sense, they do not yet understand the colonists, and they fear them and their hole in space, as do we all. They would not want Harmon having your knowledge of both Tinar firefighting and Telkai engineering, and they would not find Harmon's mind useful, as she is not a member of the human and Arrallin Inner Circle Council.

Oh, but Luuko! You have not seen the worlds she has! Admittedly, many are fantasy, but she has traveled the stars, as well as both Earth and Arralla, and she understands much of her worlds—the interactions between people, and their metal ship engineering too. If you had touched her mind, you'd be drawn to her like a kimul bird to the fruits of the highest trees. Goothib's tone was flooded with admiration, rippling through the images in waves of blue and green.

Luuko wiggled his ears in the darkness, *Goothib, not that I speak from experience, but it is not a Sun Ceremony candidate that you have found in Harmon.* He suppressed the yellow and orange colors of mirth that ranged through his response.

She is worthy of the Sun Ceremony! She is the most powerful mind I have ever encountered, even more resonant and strong than the starborn psis, and many of our acolytes. Goothib was indignant, and in the dim light, Luuko could see him raise his head and lay his ears back. *Well, if she is not a Sun Ceremony candidate, then what is she? You tell me now.*

A mate. You're in love. Luuko felt his shock, but didn't know how to cushion the blow. Goothib was in love, but was not yet ready to admit that he wished to spend his life with Harmon as a partner. He wanted Harmon with him, in his thoughts always, and thus, he thought he wanted the Sun Ceremony supposing that he had perhaps been sun-struck by a Great Mind. Luuko chuckled again. What Goothib really wanted was a mating ceremony. Harmon was not a Sun Ceremony candidate, that much Luuko knew truly. Sun Ceremony candidates were like brilliant powers, more commanding than Leaders, braver than Tinar heroes, and as intelligent as Telkai herself. Harmon had only had this effect on Goothib, and no other Dimar in the camp or out of it had noticed her at all. It was a sure sign that only Goothib was love struck.

Feh! Goothib sent an annoyed farewell, with a troubled undertone, and returned to his restless thoughts.

Luuko returned to his disgruntled slumber, a bit jealous that the only mate he'd found yet was the Wind, and that even it's constant contact was not enough to sate him. He watched the night colors flash across the sky, letting the patterns mesmerize him into a light sleep. Hours passed, and the creamy crescent of the largest of Dimar's two moons slipped down behind the horizon.

An explosion, followed by another even closer, rattled Luuko's perch. He came fully awake, and looked for the moon. It was well set—much time had passed since he had settled and the sun would rise soon, but Rank 5 and Liur's half of Rank 1 were not back from the fire line. He reached out curiously to find out how they were progressing.

Liur? Why aren't you back yet? The light will hit this valley soon, and the other Leaders may be watching. He reached out toward where he thought Liur would be, shocked at the images that flooded back to him.

No time to talk, Luuko—we just lost the last line before the Valley. IT'S GOING UP!! Rouse your half, and get Rank 4 in the air now! Summon Telka—the colony will not survive without help! Liur's panic was more than just his fear that he would fail in his Tinar—he too had come to see the waters-lost of the colony as his own barryd. Luuko's own fear sent him blasting up through the branches of his tree and into the air, bugling a summons to all Ranks and Telka. Looking west, he could see the valley, with no streambed in it that ran alongside the valley in which the colony lay. Gouts of fire burst out along the walks of the canyon, moving toward where the two valleys met.

Spinning, he assessed the colony valley condition. The dry season had progressed even further, and the few storms that had passed through the region had missed Telka and Mulkol provinces. It had been a very bad year for early rains. The stream that protected the swath of green around the ship and membrane-buildings was barely a trickle, and the plants at the top of the ridge were brown and had dropped much of their foliage.

Humans and Arrallins streamed out of the ship, stumbling toward the clearing that served as a center for communication. Tara, dressed in her ripped fatigues, burst forward from her tent and swept the dark encampment with a hand-light.

Luuko angled his wings and swept in to land on a branch near the encampment. "Honored colonists! The valley of which we warned you has caught fire now, and you must prepare yourself to defend this ridge." He swung his head toward the sloping, craggy rise that separated the colony from the dry valley. Fire was already climbing the ridge, igniting the trees along the top. "We will fight with you! Our ranks are coming to help!"

With that, he swept over a ridge and took his place in the newly forming fire line. In faltering transports with water cannons mounted on the front, human and Arrallin teams swept along the top of the ridge, soaking the trees with water. Other crews foamed the ground, smothering the fire as it blazed through the underbrush that had not yet been cleared by the crews.

Relieved, Luuko could feel group after group of Telka's Tinar ranks assemble at the barryd and move south toward them. The Great Mother had awakened to guide the effort personally, and many acolytes were flying in the honor guard that would bring the foam and Water litas to aid the final effort to stave off the destruction of the colony. This would be a firefight worthy of a mural in glass, but Luuko knew that even with all the ranks Telka could spare, the colony was not well enough prepared for many long days at the fire line. He scanned for storm clouds in the dawn light, listening as colonists and their dogs herded their frightened animal charges into the pen at the nose of the ship for protection. It took the largest dogs to keep the morraks from trudging up the far ridge to move away from the fire, as they instinctively wished to do. The other side was just as perilous—but it had not caught fire yet. It wouldn't, providing the barryd...not barryd, he corrected himself, colony, could find time to fortify that side before it ignited.

Sweeping in on gleaming silver-tinged wings, thousands of Dimar took positions along the walls of the burning valley, sweeping down to douse fires as they blazed into walls 40 meters high. The heat was stifling, even from the valley in which the colony lay, but the ranks held the fire line. Luuko slipped himself into the front line with Rank 23, bolstering their faltering upper edge.

A scream punctured the roaring of the blaze as a hovercar smashed against the ridge and into the flames. He did not know the people aboard well, but he knew them. Against all training, he ripped himself free of the 23rd's fire line, blasting out a burst of Wind to hold the flames as others of the Rank closed in to seal the line again. Like a hatchling burning velvet, he swept into the flames, grabbing the unconscious bodies of the four pilots, two Arrallakeeni, two human, in his front legs. The heat nearly melted his scales to his sides as he shot up into the burning air above. Reaching out to locate Liur, he blindly pulled himself through the flames and flipping on his back, he shot through the wall, through the fire line and into the clearing. Gently, he placed each of the four figures on the ground, calling the honor guard.

They did not answer.

Furious, he screeched out for them to come, scanning the horizon for the honor silks. *Honor Guard! WE HAVE INJURED! I will personally flay you alive if you don't get here now!*

A single guard flew in from the west, dropping a half full lita of Water on the ground as she skidded to an exhausted halt. *What? Do you think these four are the only injured? We come as fast as we can, but we have lost three members of the honor guard as it is already! I left the other four in a dangerously weak line to go through the flames to you here. Flay me if you like—the blame will be on your head.* She was gray-brown with charcoal smudges all along her sides. One wing was partially burned, and in serious need of the Water itself. Still, she poured the water on the four on the ground.

Only one Arrallakeeni awakened. The other three—two humans who were mated and an Arrallakeeni of Rakal's family, were dead. And it was only the start of the firestorm. Luuko could not hold back, releasing a fervent mourning song into the air and he returned to his position in the 23rd to hold the line. His 'mates to either side did not acknowledge his return, they were so focused now on the fire that raged.

Roars caught his ears as parts of the fire line fell away to the south and west.

Liur—I can't get to Rank 1, and Rank 23 needs support, so I'll be staying here. What ranks fell back? How many have we lost? Luuko took advantage in a momentary lull in wind, and a strong surge in the Wind to project to Liur, who was coordinating the effort of the ranks with four acolytes.

He could feel that Liur was also having difficulty settling the line and holding it back, but that they were succeeding. *The five ranks fell out of the south to re-enforce the flank. It seems to be working. We'll lose that grazing area for the animals, and some of the membranes to the far south, but that wall will hold, I think. We lose a battle, but win the war.* Even through his physical strain, Liur's strategy was clear and well thought out. Luuko could catch echoes of respect from the acolytes that echoed his fire line orders, outlining the design to rank after rank. They might just survive the day.

‹⸆•‹⸆•‹⸆›

As the sun reached it's zenith, the fire line was well entrenched, and the colonists, although exhausted, had honed their spot-dousing navigation to exceed even the exploits of the honor guards. Luuko reached out toward Telka to see how the barryd was holding out, knowing that the lines there too were severely strained, but could read nothing from the mind-tones of the few acolytes he was able to reach.

Luuko wavered in his place in line as a set of newly-burned hatchlings emerged from a wall of fire in the distance. *They choose to burn their velvet NOW? Who allows this? The line is not yet fully stable!* Luuko echoed his concern to Liur, hanging at the top of Rank 1, visible occasionally when the smoke blew away from the colony.

I allowed them. We are settled here, and they know not to target the side near the colony. I've also cautioned them about trying for a Firebirth — having a flaming hatchling smash into a fire line in it's dying breath would cause some difficulty. Liur was impassive, but a fleeting spark of respect flickered through his thoughts about the young daredevils from

Telka that would shed their velvet on this historic day to become full-blooded Dimar adults.

Oh, Liur! Be serious. You know at least one of them will try for a Firebirth. Knowing that lot, probably half of them will. And most of the appropriate flame-wells are near the lines. You should have told them to wait until tonight or tomorrow. Flying at night is considered more daring anyway. Luuko snorted with irritation, watching another pack of youngsters dive through wall after wall of flame, exposing the rich pearlescent sheen of fresh firescales.

As if it was injured, one dropped down into the heart of a fire geyser, screaming as the intense heat and roaring rise of air ripped layers of velvet off her sides. She had to veer off before she could touch the source of the geyser, and she shot toward the cooler portions of the flaming field ahead of her. Luuko chuckled. She had been very close to hitting the heart of the flame. He wondered if any of the others had done that well. *Liur, I JUST saw a female—looks like she'll be a golden-brown, go for Firebirth, right in front of my already taxed line. Like I said, this perhaps should have been scheduled for later.*

Liur's answer was distracted, *Yes. Right.* He let out a mental cheer that rippled through the ranks. *Tewi's sister's hatchling did it! She made it! She's fireborn! Now, we'll see if she turns out to be acolyte material.*

Luuko chuckled, torn between pride for Tewi's family and the little one who had managed to touch the heart of the geyser, and irritation with the lightheartedness with which many in the line were treating the situation. *If it were YOUR barryd, you'd fight harder.* He growled inwardly, careful to shield it from his 'mates to either side. A burst of flame ignited to his left as yet another tree burst into flames. The tent near it began to crackle and melt from the searing blast of air that ripped at its sides. Furious, he moved his segment of the line back, smothering the flames, but the tent was lost. It had been a medical tent, stripped and abandoned because of it's proximity to the encroaching fire, but Luuko was enraged that the 23rd had let even it fall.

Sullenly, he redoubled his efforts in the line, bolstering his 'mates to either side, who truly were struggling against the heat and force of the flames before them.

‹⟨·⟩⟨·⟩⟨·⟩›

The day passed, and the line held well into the evening of the second day. The cool air had brought some relief to the remaining 23rd, but not in time to prevent dire injuries to the line. Out of the 40 Dimar that flew in the 23rd, which was a much larger Rank than the 1st, only 14 were left holding the fire line. Luuko had been seared twice, but not badly enough to warrant a break, and using his strong grasp of English, he rallied the now exhausted human support forces to re-douse the fire line and take some of the strain off the 23rd and 30th ranks that held the southwest portion. Screaming, of both Dimar and colonists, filled the air as the fire took its toll up and down the seventy-kilometer stretch of flame, but the line was holding. Luuko pointed his nose skyward, focusing on the now rising moon for strength, when a scream from the southern portion of the large 30th rank broke his reverie.

That was not a scream of one who has been burned... he commented to Ruulamar, the smoky green Dimar to his right. Craning his head around, he could barely make out in the dim moonlight the silvery glimmer of wings gliding in from behind them. A foul current in the Wind reached his senses, and he bugled a war cry in response.

Mulkol!! Mulkol at the southern flank! Liur! They're attacking! The pain of the exhausted Dimar that fell one after the other to the tusks of the war Oolars shot through the line like a spike. Furious, Luuko and his 'mates broke formation and sped toward the battlefield that was forming to the south.

Instinct grabbed him as he came upon the first black and gray striped Mulkol warrior, who was struggling to dislodge his tale-blade from a fallen Telkan. Luuko shot a blast of Wind at him, momentarily stunning him, and landed with all four legs on his throat as the thick, heavily scaled head snapped back. He whipped his own tail-blade into the open mouth of the Mulkol, striking surgically where the base of the skull met the spinal column. The heavy warrior's body went limp, and fell back upon the Telkan beneath who had already expired from his injuries. Luuko let out a cry of fierce triumph, and leapt into the air to seek another victim. A female, flanked by two war Oolars hung back from the massive Mulkol front line. She was a deep blood red, visible in even the dim light of the new evening, striped with brown and black. She wore honor war silks, and the sight of her made Luuko's blood roar in his ears.

He ducked down into the flaming forest, under the top canopy, and stealthily moved in on the female, hoping that the burning smoke of his chosen route would mask his smell and movements. *I too can fly in from behind, you Mulkol pustule.* The smoke was both blinding and choking him, and the heat sapped his energy as he moved, but he pressed on, avoiding the corridors of cool, unignited forest. Finally, he looked up, and felt he was in position. He buoyed himself on a blast of Wind and shot straight up through the canopy...

As he rocketed into the clear air, the target he expected to find in front of him was not the back of the female, but the back of her second oolar, perched in a treetop. He knocked the beast into the flames below and turned just as she grabbed him by the throat. He lashed his tail, cutting a swath in her dark, mottled wingsail, and his tail dug into her side between two firescales. As she pulled him closer to her gaping jaws, he worked his tail in deeper and deeper into her side, prying apart the scales to cut through her thick war-toughened hide to reach her second heart. Luuko realized that she could, quite cleanly, bite his throat in two, and he needed to make more time to finish his work on her side. He snapped his wings open to generate a blast of wind to stun her, but the second Oolar latched onto one wing, snapping it at the elbow. The first Oolar survived the flames and had climbed back up the tree. It was working furiously to pry his tail out of her side. As he screamed in pain, the female's jaws clamped down on his throat and began to rhythmically saw through his firescales as if they were the bones of a fish.

You dare challenge me, stripling? I will devour you and hang your head on my wall... She ripped into his mind as he lashed out mentally for some form of help, giving one final mental and physical scream before she closed off his windpipe with her jaws.

As if to answer, a thousand stars shot up from the forest

below, ripping through the Oolars, but missing him and the female. Distracted, she hesitated in making the final few bites that would fully lacerate and sever his head from his neck. As she raised her head and turned, a hovercar, with what Luuko knew to be a water cannon rose up out of the forest below, but instead of water, a glob of intensely hot material shot forward and charred her head right on her neck. She fell, dragging Luuko down as the hovercar pursued them into the canopy.

He grabbed onto a passing tree branch, wrenching his tail from the side of the female as she fell crashing into the flaming jungle beneath him. The hovercar slowed, and Tara, of all people, leapt out carrying a lita of Water. She had an expression that gave Luuko chills — she had the look of a Mulkai that had made first blood.

"We sure showed that fuzz-lizard who's boss of this place, eh Luuko!" She grinned down maniacally at Luuko as the Water worked to mend his lacerated throat and tail. "Go pick off a few more and come back for me, Susan. I want to take out another general myself!" She waved as the hovercar sped off, faltering as it passed low over the trees toward the still raging battle. Her expression softened as she regarded him. "That was a brilliant maneuver, Luuko. I could see it on long-range, the way you used the fire to sneak up on her like that. Taking out the boss often sends the ground troops running, same way as if you cut off the head of the snake, the body..." She looked at Luuko's neck and patted his side. "Well, never mind. Bad choice of example." She smiled.

"Tttsssank oooo" he managed in a barely audible whisper, struggling to translate her words through the pain of his wing. He felt the order to retreat ripple through the Mulkol ranks as thousands of Telkans descended upon the field, backed by a tiny but fierce contingent of Ekal warriors. "Tsssssey gooo now" He pointed toward the fleeting silvery glimmer of wings beating the air toward the west.

"We won the war, but lost the colony." Tara muttered, kicking at the branch with one foot.

Luuko's spirits sank as he imaged the tiny membrane-buildings engulfed in flames, and he warbled a high-pitched painful note that whistled out through the slowly closing holes in his neck.

"Hey, hey, hey, there, Luuko. It's not that bad. Most of our supplies are still starborn, and guess what? We'll be taking that offer to move to Telka. You get to go home!" She smiled, but Luuko knew enough of human expression to sense that it was forced.

He could barely hear the orders being broadcast by the acolytes, but he could hear the frightened screams of the colony animals as Dimar swept in to recover those that had survived the fire and the battle in the interior parts of the ship.

The honor guard swept in to douse the base of the trees next to Luuko's, and a band of Ekal warriors from the tiny barryd to the northwest landed to gently lift him and carry him back toward Telka. The war leader dipped his shoulder to Tara, who hopped aboard, and together they sped off ahead toward the northern barryd. Luuko suppressed a surge of jealously that he would re-present himself at Telka not only injured and unable to fly the Leader back, but in disgrace at having lost the firefight to save the fledgling barryd that she and Rakal had forged. Rakal? A pang of worry filled him, making his wing burn. He wished Tara had remained so he could ask what had become of the Arrallin during the battle, but allowed the Ekal war-party healer to lull his mind into a half-sleep.

Chapter 14

The refreshing tingling of the Water in the central pool awakened him, as the war healer and two Dimar that had carried him in let him go over the softly glowing green pool beneath the southern Spire of Telka. He fell in with a splash. The active cells quickly went to work on him as he let himself sink, patching the remaining membranes of his left wing, forcing the muscles to release their contraction that had pulled the shattered bones across one another and through his punctured skin. A healer leapt off a ledge above and dove smoothly into the water, drifting down to where he lay at the bottom of the pool to oversee the setting of the spar bones and to numb his pain. The healing process was excruciating at first, but, as Luuko knew from many visits to this very pool, the pain would soon subside and the glowing tingle of newly generated tissue would replace it. His wing would be more sensitive for quite a time, but eventually, his awareness would adapt.

He sighed, letting out a torrent of bubbles, and let his tail drift lazily from side to side as the active cells made their final repairs to the work started by Tara back on the tree. *Well, at least I get to come home and enjoy my usual swim in the Water, regardless of the shame of my defeat.* Comforted by the familiarities of home, he lapsed into a deep, dreamless sleep as the Water swirled around him.

⟨⊹•⊱•⊰•⊹⟩

The sunlight filtered down through the murky green Water,

forcing Luuko to open his eyes. Spreading his wings, he gently rose, calling the Wind to carry him through the thick liquid to the surface. He blinked against the sunlight, and turned to question the healer on duty. *How long was I under, honorable barrydmate?*

Four days, Luuko. Quite a while, but no record, I'm afraid. Your colony 'mates have been asking for you, but the Great Mother would still not let them near the healing pools. The healer sounded irritated.

She still does not trust them to respect the Water? Why did she bother to take them in, then? Luuko dragged himself onto the wooden overhanging root that served as the side of the pool and shook the water out of his under fur. He hopped into the air above the main pool to check his reflection, and to his dismay, each injury was marked by glaringly greenish-white scales. He had a ring around his tail, and a double ring around his neck, as well as a long band running off his left wing and into the membrane. He might have the nila for some cosmetic healing, but that would mean another day lost in the pools. *I always either have nila, or time, but never both.* Frustrated by both his injuries and the enigmatic decision of the Great Mother not to allow the colonists into the Water, he growled. There were still a half dozen other Dimar in the pool completing their healing. Despite cosmetic setbacks, he had been lucky. With nila from the next Mirrai festival, he could always come back to have the scars erased later, and have his older scars tended as well.

She'll eventually have to let them use the Water. They suffered severe losses, and many deaths occurred because the litas just don't have the capacity that a full pool does. The healer's mental tone was troubled. Luuko caught an image of humans and betas lying outside the barryd, suffering through a long slow healing process outside of the pools. *For many of them, death would be preferable at this point to the treatment we can offer with the litas.*

Did you see this colonist in the healing rooms, 'mate? Luuko projected a clear image of Rakal, nervously preening a wing as the healer recalled.

No...He was not among those I worked on, or in the rooms to the south. You should take to the air and see if he's in the residence halls. Those who survived the battle unscathed were moved immediately into their new quarters and are now training to fight the last of the fires before the rainy season starts. The healer flashed pictures of the long, leaf-lined vine-beds that had been set up in some of the smaller unoccupied residence rooms. *They are an industrious lot, the colonists. Especially the furred ones. They pour over the barryd and poke their muzzles into every open door. It can be...frustrating.*

Arrallakeeni love new things, 'mate. If our world were not considered highly advanced by them, they would not be so curious. They are in awe of us, and want to learn as much as they can. It is more an honor. When you can teach your healing arts to them, you may feel differently. Luuko tried to help him see the Arrallakeeni as people, and not as the flat, animalistic images the healer had projected with his complaint.

The healer just shrugged, and continued filling litas for the injured.

Luuko took to the air again, and rose through the southern spire to land at the residence levels. He could tell from the musty smell that there were Arrallakeeni all over this level, but he was still too tired to reach out to find Tarrin and ask about Rakal. He ambled down the hall, poking his head into each room to find an appropriate Arrallakeeni to ask. The floors of every residence room were strewn with litas, cooking implements, seeds, shelter seedlings, and equipment from both the colony and Telka itself, and hundreds of furred bodies piled through the wreckage, exploring each item in turn, discussing back and forth in a cross between excited Arrallin and English speech.

"Excuse me. Where is Rakal?" He strode into one room that still had enough space for him to stand comfortably. A white-faced Arrallakeeni with brown speckles poked up from a jumble of papers and drawings, and pointed out the door and up toward the central spire. Before he could even offer his thanks, the little face disappeared into the pile of notes, purring absently as it worked.

He strode off, rumbling happily that the new residents were making such an industrious effort to learn about the barryd. Trotting to stretch his still-sore muscles, he made a running leap off the residence hall platform and rose smoothly toward the fire watch platform. Relieved, he could make out the familiar forms of Tara, Tarrin, Rakal and the Great Mother and her acolytes all resting in the shade of the blossom spire. Calling out a warm greeting to them, he swept in to land.

"We are going to have the ceremony, and that's final. All honor and grace to you, Great Mother." Tara's brows were furrowed with consternation. Luuko warbled with concern—they had all looked so comfortable from above. He called to Tarrin to find out what the problem was.

Seems the Great Mother doesn't want us to perform a common and celebrated post-battle ritual that we have. Says any celebration of Mulkai tradition in this barryd is forbidden. She's being pretty tough about it, too. Tarrin sounded annoyed more than concerned, leading Luuko to conclude that this was another of the Great Mother's attempts to test the resolve of the two colony Leaders. Telka did not have a formal ban on the celebration of Mulkai teachings, they just chose not to reward particularly warlike actions to discourage in-fighting among the youngsters of the barryd.

"You will do no such thing beneath the sheltering branches of Telka, Leaders Tara and Rakal. It would cause pain to the spirit of the gentle Telkai. It would be an insult to our traditions of non-violence." The Leader's English was flawless—she had been practicing! Luuko flashed her a greeting, suffused in appreciation of her language skills.

Tara countered angrily. "HA! If what I saw out there is an example of your non-violent nature, I'd love to see what your war-mongers are like." Tara turned and openly glared at the massive purple female. The Leader just hissed. Tara was not impressed, and continued. "Your people fight well, and you defended us at great cost to your own lives. That should be rewarded—not as an act of a military appreciation, but of appreciation for the bravery and fearlessness you all showed for our sake. I'll hold it at the site of the colony when the fires die down, but I *will* hold it. Discussion closed." Grinning to Rakal, she muttered, "Upidstay uzzyfay-izzardlay."

The Leader's eyes narrowed, and Luuko could sense her fury at being unable to understand their jokes. Tarrin caught her feelings clearly too, and moved back a pace.

Rakal half-smiled back, but seemed lost in his own problems, unwilling to speak. His tail swept along the ground under his branch-bench, pushing along the dry leaves that lay scattered around the platform.

Tara rose stiffly, refusing to look at the Great Mother as she walked toward the edge of the platform toward Luuko. "I've got a colony to look after. Thank you for the lovely talk." She kept her eyes focused on the distance, and her back to the Leader. "Luuko, it's good to see you again. Want to come and get the grand tour of our new quarters?"

Luuko warbled happily—he had not lost face in the eyes of the Leaders of the colony, despite the fact that Tara had had to save him from the Mulkol female. She looked genuinely glad to see him. "Sounds fun. It would be an honor, Leader Tara." He dipped his shoulder, letting her climb aboard.

The Great Mother's rebuke almost caused him to lose his concentration as he lifted them both into the air. *Do NOT let yourself be seduced by the alien colony, Luuko. They are far from true barrydmates, these Leaders.* Her hostility was tinged with desperation. Luuko was puzzled, and looked forward to seeing why the colonists were causing her so much insecurity. Without answering, he flew north as Tara instructed.

They cruised along slowly in the clear air, conversing as they skimmed in and out of the canopies and smaller spires that comprised the roof of the barryd.

"Thanks for taking me off that platform, Luuko. I mean no offense, but I wanted to punch your Great Mother right in her fuzz-covered nose for a while there. She's a mother, all right." Tara patted Luuko on the neck with one hand, keeping hold of his mane with the other.

Luuko struggled to understand Tara's colloquialisms. "She's a mother, yes. Is she more of a mother because she disagrees with you?

Why are you both so…"

Luuko struggled for the right words, but Tara completed the sentence with a laugh."Argumentative? Impossible to deal with? Uncompromising? Stubborn?"

"Yes. But I mean that in a good way." Luuko wiggled his ears and rumbled amusedly.

"It's just that I *know* she has no reason to keep us from giving our awards of valor. She's just doing that to see if she can get my goat. Tarrin researched the feasibility with five different acolytes before we proposed the whole party in the first place." Tara slammed her free hand onto her thigh, but retained a comfortable grip on Luuko's mane.

"Get your goat? You have many goats still. Give her one." He wiggled his ears again, hoping his joke would amuse the distressed Leader.

"I wish it was that easy, guy. I really do. She could have the whole darned herd if she'd just lighten up. Oh…there! See that platform with all the betas on it? That's the top level of the main complex. Down below," she hesitated sadly, "are the healing rooms. We took some heavy losses, I'm afraid, and the Water is working slowly, if at all."

Staying level, Luuko made a neat landing on the crowded platform, disheartened by the eerie cries of the mourning Arrallakeeni on every level. "How many did we lose?" He whuffled to an Arrallakeeni he recognized from the colony building team who was wailing with the others. He paused and went nose to nose with Luuko.

Tara slid off his back onto the springy wood, "Out of 764 colonists, we now have 520. Most of those lost were either in the south field, trying to preserve the fuel reserves, which blew, killing the lot of them, or they were in hovercars or along the north and west faces doing ground patrols. These fires are unnaturally fast and explosive."

"Did the Mulkol kill many?" Luuko wasn't sure if he wanted to know the answer.

"Heheheh...not as many as they'd have liked. And they took no prisoners, we can proudly say, thanks to the excellent counter attack you and our forces together were able to make. They weren't expecting such resistance from us, I'd wager. Firefighting, we're not so good at. War, now THAT is where we excel." Tara smiled up at Luuko smugly.

"What did you use to repel them? What were those stars I remember?" Luuko looked around cautiously. It was obvious that the colonists were from a strong Mulkai tradition, and such open pride in Mulkai arts was discouraged. Mulkai skills were something to be learned because they were required only. They were not a celebrated art.

"Our water cannons aren't water cannons at all, Luuko. They were originally meant to serve as multipurpose high-powered propelling systems, for drilling, or for pumping water, but mostly they were meant for combat. We take whatever we can't use, melt it down to plasma with a superheater, and blast it at whatever comes our way. It's not as good as a dedicated plasma weapons system like our plasma rifles, but they'll do in a pinch, and they convert quickly from one use to another. Because we had only been using them for water, the Mulkol had no way of knowing that they were actually weapons. We sure surprised them!" Tara grinned widely up at Luuko. He shuddered, remembering her face as she had found him on the canopy top. She was Mul.

"Tara, I have a question." He proceeded slowly, not sure how to breach the subject with her. He followed her down the hallway past large chambers lined with supplies, or cots and personal belongings of both Arrallakeeni and humans together.

"Mmm?" She turned into a more formally appointed room with a small stained glass mural on the inside wall. "This is my place. Not bad, eh? I only have to share it with three other people and one Dimar." She flopped down on her woven vine-cot, which had been hastily coaxed to grow out of the barryd wall. The smoky, half charred remains of her morrak slippers were tucked neatly under the cot, much as they had been at the colony.

"Are you Mul? Do you love war?" Luuko nervously preened at

his injured right wing with his broad, flat tongue.

"Me? Naw... I have been trained to fight since I was young, and I do enjoy the thinking part of a battle, but death has never set well with me, and injuries bother me even more." Tara amended, "Not injuries to me—that I'm fine with. But injuries to the people in my command, those are the most disturbing. Most of our folks aren't fighters. I'm one of the few, but they'll do whatever it takes to see this mission through."

"You enjoyed killing the Mulkol female that was defeating me?" Luuko used a curious tone, not an accusing one. He did not want her to be defensive about things. It was much harder reaching a non-Talent once their walls went up than it was mind-speaking to another Dimar or colony Talent.

"Yeah. I did enjoy that. She was going to kill you, a member of my team, and in such a gruesome way! I enjoyed removing her from the gene pool." Tara chuckled. "Humans will fight like mad dogs to save their own, and I haven't shied away from a battle yet. It must be some weird parental instinct in me. Everyone in the colony is one of my own."

Pride welled up in Luuko. She considered him a member of the colony! He remembered the Great Mother's rebuke, and wondered if the two barryds would ever form one cohesive whole, as Rakal and Tara's groups had. He would encourage them to work together, and perhaps, one day his two families would finally consider themselves one.

Chapter 15

"Well, today's the day. How do I look?" Tara surveyed her uniform in the mirror, fingering the smooth silk honor-band that hung from her rank insignia. She'd waited two months for this day, and had fought the last three weeks with the Great Mother to make sure it would happen. The final colony shipment of supplies, and, most importantly, of the three other Arrallin mated pairs and Kiralla, would be splashing down in the Big Easy in an hour. "Telka colors do a lot for these old grays."

"You look great." Rakal's tone was distracted as he worked through his own thick fur with a Dimar mane-comb. "How do I look? Today is the day, and my social life is riding on a good first impression. I haven't seen Kiralla in person for three years."

Tara frowned, careful that Rakal wouldn't notice. "She's seen you in the video-comm. She knows what to expect. Hope she doesn't mind that you're shorter looking in person." She turned, grinning maliciously, and grabbed her side arm for the welcoming.

Rakal turned in stunned shock. "I look..? YOU! Stop doing that!" The hair on the top of his head had bushed out as he reacted to her jibe, and he worked to get it to lay flat again. "Now I'm all fluffed up. I look like I've just been through an air blower."

Tara just laughed. "It's dramatic. I can't wait to see you fluff up when you have your full mane grown in. If only Landry can get that good-for-nothing tub of his through the gate and crash it..." Grabbing a report from the Dark Hope, she flipped through the

engineering progress reports. "They should be able to head back
through and shut it tonight, adding fireworks to our little party,
providing the third fuel cell holds. That's the only system here that
looks like it really needs work."

"Good. And, if worse comes to worse, we can always have the
Arralla's Pride tow it into the gate to launch the crasher and out, and
let that little toady Landry keep it. I hate to lose my ship, though.
We'd be permanently moored here without it." Rakal fluffed again at
the mention of Landry, and gave up on trying to appear unruffled for
the celebration.

Tara nodded. "Whatever it takes." She and Rakal exchanged a
long look for a moment, and headed out toward the residence hall
platform to meet with Luuko and Liur.

⋖⫶⟩⫶⟨⫶⟩⋗

"You both look fancy. Rakal—I like that fluffy look you're
sporting today." Liur wiggled his ears, rumbling deeply as Rakal
slapped his side, fluffing up even more.

Tara laughed and climbed aboard Luuko's shoulders.
Instinctively, she felt around in his mane to make sure there were
no young stow-stowaways aboard. She'd been surprised more than
once when she had accepted rides from well meaning barrydmates
who were carrying hatchlings. Hatchlings had a propensity to sample
with their teeth anything put near them, and Tara didn't want a large,
embarrassing hole in the butt of her dress grays today.

"Hello Tara. Welcome aboard." Luuko turned his head to regard
Tara with his large golden eyes, and warbled good-naturedly. She
could tell that he was looking forward to the ceremony as much as
she was. *You, my big fuzzy friend are going to get a surprise today.* She
mused, chuckling to herself.

"Thanks, Luuko. Always a pleasure to fly Luuko Air." Tara stated
with a smile as he wiggled his ears. Luuko had been fascinated with
the stories of old Earth airlines before hovercars, and had taken it
upon himself to act as a ferry for the residents of the colony wings
of the barryd while the stairs were being built. He had affectionately
become known as 'Luuko Air' to Arrallins and humans alike.

Exhilarated as always, Tara caught her breath as Luuko padded along the platform and launched himself into the wind. Liur and Rakal sped along beside them, Rakal's long tail flying out behind them as the air rushed by. She chuckled ruefully, knowing that what grooming he had managed to maintain would be long gone by the time they reached the coast.

Herds of various Dimar animals grazed below them as they passed out of Telka's territory and into Ekal's coastal region. Flocks of Dimar's native birds and flighted lizards spooked and took to the air in blinding masses of color as they flew low over the canopy top, which was divided by huge swatches of charred stumps and the firebreaks dug by Ekal Tinar firefighters. To the southeast, the fires still raged at the colony site, which was now a deserted neutral zone in Telkan territory. Tara sighed. The forest thinned, giving way to a stretch of prairie and then dune. The brightly decorated landing rock came into view as they turned south and moved down along the coast, and Tara could barely make out Mason, Tarrin, Harmon, Goothib, Tewi and the others in a close knot in the shadow of the rock. Luuko swept in, seemingly unaffected by the strong onshore breeze and landed on all fours on the flat top of the red rock bluff.

"Just in time!" Tara slid off Luuko's shoulder as Mason scrambled up the rock to report. A glimmering star, the Arralla's Pride, was already in view, making its final approach to splash down in the gentle currents of the western sea. "Any news about the Dark Hope, Mason? Will it be ready by tonight?"

Mason snapped a salute, and his eyes clouded. "They're going to work right up to the minute to get that last fuel cell in order, and they think they'll make it." He glanced at Rakal, who was deep in a discussion with Tarrin and some of the other betas, and mumbled, "We'll have our fireworks. Kiralla is not aboard the Pride."

"Shit. We don't have time for this. The Great Mother is going to have a field day with this one." Tara gritted her teeth, groaning inwardly that the Telkan Leader would have yet another bone to pick with her for being unable to 'control her children.' "I'll go talk to Landry and find out what's really going on." She strode purposefully to the edge of a rock, and called to Tewi, who was nearby. "Tewi, can you give me a lift down?"

"Sure thing..." The tall female stood on her hind legs, providing her front legs and knees as stairs down from the high rock. Tara was glad that the Dimar had no reservations about being used as all forms of furniture and transport by their new 'mates.

"Thanks, Tewi! If I ever can return the favor..." Tara winked at the green Dimar, who rumbled back at her. *I've got a surprise for you too,* Tara mused.

She slapped the comm, "Landry, report."

Landry looked calm and collected, as always. "We're not going to make the window, sir. There's no way. We lost 2 cells... again."

"Wrong answer, Landry. We'll send the pride up, and we'll tow you through the gate, then. That gate must close tonight or we'll be torn to shreds by the fuzz lizards." Tara didn't mask her annoyance — enough was enough. She knew from Kiralla's progress reports that the ship would have been spaceworthy, and strong enough to survive the gate crash operation by tonight. He was stalling, but why?

"All right then, I'll institute plan B and get the ship ready for a tow from the Pride." He shrugged, his angular features remaining unnaturally controlled as he glanced to the side of his console.

"Fine. Tara out." She slapped the comm panel, and the screen blanked with a flicker.

Waving to Tewi to give her a lift, she strode toward the stone platform, wondering how to break the news to Rakal yet again. Rakal turned and regarded her eagerly as she strode toward them.

"I'm sorry, Rakal. Two cells are once again out, and Kiralla is again not aboard the Pride." She backed away instinctively as his fur again fluffed out. He let loose a blood curdling shriek, and snatched a sidearm from one of the flag bearers standing nearby, nearly knocking the small man off the bluff. The disturbance was broken by distinct boom and hissing as the Pride made what would have been it's final splash down in the cool waters of the ocean.

"I will return to orbit with the Pride, and this time, I fly." Rakal stood on his hind legs, tying the sidearm into the thick fur on his sides deftly, obscuring it from view. "I will escort..." He paused, realizing that not all the people on the platform were inner circle members, "the overdue engineering team back here to the colony personally, as your Ir'est, your first officer, Tara." In a loud voice, he announced, "Those engineers have dishonored us by failing again to repair the ship. I will deal with them personally."

The Arralla's Pride powered itself toward the bluff, gradually growing larger as it coasted in on water pulse engines. Tara turned her head slightly to the northeast, and as she expected, could see the honor guard's banners, and the violet form of the Great Mother sweeping in to attend the festivities. She wondered just how festive this was going to be.

Distracted, Rakal turned and greeted the Great Mother, his tail lashing from side to side. Her disdainful Dimar expression for his irritation did not make matters any better. Resigning herself to the fact that this celebration would not provide any of the much-needed rest for her and Rakal, she braced herself to put on a good show for all the colonists. This was for them. They'd suffered the most these past weeks, and this celebration had provided them with a much needed morale boost.

People, betas and Dimar emerged from the woods, sailed in along the coasts, and landed all around the raised bluff platform. Tara was pleased to see that many of the colony's humans did arrive with various Dimar barrydmates, but noticed that there were many distinct groups of humans and a few betas that carefully avoided mixing with their larger hosts. She'd have to find a way to accommodate those who just couldn't adapt to barryd life.

Scanning the surrounding beach, she could tell that a majority of the colony not on fire duty, and a significant number of the Dimar from Telka were patiently waiting the start of the presentation. The few children and young betas, seated near to the bluff so that they could see clearly, burbled with excitement. Various classes and wings of Dimar flew lazy circles, proudly displaying their various identification silks and challenging each other in mock territorial game-dances. Crowds of humans and betas sat in dunes, or under the shady mangrove-like trees that provided shade near the bluff, munching away on a variety of fresh barryd foods. Despite the problems on the bluff, the crowd was festive.

The Pride pulled up to the bluff, and two young Dimar pushed the pontoon dock up. No sooner had the dock clicked into place, Rakal and one of the Pride's secondary crews climbed onto it and began refitting it for another takeoff, quietly working out of sight of the crowd. It would take at least an hour to clear the engines and reload the fusion reaction chamber with appropriately dense material to power it back into orbit, even with Rakal's best team working on it. It would be another two hours to fix the tow rig, and to position Dark Hope to successfully drop the gate crasher. Tara worked to think of ways to lengthen the ceremony so that the gate crash would coincide with the end of the presentations. Scanning the bluff crowd, she noticed that an entire division of people to whom she had planned to award medals were conspicuously absent. She hoped perhaps they'd provide the delay she needed.

The door of the Pride opened, and one by one, the final colonists and crew from the Singularity II filed down the dock and up the stairs to the bluff. Excited yips and purring from the newly arrived betas exiting the ship elicited a joyous cheer from the crowds below, and a few celebratory whoops from the human colonists inside. Tara watched the six disguised Alphas exit the ship, and exchange a short but meaningful glance with Rakal. Stooping slightly to hide their greater height, they quickly moved up the platform to mingle with humans from the Inner Circle on the bluff. Following, the remaining humans filed out behind, their faces glowing with the elation of being off a starship and out in open, unrecycled air. A few faces fell upon seeing the size and number of Dimar all around, but they quickly forgot their discomfort as they were reunited with long-missed crewmates and friends around the bluff.

Tara turned to the Great Mother, surprised to find her not ignoring the proceedings as she had expected. Her lavender head, grizzled with white hairs indicative of her age, had an open, welcoming expression as she looked from one arrival to another. She rumbled to herself absently, seeming as pleased with the new arrivals as she might be with a returning rank of her own Tinar firefighters returning from the line. Noticing Tara's scrutiny, she snorted and turned away.

The Great Mother turned back toward her. "Ssould I begin the ceremony, Leader Tara? All the new arrivals are here." Her tail flicked back and forth with her annoyance. Tara wondered if she was annoyed at having mispronounced the 'sh' sound, or at having to refer to her as a Leader. She didn't have time to wonder.

Rising on her hind legs, and spreading her iridescent wings wide, the Great Mother let loose a loud "OOOOOLAAAHHHM!" The new arrivals on the bluff nearly dove into the water, scrambling for sidearms. Other members of the crew on the bluff quickly silenced them, careful to keep their rifles clipped and the safeties on. Tara clicked on her amplifier set, and strode purposely to the edge of the platform where she could be seen by both sides of the crowd. Shaking, she pulled out her notepad. She was accustomed to addressing large crowds, to prepare them for battle with a rousing speech. She'd never addressed a crowd of civilians, or a newly discovered alien species.

"Three months ago..." She began, her voice cracking. "Three months ago we colonists were all running. Running from Earth Command, debts, imprisonment, slavery...the drudgery of what has become life on Earth, Arralla, and the Fleets. Three months ago we were searching—searching for a new way of living, wishing on distant stars for elbowroom and a place we could call our own home. Today, our running is over." A cheer went up from the crowd, punctuated by the various wisecracks from those who Tara recognized as living in the third level barryd rooms, which were the most crowded of the temporary housing. "Level three...I can hear you!" She jibed, eliciting another roar of applause from the crowd. She paused, waiting for the crowd to refocus its attention once again on the bluff.

"Today we have a home. And, as we all knew when we joined this team, we have a lot of work ahead of us. As the people of Dimar have embraced us, so must we embrace them and work together to ensure our continued mutual survival. Without them, we'd have been burned alive. Without us, they'd be enslaved by their neighbors...or worse...Earth Force." The crowd quieted at the mention of Earth Force, knowing that until the night sky lit up with the explosion of the gate crasher closing the star gate, they were all still very much in danger. Liur cast a worried glance skyward, and quietly slipped off the bluff and glided back toward Telka. Tara didn't have time to worry and continued on.

"Together, we will form a new Telka, as well as new colonies all around Telka territory — strengthening it against attack and against fire. We will be a part of the Dimar Plan. We will make this world our own, and it in turn will become a part of us." She saw eyebrows rise in parts of the crowd with the mention of new colonies. Many of the colonists were itching to rebuild the first settlement, and to claim their own pieces of territory free from the constraints of the barryd. "We all will find a space on Dimar that we can call our own home, where we can determine our own will and our own way, in the great barryd and out."

The colony crowds cheered again, but the Dimar didn't echo the sentiment as loudly. Tara was walking a tightrope by pushing the colony concept and knew it. She continued, keeping the speech fluid as she altered it. "Our way will be a new way — the Dimar way. We will honor the great Plan that the Telka and all peaceable barryds have laid out. We will not deadbuild. As the true children of the Water, the Telkans will guide us as we become a part of all of Dimar. We will take the best from all three societies — Arrallin, Human, and Dimar — and together build a new, better world for our children." Most of the humans were not part of the Inner Circle, and the comment about the three societies started an undercurrent of discussion. Arrallins were no longer considered a society by humans, and using Arrallin instead of Lupine or Furry to refer to them was questionable.

"Now, to celebrate this momentous day — the arrival of the last of the Singularity II — I would like to begin by recognizing individuals who have shown particular valor during the first tenuous months on

Dimar. First, the fire crews—Tinar 1, 4 and 5, and our own firefighting teams..." She beckoned for Mason to bring forward the award case. All heads turned as a howling whine issued from the back of the crowd. The Great Mother wiggled her ears and whuffled loudly, laughing as the Tinar ranks rose out of the forest well behind the crowd and glided toward the bluff. The whining noise became more familiar...it was bag piping, but it was horrible! Tara cast her glance up to the ranks moving in to see if they were the source of the noise. Each lead wore honor silks—but unlike any Tara had ever seen. They were plaid! They each wore a hideous mix of Telka colors, green gold and purple, arranged in a tartan pattern. As the ranks approached, the crowd parted, revealing the three dozen human and beta firefighters, dressed in full kilts made of the same hideous plaid silk, playing bagpipes fashioned from old lita-sacks. A roar rippled through the crowd, and those Dimar still hovering in the air dipped and swooped in a fit of sneezing Dimar laughter. Liur landed next to Tara, and announced, "The first integrated Tinar rank reporting as ordered, sir!"

Tara recovered her composure enough to manage a reply. "Well, I can see you all haven't lost your sense of humor, but I won't comment on your taste in fashion." Sean MacNamara, a true Scottish fanatic who had headed the southern border fire-defense at the colony, strode purposefully up the stairs and onto the bluff. "I should have known, Sean. But next time...give your crew time to learn the bagpipes before you let them play." A few kilted betas had already fallen over with the effort to maintain the howling off-key bagpipe note they'd managed all during the procession. "Kill the bagpipes, Tinar!" Tara motioned.

Happily, the howling died down with a sickly moan, and the Dimar in the air above the ranks landed and filed in with the betas and humans below. "To each of these brave defenders, I would like to present the Order of the Flame, for their dedicated service to the barryd, the colony, and to one another." The crowd cheered as one by one, humans, betas and Dimar filed up onto the platform to accept each of the small silver pins. "And, to the Great Mother, and her Tinar ranks who selflessly gave each night to the colony to dig firebreaks despite direct orders from the council of Leaders, I would like to present this token of our esteem." She signaled to one of the unloading crews, and they brought up a large white box. "This was made onboard the Singularity II while it was in orbit by one of our own artisans, Kelsey Dreslough. We snuck the materials up with each of the Pride's shuttle runs." She pulled away the container cover to reveal an intricate metallic sculpture depicting a graceful Tinar line hovering before a wall of carved rosewood flames. Tara grinned as a number of Dimar artisans near the platform rumbled approval of the work.

"It is most beautiful. Perhaps our own artisans can learn from yours, Tara." The Great Mother strode forward and took the sculpture carefully in both paws. Holding it before the crowd, the Dimar joined in a chiming song of thanks. With perfect timing, one of her acolytes came forward and spirited the sculpture back to the barryd, skimming noiselessly over the crowd. Tara noted with a spike of jealousy how handy psionic communication was for these ceremonies. The Great Mother retook her place in the back of the platform, and nodded to Tara, signaling her to continue.

"Now, it is both a human and Arrallin tradition to recognize acts of bravery and ingenuity whenever they occur—even in the heat of battle." She saw a few puzzled looks from the various Dimar in attendance. "During the course of the attack on the colony by the Mulkol, many individuals showed exceptional self-sacrifice by risking themselves to save our colony, even though it was not their own home. For their bravery, the colony would like to recognize three Telkans—Luuko, Tewi and Namalki for their efforts to defend the colony from the attack and hold the fire lines." A buzz went up among the Dimar in the crowd, and all eyes were on the Great Mother.

She stepped forward slowly and gracefully, towering over Tara. It was clear from her expression that she was psionically explaining the situation to the Dimar, quelling their protest. Speaking aloud for the benefit of the non-Talented, she roared, "As the colonists honor our traditions, so must we allow theirs. These awards are not for Mulkai action or Mulkai thought, but for bravery in a crisis. These individuals did not kill cruelly, or choose the Mulkai path, but instead chose, as any of us would, to defend the colony as if it were our own barryd. That is within keeping with our own Telkai tradition. We will accept this. There will be no questions." Her tone was final, and the Dimar were silent.

Tara stepped forward to Tewi, her mate Namalki, and Luuko. "Tewi and Namalki—for risking yourselves and your unlaid eggs for our colony, I present the Order of Kinratta. It is an ancient Arrallin award reserved for Alphas carrying children who go into combat." She placed a blue silk ribbon bearing the golden insignia around each of the females' necks. She wondered about the frequency of same-sex pairings in Dimar culture, but had her attention snapped back to the business at hand.

"For you, Luuko, who bravely endured flames to try to drive off an entire Mulkol rank with minimal loss of life by engaging the rank leader, I present the Silver Cross. It may not be commonly known to Telkans, but by driving off the leader of a group, you can sometimes break the entire formation and force it to retreat. In attempting to do this, Luuko was not only saving the lives of those defending the colony, but also sparing those lives of the young Mulkol in the first line of the battle who were ordered to retreat when the rank leader fell." An appreciative singsong tune rose up from the Telkans in the crowd, and Luuko bowed his head modestly.

She glanced back at the Pride, and saw Rakal's signal that they were ready to take off. "And now, for the first of two sets of fireworks for this evening. First, the Arralla's Pride will take off again—a spectacle with which we are now all thoroughly familiar. And, with the Pride overseeing the operation, in a few hours, we will all be able to view the closing of the gate, which promises to be something to remember." The crowd, Dimar and colonists alike let out a strong cheer at the news. "We'll spend the remainder of the evening enjoying a wide variety of new recipes, and hearing reports from all divisions of the new barryd-colony."

The Pride detached and pulled away on water-pulse engines, working toward takeoff speed. As she watched it go, Tara was filled with a sense of foreboding. She scanned the crowd, trying to figure out what was triggering her nervousness, but with no luck. She clicked over to the Pride's communication channel. "Rakal, is everything okay on board? You got that fuel transfer done in record time, which isn't exactly a good thing."

"The Pride is as good as ever, and I'll throw it into orbit myself if need be. We'll be off this rock in 10 minutes, and I'll be with Kiralla in another five. I could fly without a ship right about now. I'll keep you posted on how the operation is going, relativity allowing. Rakal out." His voice resonated with a familiar confidence as he piloted the craft out into the calm water. Tara wondered how much he would miss long years in space, piloting the more challenging destroyer class ships.

Still, Tara could not shake the apprehension she felt as the ship moved out of view. She concluded her presentation and prepared the crowd for Mason's important biological survey information. He took the broadcast channel, and she tuned back into the Pride's communications frequency nervously. She scanned the horizon, watching for the plume that would mark the Pride's liftoff toward orbit. Rakal's voice broke her reverie.

"We're beginning liftoff, but I think I should abort...there's something big down there. Like a school of fish, moving toward the coast fast!" Rakal sounded torn between keeping the Pride and its weaponry power close to the festival and getting up into orbit and on board the Dark Hope with Kiralla.

Luuko padded up, his head swaying back and forth with alarm. "Tara, Kiralla just spoke to me...something's very wrong with her," he whispered.

"Rakal—no time for fishing. Get up there now! Seems Kiralla just told Luuko that there's something wrong up there." Tara fervently wished that Kiralla had not gone into season. Rakal's bark of alarm was coupled with a roar from across the ocean as the Pride lifted on a plume of steam.

"Luuko, give me a full report...as best you can. Did she say that she was going to mate?" Tara stared deep into his golden eyes, seeing her own panicked reflection staring back at her.

"Landry is moving the ship...and yes, she will mate very soon. He's heading for the Gate...he may not close it. He knows Kiralla is Alpha and has her alone in the hold of the ship." He blinked nervously, careful to modulate his voice so the Great Mother could not hear. She was engrossed in her own discussions with her acolytes, listening to Mason's report.

Wincing, Tara clicked back onto the communication channel with Rakal. "She's going into season, and Landry's making a break for the Gate. Damn furverts! He knows," she moaned. "I don't know how, but he knows! Get up there, and prime the cannons." She clicked out, not wanting to hear Rakal's reaction. She blinked back tears of rage, hoarsely whispering, "He'll never make it. Landry's 120 minutes from the gate and accelerating. Rakal's 30 minutes from Landry. If Landry drops the Gate crasher as he goes through, Rakal could be killed up there!" She felt as if she were watching a friend die.

Luuko whined a concerned note, and the Great Mother momentarily turned her gaze to them. Tara looked away, feeling completely drained and helpless.

"Her voice is very strange...she doesn't sound like herself." Luuko stared out across the water, as if listening. "She isn't making sense right now."

Tara bit her lip. She was under the influence of 20 years of pent hormones. And, isolated from her beta entourage and alone with Landry, she'd have little choice when she reached her mating peak. Bleakly, she turned back to the crowd to listen to the reports.

The Pride was little more than a speck atop the pillar of steam at this point, but the engine roar seemed to be getting louder. The water around the bluff became rough, with the waves getting higher and higher. The crowd went silent. The ground beneath her feet shuddered as the Great Mother screeched out a strangled cry of alarm!

Chapter 16

Rakal ground his teeth with frustration, holding still as the acceleration pushed him back into his seat. Frantically, his mind raced. Images of Kiralla trapped with that...that thing fought with images of possible trajectories and plans of attack. He whined inwardly, knowing that he first had to catch up to the fleeing ship, which might not be possible, even with the Pride's greater speed and maneuverability.

With unconscious precision, he set the ship into a slow roll as the gravity shifted from down to back toward the stern of the ship. His crew could last an hour comfortably at 2.5 gravities—another beta blessing, so he set the ship on an accelerated intercept course and gave the signal for them to leave their seats. His crew set about priming the plasma cannons. They spoke little— every beta on the Pride was a member of Rakal's own hive, and knew what this mission meant to him, and their future. Staring out into the cold blackness of space, Rakal could see the glimmer that was the Dark Hope, powering off toward the star gate. "Please...please...let those engines fail...." He dug his claws into the padded steering yoke, and held himself back from howling out loud.

"Wait! Landry doesn't know that we know about Kiralla! No one knows she's a psi...and Landry's psis are all offship!" The realization that he may still have a trick or two left to delay them sent up a celebratory war-growl from his second in command and the crew. Jabbing a claw into the comm panel button hard enough to leave a groove, he signaled the Dark Hope.

"Dark Hope...please advise on your engine status. We thought we were going to use the towing plan." Rakal faked a calm, curious tone that elicited a toothy grin from his second in command.

"Arralla's Pride...this is Dark Hope reporting. We did get our engines back online and decided to make all speed to the Gate for the crash operation. We understood that the situation down below was critical." The vaguely familiar voice of Landry's Ir'est sounded tense.

The Dark Hope was almost a light minute from the Gate, and moving out fast. Rakal knew he had little time to act and stop them from going through and launching the crash device. "Dark Hope...the situation down below won't go critical for another four hours, at least. What if your engines fail halfway through the Gate? The second plan is safer. Halt here, and we'll rig the tow cable."

Without warning, the Dark Hope blasted its reversing engines on full. Bits of the old ship broke off and kept going on into the Gate, but the main hull remained intact. Rakal raced to recalculate his trajectory to avoid collision with the hulking destroyer, and brought the Pride alongside the docking ring, a few hundred meters away.

Carefully, he scanned the Dark Hope for weapons activity as his own crew manually cranked the cannons into position. By not using the positioning hydraulics, the Dark Hope's own defense system would not detect the lock-on. The ship was not gearing up for defense. In fact, damage reports from the various levels showed that the quick stop was not planned.

"Dark Hope...report. Our scans show significant damage to the outer positioning rings. Who's flying that crate of yours? Tell Landry to report immediately...we're coming aboard!" Rakal vented some of his pent fury into his admonishing tone.

The voice that answered was different, and almost groggy. In the background, Rakal could hear the distinct keening whine of an Arrallakeeni mourning a death, as well as swears and moans. "Sir...sir...that stop was not planned. The helm refuses to respond...we will need that tow now. No need to come aboard...we can handle the damage. Please prepare the Pride's tow line, and wait for our signal."

"You've got injured aboard...and dead. We're coming over now. Open your docking clamp on strut #3...it's still functional from what we can see." Rakal tried to remain patient. If worse came to worse, he'd have his crew cut a hole above the hold where Kiralla was, and he'd suit up and float over.

"No, sir. This mission is our duty and our right. We will perform it unaided. Do not try to board." The voice was strained but resolute, and the rotation of the Dark Hope became erratic—a common tactic to prevent a docking lock or forced link.

Rakal had no choice. He could hide his Alpha identity no longer. He slammed his paw down on the comm button and in his strongest command voice screamed, "Regulate rotation and open the clamp...NOW!"

A minute passed...the longest minute Rakal had ever experienced.

The ship's rotation did not regulate, and suddenly, the Pride went to red alert. They were going to fire!

Before Rakal could even give the order, his crew clipped away each of the gunnery ports within range of the Pride, working to dispatch new ones as the ship rotated, exposing new turrets. He unbelted himself from the pilot's seat, and, using weightlessness to his advantage, shot himself headlong toward the pressure suits at the end of the small Pride cabin. "We're going to do this the hard way...Sadir, take the helm, and start evasive maneuvers if they do manage to get a decent shot off!"

Struggling into his suit, he hurriedly began to check each gauge. Dying in the coldness of space, just meters from Kiralla while Landry had his way with her was not in his plan. He watched his crew expertly cut a hole in the hull with well-aimed plasma shots, careful not to breach it on the level where Kiralla was imprisoned. Burst after burst struck the hull, creating a pockmarked circle. With a final shot to the center, the metal plate was knocked spinning and then out into space as the hold depressurized. Rakal fervently hoped that Kiralla was not in that bay. Regardless, they had to press on. Other members of his boarding team struggled into suits, as intent on victory, or at least some kind of resolution, as he was.

A turret on the Dark Hope turned to fire, and Rakal barked out an alarm call as their return shot missed it by inches. Expecting the rollicking impact of a plasma burst against the Pride, Rakal desperately grabbed for his helmet, slamming it into place with a clatter. Amazingly, the gun not only didn't fire—it overloaded and exploded. Rakal raced toward the airlock. What the hell was going on inside that ship!?

He filed in behind his second in command, already suited and armed with a plasma rifle, and clipped onto the rescue cable. Gnashing his teeth, he imagined his Kiralla, alone in a dark hull with the hulking specter Landry looming over her like a vulture over a fresh kill. He probably had her bound like some animal, waiting for the full onset of her season to take effect before he...

He blinked back his rage as the airlock door slid away and the escaping air whisked them into the silence of cold space. She'd have no choice, alone in the hold with him. He rued the fact that if Arrallin females did not mate, they'd go into a psychological shock that always resulted in insanity or death. For the first time, he wished Kiralla had been born a male. Images of Kiralla from their childhood flashed before him—her laughing, her gentle understanding, and her fury at the conditions in which she and the other Arrallins had to live. Now this. Would Kiralla's fury at being used by a human so undeserving eat her alive if he didn't reach her in time?

A plasma blast whizzing by his left side broke him out of his bitter reverie. Two suited Arrallakeeni from Landry's ship were firing haphazardly at the boarding party out of the hole they had cut in the hull. The hole rolled away before they could attempt a better shot, and on the next go-round, Rakal's forces would be ready for them. He issued commands, setting two guards at either side of where the hole would approach. Leaving them in place to convince the hull-defenders that the boarding party had not yet entered the ship, he and his second in command slipped into another hull breach the Pride had created when it began firing on the crippled ship. He didn't know the deck layout of the Dark Hope well, but he knew enough to get down to Kiralla's level. Breaking off radio contact, he sent his second toward the bridge, and speeding off on all fours he made his way into the dark, twisted wreckage to find Kiralla.

Chapter 17

Shots rang out through the forest behind the bluff. Tara spun away from the churning foam to find acolytes falling to either side of her. The carnage was almost incomprehensible. As each barbed globule struck, the firescales and skin of it's target seemed to slough away, as if liquefied. One acolyte fell into the now slushy wing of another, and it itself started to dissolve. Both fell away off the bluff and into the water, carefully avoiding the Great Mother and her guardians.

Out across the treetops, massive forms churned toward them, preceded by a pressure wave of wind that knocked Dimar in flight out of the air and down into the trees. Tiny petals dropped from the underside of the flying vehicles, blossoming into parachutes. Each carried a fearsome looking cargo that either erupted in a shower of projectiles, or sprouted legs. The mobile vehicles scuttled through the forests like spiders, impaling Telkans on their barbs as they crushed through the underbrush at lightning speeds. Tara had seen enough, and grabbed a plasma rifle instinctively.

"Damn Landry's timing! We need the Pride down here. What the hell are those things!?" The sea-borne vehicles, now amphibious, were making good speed up the beaches. What Telkan resistance there was did little, but the plasma rifles did seem to slow them down. Tara picked off the front legs of one of the smaller craft that was making a beeline for the bluff.

Acolytes crowded around the Great Mother. They carried her

off the bluff and down into the relative safety of the lee side. She was motionless, sitting in her customary position for commanding the fire lines, but her face lacked the sanguine expression she usually wore. Furrowed with concentration and raw anger, her muzzle had pulled back to reveal rows of sharp white teeth, and her eyes flashed. All around, Telkans formed the familiar and orderly battle lines from their territorial dances, as if propelled by an unseen hand. As each rank formed, it let loose a furious battle cry, and swept off to engage each of the approaching crawlers. Tara couldn't bear to watch to see how well they fared. It was the equivalent of naked humans trying to bring down hovertanks.

Luuko leapt up from the Great Mother's side to sweep Tara off the bluff as a barrage of barbed globules rained down from an approaching paratrooper.

Betas, working frantically in a coordinated mass, had dug a cave in a matter of minutes. Others clumped around the Alphas creating a perfect sphere of living protection for each pair. A giant mass of fur, they rolled like some giant dust-bunny into the opening, suffering the impacts of spiked projectiles noiselessly. A snarl still evident on her face, a tan Beta, dead from a direct impact to the chest by one of the barbules, fell out of the clump and to the ground.

As they rushed by, Tara noted that the viscous fluid that had caused such damage in the Telkans had no effect on the Betas struck by the projectiles. The Mulkol were using some kind of biological agent to digest the Telkans alive. But, it was either sparing, or unable to affect, the colonists. The spikes were still solid, and as sharp as razors, but at least the Arrallakeeni wouldn't start to melt and infect others as the acolytes had.

One of the nightmare machines climbed over the bluff, looming down over them and the Great Mother's entourage. Tara gave a warning yell and fired five shots into its center. It faltered, seeming to writhe for a moment as if alive, and backed off. Screaming to the acolytes to move out, she knew it wouldn't be long before another and another of those machines came tumbling over after them.

She ran into the woods in a zigzag pattern, firing on the ground-troops and foot soldiers of the Mulkol as best she could. "A hovercar, dammit! I need a higher capacity weapon!"

What hovercars were still working had already taken to the air. Some blasted away, working to defend the bluff from attacks from all sides. With a deep resentment, Tara watched two hovercars blast off back toward the old colony site to the south, firing no shots as they went. If she lived, she'd execute those traitors personally.

Fury goading her on, she deftly leapt over bodies of fallen Telkans, now decaying into pools on the forest floor. She fired away at the armored Mulkol, doing little damage and avoiding them in the complex root systems and underbrush. Again, she wished she could get airborne. She was a pilot, and could do more damage from the air—with the right weapons.

She skirted a clearing where a wing of the Telkan defenders had engaged a crawler. Each had dug its tail-spade into the side of the vehicle, and was working to pry one of the shell-like panels loose. The vehicle was covered in barbs that dug into each Telkan, infecting them with the liquefying ooze that had so completely destroyed the acolytes on the bluff. As if ignorant to the pain, the Telkans worked on...their sheer weight dragging the crawler to its knees and flipping it.

A Mulkol foot soldier approached to her left, not noticing her crouched in the underbrush. As it latched onto a dying Telkan and worked to pry it loose from the crawler, she quietly took aim and neatly shot a hole through the Mulkol's skull. The foot soldier's efforts were misguided, however. The crawler's own biological defenses were making quick work of the Telkans. They were simply turning to jelly and sliding off in half-digested pools, flailing ineffectively at the vehicle as it regained it's footing and righted itself.

Tara swore in frustration. Noticing a fire-scorched tree leaning in toward the clearing, she took careful aim. Blast after blast blew hunks of wood out of the bottom of the tree, and finally, with a resounding crack, it fell, crushing the crawler. The machine stopped moving, leaving Tara with only the distant sounds of battle.

The sudden stillness of the meadow, littered with colorful pools of the dead was too much for Tara. Her head swam, filled with a thousand frantic voices and cries for help. Dropping her rifle, she fell to her side in the grass. In vain, she covered her ears to block out the voices—voices, she slowly realized that were only in her head. An almost overwhelming feeling of guilt swept through her. In her exhaustion, she realized that she may be dead, and that these were the voices of all the Arrallins and people she'd killed in battle before she met Rakal. Before she understood just how wrong what she had been doing was. "I'm trying to save them now! I'm trying to save them now... I'm trying..." she screamed as the voices grew louder and each cry more distinct.

A frantic shake on her shoulder knocked her out back into reality. She rolled to find Harmon staring down at her, stunned. "Tara...you've got to shut down your broadcasting... They're combing the forest for that voice now!"

"Harmon...I haven't got a radio. Dammit, I need a hovercar to do real damage, and to coordinate the counter attack!" Tara sputtered, clamping down on her previous wild emotional outbursts to again take command of the situation. "Contact Tarrin...find out if there are any hovercars left near where they took the Alphas. We need to set up some kind of communication net...the Telkans' efforts are just damned useless!"

Harmon locked eyes with her in a steady, searching gaze. "Tara, you were broadcasting...you have Talent. I can see it plain as day now. You've got to keep it hidden or they'll find you for sure." Without moving her mouth, Tara distinctly heard, "Can you hear this?"

"Yes, but..." Tara answered verbally, still too shaken to know exactly what had just transpired.

"Okay...next test...can you see this?" Harmon closed her eyes, concentrating. "Don't get frustrated...I can sense you blocking. Okay, what do you see in your mind now?" Images, first of basic shapes, and then colors, and different scenes in combination flashed into Tara's mind.

"The blocks...circle...pyramid...blue...green...red...the Colony, Telka Barryd, the goat pens...the horses running in the grass courtyards at Telka." Tara struggled with the unfamiliar flavor of the images. Despite their bucolic and peaceful nature, the very presence of the odd images was disturbing. Feeling the need to counter, she responded with her own. She pushed out an image of her favorite horse, Tsarina, leading the herd back at the colony, feeling the warmth and pride she had felt when she first let them run after many long months in the ships.

"Whoa...okay...we've established that you can broadcast and receive. Figuring your effective range we can do later. Our first task will be teaching you how to avoid detection. If they know you're a psi, they'll catch you for sure to lead the non-psi slaves." Harmon's tone was caustic, and she glared out toward the wings of Mulkol foot soldiers that swept low over the forest, carrying off colonists and Dimar alike.

"Slaves? What? This battle's not over...we've got to regroup and set up a battle plan." Tara struggled to her feet, shouldering her plasma rifle. Emotionally, she was swept with wave after wave of an unfamiliar feeling—the feeling of defeat. It emanated all around her, an unfamiliar presence that she could never detect before.

"No...From what I can tell, the battle is over. Reports from all over show that what Telkans resisted were quickly killed, and those that didn't resist were enslaved. Seems that that's the way the Mulkol do business..." Her bitter tone told Tara that this was more than just a lost battle, but a personal loss.

"Is Goothib...?" Tara slumped back down into the long grass.

"No...He's alive, but enslaved. Seems his skills will make a valuable addition to the Mulkol's failing Telkai and Tinar branches. They're not good at much beyond war." She dug her fingers into the roots of the grass, pulling at them angrily.

Tara sat bolt upright. "The Great Mother...is she dead?"

Harmon let loose a rueful chuckle. "No...No no no...they've got something special in store for her. I'm not sure what, but from what little I know of their history, it won't be pleasant. At least she's still alive though. As long as she's around, the Telkans are willing to at least put up some resistance."

"What about Luuko, Liur, Mason and the others? Any news?" Tara was already forming a possible counterattack plan, but she'd need willing resistance from the Telkans who survived, and she'd need field marshals she could depend on. "Who's left to finish this war on our side?"

"Luuko suffered some serious damage, but didn't get hit with a snot-gun, thanks be. He's getting watered-up at Ekal with the rest of the resistance. Liur...Liur was lost trying to defend the Great Mother, as were Tewi and her mate. About half of Telka's population was killed...the rest enslaved. Mason was captured, along with about five dozen other humans, I suspect for experimentation purposes. Telka is Mulkol occupied now...we can't go back, so we've lost most of our equipment. Luckily, because the Arrallins and humans aren't psi, and aren't considered very valuable by the Mulkol yet, most of the colonists did escape into the woods." Harmon looked dubious at the mention of a counter attack, but gave her report dutifully. "It's not enough to stand against the Mulkol and these ancient war-machines of theirs. It just isn't."

"We've got three ships in orbit, and if need be, I'll drop all three straight on Mulkol's head. But, a direct attack is never effective at this point in the game. We're going to need backup to get out of this. We need support from other Barryds." Tara knew she needed more information, but Ekal was more than a day's march from the bluff, and the colonists were scattered. A twinge of guilt for having left the Great Mother's side passed through her, but she crushed it down.

"I felt that guilt as clear as rain on my head, Tara. I've got to show you how to block...they'll hear you a mile away at this rate." Harmon shook her head, chuckling sardonically. A wing of Mulkol soldiers flew low over the forest near them, and turned their way as Harmon began the lesson.

Chapter 18

"Keep your eyes peeled...one of them's an Alpha. The Boss will kill us if he gets through to them before they mate." The speaker crackled, but the message was clear.

Rakal bristled at the intercepted radio messages from the Landry's Arrallakeeni, now combing the ship for him and his tiny invasion force. The little sugtrats knew that Kiralla was an Arrallin female! They knew, and still, they'd give her up to that *human*! Rakal padded forward, quickening his pace. If Landry had enough sway to make Arrallakeeni heed him over a full-blood Arrallin, he was a force to be reckoned with.

Rakal cautiously slipped around a twisted bulkhead, avoiding the jagged points that could tear his pressure suit and end his search quickly and painfully. Damning the loss of atmosphere on the level, he rushed through a long corridor and into a still-functional transport tube. "If I could just use my nose, I could find Kiralla in an instant! This is going to take me forever."

He zipped on to the next level, relieved to find that atmosphere was indeed intact here. The pull of the slightly heavier gravity informed him that he had reached the outer edge of the ship...and should be very close to the hold where Kiralla was trapped. He pushed the image of Kiralla's sparkling green eyes from his mind, and leapt across the wide hallway in a single leap, plasma rifle ready. Shots rang out behind him, as the guards in the long corridor ran toward him. Landing safely in the hallway across from the lift tube, he rushed for the far door...just to find it opening as he reached it.

He made quick work of the first guard, using the decorative plastic claws on his suit to separate the Arrallakeeni and his throat. The claws weren't strong or sharp enough to rip his suit, but when propelled by one angry full-blood Arrallin against fur and hide, they did the job admirably. Using the corpse as a shield, Rakal traded plasma fire with the second guard with less success, taking a hit to his lower left leg. More guards clattered toward him from down the hall. Once they rounded the corner, he'd be easy pickings. Frantic to finish off the second guard and seal the door behind him, he flung the bleeding body headlong into the guard and shot the last of his plasma into the locking mechanism. The door closed with a sickly whoosh, sealing him in the chamber. "I hope for your sake that Kiralla is beyond this doorway," Rakal growled as he leapt toward the stunned Arrallakeeni on his three good legs, smacking him squarely in the head with his visor. The force was enough to crack the shield, making visibility poor. He clicked the throatlatch and flung off the helmet as the Arrallakeeni made a grab for his rifle.

Instinct upon smelling Kiralla's distinctive odor seized Rakal. Struggling, he kept his wits, determined to finish the guard. He clamped his jaw down on the guard's arm, snapping the bones. Through bloody teeth, he spat, "I was saving this for your Landry! Enjoy!"

With lightning motion, he clamped his jaws onto the throat of the guard, closing off his windpipe. Digging into the guard's soft underbelly, he gutted him with his right hindfoot, ignoring the guard's attempts to scream. The bulky form went limp beneath him as Rakal stumbled back from the corpse. Shock at his own cruelty stunned him momentarily as the blood from his partially charred hind leg mingled with that of the hapless guard. A second whiff of Kiralla's scent brought his hackles up and dulled the pain in his leg and his mind. He had to reach Kiralla before it was too late!

Working frantically to find the keycard on the dead guard, Rakal could see the hallway guards burning holes through the bulkhead with their rifles. It wouldn't take them long to burn a set of perforations in the door and knock a hole through, if the plasma from the shots didn't kill him first. "Where is it, damn you! WHERE IS IT!?" He turned to face the entryway that was quickly becoming slag as the guards worked on it, dodging flying shrapnel and red-hot plasma as he tore the guard's gear apart.

The distinctive buzz and whoosh of the door to the room beyond opening brought him up straight, and he spun to face the new enemy. Taught muscles under a silkily furred body slammed against Rakal's ribs, and he fell hard against his bad leg. The scent that rose up from the body on top of him was overwhelming, making him immediately aware of the burning sensation growing inside of him, and his need... The smell of her, the smell of blood, his own pain was almost too much. He flung his attacker away, screaming out for Kiralla. He would reach her, or die trying.

"You idiot! Has it been so long that you don't recognize me when you see me!?" He sprang forward through the doorway as the familiar voice, somehow deeper now, called him from behind. The carnage inside the room was nothing like Rakal could imagine, but Kiralla and Landry had been the only ones in this room.

"What in five hives did you do, Kir?" Rakal turned back toward the door, to find his assailant, Kiralla herself, facing him in the doorway. Her tawny fur was drenched in blood, and it coated her grinning muzzle.

"Do you like it? I call it 'Landryburgers'. The little pervert had cameras set up all over the room...I got the whole thing on film." She chuckled smugly. "Now let's get rid of our party crashers at the door, eh?"

Her sidelong glance set Rakal's heart pounding, and made him imminently aware that his pressure suit was too confining. As she turned, swishing her long, graceful tail in the doorway, the scent nearly bowled Rakal over. Like a kit, he toddled after her, shrugging out of his suit.

"Kiralla...am I too late?" Rakal bleated, desperate. Judging from the total carnage in the other room, he knew that Kiralla might already be in the throws of mating psychosis. If she had already passed her season without mating, she would soon die.

Her tone was gentle and reassuring. "No. no, Rakal. You're just in time. I've got about another 20 minutes before I'll be ready." Using her command voice, she ordered Rakal to the other side of the door to await the guards. Rakal followed her every word, floating on a cloud of elation. She had killed Landry, risked death, to mate with him!

The door burst open, and using the butt of his rifle, he quickly knocked out the first guard as he poked his head through. The second managed to get an ineffective shot off, but Kiralla grabbed the rifle barrel, and pulled him into Rakal's range. Another quick knock to the skull, and Kiralla and he were alone, save for the sounds of the ship and the rasping breath of the two guards.

"C'mon...Landry has some nifty toys we can use to keep these guys restrained." Kiralla giggled, striding into the back room on two legs.

To Rakal, she was luminous. Her golden-brown fur seemed to glow white in the dim flickering blue lights of the hold. She came out, suggestively swinging the spiked chains and leg irons, a scene that sent Rakal's heart rate through the roof. He licked his chops, trying to wet his parched mouth. Embarrassed, he averted his eyes, resting on his belly to obscure the physical results of his thoughts from her view. This was Kiralla he was thinking about!

She laughed as she bound the two guards and flipped a loop of the chain through a hook high on the wall. "Rakal...grow up and give me a hand." She used the butt of an empty rifle to beat the metal hook closed.

"Kiralla...if I hadn't saved you, you would have died." Rakal chided her, furious that she would have risked her life to avoid a first mating bond that she didn't approve. He could have killed Landry and she could have chosen him as her second mate, with the same results achieved.

She spun on him, her green eyes flashing. "You saved ME? You SAVED me?" She paused, slamming the rifle to the ground with a clatter. "When I had to jury-rig this ship to stop before the gate, to blow turrets when it tried to fire on anything with an Insurrection identification beacon, as well as locking off five floors and sleep-gassing the rest of the crew...all FANATICALLY loyal to Landry, to keep them from eating you alive?! You saved me, eh?" She snarled, showing rows of sharp white teeth. "I wasn't planning on dying...I was just planning on NOT mating with that good for nothing whoreson Landry. One of these Arrallakeeni would have done me fine, babe...and the option's still there if you've got a problem with my judgment!"

Rakal was taken aback, ashamed that he had questioned her at all. He wondered if he had been in the same situation, if he could have survived being bonded with a mate like Landry. He would have chosen death.

She spun, refusing to face him. Her voice cracked with emotion. "I know what being raped does to a human. I can only guess what it would do to me. Landry wanted me as his slave, to do...You don't know what he said...what he described! I couldn't survive that. For twenty-one years now I've suffered, letting other people make my choices for me. This, this is my choice and only mine. On something this important, I refuse to compromise." She sank to her haunches and whined quietly, holding her face in her hands.

He padded over to her on three legs and sat next to her, saying nothing, careful to keep his nose upwind from her tail. Not knowing what else to do, he tried to comfort her by stroking her shoulder.

Her sobs subsided, and after a few minutes she turned to him, her green eyes full of emotion. "I love you Rakal...I have since that day on Arralla when we hid in the abandoned hives with Rinnar and talked and talked. You're the one I want...you are my choice for this mating, and for all to come. Know this, and trust this." With that, she leaned over, clamping her jaws on his shoulder, easing him back onto the floor. Her tail brushed up, encircling his muzzle with heady female scents, and instinctively, he gently gripped her shoulder with his jaws. His need for her burned within him, but he would wait until she was ready. Finally, she pulled herself to him as their tails twined.

Kiralla had made her choice.

Chapter 19

Luuko crowded into the Water with other survivors from Telka.
It was dangerous, as the Water might confuse one Telkan for another
and start rebuilding each incorrectly. Luuko's cousin got a green
patch of scales mixed in with his original blue ones when he had to
be healed in a crowded pool after a particularly nasty day in the fire
lines. He was lucky...others have been known to receive limbs in the
wrong places. His cousin...he wondered if he had survived. Luuko
tried not to think too loudly about the dead, or the possible trouble
with the healing pool. Most of the others in the pool had severe
internal injuries and would die if the Water failed. He had only a little
more time to go before he could continue his healing outside the
pool, and could find time to think then.

An Ekal healer nudged him from above, requesting that he
move to the left. Her mind-tone was resonant with confidence in
her abilities, even as she added yet another twisted Telkan body to
the pool. Luuko turned to peer at her from beneath the green-tinged
water. She wore the honor silks of the first rank of the healing class
for Ekal, as well as the graduate band from the Ekaokai Barryd.
Ekaokai was the premier healing Barryd, and competition for space
in their healing classes was intense. Luuko no longer feared for the
residents of his pool, and broadcast a wide, confident beam to those
in the throes of recovery.

Luuko, we have a friend of yours here to see you. You can come out of
the pool now. Your injuries are no longer critical. The voice of the healer

sounded in his mind, and he wondered who he knew who may have survived the massacre and escaped enslavement.

Curious, he popped his head above water and looked around the edge of the pool. *Where? Who?* Grabbing the pool ledge with his recently regenerated forelegs, he miscalculated and slipped back down into the water. *Ach! It's going to take me quite some time to get used to these new limbs. I hope I don't fail your beautiful work, Healer.*

He opened his wings...one which was also completely reconstructed. Even with the disadvantage of the new, untrained wing, he could feel the Wind flowing through the Water and through the stones. He rose smoothly from the pool and set himself on the edge.

You seem to have taken to those new wings, I see. The healer's approval was partially suffused in pride in her own craftsmanship.

He stretched the silvery-white expanses of glossy membrane open for her inspection, noting that she had even done some color work to hide the places where new membrane had grafted itself to the old. He warbled happily, broadcasting the quality of this healing team's work to those still underway in the pools. Relieved echoes filtered back to him through the Water.

All honor and grace to you, Healer. Telka is honored by your skill, and is in your debt. Luuko bowed his head to the healer before he rose into the air to find this friend on the levels above. He wondered if he could bring Tara here to finally have her discolored side treated by a true master in a proper pool. He shook the thought from his head...now was no time to be thinking of appearances or the nila needed for luxuries.

All honor and grace to you, Telka. I'm sure we can find a way to repay the debt next fire season. Our healers are good, but your Tinar ranks are the best. The healer whistled a farewell to him and turned back to her work.

Luuko rose up through the central passage of Ekal's single spire. It was still an immature Barryd, and would develop it's second set of healing pools and second spire in the next 10 cycles, when Ekal's population had risen to the point where it needed it. He stopped

at the courtyard level as instructed by the healer, and glided down
the passage to the third dining hall, not sure if his new legs would
be willing to walk him there. Coming down the hallway, the familiar
babble of colonists caught his attention. He sped headlong down the
hallway, almost bowling over one of the Ekal coming out of a side
chamber.

Into the hall, he swept up, bellowing greetings to the colonists
crowded into the huge room. "Hello! Hello! Nice to see you again!"
His cheerful greeting was met with less enthusiasm. Injured colonists,
Arrallakeeni and humans, were laid out on tables and on the floor as
other humans poured lita after lita of Water on them.

"Luuko! I heard you were nearly killed..." The familiar voice of
Tara made Luuko swoop in mid-hover.

"No, Leader Tara. I survived and healed well." He stretched his
wings a little wider, trying to show the greenish patches. He landed,
chiding himself inwardly for this silly sympathy ploy, realizing that
without use of full Water pools, the colonists would have a much
more painful times healing, if they survived the first day at all. He
felt a probing presence in his mind, and quickly shielded images of
the Water pools lying below the ground levels of the Barryd. Ekal
knew from discussions with the Great Mother that there was great
concern about the colonists knowing about the Water, even if they
did become full Barrydmates eventually. He tried not to think about
the Great Mother, dragged aloft by her throat by one of the winged,
armored Mulkol death vehicles while still holding her position
guiding the defense of Telka. Something inside of him pulled at
him, wanting to review the images. Maybe there was something he
had missed...some clue that could help them rescue her before she
was executed. The image of her, frozen with concentration even as
the tractor arms jabbed barbs through her throat to get a firm grip
pushed itself into his mind. He hung his head down unconsciously,
feeling guilt at his own inability to dislodge the barbs. Her firm
commands still rung in his mind, cluttered with the echoes of
hundreds of other orders ringing out from her to all Telkans, but as
he grabbed the barbs, they reacted to him, dissolving his flesh. He

worked fervently with Tewi and Liur, exactly as she had instructed, but she was still dragged up into the ship and out of mind-reach. He was still alive when the Mulkol peeled him off the side of the ship and cast him toward the sea, but Tewi and Liur were dead. He remembered how he had half-consciously caught the wind, following the only safe path he knew to Ekal's border.

Tara was staring up at him intently, looking sad. He shook away the thoughts, cursing himself for having so much trouble pushing them away. He had the colonists to think of now.

"She's still alive, isn't she?" Tara patted his neck and stroked his mane soothingly.

"Yes." Luuko sighed, marveling at the colonists' ability to sense trouble just through bodily expression. "She will be killed, and Mulkol's Great Father will claim Telka as his own."

"When is this going to happen, or is it too late?" Tara looked off into the distance with that peculiar look of hers, and Luuko felt his hope rise.

"No, no...It won't happen for two days. It's a big ceremony, the transferring of Barryd leadership, and usually takes place when a Leader is old and about to die naturally. They'll take their time with this. They've been waiting for this day since the other Barryds went Starborn. Telka has always been a thorn in their side, and they've been wearing us down for hundreds of dozens of cycles." Luuko waited for Tara's reply anxiously.

"I don't have enough information...can you get me schematics of the Mulkol complex? Can we get in there, get her and get out?" Tara strode over to one of the colony hovercars, now working as a medical power station for the humans' healing and monitoring equipment.

"We can give schematics to Harmon...and Ekal's craftspeople can make real representations of Mulkol for you." Luuko regretted now more than ever that Tarrin had been lost defending the Alpha pairs. He was Inner Circle, and would not pose as much of a security threat as Harmon. He sent a hurried request out to the Craftsmaster of Rank First Ekal to commission the schematics of Mulkol in some visual form for the colonists, disturbing him as he worked. Echoing and understanding the nature of the situation from Luuko's excited tone, the Rank First sent back an abrupt agreement.

"Have them start right away. I need to know more about Mulkol custom in these situations. We've got small size and plasma firepower to our advantage, and with luck, we'll even have the Pride back..." Tara stopped, glancing at the burnt out communications console in the hovercar. "Damn..."

"I can reach Kiralla, if she's still on this side of the space hole, Tara." Luuko reached out the moment he realized what Tara was looking for. "And the artisans have begun creating a visual model of Mulkol for you. It will be ready by morning."

Chapter 20

"You can't be serious!" Cries went up from all sides, human, Arrallin and Telkan as Tara outlined her plan. Her new psi senses were proving a mixed blessing, preventing her from simply ignoring the loud mental and vocal protests from the Telkans as she normally would have.

"Look. We've been over this. We can't beat them straight out. We need to get in there and surgically cut them down, starting at the top. And, if we don't get the Great Mother back before Mulkol takes control of Telka, we lose the Telkans. It will be humans and Arrallins only." Tara wondered if she'd know when the Patriarch of Mulkol had taken the position of Leader at Telka. The ritual would somehow link his mind to each Telkan, and although it did not grant control, he might have access to any of the plans they'd seen so far. "We have to act fast, and the number of Telkans filing into Mulkol through the slave trains is beginning to dwindle. There is no time for debate." She paused, sensing the despair in Telkans. Many of them would not return from this mission. She surveyed the faces of the humans there. A few seemed nervous, but most just had a look of angry determination.

Terrimin stepped forward. "General Ir'tarku Tara is correct. Our forces will support her. Her plan is sound." The Arrallakeeni growled a low note of support. "We'll have support from the Pride, which will engage the majority of Mulkol's defenses, if not destroy them. We need to assassinate their Leader. It will cripple them, leaving us time to liberate what Telkans there are left to save."

One of the human men stepped forward. "The plan's great. It's climbing into one of those Dimar kangaroo pouches that I just can't stomach. Fighting I'll do. But in no way am I riding around inside one of THEM." Tara recognized him. He was part of the separatist group that had been scouting the southern coast for a human-only settlement. Tara wasn't sure how to deal with him, but, considering his background in humiliating others, she tried a dose of his own medicine.

"What? Afraid to do what every baby Dimar on the planet does for three cycles? What a brave fighting man you are." She dismissed him with a laugh. "Okay, then, you get to spend the next week as a guest of Ekal until operation Trojan Dragon is over." Harmon nodded to two Ekal honor guard, who scooped up the protesting man and spirited him up into the higher levels of the Barryd.

The humans looked stunned.

"Every person who does not wish to be part of this mission will be detained here, in luxury, I might add, until the mission is over. Then, you'll be released to try to start a colony in the shadow of the Mulkol. I wish you luck. You may be the only ones that survive." Tara stared into the eyes of each human there. Most were Telkan-sympathetic, and had a look of resolve. A few in the back quietly slipped out. Harmon was careful to dispatch an Ekal guard to transport each one. Harmon was seeming more and more like inner circle material every minute.

"Luuko? The envelope, please." Tara turned and regarded her big blue-green friend. She wasn't looking forward to this. "A good general doesn't ask her soldiers to do anything she herself isn't willing to do", she muttered as Luuko dipped a shoulder to her. "Tell me if the rifle or any of the gear is uncomfortable, okay?"

"Will do, Leader Tara." Luuko's voice didn't hide the discomfort he was trying to mask from other psis in the room. Tara chuckled. There was definitely something to being a 'closet psi'. Gritting her teeth, she slowly slid herself into the pouch, hunkering down in the silky white fur. She had expected it to be slimy, but it was actually quite comfortable.

Outside, she could hear the chatter of the Dimar as other humans followed suit and climbed inside the various pouches.

She could feel the muscles ripple along Luuko's back as he strode and lifted into the air. They were off.

Through her tiny peephole in the deep downy fur, Tara could make out some of what was going on. Her psi-talent gave her the additional edge she needed to assess Luuko's work as leader pro-tem as they made their entrance.

Luuko guided the group along the fire lines toward the southern entrance to the Mulkol complex. The distant sound of fighting as the Arrallins engaged the main defenses showed little effect on the activities of the Mulkol here from what Tara could see from her perch. Finding a slave train into Mulkol wasn't difficult. The Mulkol were eager to have servants after so many cycles of fending for themselves. Luuko ordered the group back, telling them to roll in the mud before proceeding. Their recent healing marks would give them away.

Tara hugged her weapons tightly inside the pouch as Luuko rolled in the mud. An accident now for either of them could spell the end of the operation. She cursed inwardly, regretting pairing herself and Luuko together. All her eggs were in one basket, or pouch, and if Luuko fell now, so would she. They had to somehow reach the leader. She could hear Luuko's thoughts churning away as he worked on the problem.

Heads down, and thoroughly muddied, their group of seven shuffled along the muddy field. Some faked injured wings, and others exhaustion. Luuko took up a faltering flight, falling and flapping to regain position in the air. They joined the end of the train and blended in. The two Telkans ahead of them turned back, and Tara could feel their defiance as Luuko and they had a heavily shielded exchange. There was still plenty of fight in the Telkans, even the slaves, after all.

One of the Mulkol enslavers swept down over the line, barking insults and commands. Tara could only hear the muffled guttural sounds and see the flash of brown-gray wings through her tiny view slit. She felt a spike of fear in Luuko as the enslaver paused near him. Tara, trying to be as still as possible, slid her rifle up to the opening. They were almost inside Mulkol, and she didn't want to risk detection until she was within striking distance of at least their top generals. A piercing mental search passed over Tara, and she blocked, summoning all her energy into Harmon's blocking technique.

Her cradling pouch contracted as the enslaver struck Luuko across the head. She felt Luuko's shoulders droop, and felt his despair wash through every thought. Careful not to give herself away as a psi, she tried to emanate positive thoughts.

The enslaver grabbed Luuko by the horns, forcing him to the ground in a hard dive, driving his nose into the mud and holding it down with a hind foot. Tara struggled to keep from clambering out of the pouch and dispatching the brute right there. In a roaring laugh, he announced to his 'mates, *This one...this one here is the bloodkin son of the Great Mother! He's come to save his mahmar! Isn't that precious!* The gray Mulkol wrenched Luuko's head up and struck him again so he fell on his back. Inside the constricting pouch and under the weight of her gear and Luuko, Tara struggled to breath under the pressure.

Well, little hatchling...you'll get to watch her die. The Great Father is still planning on how to dispose of her. Perhaps the acid pools would suit her well. She could follow in the steps of your beloved Telkai. But that was a torture from so long ago! We've improved that technology since then. You'll appreciate our new designs, I'm sure. He wrenched Luuko up by one horn again, dragging the much smaller Dimar along behind him like a rag-doll.

Tara stifled her fury as she felt Luuko's pain and humiliation. The Great Mother really *was* his own mother, and he was frantic to see her one last time before she was lost, but not like this. Tara felt his spirit wane as he resigned himself to his fate. She half whispered-half thought, "Luuko...this is not how it will end. By my name, and my honor, Telka will live again."

Chapter 21

Luuko wasn't sure exactly what he heard, but the message was clear. Like the unseen constant Wind that swirled around him, a voice sounded in his mind. He struggled to ease the strain on his one horn with what lift from the Wind he could summon while keeping the pouch and Tara as steady as possible. Each time the enslaver's tail came down to lash his back and sides, he carefully turned so the pouch would not be struck. If Tara's weapons went off inside of him, they'd both be lost and all his suffering would be for nothing. He had to get them to the execution chamber...he had to see mahmar again.

"Sirma? Dinhit?" weakly, he reached out for other members of the assassination party, but they were out of range. The very walls of this Barryd discouraged psi communication...he could feel his cries bounce back at him, the desperation in his own thoughts galling him. The little voice inside his head never stopped, though. "You can do this...you have to do this...just hold on a bit longer."

The enslaver turned back, "Hrrrm? Quiet you!" He slammed a hind foot into Luuko's side, slamming him against the wall of the corridor. Each breath sent fire through him, but he had to stay conscious. If he blacked out, Tara would fall out of the pouch before they reached the chambers.

Through corridor after corridor the enslaver dragged him. His limp body slammed painfully into the corridor sides and platforms as they ascended level after level in Mulkol Barryd.

Finally, the enslaver pinned his head into a stock and clicked it shut. Luuko could barely hear him over the throbbing ache, but he knew he had made his objective. *This one's the blood kin of the Great Mother herself, Great One. Seeing her die by your hand will be the final blow to the Telkan spirit. Hundredcycles of freedom have made these slaves resistant...even this one gave me trouble on the way up.*

Cautiously, Luuko opened his eyes. *I must be dead!* Beautiful colors filtered down through the ceiling panels, flooding an elegant room in an ancient style. His mother lay on a stone couch bathed in a soothing golden light, looking almost comfortable, asleep. He could see no restraints, no injuries on her. A soothing hum filled the room, an air of expectation.

As his vision cleared, he could tell that her breath was labored. The pain in his side quickly brought him back to reality. He was not dead. Death would have eased the pain. A large mottled gray figure loomed into view.

Is that so, Krallik? Poor sod. Came to avenge her, did he? The Leader of the Mulkol regarded him, it seemed to Luuko, with curiosity and even a touch of remorse. *Well, considering where they come from, we should expect some spirit.*

Looking left and right he could see the primary acolytes of Telka at either side. They had all been brought to witness the final transfer of Telka to Mulkol. He would live to see tomorrow, he mused bitterly, to die for the amusement of the Leader, no doubt. He felt the load in his pouch shift carefully. Tara! He had forgotten! The voice chimed in again, stronger. *Don't lose hope...*

The leader walked back to mahmar, stroking her head softly. The caress was almost affectionate, as any mate might lavish on a partner. With the other hand, he readied a wicked-looking device—a combination of a main blade fitted with barbs seeping a thick red liquid. The scene was too much for him. Luuko screeched with fury, struggling against his restraints. Krallik kicked him in his bad side, and his bellow died, echoing hollowly in the chamber.

Groggily, the Great Mother opened her eyes. As she lifted her head, Luuko could see how she was restrained. A series of tendrils reached up from the couch right under her scales. He could see them now more clearly, writhing within the tufts of her fur. She looked around the room. Her usually piercing gaze was glazed, but she knew her enemy when she saw him. Struggling against the thousands of tendrils that dug into her neck and belly, she growled and snapped at the Mulkol.

The tendrils wrapped around her muzzle, pulling her head down. New tendrils sprang forth from the dais, pushing under her eyes, inside her ears and into her nostrils. She screamed in pain as they reached her brain, and Luuko again struggled, crying out to her.

Don't give up! Don't give up! Don't give up! He echoed the only rational thought in his head to her, and together he and the little voice reached out to her. Something was blocking them. Mahmar didn't want him to feel her pain. *I have to do something!* He roared again, and felt a restraint come loose...

As the Mulkol, now enshrouded in a cloud of white tendrils himself, brought the blade down toward her head, Tara began to struggle in the pouch. Krallik brought a hind foot down on Luuko's muzzle, breaking it. The pain was too much...the piercing sensation blasted him into unconsciousness.

Chapter 22

Tara kicked free of the pouch as Luuko fell back against the stocks. Krallik spun, his eyes wide with the shock of her sudden appearance, and let loose a startled bark. He galloped forward, charging back toward her. She rolled off Luuko, clicked the actuator on one of her grenades and flung it into Krallik's gaping maw. His jaws snapped just inches from her head as she rolled under Luuko's limp foreleg for protection. Krallik barreled on, skidding to a stop to turn just as the grenade activated. The blast ripped through the chamber, shattering some of the windows and damaging the stocks. The acolyte to the left, dazed, struggled against his remaining restraints.

"So much for a stealthy entrance" Tara yelled as she fired at the doors to the chamber. She knew she had to seal them shut or they'd all be lost. The membranes shut protectively against the plasma blasts.

Tara spun to see the Great Mother's tail lashing from side to side. The blast had partially destroyed the dais, and severed some of the tentacles. The Mulkol worked on, slowly working the blade and barbs into the Great Mother's neck as she ripped away tendrils with each slash of her bladed tail. She fired a few shots into the mass of writhing whiteness in the center of the room, but each shot that struck the Mulkol elicited a piercing shriek in the Great Mother. They must somehow be joined!

Tara charged forward, grabbing handfuls of the tendrils near the Great Mother's tail. *Hold on...Can I remove the head tendrils safely without killing you, Great Mother?* Tara gave up her non-psi charade and reached out mentally, blinking against the despair in the Great Mother's mind. It overshadowed even the pain in Tara's hands— grabbing the tendrils stung like grabbing a Portuguese man-of-war but she continued to grab more and more.

You...No, Leader Tara. I am lost, but I will not be forgotten. Her shock at feeling Tara's mind echoed in Tara's head, but quickly gave way to the firm resolve. She whipped up her tail blade, jabbing it viciously into the Mulkol's throat. Each thrust of her tail jabbed the blade deeper and deeper into the Mulkol's neck, and at the same time elicited a high-pitched shriek from the Great Mother. As she killed him, she was killing herself. *Two Barryds die tonight! Damn you, Mulkol! Damn you!*

No Great Mother! Telka must not die! The acolytes still pinned in their restraints flailed madly against them. Tara ran to them, firing at the heavy wood, blasting away at it bit by bit.

No, Tara...there is not time. The acolyte was right. Noise in the hallway and outside the chamber was getting louder as the remote audiences of Mulkol struggled to get into the room. *Get Luuko, Ditwer over there. Anyone...get them into the tendrils! Save the Barryd! Do not let it fall into Mulkai hands...*

A snot-barb landed squarely in the acolyte's back and melted through his spine. He went limp just as Tara finished freeing him from his stocks. The Mulkol were forcing their way through the doors, firing snot-guns into the chamber.

Tara...come here, Tara... The Great Mother's voice was barely audible in Tara's mind. She raced to her side, ripping tendrils free from her tail. Blood gushed from the Mulkol's mouth as he struggled to finish his work with the blade.

To think I wanted this to be painless for you, Telka! The Mulkol's mind-voice was white with fury.

Fool! You have given me the advantage I need to defeat you. Weak slaves, Mulkol? No better than animals? Her voice jabbed viciously at the Mulkol's mind, and she punctuated each thought with a jab from her tail. *Tara, you must lead us back to the way of Telkai. You must save our home. You must never let them be enslaved again...* Her fierce words were the last thing Tara remembered.

As the Mulkol's last drop of lifeblood spilled out onto the dais, the Great Mother loosed her tail from his throat. She swung around and dropped it on Tara, pinning her to the couch as the tangle of tendrils engulfed the three forms.

Chapter 23

Massive nightmare ships spun through Tara's mind. She was adrift in a kind of space — a starless inky blackness — spinning out of control as the ships descended upon the delicate blue globe below. A voice in her mind screamed out for them to stop. Lightning flashed.

Her point of view shifted. She was on a blisteringly hot surface as those same ships ripped up from the ground in fiery archs, disappearing as pinpoints of light atop pillars of deceivingly peaceful white smoke. There was incredible power there, and danger. Presences within her head resonated with variations of fear, pride and wonder.

Another shift. The massive red wood walls of what she instinctively knew to be a War Barryd rose before her. She could see them moving, stretching upward out of the flames toward the sky. At her feet, a tiny shoot had taken hold, and was blooming. The ground around it was cooling and healing within the tiny grasp of its white roots. A protective need washed over her.

She found herself falling toward the tiny plant at her feet, falling into it. The scene blurred and she found herself lying on her back in a field. Dizzy, she sat upright and took in the scene. The familiar shapes of trees filled her with a sense of peace. She was home, back on Earth. It was a scene she hadn't seen since she was five. The tree shifted, and grew into something quite alien, but it still felt like home. The plants around her grew brighter, with broader leaves, reaching up around her to caress her. The forms ahead of her, once trees, finally became recognizable. It was the twin spires of Telka. Her horse ran by, through the thick Dimar field. She found herself running in slow motion, chasing after the horse as her white form vanished into the thick brush. The trees blurred by as she leapt through the brush, laughing.

Breaking clear from the thicket, she stood before the same walls of the War Barryd she had seen growing from the flames. A massive oolar leapt from the front gate, claws and fangs bared, but she felt no fear—only pride. It landed before her and touched it's nose to her hand. She regarded the Barryd for a long moment. It too was home. A familiar brick pattern from Earth flickered within the wood grain, but she couldn't place it.

Telka she knew well, but this new place that was home begged some exploring.

The scene shifted again, and she found herself and the oolar drifting down toward their own reflections in a set of deep pools. They passed through the mirror-still water below them into a murky green pool. There was no difference in temperature or sensation, and they kept falling, straight through the bottom of the pool.

The wall-texture changed to a grayish, softer, less wood-like tone. A chorus of voices and ghostly forms welcomed her, each with a story to tell. Stories of great battles, of a strong race ruling with power and justice over its creations, echoed in her mind, and a feeling of pride and superiority welled within her. She swirled through the different stories as if through a dance. A singular, strong call was pulling her back, and regretfully, she parted with the vapors.

She followed the high musical voice back through the wall, and through the ground and back up into the open air. She was air now. The oolar stayed beside her, keeping pace with its loping gait as they raced back toward Telka. At the gate, a morrak charged out, it's head low and hoofed toes flashing. The oolar charged ahead leaping up to bat the creature aside, but the morrak slammed it and sent it tumbling through the air. It landed with a crash behind Tara, who continued to drift toward Telka. Shocked, the oolar raced back behind Tara barking hollow threats.

The creature that stood before Tara was no ordinary morrak. It gazed at her with an intelligent and steady eye. She approached and touched it's nose with her hand. She found herself moving with the morrak in the lead and the oolar in tow through the walls of Telka and down, into it's room of vapors. Again, she danced with the voices, each with a story of achievement and invention, power and creation. A single form, a darkness where there should have been light, hovered in a corner.

The morrak and the oolar studied each other intently, and then looked toward the dark form. Tara found herself no longer pulled or pushed, but under her own direction as the morrak and the oolar exchanged unreadable thoughts. As their exchanges continued, the darkness grew.

She moved toward the dark figure as it tried to evade her. She took control of her lucid dreaming state and willed herself into the darkness.

The scene shifted again. Images of torture, of humiliation and torment faded past her, and she found herself drifting in the starless sky again. The monster ships roared past, and she reached out toward them with her mind. No answer. She looked ahead to where they were going and saw Earth.

Chapter 24

Rakal stretched luxuriously and rolled on his back. Kiralla was curled, sound asleep, with her tail over her nose, but he could still see her faint smile through the downy fur. Rakal lay there for a moment, regarding her as she slept. The blood from Landry was still caked on her paws and muzzle.

The approach klaxon broke the quiet moment. Kiralla awoke with a start and leapt straight to her feet. "The jump gate! Time to get back to work. I trust, Rakal, that your team had the good sense to secure the crew of this tub? I doubt now that Landry is gone that they'll be particularly keen on us deploying the gate crasher."

Rakal chuckled at her discomfiture knowing his crew had already made quick work of the demoralized Arrallakeeni left on the ship. Faking nervousness, he reached for his uniform helmet. "Sidal? Is the Dark Hope secure?" He used an uncertain tone that brought Kiralla's furious gaze toward him. The comm crackled to life. "Yes sir. Crew quarters have been sealed, and the gate crasher is being checked for final deployment." Rakal faked a sigh of relief and she moved toward him to scold. Raising a paw in playful defense, he chided her, "You don't always have to do everything yourself, you know. Some of us are fairly competent." Kiralla laughed.

"You're one lucky bastard. God is in the details, as the humans say." She tinkered with the broken door lock and it opened with a whoosh. She grabbed a piece of what had been part of Landry's uniform and wrapped it tightly around Rakal's injured leg, tying it in a knot. "Sanitary? No. But effective. We'll get you to med lab after we crash the gate."

Rakal ignored the pain in his foot and worked with his helmet. "Thank you Sidal...Have you had any communication with the colony?" He removed the comm piece from his helmet and looped it over one ear.

"No sir. Nothing at all."

"Kiralla..." He bounded after her on three legs. "Time to use your little gift, eh?"

She glanced back at him, "Well, I've used your little gift all up. I guess I'll have to use mine now." She laughed and continued ahead.

"Hey!" Rakal grabbed her tail with his teeth and gave it a tug, still swooning a little from her musky smell. She ignored him...she was concentrating.

"I don't know if I have the range for this, but someone there, if they're listening, can make up the difference." She stopped suddenly, and Rakal skidded to a halt behind her. She stared blankly at the wall, as if listening. "I've got someone. Ekayim Barryd, a healing place to the north. I've got the second acolyte on. There's been a war...Telka and Mulkol. Telka lost about half it's population...Mulkol won, but the 'Archs were killed. Tara is alive...she's recovering but not fully conscious." She paused, and stopped relaying, but continued talking as if to someone in the room. "They fear the Barryds are lost? I don't know what you mean. Can you explain that?" The sound of her tail swishing from side to side was the only noise in the corridor as she listened to some unseen voice. "Thank you...Yes, we're going to close the space hole...yes... thank you...BYE!" She growled.

"What a bunch of yammerers. You get 'em started and they just don't shut up. I just don't understand what they're talking about. How do you lose a damn city? Shaggy dragons. Fuzz lizards. And, if the leaders are dead, then Mulkol did lose, if you ask me." She gave Rakal a playful bite on the nose. "Tara's alive, as are many of the colonists, and the other Arrallin pairs are currently the guests of Ekal, and are fine. If Mulkol is 'lost', whatever that means, it won't be any more trouble to us."

She continued on down the hallway and into the lift. "Cargo 2." The gravity lightened as they moved toward the center of the rotating ship.

"I'd rather take my chances on Dimar than have this litter end up just another addition to the fleet crews." Rakal fiddled with the bandage on his leg.

"Agreed." Together they strode into the cargo bay, greeted by the throaty rumbles and cheers of Arrallakeeni waiting for them.

Chapter 25

Onlookers, both Mulkol and Telkan hovered around the healing pool where Tara was recovering. Both barryds were in a state of stasis, confusion, waiting to see what was left of the link between Dimar and their respective cities. Luuko looked across the pool at the grizzled, armored faces of Mulkoli foes. They were young warriors, just as he was a young Tinar, but Mulkol developed a rough all-over armor that they never lost. A momentary flash of curiosity of what it must be like to never feel the joy of wind in light fur, or the coolness of water as it penetrated the deepest down crossed Luuko's mind, but faded as he scanned the onlookers. He saw the hollow look that haunted his own barrydmates. It was much like the hunter and the prey giving up the chase in the midst of an earthquake. A greater calamity made the war between the barryds petty and insignificant. Neither side had ever expected to completely lose the precious and vital link between their city, the barryd, and it's residents regardless of the outcome of the battles. They were both facing complete annihilation of their cultures if the barryds had rejected Tara.

Luuko looked down into the murky green pool. The bubbling and foam along the edges, and the opacity of the Water was an unclear sign. Some took it to mean that the Water had rejected Tara completely, along with the barryds, but none of the telltale signs of Barryd loss had set in on the upper spires of either Telka or Mulkol. The blooms weren't growing, but they weren't dying either. It was as if both cities were waiting.

The Water bubbled, sending tiny ringlets of white froth out in waves to the edge of the pool. In a momentary, fragmented exchange with what was left of Goothib, Luuko had been given an insight into another meaning for the sign the Water gave. The active cells of the Water had had little contact with humans. Humans were a completely new structure and composition for them. The barryd Waters of Mulkol were working to figure out just what exactly it was they were to repair. Luuko hoped fervently that this was the case. The healers had avoided the pool, leaving Tara's still form in there alone to avoid any confusion of the Water. Experiments had proven that confusion happened quite easily, with dire results.

Luuko's thoughts returned to Goothib. He should go visit with him again. Perhaps the warm mind-touch of an understanding friend might bring more of his clear thinking back and pull him out of the nightmarish world of dreams that consumed him. Harmon was with him night and day since the invasion of the Barryd, but even her love had not had much effect on the battle-scarred engineer.

A hand, healed and in one piece, broke the surface. The fingers reached out of the water frantically, grasping at the air. Tara burst forth from the pool, grabbing at her throat, kicking frantically for the side. With unexpected tenderness, a Mulkol healer scooped her from the water with his massive hands and wrapped her in a leaf from the tallest spire of Mulkol. It was a luxury reserved for only the most important members of the barryd, and the warm, soft membrane of new leaves was known to have superior insulating powers.

Oblivious to the honor, Tara proceeded to vomit. The Water cleared from her lungs and stomach, and she gasped in air with rasping breaths. Luuko tentatively reached out to her mentally, unsure of what he might find. He felt every presence in the room reach with him, desperate to feel the life of their cities in Tara. She opened her eyes and sat upright on the leaf, and the cities answered.

A shudder ripped through the walls of the Mulkol healing room, sending technicians from both Mulkol and Telka soaring up toward the spires and into the tunnels to the lower root systems. A full minute of shaking brought frescoes and stained glass raining down in the healing room, sending up cries of alarm all over the barryd. Luuko fell hard onto the floor, but refused to flee the room with others. He just watched Tara, who sat on her leaf, looking as if she was listening to something. He listened too.

"*Unprecedented growth on the west side! Telka's sprouting on the east...the blooms are growing again...*" Engineering reports from both Mulkol and Telka channels rang through the air as the shaking subsided. Luuko looked at Tara, sensing a sure resonance from Telka and a new resonance from Mulkol. He let out a whoop of celebration and launched himself into the air. Both Barryds were alive!

Tara stood and shyly wrapped herself in the leaf. Onlookers hovered in the air, eyes closed, as they drank in the emanations from their home barryds. Some Telkans, Luuko could sense, were pouring themselves into the light of Mulkol, flowing freely out of Telka's radiance. Mulkol flooded in, especially curious about the technological advancements Telka had made in the many years of separation. They were oblivious to Tara, who quietly padded off down a tunnel. Luuko silently followed, letting the wind carry him noiselessly behind her. He couldn't tell what she was after, but she was intent on something in the lower pools.

The tunnel was dark and the floor of the passage was uneven, but Tara made her way quickly. She darted through the twisting tunnels and passed her tiny hand over the membranes of the recognizers, opening each one she passed and leaving it open. Luuko refused to look into the chambers beyond; these were the Mulkol's fabled experimentation pools. Tara slowed as she approached a large, well-lit doorway. She turned back toward Luuko, and brushed his mind with hers.

"*I have to be present for as many hatchings as I can, don't I?*" Tara looked up at Luuko expectantly.

"*I am not an acolyte, Tara, and I can't speak for Mulkol tradition, but by Telka standards, yes. But, this can't be a nest room, can it?*" Luuko carefully reached out to Mulkol, looking for their layout in the record resonances. Their system of information storage was the same, but the layout was different. He had no idea where to start looking.

She waved her hand by the recognizer and slipped into the chamber. Luuko hesitantly moved inside, sizing up the room for any signs of danger. Tara launched into a halting rendition of a hatching song, but only parts of it Luuko recognized.

Goothib sat in a corner, rocking wildly from side to side. Thirteen marks had been dug into the walls, each marked with stains of deep red-brown. Harmon hugged Goothib's shoulder, rubbing his foreleg protectively. She looked haggard, and gave Tara only a passing glance. Her eyes were on the large mass in the center of the room. An egg shape, covered in gently moving tendrils, was set on a makeshift nest beside a small Water pool.

Nervous, Luuko tried to regain mental contact with Goothib. *...thirteen gone...he'll live...he'll live...thirteen gone...I haven't failed...thirteen gone...* Goothib was chanting to the tune of a hatching song, concentrating on the egg. Harmon was concentrating on him, lending him as much energy as she could to stay awake. Not knowing what else to do, Luuko began to carry the tune as well, re-enforcing Harmon's support of Goothib, but avoiding Goothib's horrific thoughts.

The egg shattered as a rusty-brown form emerged. It slid down the side of the nest pad, and frantically scratched at its face to remove the birthing material. A combination of fear and fury emanated from the creature, but the emotions muted as Tara began to converse with it. Horrified, Luuko realized that this was Mason.

"You're not the only one who was taken, Cy. The barryds have taken over as much of me as you...they're just linked to my mind is all. We knew there was no going back, and now there can be no doubt." Tara's voice had a desperate edge, but was resigned. She continued the hatching song tune as a background to her thoughts.

Mason? Luuko touched the creature's mind, and did catch a very familiar set of memories of the colony, but from a different viewpoint. Mason was furious, and his mind was bathed in pain.

"Yes, Luuko. It's me. It seems the Mulkol were curious about how humans would react to the Water, and decided to see if we could take a useful form for them. They didn't see much use in our ugly, hairless, bipedal

configuration and figured it would be a great favor to convert us to more Dimar standards. So, HERE I AM. It only cost the lives of THIRTY-SEVEN of my crewmates!"

Goothib continued his frantic chant. *"Thirteen gone...he'll live...he'll live...Thirteen gone...he'll live..."*

"Goothib, SHUT UP!" Mason swung his head backward, flailing blindly. Goothib halted his chant, but continued rocking back and forth. Striking his head against the rough surface of an egg fragment shocked Mason into opening his eyes. *"How the hell do you coordinate all these limbs! This is insane..."* He kept his head up, unwilling to see what Goothib and Mulkol had done to him.

As he slowly gained some use of his limbs, Luuko noted that the new Mason wasn't a far cry from a true Dimar. He looked like he was half way to adult, sinuous and lanky, and even had signs of firescales forming beneath what was a rougher version of true velvet. His wings glittered with newness, exposing tender membranes as he opened and closed them. His wings had a complex pattern of gold, green and brown shades worked into them, like a Mulkol, but lacked the tiny scaled protection Mulkol wings had. His eyes were no longer human, but were a brilliant blue with catlike slits. They were Mulkol eyes, adapted for both day and night vision, unlike all other Dimar, who could only see well in daylight. His horns, however, were regular Telkan...graceful spirals with no offshoots or points.

"As soon as possible, Goothib. You have to change me back. I can't live like this." The pain in Mason's mind had abated, and he was examining his foreleg. *"At least I still have only five fingers."* Curiously, he extended a foreleg and flexed a hand. Turning his head back, he stretched one wing and then the other. Unused to psi communication, he made garbled conversational tones as he thought, still trying to use his voice as he would have before.

Goothib collapsed in an exhausted heap, and Harmon sank down next to him. "Only three more to go. I don't think Goothib can take much more of this. The next one hatches in two days, and it's an Arrallin. We'll probably lose her. He's lost 24 betas so far, and 13 humans. Mason's the first one to live through the process. Every death rips at his mind."

"And yours, Harmon. Get some rest too. I'll rally the acolytes to bolster him when the hatching time starts for the others. You're not working alone now. Things are going to return to...well, I hesitate to use the term 'normal'. But, order will return." Tara scrubbed at Mason's sides with a bit of her leaf, drying him as he recovered from the hatching process. He quickly fell into a deep slumber at the side of the pool.

Two acolytes, one Mulkol and one Telkan tried to burst through the same doorway calling for Tara. The sounds of scuffle began in the hall as they fought over who should enter first. *"We MADE you...so stand aside, Telkan! Heed your superiors..."* The Mulkol acolyte's tone was caustic and self-righteous. *"We're from the same stock, you morrak. And, it just so happens IF you made, you made us smarter."* The Telkan's tone was inviting a fight, and the Mulkol rose to the challenge. As the Mulkol reared back to strike, the Telkan slipped into the chamber first.

"Telka fifth acolyte, reporting Leader." Smugly, the Telkan took a seat placing Tara between him and the massive Mulkol. The larger acolyte burst in from the hallway, fuming from the deceit. *"Just like a Telkan to run from a fight."* She asided to her rival.

"Mulkol FOURTH acolyte, reporting Leader." She eyed both Luuko and the other acolyte with contempt, but regarded Tara with only expectation.

Tara eyed them both sternly and crossed her arms, hugging her leaf closely to remain covered. Giving orders dressed in little more than an oversized houseplant wasn't her usual style, but she could tell by their gaze that when they looked at her that her uniform didn't matter. They didn't see a human, but the embodiment of two whole universes-Mulkol and Telka. She could probably get away with wearing her morrak slippers and nothing else with the Dimar now. A presence at the back of her mind waited expectantly as well. It was the Telka-Mulkol barryd plant, with all its knowledge and wisdom of ages of growth and the growth of its people. It was like having the entire Earth United Libraries system hooked to her head, ready to answer even the most minute question and bend to whichever directive she sent it. She mused to herself, chuckling, *Wow...I could really screw this up.*

She immediately turned to the only reliable source she could find—the barryd. Leafing through image after image of ritual, speculation, design, tradition, all displayed to her without opinion or pretense, she worked to find some precedent that matched this situation, and a way out of it. There were ceremonies to pass barryd control from usurpers or retiring matriarchs without loss of life. There was a very common convention of doing a half-transfer to an acolyte if the Leader had to leave the Barryd confines for any reason. The Telkan side revealed all this the moment the thought entered her mind. The Mulkol side had a number of options as well, and presented them in turn. She breathed a sigh of relief and continued her research. There was an identical retirement ceremony on the Mulkol side, as well as joint control.

A tingling sensation caused Tara to involuntarily blink. An obscured set of images relating to Mulkol barryd leaders caught her attention. Something was pulling those barryd pages out of her reach, but she managed to catch them before they were gone entirely. An ancient and complicated ceremony for relieving a barryd leader of duty for rejoining with a Starborn craft, with most of its details intact flipped through her mind. Nearly instinctively, she stored it in a remote section of the Telka barryd data stores. There were Mulkol forces at work that didn't necessarily follow the straight and narrow line outlined by their Leader. She wasn't surprised...the Mulkol had a deep history of feudal organization by family and clan. Mulkol families within the barryd were probably at this moment taking their family histories and knowledge and breaking off from the core of the barryd knowledge base. Realizing that as time progressed Mulkol was probably splintering even further, she took a seat right at the edge of the pool and worked to snatch as much information as she could.

"Tara? What are you doing?" Harmon began to approach, but the two acolytes bared their teeth and blocked her path.

Tara continued her research, chasing image after image and

storing it away as quickly as the unknown Mulkol could pull it from the Mulkol core, only peripherally aware of the conversation that began around her.

"She communing with the barryd and should not be disturbed," the acolytes chimed in unison. More annoyed at the similarity of their replies than Harmon's actions, they turned to face each other and growled.

Absently she shot a command at both *Explain it to her, and politely, or you'll enjoy a stay in the muck room.* She pulled more and more Mulkol data into Telka, swapping out some of Telka's information as the core had difficulty creating unoccupied cells. She was wreaking havoc on both plants, and what little Dimar restraint had been passed to her wasn't enough to keep her from knowing whatever it was the Mulkol so desperately needed to hide. She could sense engineers from both barryds drinking up the mixed information and untold Telkai secrets now laid bare by Tara's exhaustive pursuit. Goothib's personal bandwidth wasn't far behind her own, racing through the core of Mulkol to find the culprit.

The Telkan acolyte deferred to the Mulkol with a mischievous wiggling of ears, "Age before beauty, Mulkol. You try explaining this to the human."

The Mulkol hissed at the Telkan with annoyance, correcting him. "Don't call me Mulkol, Telkan. It's improper! Mulkoli if you like, but not Mulkol—especially in front of the Leader. My name is Freia."

The Mulkoli regarded Harmon, not sure how to proceed. "She, Tara, is one of us now, and she is the only one who should be called Mulkol. She's not a tiny single-minded grub like you anymore, so you can't treat her like some mate you'd just approach and pester. She's the barryd. We are all the barryd, but she is closest to the whole, so when she communes and you disturb her, you threaten us all." The Mulkoli swung her massive head down to view Harmon squarely, and bared her teeth.

Harmon just stared blankly at the Mulkol acolyte.

"Oh, good one, Mulkol-eee. That was a polite explanation? Did your Leader study these beings at all before you decided to raze Telka?" He snorted and slapped the huge Mulkol acolyte's side with his tail teasingly. "I, Karti, will explain–in my best understanding of human terms. I am thankful that you, Harmon, are blessed with a full mind–a psi." He paused to regard the Mulkol.

The Mulkol acolyte fell into her own reverie as she raided the Telka barryd's informational stores for information on the colonists. She slapped the ground with her right paw in a Mulkol gesture for the Telkan to continue in her place, but the Telkan did nothing.

The Mulkol's scale encrusted ears wiggled with unaccustomed mirth as she made her own jibe at the sarcastic Telkan. "This gesture, Telka, means continue. It is clear that you did little studying of your closest neighbors over the last few, oh, thousand cycles or so." She slapped the Telkan's side with her tail in a friendly manner, but the force sent the Telkan rolling to the side. He hopped up and returned to Harmon, taking a seat on the Mulkol's tail.

"When you colonists look at a flower, you see the flower only. You don't always see its dependencies–both internal and external. When we Dimar," he paused to emphasize both Mulkol and Telka in the term, "view a flower, we see the soil elements–minerals, bone meal, fertilizer and dried animal blood, as well as live elements like active cells in the soil," he showed microbes at the roots, "but we include in the definition of flower anything that lives on it that it can't live without. Bees would be a dependency of flowers, and flowers of bees. It's simply an emphasis on relationships between entities, rather than the entity itself. A flower cannot live without a bee, and a bee cannot live without a flower. They tend each other. The bee is the eyes and arms of the flower, and the flower is the stomach and mouth of the bee."

Harmon nodded, continuing the thread, "So the Dimar are part of their barryd, and the barryd is part of the Dimar. You tend the barryd, and it feeds you. So Tara is now fully integrated into the dependencies of the barryd, whereas we other colonists aren't."

"Exactly, but there's more." The Telkan continued. "Imagine there was one live being that could embody the condition of the entire whole. A barryd is a whole so complex that it is nearly aware, like us. The leader serves as the voice for the barryd plant...animal... whole" the Telkan couldn't find a word or simple tag for the idea even in his advanced English vocabulary. "Tara is now that voice, and she is having a conversation with the barryd. If she is interrupted, and her orders misdirected, the whole suffers. It is dangerous to interrupt a Leader in this state. Learn this state, and learn to protect your Leader when she is in Reverie."

"She looks like she's watching TV." Harmon winked at the Telkan, who wiggled his ears and whuffled.

The Mulkol acolyte broke into the exchange with an excited whoop. "These colonists! What history they have...I will enjoy this post greatly." She flashed images of medieval knights, Samurai, Zulu tribesmen, Aztecs with blood rituals. Proudly, she displayed an image of an Afghanistani rifle, covered in intricate hand carvings and decorations. To her, this image said it all–that war was not a battle for land, but an art and a holy calling. She flipped through images of the machines of war through the ages, reveling not so much just in the destructive power of each, but in the grace and care with which they were built. "See, Telka...your colonist friends have a strong and proper Mulkai tradition. You should learn from them."

The Telkan turned back to Harmon, and commented wryly. "Correction. Telkans are nice regular bees, and Mulkol are nasty killer bees. But, the barryd plants we are part of are the same, as much as a cactus and a rose can be considered the same."

Goothib emerged from his reverie, refocusing his eyes on Harmon. He lifted his head to Harmon and the Acolytes, *Remember this signature mark...find the Mulkoli who bears this signature mark. They are renegades.* He clearly broadcast a colorful band–a kind of psi signature left on images to identify the source.

Tara broke her trance and stretched. "Well, I think I've made quite a mess of things, but we have much more to learn from our Mulkol friends now than we would have. Yes...yes...if you find the renegades, let me talk with them. Time to smooth things over with my internal and external dependencies, as it were." She rose, as an acolyte entered with her careworn dress-gray uniform. "Now, if you all don't mind, I have to figure out how keep the Leaders of all the other barryds on Dimar from wiping all of us-Mulkol, Telka, Arrallin, and Human-off the face of the planet. Our nosy neighbors have been watching the events of the last few days with some interest and even more concern." On a restricted frequency, she sent word to Ekal where the three planet-based mated pairs of Arrallins waited for the results of the raid on Mulkol. She gave explicit orders for them and for several human colonist groups to move out and settle as far away from the barryds as was possible. Current events not withstanding, she would not fail in her mission to provide the Arrallins with a new home world in co-habitation with humans. She thought of Rakal, who seemed years as well as light-years away now.

Dressing quickly, she made her way down the elegant slightly arched hallways toward a Mulkol spire that she only knew from a borrowed memory of the barryd. She had never seen these halls with her own eyes before, but they seemed more home now than her own ship ever did. The reverent memories of Mulkai who'd gone to the stars reverberated in each panel of the corridor walls. It gave the whole barryd the soothing air of a museum or memorial to heroes long departed. Although she felt at home, the atmosphere didn't ease her worries about Rakal, or Earth.

Chapter 26

"You've got to be kidding. Look...I don't know who this is, or what kind of a joke this is, but enough is enough." Kiralla threw a wrench against the hull wall and it bounced wildly in the weightless chamber.

Rakal turned, ducking as the wrench flew past his head. Deftly, he snatched it with his tail before it could strike the Arrallakeeni diligently putting the finishing touches on the Gate crasher. He looked over to see Kiralla staring crossly at the wall. "Prank caller, again?" Rakal whuffled, glad for once that he wasn't psi.

"You won't believe this one. Says she's Tara, and that I should send a capsule through to Earth before I shut the gate. A capsule chock full about information on our location's relative star brightness and nearest neighbors, military strength, Dimar— the whole operation. Yeah...right." Kiralla shook her head, spinning lazily on her tether.

"It could be worse. It could be that two cycle old stripling who decided her favorite hobby was repeating the word 'Chicken' to you a hundred times. I don't know what Tara's feeding these fuzz lizards about Earth, but they're getting strange." Rakal rechecked his calculations, doing a final check on the amount of exotic matter needed to pierce the gate wall and close it without negative side effects, like loss of the solar system they were near.

"You didn't tell anyone you're an Alpha, did you?" Kiralla eyed him closely.

"No..." Rakal paused, his tail fluffing automatically at the mention of his being discovered.

"You didn't tell anyone I was an Alpha, did you? And Quiltan Hive, Keina Hive and Barstol Hive's leading Alphas didn't even know we were Alphas..." Kiralla's fur stood on end, and her tail wrapped around her tether nervously. "This has got to be Tara. No one else could know this. No one..."

Rakal and the Arrallakeeni paused, watching. Kiralla remained, staring at the wall, clutching a wrench to her chest protectively, lost in her exchange. With a low bark, he sent the Arrallakeeni back to work and continued his calculations, keeping a curious eye on Kiralla.

"Well, it seems we have a choice. I still can't verify that that was Tara, nor can I explain how Tara might even be able to reach me being a non-psi, but Harmon is unmistakable." Kiralla pushed off the wall toward Rakal, drifting to the gate crasher pod. "From what I can tell, we can warn earth about the Mulkols and their space-fairing brethren who haven't been seen or heard of since they left 2000 odd years ago, or we can just leave Earth in the dark, where I personally feel it belongs." She snorted and tweaked a calculation on the pod absently.

Rakal waited until she'd turned her back to tweak it back to its original state. "Either way, we have to crash the gate. Not closing the gate between Earth and Arralla cost us our home world once. I'm not going to let that happen again. We need a little breathing room between us and 20 billion humans to recover from our last Contact. It's hard enough dealing with the Dimar." He closed the panel before Kiralla could do any more damage to his work. "What do we owe Earth anyway?"

"Admittedly, without Earth opening that damned gate on our doorstep and distracting every Beta on the planet, we wouldn't be way out here. But, you and I would be about 30 years to being primary Alphas of our own Hive, you know. In a way, we owe Earth our meteoric rise to power." Kiralla whuffled as a nearby Arrallakeeni, Malry, laid his ears back at the distraction comment.

Malry drifted up next to Kiralla quietly, out of earshot of the other members of the work crew. "I'll give you a possible answer to your quandary if you promise to make me a member of your court—or a steward of a Province." The sharp-eyed golden face peered up at Kiralla expectantly.

Rakal nudged Malry good-naturedly, and whispered to them both carefully, "This place is already getting more and more like old-time Arralla. The politics have begun already..."

Kiralla bared her teeth in a ferocious Arrallin grin, "If your answer is a good one, you're going to be my Court Ir'kalan. Then I can come to you for all my ideas. If your answer is bad, you get strapped to the crasher. Now, let's hear it." Kiralla slipped the pod into the launch locks.

Malry bounced off the far wall and propelled himself back toward the crasher with the ease of a long-term space faring Beta. "Well, if humans think opening gates is possibly a bad idea that will lead them to worlds which will devour them as they devoured us, they might actually slow down..." His wrench clacked against the metal couplings as he ratcheted the pod into place. "But, knowing humans, they won't slow down at all...they'll just give themselves stress ulcers worrying about the day they open the gate onto a planet of ravening fuzz-lizards. I like the idea of causing them worry. I really do." He paused, his tail lashing from side to side as he pondered. "And, if we gave them the idea that the gate to Dimar actually had opened onto a pack of ravening deadly lizards bent on the destruction of the human race, they'll think twice about trying to aim a hole at us again, if and when they ever bother to figure out how to aim the things at all. It should keep them off our doorstep for a good long while."

Rakal paused, and then continued on his line of thinking, "But for that to work, we'd have to send through information that contradicts our false pod, and it would have to have data conclusive enough to prove that our ploy wasn't just a ruse. Why bother letting Earth know that a few precious Breeders slipped out of their hands, if some day they could aim the gates and come after us?" Rakal waved the idea away and did a final check on the crasher. "However, you get significant points for creative thinking, Malry. Expect the pick of the first litter."

Malry couldn't resist a celebratory yip at the news, and lost all composure. The other Arrallakeeni in the room took notice, but continued their work.

"What about Tara's order, though?" Kiralla mused. "She's going to be pissed when she finds out we've just completely disregarded her wish to inform her species of a possible impending threat."

"Sever all ties, she's always said. She should follow her own advice. We're free now...on the other side of the gate. We need to follow our own orders and rely on ourselves. Tara is an excellent leader and deserving of all deference, but the time has come for our Hive to stand apart as a free Hive. Let the Earthers and the Traitor Hives suffer together on the other side of the gate. We need to make a clean break now and stabilize the situation on Dimar, and that means crashing the gate as soon as possible. We don't have time to assemble some pod for Earth." Rakal slapped the door panel and the work crew floated into the hallway.

The door whooshed shut as an approach alarm sounded in the hallway. Sidal's voice crackled over the comm. "Arralla's Pride to Dark Hope. One Earth scout, coming through the gate...now! Within firing range in two minutes!"

"Poor bastards...well, we can't let them stop us from closing that gate. Decision settled—there's now less than no time for a message pod." Rakal propelled himself toward the panel. "Dark Hope to Pride-Disable the scout, or destroy it. In any case, keep it busy. We're going in to close that gate now...all preparation is complete."

"Acknowledged...we're already on our way." The comm light flicked out. Kiralla was already racing to the crash control room to launch the pod.

Rakal slipped into the control room just in time to see the Pride disable the scout's engines, leaving it hanging in space. The yellow light and gate crasher launch siren sounded as the last flash of plasma faded on the hull of the now disabled surprise visitor. The Dark

Hope creaked and shuddered with the pains of its labor as the gate crasher shot from the bay and raced away from the ship.

The pod glimmered like a wet diamond in the black velvet maw of the gateway.

The combat hymn of the second house of Arralla, Kiralla's ancestral Hive, rose up from the back of the room, mixed with the chants of several other long-lost Hives. The hope and anticipation in the room was palpable.

The Pride moved in, attaching a towrope to the disabled ship. Rakal grabbed a rail and gave the order to accelerate away from the Gate as fast as possible. "Our place in history is secure, but I'd prefer not to die in the backlash of a closing gate, thank you very much."

The tiny beacon finally disappeared into the center of the singularity. A moment later, a brilliant flash filled the view screen with a colorful cascade of shock waves and sparks. The ship rollicked in the blast, but remained intact.

All the comms went on as roars of victory rose up on all the ships. Weightless in the control room, Kiralla, Rakal and the entire work crew smashed together into one giant ball of elated fur, howling and thundering together with joy. The hope of one new free Hive, in balance with humanity, was alive!

The cheering continued unabated as the crew split apart and raced down the hallways to confer with crewmates. Rakal and Kiralla had the control room to themselves as they watched the last waves of energy from the gate wobble and flash out into the cosmos. On another screen, they could see the pearly white clouds on Dimar swirling over the verdant green of the Mainland continent.

Rakal regarded Kiralla for a moment as they both listened to the channel chatter between the ships. From the scout ship from Earth they had just disabled, there were no voices...only the repeated beeping of the distress beacon. He looked at Dimar again, and back at radiant Kiralla, "We're free from Earth, but like the little scout, we're still stuck with Dimar. The work's not over."

"Party pooper," she grabbed him by the muzzle and pulled him toward the door. "Fuzz lizards can't be any worse than humans. We'll

make a home for ourselves, even if we have to live on this bucket."
She slapped the dingy wall of the room. In a regal voice she reminded
him, "Our kits will be provided with no less."

"Agreed." He hugged her close, rubbing the soft downy fur on
her belly, which warmed the future of their Hive.

Chapter 27

The rains held off just long enough for the residents of all of Dimar to enjoy the lightshow provided by the death of the dreaded Gate. The end of the Gate and the start of the rain provided a needed catharsis for everyone. Tara relaxed by one of the interior barryd pools and consulted with acolytes from both barryds, Luuko and her trusted colony advisors.

Lazily, she hung one leg down into the cool water as she rested her chin on her knee and listened. The rains raged and poured onto the upper levels of the Barryd, but they were barely audible where the group was. She knew it was raining torrentially from the tingling on her skin. The constant stream of information the Barryd provided her about its condition had mild physical side effects, and this was one of the more pleasant ones. Here in one of the lower levels of the complex, water from above trickled down in a constant stream filling the pool and hundreds below it. The drone of the water was comforting in the face of dozens of bickering acolytes. She listened, stifling her irritation.

"No offense, Great Mother, but the leadership commotion has cost both barryds terribly. Poorly maintained fire lines resulted in the loss of two thirds of the outer agricultural settlements and two sub barryds." The only surviving Telkan first acolyte eyed her Mulkol companions in the meeting with contempt.

The tone in her voice was not lost to the two Mulkol first acolytes present. "Luckily, the many deaths from the inter-barryd war had left almost all of these areas uninhabited. Good thing we live right next door to provide you with such a necessary service." A gray-blue male Mulkoli wiggled his ears in delight at the Telkan's fury, and raised his tail in challenge.

Harmon signaled the non-psi humans and arrallins to move back, and all psis in the room jumped.

The Telkan lunged at him, screaming and roaring at his disrespectful regard for their dead. "How dare you...!" A slash from her tail landed cleanly and left a gash in his nose, and he reared back to strike.

"ENOUGH!" Tara leapt from the side of the pool, furious, but wanting to quickly defuse the situation. "Yttea, Wrarthim...you are both fired! Demoted! Report to the relocation commission for new quarters...as of today, you are no longer acolytes...you are MUCK ROOM PARTNERS."

One of the other Mulkol acolyte's eyes widened in surprise, and then narrowed in fury. Tara caught her attitude before she could block it, and turned. "Do YOU want to join them, Olitar?" The Mulkol bowed her head, saying nothing. "I didn't think so."

Tara surveyed the crowd, catching vibrations from all around the room. Discord, shock and fury echoed from most present—all except Luuko, and a handful of Dimar who'd made the adjustment to the co-barryd situation, who seemed more confused than negative about the demotion.

Suddenly, like a bright dapple of sunlight on a dingy wall, she felt the psionic echoes of someone in the room who was actually laughing. She turned to regard the Mulkol first acolyte, Olitar, who might be celebrating the unexpected rise to the power of being the only first-rank acolyte left in both Barryds, but she was still fuming over Tara's threat to demote her. She scanned the room, not angry that someone was amused in the midst of all the tension, but curious.

Giving up on her psi senses, she resorted to just plain looking around. Freia and Karti sat far in the back of the crowd among several other fourth level acolytes. Tara scrutinized Karti closely. His ears were trembling with the effort to keep from wiggling, and Freia had simply resorted to clamping her paws to the sides of her head.

"Frick and Frack back there...is there something you'd like to share with the rest of the class?" Tara smiled at Freia, who looked mortified to have been noticed.

"No, Great Leader! Our apologies!" She bowed her dun colored head low, but continued to hold her ears to stop their uncontrollable wiggling.

"Apologies for you and who else?" Tara already knew it was Karti, but wanted to see if Freia would readily admit having a Telkan compatriot.

Karti spoke up before Freia might have to take the fall for both of them. "I'm afraid I'm to blame for the disturbance. We though we were being quiet, but I was too loud. I will go to the muck room."

Freia's head shot up, "No! It was my fault. You shouldn't go to the muck room. I was laughing too loud." She looked mortified that Karti might have to take the entire load of the blame.

Tara couldn't get them to conclusively acknowledge each other, but she had to know. "So, you both admit to disturbing this very important meeting with your own amusements?"

Freia looked around the room self-consciously, but rose up to her full height. "Yes."

Karti rose up too and nodded assent guiltily.

"Then you'll both take your punishment together. Come forward." Tara beckoned them to the pool. The crowd parted and whispers both audible and psi rippled through the room. Like nervous striplings, the two scuttled forward, avoiding eye contact with angry barrydmates.

"Freia and Karti, I am going to make an example of you." Tara crossed her arms and glared at them. "You think everything is funny. You two find something amusing at every meeting."

"...but our rank has an excellent efficiency rating! It's not that we're not serious about our duties..." Karti stammered.

"Silence." Tara pointed toward the ground, and they lowered their heads. She put a hand on each forehead. "I will now pronounce my sentence upon you."

The crowd's approval of punishment for the two was obvious. Tara didn't mind disappointing them.

"For getting along well together, performing above expectation, and for keeping a steady and positive perspective on your work, I promote you both to Acolyte First. You'll report directly to me now."

She pulled her hands back, looked down at them and smiled.

"Like I said, I'm going to make an example of these two. If you don't get along with your co-acolytes—fine, but deal with it on your own time and make sure your work gets done. If you do get along, expect great rewards." Tara hopped up on the ledge of the pool and spoke loudly over the chattering of disgruntled acolytes. One of the acolyte second rank just turned and strode indignantly from the room.

"Results equal rank—not time served. If you seconds ever want to make first, you've got to show some results. The fourth rank, headed up by these two, has shown real results. We'll have plenty of fresh fruit this winter thanks to the fourth rank's work with the vines guild and the first acolytes. However, we're low on meat and will be until next spring, NO thanks to the second rank in charge of aiding the fourth rank and the morrak herds guild." Tara's stomach grumbled as if to emphasize the point. "Results. You can't coast to the top anymore. You've got to work together. Now, I'm hungry, so this meeting is adjourned. Karti and Freia...members of the first acolytes rank and I look forward to dining with you in an hour at the front table. We have much to talk about in regard to revitalizing the entire structure of both barryds."

She nodded curtly to dismiss the group and sent the stunned pair on their way.

Trying to keep a brisk pace in the flowing silk gown the Telkan weavers had made for her wasn't easy. She grunted with annoyance at having to constantly pick up the sleeves and skirt as they tripped her. It was a beautiful piece, a forest green background color with raised brocade flowers of purple and gold, but it was designed for looks and not practicality. Tonight she'd be dining in the Mulkol half of what had become nearly a single Barryd, so she'd opt for something a little more military anyway.

Rounding the bend in the hallway, she came to the central spire passage, with its precipitous drop toward the pools. A young Mulkoli rested on the ledge, marked with the silks of an air-lifter. He was asleep and didn't notice her approach. Rather than having to suffer with the usual formal greeting, she simply climbed onto his back, settling on the quilted pad strapped between the two spiked plates along his spine. She wanted to get where she was going quickly and with as little pomp and circumstance as necessary.

"Sir...I see you are a lifter. Will you please carry me to the second level top?" She prodded him gently with her foot and poked at him with her mind.

He grunted his ascent, and without even looking back, slid off the ledge into the open air. He rose quickly, with some jerkiness, trying to get his errand over as soon as possible to return to his ledge and await his replacement.

He swept past the level and braked with a customary Mulkoli maneuver-grabbing the heavy rail with his hind feet. This brought him whipping into the second level hallway, but he was careful not to fling Tara off. He chuckled to himself, turning back to see how his cargo had fared.

Tara, arms crossed, was grinning from ear to ear. "I hope you only treat the teenaged humans and the older Betas to that kind of landing. It's a bit like an amusement park ride from Earth." She had honestly enjoyed the ride, but didn't want him thinking all humans liked a roller coaster trip from level to level.

His jaw dropped, and his eyes went wide with alarm when he recognized her. He brought his shoulders down carefully, as if he was carrying a youngster in his pouch. "Sincerest apologies, Leader Tara! I will be more considerate in the future."

She slid off to the ground and smiled at him, reassuring him that he wouldn't be sent to the muck room and that no harm had been done. "Hey...I'm not made of glass. Land as you like. I very much enjoyed the ride, and may just come later to see what other flying skills you have." She remembered his despondent boredom at the beginning of the flight and wondered if it was time to give the Mulkol something to think about. Cryptically, she added, "We'll be having need of good Mulkoli flying skills soon."

She saw the catlike pupils narrow and then widen at the mention of Mulkoli flying skills in particular. He didn't miss the hint that this could mean combat flying.

She winked and headed down the hall, knowing that she'd have to weather a storm of controversy once this lad's gossip got around. She hadn't really told him anything—Tinar firefighting took good combat flying skills. She could leave things up to interpretation for a while and then quash any rumors.

Somehow, she had to find a way to release Telka and Mulkol from their bonds and back to their natural states, if only the two cities could hold out long enough for her to bring her plan into action. And only if she could keep the rest of the Dimar Barryds from wiping them off the face of the planet...

She pressed her hand to the membrane of the door and it slid open noiselessly.

Rummaging through the interesting selection of garb the weavers had provided her and the other humans, she selected a sleeveless red overshirt with Mulkol traditional patterns woven into it, loose fitting silk pants that gathered at the feet, and a pair of black sandals. She pinned the triangular Arrallin military insignia to her shoulder, and used it to hold a silk strip of the two Telkan and two Mulkol colors in place. The green and purple clashed with the black and red of Mulkol in a perfect example of art imitating reality. Tara mused over the possibilities of her plan. New colors could be chosen to match the new organization.

Despite the coming of the rainy season, things hadn't cooled down much. They'd just gotten horribly humid. She glanced down at her watch, and decided to take the last 15 minutes to rest from the heat and enjoy a little of the fruit drink the humans had come to refer to as Bug Juice. Luuko would meet her at the door as always and fly her personally to dinner. Luuko was good about being prompt so she never really had to worry about the time.

She gazed up at the cathedral-like ceiling of her quarters. Each panel of the stained glass bubble-roof was a fret of the various flowers of the barryd. The panels in here didn't tell any stories; they were just soothing. The tiny blue and yellow flames of the chandelier-style branch that lit the room made the glass glitter, as there wasn't enough light from the rainy outdoors to really backlight the panels. The texture of the glass stood out more in this light, and the colors all appeared dark and vibrant.

She tunelessly hummed a barryd greeting song and swung in her nest-bed. The familiar tickle of a mosquito on her skin distracted her momentarily and she swatted it. She regarded the long-legged remains of the bug on the end of her finger.

She blinked.

"Mosquitoes? On Dimar?" She jumped up just as Luuko made his familiar noise at the doorway.

"Luuko, you have to see this. Come in. Come in!" She swatted the panel to open it and he trundled into the room.

She jabbed her finger up toward his head. "What do you make of this?"

He looked at her, and looked at her half finished glass of bug juice. "I think you need some rest. Finiss your bug juice or you'll dehydrate." Wiggling his ears slightly, he warbled, "That's your index finger."

She grinned. "No no no...look. That tiny thing on the end of my finger is a bug native to Earth only. How'd it get here on Dimar? Hmmmm?"

He looked again closely. "I have not seen this kind of bug before, but it is so small, I might not ever have noticed it."

"You would have. These things are the scourges of Earth. They spread disease and leave nasty welt-like bites on people and on all mammals they can find." She brushed the remains of the bug into an empty glass by her bed stand. "I'm going to have Cy Mason and the Telkai First take a good look at this. This may be a case of parallel evolution...or worse, one of these things stowed away on the ships."

Luuko looked alarmed at the mention of the insects being

dangerous pests, ears forward and eyes wide. "But do they not also serve some purpose on Earth?"

"Oh, sure. I'm sure some people would even say they're indispensable. Lots of birds eat them, and dragonflies and other bugs that bigger animals eat. But I think the pain they inflict far outweighs their usefulness to the ecosystem as a whole." She peered into the glass at the dead bug. "They're awful. And they'll breed out of control in this rainy season."

Luuko turned and headed down the hallway without Tara.

"Hey! Luuko! Wait... I need a ride to Mulkol's Ptarmin Dining Hall." She bolted out the door after him with the cup in hand and caught up with him at the balcony to the spire.

"Apologies, Tara. Just wanted to prevent a disaster. Mason and the Telkai First have been informed of the bug." He lowered to the ground so she could climb aboard.

"Look, we've survived with these pests for millions of years...Dimar probably won't have a problem. They'll never last in the dry seasons anyway. There will be a natural limit on them." She grabbed a tuft of his mane and settled on his shoulders, keeping the cup upright. He slid off the railing and down into the spire, taking one of the new ground level tunnels from Telka to Mulkol.

The trip from Telka to Mulkol was long-a half-hour even on Luuko or in a hovercar. The tunnel, in parts, was open, giving views to the countryside of both barryds, but also allowing the rain to pour down on them. Tara envied Luuko's innate ability to simply ignore the weather, and regretted not grabbing a rain slicker. Eventually, the Telkan transport tunnel ended, leaving Tara to enjoy a wet ride over the steamy forests and fields.

Through the foggy day, she could survey the borderlands of Telka and Mulkol. Much of it was just starting to recover from the horrible burning that occurred during the fire season. Hostilities between Telka and Mulkol had resulted in severe mismanagement on both sides and much of the land's growth had been lost. It was going to be an interesting winter. Tara took advantage of the trip to talk to Mason about recent events.

"Haven't heard from you in a long while...what have you been up to?" She reached out to Mason, who's mental signal got stronger as she approached Mulkol.

"Learning, learning, learning. We've landed on a biotechnical gold mine with this planet. I am glad that gate is closed...I can only imagine what Central Command might have done with this stuff." He sounded distracted, but Tara had come to expect that from anyone working with Telkai.

Tara continued, "I've got some news for you, which we can discuss over dinner. I think I've come up with a solution to the problem of how to deal with our Dimarian neighbors."

"Problem? I'm having a great time with the Mulkoli and the Telkans, when you can get them to stop trying to kill each other." Mason sounded confused. Tara could feel him release a bit of the Telkai concentration he'd been using. "And I haven't seen any problems between the colonists and the Dimar worth mentioning. Both Mulkoli and Telkan are getting along fine with arrallins and humans. We take up so little of their range, they don't see us as competition. They see designing colony structures with us as fun."

Tara grinned at the mental image he sent of Telkan engineers puzzling over how to make a live plant resemble stone. "Not those neighbors. You're right...except for the infighting between Mulkoli and Telka, things are going well between us and the barryds we're in. It's our neighboring barryds I'm worried about.

"The acolytes have been keeping a quiet ear to the Wind, using what friends they have in far off places to keep tuned into the political situation outside. Reports from all sides show the other Barryd Leaders are scared witless of Telka's engineers combining with Mulkol's warriors. If they ever could get along, they could take the continent handily."

"Heh! Like any two groups fighting this much could raise an army. They're too busy taking each other out in blood feuds." Mason retorted sarcastically.

Tara wondered how much longer the two Barryds could hold together. The murder rate was high and getting higher as disgruntled

Telkans or disgraced Mulkoli warriors took action against their perceived enemies. Both Barryds could eventually depopulate each other enough that the core plants could not be maintained.

Mason interrupted her thoughts, "So, what's the plan? Or do you want to tell me vocally so that curious psi-ears don't pick things up early?"

"Over dinner...I'm almost there." She looked down into the bushes below and spotted the guarded expressions of older Mulkoli watching her pass. Luuko flew carefully over the observers, staying above fields and avoiding the fortified outbuildings the Mulkoli kept. Tara had been on him once before when young Mulkoli pranksters had knocked the Wind out from under them.

As they moved in toward the main Barryd, Tara began broadcasting an arrival song to prevent anyone from taking pot shots at them. Being the physical manifestation of two entire cities had it's advantages, but Tara wouldn't miss the drawbacks when she could finally relinquish her post and be just Tara again.

Tara continued her song, enjoying Luuko's skill in approaching the hall. They made their way over the roofs and branches, finding a convenient entrance in the third hall spire above the Ptarmin wing of Mulkol. Tara's barryd-given knowledge of the layout helped her direct Luuko along the shortest route to the hall and the front table.

Saluting Olitar, then Freia and Karti, Tara made her way down the table. Mason was seated to her right, and was shaping up to be one of the most striking Dimar in the room. He had burnished his velvet in one of the heating chambers of Telka, exposing firescales that seemed translucent, as if cut from sheets of a ruddy amber stone. The yellow glow of the hall lights gave his sides a warm yellow tint, bringing out the deeper stripes of rusty browns that could camouflage him in deep cover. He stared off at some unseen plan with his sky-blue Dimar eyes, oblivious to the room. Tara tugged his tail on her way by to get his attention, and he reluctantly released whatever he was working on to watch the opening of the meal. She handed him the mosquito sample on her way by, muttering, "Tell me this isn't what I think it is..." but Mason had little time to respond.

Reaching the end of her table, she picked up her glass. The room quieted and watched intently. Per Mulkol tradition, she walked down into the room, moving table to table. She recognized a young Mulkoli female who had been doing quite a bit of studying at Telka and was making friends there. She had only spoken to her once, but liked what she'd seen. She placed her glass on the table before her, and wordlessly took the large bowl the Mulkol used for drinking, and returned to her place.

It was a mark of trust and respect for the Mulkoli to be chosen to trade for Leader's cup. Poisoning was a long-standing tradition in Dimar wars. Of course, Tara's tiny cup could not hold nearly enough liquid to be useful to the Mulkoli. She would just take the cup home as a trophy, and would receive another bowl at the serving table.

"Oohlam!" Tara signaled, and the meal began.

Chapter 28

Luuko greeted the few familiar faces in the Mulkol dining hall that night as he swept in for a quick landing. Tara slid from his shoulder, tugging his mane in a customary thank-you. She seemed more distracted than usual tonight, but it had been an unusual day. Luuko felt more curiosity than worry in the Leader's mind, and was relieved. He moved around to the far side of the table quietly as Tara began the evening ritual to begin the meal.

Luuko rumbled approvingly as Genar accepted the Leader's trade. It was a wise choice, as Genar was popular with both her Mulkoli mates and the Tinar ranks at Telka. He settled in his customary spot to Tara's left, and grabbed a mirul steak as the platter passed, ruing the fact that this might be the last steak served this winter thanks to the war.

"So, Mason...what do you think of this little stow-away?" Tara leaned on her elbows watching Mason, who was peering into the glass at the bug.

Luuko fidgeted nervously, wondering how Mason would react to the horrible bug.

"It's a mosquito all right. Aedes grossbecki, I think. But I'm not a mosquito expert, really. It must have stowed away, but how could it have gotten from the colony ships all the way to Telka? There must have been two-which means we now have a new colony species to introduce." Mason seemed unconcerned, but Luuko had come to know that Mason was fond of taking chances.

Tara was munching on a slice of bread when suddenly, she sat bolt upright. Surprise more than fear emanated from her as she pointed down at the platter. Luuko followed her hand down to the plate and saw tiny black dots hovering. Curious, he lowered his nose to the plate and sniffed.

"Luuko! Breathe out! Breathe out!" Mason rose up on his haunches and grabbed Luuko's nose with both paws. "Snort if you have to–I need to see those bugs!"

Luuko snorted out, and quietly hoped he'd avoided eating the garlic-spiced slices of the meat for Mason's sake. Mason grabbed at the air in front of his nose and stared intently at the black dot on his palm.

"Flies. The usual garden variety late summer flies." Mason looked at Tara, and then around the room suspiciously. "I did the preflight checks of all the ships, and Tulera oversaw the radiating of the cargo. This is no fluke. One mosquito getting by us I can see, but flies we would have discovered. Someone's making Earth pests."

Luuko wondered if these were machinations of Earth warfare, but the word 'pest' didn't carry that kind of weight in his mind. He thought for a while about who might be interested in Earth species, and offered helpfully, "Goothib was reading a golden disk from the metal tree ship that was about Earth animals."

Tara and Mason both just stared at him. Tara dropped her bread.

Slowly, they both looked at each other and spoke in unison: "The Ark!"

"Ark?" Luuko asked, while sending out a search broadcast to find Goothib.

"The Ark is a disk sent on all Earth starships. It contains encoding of genetic samples for every major animal and plant species on Earth. It's meant to be enough information to re-create Earth if those that find the disks understand the system of DNA most Earth species use." Mason answered Luuko's question quickly and scientifically, while joining his search band for Goothib. "Earth technology can't do much with the information. Our technology isn't to that point yet..."

Tara broke her stunned silence and helped Mason explain the political angle, "Those disks were only installed on ships as a conceit to get funding from United Canada, who's prime minister at the time was...well, how can I say this delicately? He was crazy. Crazy McCray. He mandated the disk program after watching an episode of a science fiction entertainment show. The deal bankrupted United Canada, but Earth Federal Council got its ships, and Minister McCray got his disks."

Groggily, Goothib answered their call from Telka. "Tara? Mason? What has you knocking on my mind at this hour?"

"It's dinnertime, Goothib...Harmon's letting you stay up too late." Luuko wiggled his ears at Goothib's indignant reaction, audible even over the distance.

Tara broke in. "Um...Goothib. Do you know anything about a rash of insect sightings that's been happening in Mulkol? These are Earth insects...not Dimar natives."

Goothib was quiet for a long time, but finally he spoke. He mind voice was suffused in Telkai pride, which made Luuko wince. When Goothib was working for the greater glory of Telkai, bad things could happen.

Goothib proudly pronounced, "I have integrated 1812 Earth species into Dimar biosystems successfully so far. As a true child of the Water, I am striving to bring the dependencies of Earth's Barryds into harmony with Dimar's. I'm making your barryds here."

Tara picked up the mosquito cup, "Just which 1812 species have you brought into the ecosystem? Are they all bugs?"

"No. I started with bacteria and lower forms. They are doing well, and many have Dimar counterparts that are nearly identical. Earth and Dimar are quite similar." Goothib sounded as if he was about to launch into one of his scientific dissertations. Luuko began to tune out and search for Harmon, who might be able to shed some more light on exactly how much damage had been done.

Mason lit into Goothib like he was one of his assistants. "Goothib, you should have TOLD us about this! You know you should have told us about ANYTHING you took off the colony

ships. You might introduce something that this planet can't handle...
how can you simulate the effects? The barryds can't do that kind
of calculation." They continued arguing over the disk on a private
channel.

Tara took her seat and resumed munching her bread. "Any luck
raising Harmon, Luuko?"

"No Leader Tara. Not yet." Luuko listened carefully to Telka's
responses but continued his conversation. "You seem calm. Does the
bug no longer bother you?"

"No. It bothers me very much, but what can I do?" Tara regarded
the salad on her plate dejectedly. Luuko wondered that perhaps she
had finally just snapped under all the pressure.

Harmon's answer broke Luuko's concentration, "Harmon here.
Time for me to do some explaining, I guess..."

"Harmon, tell Goothib to give us the disk. This little science
project of his could kill us all." Tara's tone was final, and tired.

"I'm afraid I can't do that. This is what I knew would happen."
Harmon sighed. "Look, I know you'll never understand, but we
Earthlings need the species on Earth. It's the same as the barryds
needing the Dimar, and the Dimar needing the barryds. If we don't
establish a valid Earth ecosystem on Dimar, our species won't survive.
This program has to continue. Period."

"Arrallins survive on Earth. We can eat all the Dimar foods. We
get all the required vitamins. I've seen the reports Harmon...What's
really going on?" Tara pulled Luuko in to exert force on Harmon
to reveal more. Harmon and Goothib had been less than mentally
stable after the last few hybrid Arrallin/Dimar and Human/Dimar
had hatched. Making Mason and his cousins had taken a heavy toll
on Goothib, and Harmon was just too close to him.

"Tara, I taught you everything you know about mind-tricks, so
don't even try it." Harmon's fury was open, and Luuko recoiled at
such disrespect for a Leader. "We've got the disk, and we're keeping
it. Goodbye!"

Harmon's signal promptly disappeared, and Mason raced off
toward the spire exit.

Luuko lowered his chest to the floor as Tara leapt aboard. Without so much as an explanation to the rest of the front table or the hundreds of hall spectators, they were off.

Luuko's roar and Tara's signals cleared everyone out of the spire as they whipped up through levels and out into the humid air. Mason had proven a quick study in the arts of the Wind, and was well ahead of them. His ruddy wing membranes were stretched to the limit, nearly transparent as they generated lift from the Wind. He streaked off toward Telka oblivious to Luuko's cries.

Luuko could feel Tara hunch on his back so he could make the best time with the least wind, and rain, resistance. He stretched his own wings into the Wind, feeling for the strongest fluctuations and trying to maximize his surface area to generate the most forward speed. She wasn't using a guarded frequency as she called on Telkans to find Goothib and Harmon, and curious searchers flooded from Mulkol as well. Looking back, he saw Olitar keeping pace with him, followed by Freia and Karti.

Luuko listened intently, trying to pinpoint where the signal had emanated. Tara had contacted him while he was asleep, and used a fairly open channel, so he wasn't hiding his signal through various echoing tricks the Barryd could provide, but he did sound distant.

Joining a group of Telkans they moved out toward the sea, following the last contact from Harmon.

The driving rain slowed their progress back toward Telka. The trip, even at Luuko's top speed seemed agonizingly long. Listening to the search teams—most of them his Tinar rank mates—he knew to fly past Telka, and out toward the original colony site. Tara was coordinating the ranks well, keeping Mulkol apart from Telkans, sending them both toward the colony on different routes. Luuko fell into formation with the Mulkol line knowing they wouldn't give him any trouble with Tara on his back.

Luuko crested the last ridge between Telka territory and the now defunct colony site. The Mulkol ranks broke off and began rummaging through what was left of the settled area. Charred cinders were all that remained of the few outbuildings that had been constructed, but Harmon and Goothib could be inside the ship itself, or inside the many pockets created by the fallen trees. A deep longing welled in him as the silvery mass of the metal tree ship loomed into view. The entire area was charred to the ground, but spots of green were beginning to show along the creek bed. "*If only the colony had survived.*" He positioned himself above what had been the meeting area to allow Tara the best view of the search.

It was beautiful, wasn't it? Tara's voice in his head surprised him. He hadn't realized he'd been thinking out loud. Warm remembrances of the early colony filled her visual communication with him. She missed the old colony as much as he did.

Reports flooding in from the Telkan group along the nearby coastline interrupted Tara's reverie, and Luuko respectfully broke off communication to make a gentle landing in the mud below.

Finally, Tara spoke. "No sign of the disk...no sign of Goothib, no sign of Harmon. Well, I did choose Harmon for her ability to keep a secret. I should have expected that she'd have a plan in mind if she was going to try something as hair-brained as mixing Earth's species with Dimar. Well, let's just hope that their little mission doesn't involve breeding Ebola Haarvens or one of those other incurable diseases. We DON'T need that kind of trouble down here." Luuko recoiled at the images that Tara broadcast as she spoke. In agitation, he lifted out of the mud, letting the rain wash some of the dirt from his emerging winter coat.

Tara tuned into him and patted his neck. "Don't worry, Luuko. From what I can tell, Dimar has the technology to handle that kind of a threat. Viruses are very much like your Water. They just carry a code, inject it and let it do its work. Telkai can handle it." The confidence that suffused her voice made Luuko raise his head in pride. "And, my blue friend, our colony will live again."

Her cryptic tone made Luuko swivel around to face her. She was grinning a grin that Luuko knew meant either great fun, or great trouble. He could hear her calling Mason in. "You have to keep this from Karti, Freia and Olitar, however. This must all be kept in the strictest confidence. It's so secret, I'm going to tell it to you in

English—not mindspeak. This is probably as appropriate a place to discuss this as any." She wiped away rainwater as it poured down from her hair.

Mason crested the hill and glided gracefully down into the colony valley, taking a seat in the mud without batting an eye.

"Lucky bastard. Maybe I'll trade in my form for one of you dragon models. This rain doesn't even phase you, does it, Cy?" She spoke out loud, wringing some of the water from her shirt.

Luuko took his own seat in the mud again and thoughtfully raised a wing over his back to shield her from the rain. He forgot that humans tended to use machinery to avoid problems with their environment, instead of just evolving themselves to handle it. He shook his head and bit back his frustration with himself. He should have remembered! Tara didn't need to be uncomfortable while guiding the ranks.

"You didn't call me in to talk about the weather, I suspect. Certainly not in spoken English. What's the big secret?" Mason extended a wing as well, creating a dry area for all three of their heads.

"I want you to begin producing a seed. Use half of Mulkol's compliment of plant and species types, and half of Telka's. I need it to launch within the next three weeks. Can you do that?" Luuko watched him closely as he went into his own thoughtful reverie, and listened as he called out to Telka's data stores to run the calculations.

Tara stopped him, "Wait—don't refer to the barryd yet. Our trusty cities can be made to talk, and our neighbors might move in before we're ready. Do the calculations here in your head if you can."

"Well, from what I know of the seed process...yes, it can be done in two weeks. There are several good pods at Telka that could be intermixed with Mulkol, but Mulkol will be the side that holds us back. They haven't produced an external pod in centuries from what I hear. The spire may just not be up to it." Mason doodled in the mud with a clawed finger, and his tail flicked from side to side keeping time to some unheard tune.

"We can use Telka's spire for the launch. Mulkol just needs to provide seeds. So, it is possible?" Tara's voice sounded flat to Luuko...he couldn't feel her emotions through it. Again, he cursed himself for getting out of practice with the human communication skills. Tara's becoming a psi had made his English studies much easier, but he wasn't gaining the subtle training he needed to fully understand humans.

"Yes. The timetable's tight, but there are pods well along in Telka already. And, you'd think after centuries of dormancy, Mulkol's barryd would be desperate to produce some seeds." Mason turned from his doodles to regard Tara and Luuko. "So, what's this all about?"

Luuko listened closely, and despite his best training, he peered into Tara's emotional mindset surreptitiously. Her hope and expectation for this project was strong–as strong as her feelings about the colony.

"This seed will be the start of The Academy. I haven't thought of a good name for it yet, nor have I done historical research into what this kind of barryd would be in Dimar terms, but it will a place of learning." Tara gesticulated carefully, and Luuko could feel her strain not to use her psi ability to show them what she saw. "This planet is so vulnerable to outside attack right now, it's ridiculous. This Water technology is a weapon that could change the tide of any war on Earth or Arralla–possibly on any planet with genetically encoded life similar to ours. There were once ancient Mulkai craft on this planet that could rip Earth to shreds in a day, and there are still ground based war machines on here that if in the wrong hands could destroy everything the Barryds have worked for.

"The Mulkai Barryds are dormant, and dying, but the skills they guard are vitally necessary. They're just too proud to share them with the rest of Dimar, or too short sighted to realize that their military duty doesn't lie in destroying the production barryds, but in guarding them and enjoying the products of their work in return. It will give them a place to go–a reason to train as hard as they do. Sparta will guard Athens this time around, instead of warring with it."

Tara's warm regard for the Mulkai bothered Luuko, but he suppressed his feelings.

"The Dimar live in constant fear of Starborn attacks, but do nothing about it. That's where the Academy comes in. We're going to set up a space-based defense for Dimar. We don't have a choice. The three Arrallin Hives have already settled and begun serious colonies, and will be having litters soon. Kiralla and Rakal may whelp on board the Singularity II, and up there, if anything came into orbit, they'd be the first casualties. I won't allow that." The firm tone of Tara's voice wasn't lost to Luuko, even though his English was rusty.

"We need a space based defense. This isn't a theoretical threat we're dealing with. I saw what the Mulkai sent up. I know what may be in store for us if even one of those transport ships 'rediscovers' Dimar. From what the records show, they'd expect to find a dead planet with remains of species they were familiar with. They wouldn't even recognize the new improved morraks on Dimar these days, let alone humans and Arrallins. They'd immediately think we were a new world to conquer." Tara beat her fist into her other outstretched hand. The emphasis wasn't necessary; Luuko agreed wholeheartedly. It was a great fortune that Tara and her ships had found Dimar in the first place. Fate would not give Dimar such a gift again. Luuko and Mason both nodded their heads in assent.

"We will return to the Stars. We have no choice." Luuko emphasized his support with a throaty growl. "The other Barryds must be made to see."

Mason chuckled and shook his head. "And I thought this trip would finally free me from life in orbit. But, you're right. We won't be given this opportunity twice. The debris from the Dark Hope that went through that gate before it shut has probably raised some serious concerns about what was on the other side. If Humanity can unlock the secret to aiming the Gates, we're going to get visitors. It's only a matter of time."

"You can get a cushy ground-based desk job. We need your scientific knowledge down here anyway." Tara patted Mason's muzzle affectionately. "I'll take the point on pilot training. Question is, what will we be flying?"

"I can tell you, Leader Tara." A voice, speaking English, behind them made them all spin. Luuko was careful not to unseat Tara, but the shock of their discovery only made her grab his mane more tightly. Luuko turned to face Olitar full on, and flared his wings. He could take her out if it would save the plan.

"Back down, Luuko. There's more Mulkai in you than I expected," Olitar growled, snaking her neck forward. Luuko probed her emotional state, but she was blocking heavily. She dismissed him with a grunt and turned to look at Tara.

"Leader Tara, for centuries we've been waiting for something to change. Something that would bring us back to our old glory and give honor to our family names. You will provide us with this opportunity. I respectfully request to be part of this venture." She dipped her nose into the mud in a gesture of absolute submission. Luuko could feel Olitar's fervent hope, even through her shielding.

"Olitar, rise, and drop your shields. Luuko, block for her." Tara's tone was controlled, but Luuko recognized her fidgeting. She probably trusted Olitar as little as he did. You didn't get to Acolyte First in any Barryd without making enemies, and unseating them from their positions of power.

Luuko moved in close to the large female so that Tara could grab her horns. He arched his neck back so that his horns locked with the ends of hers. The intimate contact made him bristle, but he had to be sure he was blocking her completely while Tara scanned her for signs of treachery or deceit. His shoulder leaned in against hers, and the sounds of her serrated scales rasping against his set his teeth on edge. The unexpected warmth of her side dredged up unwanted memories of his lost family, reminding him too much of the fire season. Despite his discomfort, he held his ground.

He avoided listening to their conversation, and instead focused on anyone who might be approaching, or listening at a distance. Mason also set up a mental noise barrier to help. Luuko would trust Tara's judgment. She was a strong mind, although certainly far from even as skilled as some second acolytes, but the Barryds would give her extra abilities she would need. Olitar was already obviously under great emotional duress, and Luuko could sense her emotions even through her shields. Still, he worried that she could be hiding something, or that Tara's irrational respect for the Mulkai might keep her from exploring as fully as she should. There was no dishonor in a Leader invading privacy to protect the Barryd.

"Olitar, welcome to the Academy." Tara released her spiked ebony horns and patted her nose affectionately. "She's clean guys. And, she speaks English well enough to keep up with us. Plus, she has some interesting news regarding our transportation."

Luuko continued listening for anyone approaching, and berated himself for letting down his guard. *"Foolishness, letting Olitar approach! What was I thinking? I WILL be more watchful of her."* Luuko regarded the silver gray Mulkol surreptitiously from behind his outstretched wing. She had a black mane tufting out from beneath permanent firescales along her spine, and piercing green eyes. Her scales had rough serrated edges, and spikes along her back. A shiny black plate, covered with serrated blades, protruded from the end of her tail. Luuko shivered, wondering if he'd have to dance against her in any Mirrai practices at this new Barryd. He reached out quietly to sample her emotional state, but sensed nothing. Her shielding was excellent. Her scaled ears pricked up for a second, and she broke her concentration on Tara to dart her eyes toward him. *She senses me!* He ducked his head behind his wing and resumed listening to Tara, feeling a bit foolish.

Tara continued, oblivious to the exchange, "So there's a good chance we can use the system for the walkers and the fliers the Mulkoli used on Telka to create a space-faring set of fast attack vessels. We just have to find an alternate propulsion system once in orbit. The Wind will be useless there, but we will have solar Wind. Fusion engines wouldn't fit in the designs I'm envisioning, but for the larger transports and base ships, they'll work well." Rubbing her hands together in both anticipation and to get warmth, Tara grinned. "I hope Kiralla has her kits soon. We'll need her engineering talents, and her engineering team to pull off the larger ships. And there's still the problem of getting them in orbit."

Luuko could not believe that an Acolyte First would not know the entire history of her own race. In challenge, he interrupted. "When the Mulkai went Starborn, they had a way to get the ships off Dimar. Does not Olitar have information on this system?" He peeked out again at her from behind his wing.

Olitar's eyes narrowed, and she regarded him for a long moment, giving him chills. "The Mulkai who did go to the stars didn't want followers. Those of us left on Dimar were given the sacred task of guarding the secrets of the home world, so those in space could keep the knowledge of their evolution and weaknesses secret, securing a tactical advantage." She snorted derisively. "However, there are those who believe that those Mulkai Barryds left to rot on this rock were simply being given a long and painful execution. We were the vanquished of the Barryd Wars, and we do carry this dishonor with us regardless of what the Starborn might call it." Her bitterness was unmistakable, even in her English voice.

"And, you wouldn't mind heading to the stars to finally get a little sweet revenge, if a Mulkai warship was to venture into this sector?" Tara grinned slyly at Olitar, who feigned shock at the idea. Luuko was deeply disturbed by how quickly Tara and Olitar had bonded through Tara's mind probe of her. Tara had Mulkai leanings, but he knew that she was a true child of arts other than war. *This must be an act to win her confidence,* Luuko comforted himself. Tara was exceptionally sly when she needed to be, so Luuko would rely on her judgment until given reason to do otherwise.

"The thought hadn't crossed my mind, great Leader!" The big gray female laughed, wiggling her ears wildly with amusement.

"Spite isn't the best motivator, but if it keeps us all safe and gives us a potent fighting force, I'll use it. I'm hoping that we can create ships and a team that will inspire us to do our best, instead of relying on grudges to whip us into shape." Tara wrung out her shirt again, deep in thought, and turned toward Mason.

"Any luck with those seed calculations? Olitar, do you know what condition the west spire is in? Can Mulkol provide seeds for the new academy Barryd?" Tara looked back toward Telka.

"Seeds are not my specialty, but yes. We have had seeds and pods for a long time now that could be sent over to Telka." Olitar scratched her scaled chin with a paw.

Tara outlined the framework for the plan, "Olitar, Find your most trusted allies at Mulkol and have them transport the seeds to the westernmost spire at Telka. Mason, coordinate the effort with insiders there as well. Move at night-we can't risk the Leaders of the outside Barryds finding out what's going on. They're already massing forces in the north from what our Ekal allies can tell. There may be a scuffle. You both know what you have to do, and I'm going to trust you both to work out the details, and to work with each other."

Olitar's ears sprang forward at the mention of fighting. "Should I ready our forces and machinery to repel the Barryd invaders?" Luuko nearly hissed as she licked her lips with anticipation.

Tara just chuckled. "Be ready, but only cool heads will go out in this maneuver. Think of this as holding a fire line. If as a team, we can keep an entire regiment of Mulkol craft and fighters from attacking an agitated enemy, we'll hopefully gain a grudging amount of respect in the public eye by showing our self-control. We need to demonstrate to the rest of the planet that we're willing to serve. And that's serve everyone...not just ourselves." Tara brushed away the dampness on her forehead. "And, Olitar, I won't lie to you. To gain the trust of the other Barryds, we may have to surrender without a fight. They must be allowed to inspect and understand every piece of war technology we have. They must be our allies, and they must trust us. We may all have enemies before we're ready. There is no time to be lost in petty on-planet fighting."

Olitar reared back at the mention of surrender, and her tail lashed from side to side. "That's probably not going to be possible, Leader."

"Then the Mulkol warriors will be confined to quarters for the duration. I know you understand this mission, and I know you understand what we're trying to do. If you can't make your most loyal troops see the same, then we'll deal with them as the treasonous scum that they would become." Tara was firm, but not angry from what Luuko could tell.

"Yes, Tara." Olitar settled back down, but her tail continued to twitch. She scratched her chin absently as she pondered some unknown thoughts. Luuko tried to snatch a peek at her emotions again, and she let loose a tiny vibration. She was worried.

Tara drifted into reverie, communicating with the search teams along the coast. Luuko scanned the report bands as well, but found no sign of the pair and the golden disk.

Emerging from her thoughts as the two divisions of search teams landed around them, she announced in a strong mind-voice, "Oohlam! Attention. From what I know of these two fugitives, they're going to be seeking equipment and a safe harbor to continue producing Earth species and introducing them onto Dimar. I'll know if they use any of Mulkol or Telka's main stores, so they are bound to search for private refuge, possibly in other Barryds. We cannot have the loss of face that would come from other Barryds discovering their intent, and my personal failure to prevent this calamity. For this reason, you must continue searching, but privately. Your purpose cannot be known." Luuko noticed eager Mulkol faces in the crowd, their wings trembling with excitement to be on a hunt outside their territorial confines. He thought of gentle Goothib and curious Harmon, and looked back at Tara with concern. She glanced at him, and brushed his mind gently in reassurance.

"Searchers-they must be returned to me ALIVE and UNHARMED. The disk must be found intact as well. These are my friends, and although they are errant Children, I will not have them treated with disrespect." Tara smiled up at him, and he sighed with relief. Her tone was clear, and there would be no misunderstandings among the Mulkai searchers. Harming them would be tantamount to treason.

She dismissed them, and in a tired voice, "Okay, Luuko. Time to head back to Telka. What a night." Gently she patted his neck and pulled some of his long pouch-hair across her lap for warmth.

Helpfully he offered, "You may use my pouch to stay warm, Tara." She hesitated, but acquiesced, slipping halfway inside the fur-lined pocket. He could feel her exhaustion and anxiety, even through her Barryd-enhanced shielding. He looked toward the borders, listening on the Wind. It was disturbingly quiet on the public wavelengths toward Ekal. He wondered what allies they truly did still have.

Mason and Olitar broke off from them outside Telka's boundaries. Moving at top speed, they headed back toward Mulkol, eager to set plans in motion for the new Barryd.

Luuko looked back to find that Tara had fallen completely asleep on his back. Loyalty to the tiny being from so far away welled in him, and he most carefully conveyed her back to her nest bed at Telka.

Chapter 29

Rakal chuckled, "Nothing's changed...you're still poring over reports."
He poked his head into the open door of Tara's barryd room.

Tara leapt up from her desk and rushed toward him joyously.
"You're back! You're back! You're back!" She grabbed him around the
waist and swung him around the room, laughing like she was a girl
again.

Breathless, he stumbled back as she released him, "I have to
load up on mainland food, I guess," he laughed as he caught his
breath. Always able to manage his supercilious airs, "It's unbecoming
for even one as important as the Leader of two great Barryds to be
able to lift a full blood Arrallin..."

"Oh, you!" She punched his shoulder good-naturedly. "I prefer
to think of us as shipmates before the day I was promoted to officer
status." She grabbed a report off her desk and flopped down in her
bed, as much as she might have on board the ship they both flew so
long ago, before the Insurrection.

She looked tired, Rakal noted to himself, not letting his concern
show. She had a nervous kind of energy about her, but her eyes were
ringed heavily with dark circles and her hands fidgeted. Her look
matched the mood of the barryds-anticipatory, nervous, but already
stretched to the limit.

He had to ask, "So, how's Barryd life treating you? These plants
being good to you?" He patted the mahogany seat-shelf he was on.

She dismissed his question with a wave, "Don't try to change the subject bud-you're here to report to me. Tell me everything! How's Kiralla? When's she due? Are you going to stay up on the Singularity II, or make a Hive down here like the others?" Tara pointed to her map of mainland, winking at him as she jabbed her finger toward a bay along the northeast coast.

"Kiralla's coming along fine. Two more months and she'll give birth to, from what we can tell, 27 healthy kits." Rakal whuffled with pride. "As you can imagine, the politics are unbelievable, but we only have 20 keeni up there so there's little fighting over the choosing order. They all know they're getting at least one kit. The fighting's been over who will get two." Rakal looked up toward the ceiling with mock exasperation, "An embarrassment of riches." He grinned wildly. "I'm going to transfer up seven keeni with me when I return to the Singularity II. We'll need them to start getting acclimated now so they'll be ready to take guardianship by the introduction time. You know...milk production and all that."

Tara nodded. "I've never been around a real Hive at this time, but I was wondering how long you'd need for Arrallakeeni to start producing milk." Tara flipped through a personnel chart. "I hope I'm invited for the introduction, you! Heck... can humans take guard of a kit?" She shook her head, "Who am I fooling? When will I have time to be a parent anyway! I will have more free time by then, though. I expect to be fully disconnected from these fairly soon." She patted the wall behind her. "Definitely take Timra and Whirkil. The other five you can choose however you like. Those two you'll find particularly useful. They've both developed Psi down here. With their help, and Kiralla's talent, you can stay connected with the other Hives more easily. It's the oddest thing, lots of Talent emerging in the Keeni population. The Dimar tell me it's the Wind down here. If anyone's got even a hint of psi, it will emerge if immersed in this magnetism long enough."

"Go back a step. Disconnecting from the Barryds? Explain. Your turn to report, lady." Rakal peered toward the door, pointing toward Luuko's blue hindquarters visible down the hall.

"He knows...it's fine. But, the walls have ears. Literally." She waved her hand toward the door membrane and it slid shut noiselessly. "This is the second reason I called you down here. I need someone competent-combat competent-to operate the Pride."

"What? Why?" Rakal's lengthening mane stood on end. Could he risk himself flying a combat mission so close to Kiralla's birthing time? He couldn't bear the thought of her having to become a second mate to one of the Hives down here if he was lost in the combat. Kiralla was second to no one, and deserved better than that. He was her only shot at being an independent Hive queen, and despite his loyalty to Tara, he couldn't risk himself now.

"In three days, we're launching a Barryd pod. Talks with outside Barryds have completely broken down at this point. Telka and Mulkol cannot continue as one and not be completely razed by the rest of settled Dimar. Between our plasma, Mulkol's death weapons and Telka's cleverness, we pose far to serious a threat, and the other Leaders know it." Tara leaned back against a wall and seemed to rejuvenate from the contact. "So, we have to win their trust..."

"With combat flying the Pride?" Rakal interjected.

"Let me finish. We have to win their trust or beat them into submission. Either way, the mission cannot be jeopardized." Tara ended on a low note.

Rakal knew that tone too well, but would not be swayed into risking himself or the Pride unnecessarily. For once, he understood Tara's complaints of being pulled in too many directions at once. He was in the position of leadership now, and would have to make the final call regarding his own resources, and his own ship. "Outline the mission. Let me see what we might be able to do from up above."

"This seed will be guided two days north up to that bay I showed you. What this seed is designed to be is a combined Mul/Tel Barryd, and it's going to be Dimar's first Starborn Defense Academy. From there, we're going to train up a fighting force the likes of which even the Mulkai would tremble to face. No one is taking our home world without a fight." Tara's passive posture didn't hide the tensing in her arms as she quietly stated her case.

"You sound like a Dimar, Tara. Our home world? These barryds have gotten to your head." Rakal grinned uneasily. "And how do you think the other non-Mulkai Leaders are going to take this? You're building a military force in their backyard. Winning their trust, in the face of what you're proposing, is preposterous. How do they know that you, or your successor at the Academy, won't just turn the machinery on them and enslave them again?"

"I don't see what choice they have, Rakal. The only reason they're not Earth force slaves now is because we stole the gate from them before they could find this place. It's only by sheer chance that the Mulkai that left Dimar haven't stumbled back onto it and retaken it-with perhaps a worse regime than before. You have no idea what they were like before." Tara sorted the plastic report sheets distractedly. "No, the Leaders will be made to see that there is no threat from the Academy. It will serve them, and they for their own protection will want to learn from it. All the books will be open to them. Anyone who wants to learn from what we do, can.

"Dimar got lucky once, but luck has a tendency to run out. The Telkans have been made to see it, even those so hateful of Mulkai that they can't bear to fly past the western spire of Telka these days. The Mulkol, with all their feelings of superiority, agree that they have to serve the whole. If I can get these two wretched plants to agree, the rest of the planet should be easy." She smiled half-heartedly.

Rakal nodded. He'd seen some of what she'd learned from her experiences as a Barryd Leader in her reports, and from the historians. The fighting farmer-lizards on Dimar were not going to be the problem in the years to come. The danger was from offworld. An image from one historical report leaped into his mind– one of hundreds of non-Mulkai Dimar arranged in a massive column to guide a Starborn Mulkai ship to space. He furrowed his brow, remembering the animation of the huge black ship, propelled by all the tiny wings of the Dimar toward the stars. It crushed them as it passed, and they fell back on the writhing half-dead bodies of those beneath them as they, impelled by the undeniable force of a Leader's command, continued to direct all their force up. Hundreds of thousands of Dimar slaves died with each launch-both Mulkai and non. It seemed the losers of Mulkai wars were no better off than the non-Mulkai slaves they kept. There were parallels between certain Hives on Arralla, and certain nations on Earth, but none rivaled the image of that much carnage all at once.

"We're going to use our own launch techniques, I hope." Rakal watched for Tara's reaction closely. He wasn't sure how much contact with the Mulkai barryd would change her. She certainly hadn't seemed herself in this interview.

"Definitely. However, there are rumors of another launching system. Disgruntled Mulkol have destroyed the files, but the equipment has to be on the planet somewhere. You can oversee the surveyors on the Golden Hinde for me on that project." Tara flipped through maps and heat-resonance scans.

"You're not going to use the Dimar as a launch wall, are you?!" Rakal demanded furiously. His tail lashed from side to side. He couldn't believe she would even consider it!

Tara looked taken aback. "Never! There were some Mulkai who recognized the value of life, you know. You shouldn't believe everything you see in the history reels-many were made for us by Telkans. Although, the Pillars of Flesh were actually used by the most cruel of the Mulkai culture. That's who we're going to be defending against. They make Nazis look like amateurs." Tara explained calmly. Rakal expected that she'd been through this argument before a number of times. She continued, "Some Mul, despite their choice of lifestyle, were quite ingenious. They used another technique. We just have to figure out what it is. From what the reports can tell, whatever it was, it was environmentally friendly and would augment our fusion drives. The Pride will only last so long, and we've got serious mass to lift off this rock."

Rakal sighed inwardly at the idea of his quiet little pocket of space being invaded by the bulk of a giant space station. Even orbit wasn't going to provide him with privacy for Kiralla and his Hive. He consoled himself with the idea that an Academy would mean less need for him to lead combat missions, and with this in mind, he almost enjoyed the idea of one last mission. "So, how do you need us to prepare? Should we gather up bombardment objects in orbit to aim at the neighboring barryds? And how do you need the Pride?"

"I have no idea how this is going to play out. They may try to swarm us, in which case we have to keep the Mulkol from just shredding them. I've been reviewing the ranks, and most have agreed that in return for Mulkol returning to Mulkol rule and isolation, they will restrain themselves. Of course, Mulkol is teaming with young warriors desperate to make a legend for themselves-I'd rather they fight the Pride than take out a Leader and destabilize the entire political structure." Tara rested her chin in her hands.

"Great. A friendly fire mission." Rakal couldn't hide his disapproval.

"What else would you have me do?" Tara gave him one of those 'Why should I even justify my plans to you?' looks and continued on. He bristled with annoyance. "In the best case situation, the Leaders will want a demonstration and explanation of how the technology for Plasma and Fusion works. In either case, we need an impressive lightshow. I need to convince them of how serious I am about full disclosure of this information. In any case, just have the ship around."

"Do I have to comply? More importantly, do I need to pilot it?" Rakal looked deeply into her eyes, wondering if she'd try to command him.

"No. You're a Hive King now. I can't tell you how to live your life-all I can do is ask to borrow your transport and hope you say yes." Her voice was unusually soft, but her face was impassive.

"In that case, yes. You can work the ship into your planning. I'll stay down here to watch how things go. I'll move off to Keinsa Hive tonight. I can't risk myself or any more Keeni. I'll be moving out all the Arrallakeeni over to Keinsa Hive and back up to the Singularity II over the next three days. I'm sorry if this leaves you short-staffed." His tone was curt and to the point. Rakal wasn't sure how Tara would react, but he had to take command sometime, and the gate was closed. It might as well be now.

"Fine." Tara's eyes flashed angrily, but she nodded.

Their conversation continued long into the night, but was all business. Rakal wondered if he hadn't lost a friend in gaining a Hive.

Chapter 30

Tara beamed with joy as she caressed the glistening pod. It felt like smooth warm marble under her hands. The giant egg-shaped seedpod was twice her size, and she knew from Mason's calculations that it weighed nearly a ton. She wondered if the filigree sails tucked above the pod in the chute casing would be enough to carry it a full two days north in the driving rains of the season. She fingered a rough spot in the speckled green surface, wishing that she would have more than three trustworthy Mulkol to help guard the few Telkans who had volunteered to be part of the new barryd.

In the hour, she would separate from the two Barryd plants that had become her second home, giving them each back to their communities in return for the fleeting hope offered by this Pod. Celebrations were being set all over both Barryds, both desperate to get back to a semblance of normalcy, and to see the alien that had taken command of them back in her proper place as a guest. She wasn't bitter about it. It meant she'd have more freedom to do what she knew had to be done. Just less resources. She thought of her meeting with Rakal and wondered what the future would bring for them, now that he had taken such a separatist track for his Hive. Well, the Golden Hinde was her ship, and she'd have that for the Academy. And she'd trade with him to help him keep going until he came to his senses and choose a Dimar-based site for a Hive.

She listened north, toward Ekal. The deadly quiet meant that preparations of another kind were indeed underway. There might be a fight, if she couldn't convince them that her intentions for Dimar were honest.

Freia appeared in the doorway to the spire. "Leader, it's time to get ready." Freia was already in her best finery, with traditional Mulkol leader cuffs and long red, blue and black silks trailing from her spiked horns. She would take Mulkol from Tara first, over at the Mulkol transfer chamber. She was a good compromise as a Leader for Mulkol. Her friendship with Karti hadn't made her popular with the older Mulkol factions, but Tara knew she'd settle in. Freia understood and respected the ancient ways of the Mul, and always had, but she also understood the need for a new way of thinking.

Tara turned toward the door to follow Freia down to Tara's room. She saw no sign of Olitar, who normally guarded the pod when not performing her duties as first Acolyte. Olitar had outgrown her ability to tolerate the status quo of Mulkol life and had refused Tara's offer to be the new Matriarch of Mulkol. She wanted adventure-she wanted to learn and take to the stars. She was Academy bound.

Freia waited by the door, tail twitching with excitement as Tara changed. Toweling off the cool rainwater from the spire, she slipped out of her wet green pantsuit and wriggled into the black dress set out for her on the bed. She slipped the iron cuffs around her wrists and smiled as they clacked shut. This would be the last time she'd have to wear these brutally heavy bracelets! Flipping the horned headdress up onto her head, she buckled the chinstrap. A wave of her arms verified that her silks weren't tangled. Checking herself in the mirror, she smiled. She didn't feel like wearing a black dress today... she wished the traditional transfer color was Mulkol's red. This was going to be fun.

Matching Freia's huge strides was difficult, but together they marched out to the balcony to join the procession to Mulkol.

Telka's artisans had rigged a special umbrella-cover for Luuko's back to keep Tara as dry as possible, and even with the wind resistance, they made good time to the west spire of Mulkol. Tara could feel the anticipation radiating out of both Barryds-almost boosting the Wind.

The transfer of Mulkol to Freia went by in a blur, mostly due to the special pain-numbing drink they'd concocted for Tara to prevent the amount of injury and shock she'd received in the last unplanned transfer. Peacetime transfers were much easier than wartime, as all participants involved were willing and well prepared.

Emerging from the tangle of white tentacles on the dais, Tara could really tell just how much connection with Mulkol had affected her. Mulkol she saw seemed flat and lifeless, whereas the Telkans around the room observing the procedure seemed to glow warmly in her mind. Luuko was nearly neon as she smiled at him, leaning on his shoulder as the drink continued having its effects.

"Tara, how are you feeling?" he asked quietly as she giggled and tugged on his elbow fur.

"Drunk as a skunk, Luuko. I'm great!" She buried her face in his fur to keep from laughing too loudly. Mulkol around the room snorted in disapproval, but didn't comment. They understood what was wrong, and were just glad to have a Mulkol leader again. They would tolerate an inappropriate noise from someone who could have chosen to kill their Barryd completely.

Freia was still inside the mass of tentacles, joining with every branch of her home. Only the very tip of her tail-blade was visible through the mass of white anemone-like arms that writhed around her.

The movement on the dais slowed, and then one by one, the snakelike tendrils retracted.

She watched as Freia emerged from the tentacles, as they reluctantly released their hold on their new and rightful Matriarch. A cheer and a thunderous deep song rang out all through Mulkol–the transfer was successful and complete.

Tara could feel Luuko's unease right through his fur. In a detached drunken thought, she wondered if the Mulkol, now that they were free of her, wouldn't just kill her and the Telkans once and for all. She peeked out from behind Luuko's elbow at a dark red elder who had been watching from the back. As Freia descended the dais, the elder moved forward, brandishing a gray blade. Tara listened intently, but they were communicating on a private frequency.

Luuko reared back, keeping himself between Tara and the red Mulkol, roaring and hissing in defiance.

"Oopsie...there's definitely trouble! Shoulda transferred Mulkol...SECOND...I guess..." Tara stumbled out from behind Luuko, trying to reach the door. The other Telkans leapt toward her, blocking any Mulkol who tried to move on her. She toddled between them, leaning on one and then another. A roar behind her made her stop and turn.

"MULKOL KEEPS ITS PROMISES! The Telkans will not be harmed." Freia, like Tara had never seen her before, leapt forward, all fangs bared. Tara noticed through her fog that the crimson Mulkol was in the process of chewing off Luuko's side as he desperately tried to protect Tara from his sword. Luuko had shed most of his scaled protection for winter, and his shoulder skin fell away from him in a sheet of red.

Freia's jaws clamped around the crimson Mulkol's neck, right behind his head, snapping his spine audibly. He fell away from Luuko limply as she turned and faced each Mulkol in the room. "None of you may presume to speak for me. None of you may presume to act for me. I am MULKOL. Any dissenters will be treated in accordance with traditional law. Am I CLEAR?"

All Mulkol heads in the room bowed, but one gray in the back growled as she reluctantly lowered her head. Tara had always had trouble with that gray while she was Leader, but had tolerated her. Freia was not as forgiving. Without so much as a word of explanation, she flew forward, knocking the gray back. With ruthless efficiency, she slit the gray's belly lengthwise with the blade of her tail while biting through her neck. A final gurgling cry from the gray was the only noise in the room. Freia had made her point crystal clear to the other Mulkol.

Rising from her kill, Freia strode toward Luuko, who struggled to rise on his injured three legs. "Telka, you may leave in safety. I will accompany you personally." Pivoting so she was under his wing, she helped him toward the door. Noiselessly, a Mulkol healer glided to the doorway, pouring a lita of Water on Luuko, who only winced as the water did its painful work.

Tara was stunned into sobriety, and did her best to aid the process, holding the sheet of muscle and fur that had fallen away in place for Luuko. It was risky–her genetic information might confuse the Water, but she needed Luuko in one piece for the next transfer. He was supposed to take over Telka, to provide the Academy with a strong ally in the coming years, as well as to continue his mother's work.

His bleeding stopped as the strong military-strength water did its job. Tara chuckled, reaching out to him, *"You're one tough fuzz-lizard, Luuko."*

Luuko wiggled his ears feebly as they stopped to prepare for the flight that would take them back to Telka. He managed to stand, but knew not to even attempt to use his left foreleg. To save his strength, he quickly lowered himself back to the ground. Tara could feel his strength coming back as the skin sealed and the muscles began to rejoin.

"Tara... Tara... I won't be strong enough to take Telka," Luuko moaned to her through his receding pain as Freia herself prepared a sling from her honor silks to carry him out of the war Barryd spire. A Leader's body had to be in good condition to take a Barryd, or the injury and illness in the Leader's body might trigger weakness in parts of the Barryd. Tara felt unshielded relief emanate from Luuko in waves. It was not from the subsiding pain, but instead from having avoided becoming Telka's new Leader. He hadn't been ready for it after all.

Olitar glided out of another Mulkol hallway to join the group, roaring a singsong warning as she approached. In English, for security reasons, she reported: "There's a mass of Dimar forming at Ekal. Movement's been spotted all along the perimeters. I think every winged resident of the planet is involved judging from the trails left on the wind as far out as the Twin Continents. For non-Mul, those farmer-lizards can be pretty sneaky. There were no warnings of the traffic until now." She growled, pawing the ground with a foreleg.

Tara, grabbing the long mane on Karti's back, just shook her head and laughed. It was a desperate, wild laugh. She clambered aboard Karti's narrow shoulders.

"Still on that berry-wine they had you hopped up on, good Leader?" Mason was already in the air, hovering next to where the group would launch. It would be an interesting race back to Telka for the second transfer. That was certain.

"Olitar, you know what you have to do. Launch the pod. Hide it if you have to, and prevent it from rooting–just get it out of here. Take the volunteers, and take Luuko." She was emphatic on that point. The poor guy had been through too much. He deserved to chase the pod and live his one dream. "Mason, you go too. I'll catch up with you when the transfer's complete. I have my own promises to keep." Tara waved them off, knowing that this was possibly the last time she'd see them all. Looking back at Freia, she hid her anguish, "Are you ready for this?"

Olitar gently looped herself into Luuko's hastily constructed carry-sling and lifted him off the balcony.

Freia nodded grimly, the tatters of the ends of her silks waving like war banners behind her.

"Luuko cannot go! He has to be Telka..." Karti turned his head back, looking at Tara with alarm. Karti was the only other acolyte first for Telka, and he didn't hide the fact that he didn't want the Leadership position either, especially with a force massed on the border ready to try to destroy both Barryds. Every strike to the walls of the plant would be a strike to his own body, and Karti never had been much into athletics, let alone pain.

"Don't all volunteer at once." Tara crossed her arms with frustration racking her brains for someone to take the post. She was running out of first acolytes.

"You wimp!" Freia barked in English as she smacked Karti's hindquarters. The strike sent him, with Tara on his back, skittering off the ledge and into the air. Her ears were wiggling with amusement. They'd obviously been exchanging words on a private channel, but Tara didn't see the joke as she struggled to remain on Karti and avoid falling a quarter mile into the Barryd basement and to her premature death.

"Dammit, you two..!" Tara righted herself, as Karti apologetically turned his head back.

"I will take the Leadership of Telka. Chicks will dig me." Karti wiggled his ears as he spoke the words in his slightly stilted English.

"Well, I promoted you two because you never failed to find humor in a BAD situation. This is about as bad as it gets." She shrugged and laughed. "Let's get going. I've got a pain in my leg that says that our visitors are moving in." She rubbed her calf, which corresponded to the northernmost prefecture of Telka's territory.

Karti and Freia shot up the war Barryd spire so fast, Tara knew Freia must be using some Wind enhancement trick she hadn't learned in her time as Leader. She chuckled... "So much for teaching tricks at the Academy. Will have to have Freia visit and lecture." Her head rocked on her neck as they shot into clear, wet air and took an arching path toward Telka's easternmost spire. To the north, the sky was dark with the wings of massing Dimar.

Freia and Karti both gasped and looked back at her.

"We can take 'em," Tara laughed maniacally, wrapping her hands in Karti's long mane. As they passed into Telka territory, they slowed, lacking the augmented Wind. "Freia, use that trick!" She opened her mind to Freia, allowing her to take partial control of Telka. Angry wings of Telkans, sensing the invasion by a Mulkol, rose out of their homes, but stopped midair to watch as the shadow to the north grew.

The pain in her leg had reached her knee. The force was moving in quickly. She gave a Barryd-wide order to run and not resist, but the force might be slaughtering them as it moved ahead. Telkans below her scattered, flying headlong toward the sea. They would take Telka first, and then Mulkol, she suspected.

Tara got a glimpse of the billowing golden sail, as the ungainly seedpod for the Academy launched itself during their approach. A raggedy group of Mulkol and Telkans streamed out behind it, guiding it as best they could. The onrush of the shadow was making movement above the treetop level difficult, especially for the delicate seed-wing, designed for flight only in the best circumstances.

She clamped her legs around Karti's neck as he dove wildly for the spire. Rocketing down the spire, they looped upside down and flew into the Hallway to the transfer room. Karti slammed directly into the mass of waiting tentacles. Tara leapt from his back. Landing on her feet, her right leg gave way completely with a vicious cramping pain. Frantic, she broadcast the command to flee Telka to everyone still left in the main city. The cacophony of panicked cries that rang through her mind as the swarm moved in stunned her, and she grabbed her ears. Freia grabbed her by her dress and flung her headlong into the tentacles, careful not to contact them herself and disrupt the transfer.

The spire shook as the transfer took place. Winds from the north lashed the Barryd. Pain raced through her body as the tentacles linked with every nerve she had. The tentacles felt like ice at first as they slithered along her skin seeking their corresponding nerve ending. When they linked with her, they sent waves of fire through her spine. As tendrils slithered up her dress and into her sleeves, digging into her skin, she cursed. Being asleep for this was much easier. She shut her eyes as the tentacles dug into her neck and her face, and finally her eyes. She screamed and nearly blanked out as the final tendrils took root, but once the link was complete, she could see with the eyes of the Barryd again. Adrenaline pumped through her as she half-felt, half saw the furious swarm of Dimar in her mind. She reached out to Karti, who was also linked, sensing his thoughts mingling with hers, and that of the panicked Barryd.

"It feels like they're simply crushing Telka as they fly over it. I don't feel individuals fighting...just a crushing pain." Tara winced as she felt Karti take up the pain in his right hind leg. The transfer was not going to be pleasant for him. They had to find a way to stop the wall before it reached the heart of the city and crushed them all to death. When the Barryd died, Karti died. Tara felt like a coward, giving up the ship to a subordinate when she should be going down with it herself.

"I can handle it, Leader Tara." Karti reassured her, "This is not your responsibility. You must protect us all, even if Telka falls."

She probed him...he knew about the Academy, the scoundrel!

"Of course I know. How do you hide a pod from an Acolyte

First? We don't get to these positions of power by just cracking jokes and sitting on our hindquarters you know." She could hear him laughing through their mind-link. Tentacles began to retract from her. She could feel the pain in her leg recede, along with her augmented Psi abilities. Karti grunted a muffled grunt through the tentacles as the pain reached their hips.

Desperate to stop the onslaught, she called out to Kiralla, using all the power the Barryd would allow her in transfer.

"Kiralla! The Pride... Please have Rakal send a pilot to provide a distraction! Please...can you hear me? Don't let Rakal fly it...he can't risk himself." She couldn't sense Kiralla's reaction or emotions, but did get a curt reply.

"He will fly it. You want the Pride to chase the Dimar out of Telka territory?" Kiralla answered in a flat monotone that got weaker as more and more of the barryd reverted to Karti's control.

Tara felt him boost her transmission, and managed one last instruction before she lost contact completely "If not out of the Territory completely, then keep them to the outlying areas. The twin spires of Telka's main city must stay up."

No answer. The link was lost. Tara felt the pain in her hip subside completely, and could hear Karti whimper through the muffling tentacles.

She jumped off the Dais and threw a cushion from the spectators' area of the transfer room across Freia's scaly back, lashing it in place with a strip of tapestry from a wall hanging. "She'll send Rakal to pilot the Pride, but I've got to be the one. He can't risk himself!"

She carefully grabbed some of the long black mane that tufted out from under Freia's spine-covering, and held on as best she could. She was already covered in lacerations from the hasty transfer, and didn't want to gain a new set of injuries from Freia's rough combat scales. Together, they bolted from the room, Freia's long gallop was smooth enough that she managed to hang on with only minimal cuts to her hands.

They screamed up through masses of fleeing Telkans, and felt a boost of wind rocket them into the clear air-a gift from Karti.

Tara looked out north, and could no longer feel what was going on out there. She could see the Pride screaming in, glowing with heat as it's plasma weaponry armed and the atmosphere resisted its speed. The sonic boom hit them, knocking Freia backward momentarily. And then another, and another. In the dimness of the twilight, Tara could see Rakal dropping in and out of the speed of sound, buffeting them with recoil shocks.

"Genius!" She screamed as the wind raced by her. Freia continued on, not hearing.

Like a swarm of bees after a firefly, she watched the blackened mass turn to follow the Pride.

"If they catch him, he's dead. I don't know how we'll reach him, Tara!" Karti's voice sounded in her mind. "We have to distract them from him."

Tara could feel the fury of the swarm even with her weakened psi abilities. If they caught that ship, there wouldn't be anything left to recover, and these Dimar dragons had proven them more resourceful in combat than Tara could have ever imagined.

He watched him turn the swarm west, inland, instead of choosing the easier route north. Tara knew he was protecting the Pod. Kiralla must be coordinating his efforts from orbit. They approached the swarm, followed by a defensive swarm of Mulkol death machines, which had emerged the moment they realized their new Leader was risking herself at the front lines.

"Freia, can you control your people? Can we reach the Leaders of the swarm?" Tara reached out to the distracted Leader, who was working to channel the open fury of Mulkol warriors as the west-moving swarm crossed the line between the two Barryd territories.

"It will be hard, but yes. They will not attack...they will only hold their lines." We have to reach the instigators. Ekal will ally with us. Find the green one and orange silks. We have to find their Leader. Telka will help." Freia's voice was strong in Tara's mind, bolstered by the group will of the Mulkol as they fell into rank behind a rightful Leader. Freia hissed as a young warrior broke ranks and rushed headlong into the first line of Dimar. He was instantly crushed by the force of their approach, and fell to the ground like a broken twig.

Tara could hear Freia's commands ringing out; she was using the warrior's fall as an example. "We have to stand together. You must stay in your rank, or you'll be crushed!" The machines lined up and meshed, generating their own wall of force, and the writhing mass of furious furry Dimar stopped. The Pride faltered as it passed over the line, and Tara gasped. The Wind from this many agitated Dimar would disrupt its lift generators! If he remained over them, he'd fall straight into them.

Freia passed over the mass, as thousands of angry Dimar eyes looked up. The fear from the Mulkol lines was palpable. The heart of their city was a few hundred feet from a thousand individuals, each who would gladly die to take her life. She roared out for the Leaders of the mob to show themselves so that they could talk.

In the center of the swarm, figures swathed in silk rose up. Tara looked over her shoulder to see how the Pride was faring, and was relieved to see it rocketing toward an orbital path well out of harms way, back toward Kiralla and the orbiting ships where it, and Rakal, belonged.

"I have sent our thanks to the Starborn Hive, Tara. Now, let's see how we do against the Leaders." Freia showed no fear as she approached, even though her own forces were nearly a mile away at this point. Tara couldn't help but ask.

"Nervous?"

"If they even do so much as raise a breeze against me, there will be no controlling my forces. Mulkol will be dead, and with it, any reason for its residents to live except revenge." Freia sounded like a conquering warrior coming to accept their surrender.

"Frankly, I think they can take you, Mulkol." Tara cautioned her to be a little less proud and a little more cautious. Having all of Mulkol's pride and fear running through her was probably doing strange things to Freia's judgment at this point. "Never underestimate the fuzzy farmers." She pointed out all the defensive weaknesses she had found with Mulkol in her time there, and compared them to the strength of the current force on their doorstep.

Freia acquiesced, and took a more communicative tone in her

calls as they approached the knot of leaders, choosing a place closest to the brilliant green Ekal leader, in his green and orange silks. A large white Dimar with brown marbled patches came forward, wearing silks festooned with tiny platinum circlets. Even in the dim light of the oncoming night, his white coat was easy to see. He was the Leader, Tara knew not only from his decoration, but from the way the other Leaders deferred to him. His mental accent showed that he was from the far northern island, near the Pole.

"We have come to restore order in these territories, Leader Mulkol." He announced as a chorus of approving songs rang through the mass below them.

"Order is restored, Leader Elakolul. Telka belongs again to the Telkan. Mulkol belongs to the Mulkol, and the Colonists, as agreed, have taken to the Arts themselves as children of the Waters." Freia's tone was flat in Tara's mind; she had her shields up completely.

"And why should we not raze your homes, now that you have the secrets of a fine Tel Barryd, like Telka." Elakolul's voice was tinged with curiosity, which gave Tara hope.

A voice behind them brought the Leaders forward, but they were careful to stay well out of Freia's tail range. "Because they will not use our secrets against us, the Tel, the Ela, the Barryds of peaceful arts." Karti had arrived, still a little shaky from taking on the Barryd. His right hind leg hung down limply, slowing his flight speed. He took a position among the invading Barryd leaders, not next to Freia and Tara, to emphasize his bond with them and their ways. "We have their secrets now, Leaders. It is time for the secrets to end and for all of us to take up a new Cause to save our Dimar."

"Yes. You all have lived in fear of the Starborn instead of taking arms against them. This foolishness will lead to our joint demise!" Freia's scathing tone was meant to bolster Karti's introduction to the Academy idea, but caused the swarm below to change from singing approving tunes to roaring in fury.

Karti flew forward, putting himself between Freia and the furious Elakolul Leader, who was growling audibly. Karti bapped Freia's nose with his paw. "As usual, I should do the talking."

Freia reared up in shock at Karti's disrespectful strike. Tara desperately grabbed at her thin mane to stay onboard, suffering more cuts to her hands on the serrated edges of her scales. Tara screamed out, "He's kidding Freia! He's kidding!" but she had already gotten the joke and her ears were wiggling. She nodded to him and deferred her position as speaker.

The Leaders watched, immediately suspicious of two Leaders that were this friendly with each other, but they did listen.

Karti outlined the Academy plans in great detail, using the stored knowledge hidden in corners all over Telka to clarify where the Leadership was unsure. Tara was glad she hadn't had time to clear the planning banks before she reverted control to a Telkan. Karti was a brilliant statesman, and armed with the plans, he was slowly bringing them around to see her idea.

They agreed that Dimar had been spared a worse fate by the colonists, who had never intended to make a War machine. With some convincing to overcome the ancient taboo against Starfaring, they did agree that it was fine and good for the Colonists to make a defense for their combined home, but Mulkol must not be involved.

"Not involved in the defense of the planet!? What kind of morrak refuse is this? For centuries, we've been defending against the worst both war and non-war Barryds could devise, and now this?" Freia was furious, and turned back to Tara for some sympathy as she was her only warrior companion in this discussion.

Tara just pointed down to remind Freia of their current predicament, as the mass of angry Dimar slowly rose toward them.

Freia quieted, but all eyes were still on Tara. She cleared her throat and began, "I propose, good Leaders, that a Mulkol must never hold Leadership of this new Academy Barryd. However, their skills as pilots and fighters are needed. We need the best Dimar can provide, and the Mulkai would be ineffective as farmers, Telkai, artisans and guilders, or for any other purpose." Tara racked her brains, trying to find a way to reassure them that destroying Mulkol, or locking them and the other Mulkai Barryds out of the program. She chattered on, listing all the things Mulkol weren't good for as she searched for an Earth corollary or solution.

Freia interrupted, "Well, you don't have to be that detailed about it, good Tara. We are good for something, you know!" The big Mulkol snorted, looking back at the tiny charge on her shoulders. Her ears wiggled slightly, and the other Leaders suppressed their amusement.

Tara decided on a compromise, and offered, "The Mulkai may never have Leadership of the Academy–only Mulkai Barryds and Barryd townships." She wondered how Olitar would handle this news. She'd been guarding the pod with the expectation of being the new Barryd Leader of the Academy. She shook the thought from her mind and continued on, as she sensed her audience liked this idea very much. "However, in return, you all need to agree to fortify your residences more. Just a bit. Mulkai may be sent to serve as consultants for this purpose, and in payment, you must agree to trade knowledge of other Arts with them if asked. Academy Barryd seeds may serve as strong additions to your existing plants, giving a living space that can accept both Mulkai and others as members. They can form a living web of protection around all Barryds, which will be protectorates of higher study of their chosen arts." Tara reached out, sharing images of ways Academy seeds could be integrated to provide war-shelters and defensive fortifications. She tried to remember a simulation she'd run of an Earth attack on a fortified Ela Barryd-one of the most spread out and weakest in design, but couldn't remember all the details. Karti chimed in, taking over displaying the files for her.

"Mulkai would serve us in these Academy Barryds? Preposterous. They will just overrun us." One of the southern islands Trade Barryd Dimar moved toward Freia, growling. Others hovered over to his side in agreement.

Freia answered his challenge in a quiet voice. "That would not serve our purpose. For centuries, we've been losing territory because our artisans and farmers have no skill. We need to be supported by those who practice other arts so we can continue to survive. But, you need us as well. We wish to pursue our arts, and as the arrival of Tara and her kind proves, we are needed by planet Dimar as much as the

Plan is." Freia drifted forward into the center. "If you do not believe me, then you can scan me."

There was silence. Tara wondered if the Dimar were ready to know the secret history of the Mul. She also wondered if Freia wouldn't drop out of the sky like a rock, with Tara on her back, if they scanned her now.

"Scan me first. It will help you understand better." Tara offered. "I have seen both Tel and Mul, and I come from a world where there is very little separation between the Arts. And, I'm expendable."

Tara knew from her time in the Barryds that if even one of the Leaders who scanned her decided to, they could leave her mad or dead. They could leave suggestions, ways to control her. Letting Freia, no matter how strong her mind was, risk that with all of Mulkol's power at stake was too much.

Karti nodded. "I will oversee, to make sure none of you try anything. However, there must be preparation. This is not the place for this procedure." He nodded back toward Ekal. "Do we agree that Ekal is a neutral site and will make the appropriate setting for this?"

"Agreed. Ekal, do you agree to this?" Elakolul turned toward the stunned face of the smaller green leader.

"I would be honored!" He dipped his head.

"We shall disperse, but we will keep Tara as collateral. She will be scanned first, and then you Mulkoli." Elakolul grabbed Tara off her back with both paws.

"Wait, Elakolul. If we are going to offer up an active Leader of one Barryd, and a former Leader of two...three Leaders must also agree to be scanned." Karti interjected. "An Ela, a Mir and a Olu."

There was a long pause, but finally, the ringleader bowed his head. "Agreed. I will serve as the Ela. I could not ask of you if I was not willing to undergo it myself."

The leaders of Mirkal, an animal breeding barryd and Olunali Barryd, an arts barryd, agreed to scans, sealing the bargain.

"Agreed," Karti nodded in final agreement. "Now, get all these Dimar off my foot." He pointed down at his limp leg, chuckling. The leaders laughed, and called for the swarm to disperse with singsong cries.

Groups of Dimar broke off from the huge mass as it slowly dissipated. Many had days of travel ahead to return to their home Barryds, and all had stories to tell.

Tara looked down, preferring to sit astride a Dimar rather than be carried in their paws. Elakolul raced along the treetops, but was careful not to let his paws drift too low to the trees, which might injure his charge. The ground beneath where the swarm had been was crushed flat, but only the animal life and some trees seemed to have suffered. As soon as the force of the crowd was off them, many plants sprang back to provide cover for those animals that would soon return.

As the longhaired Dimar cruised in toward Ekal to the north, they flew over some of the worst damaged parts of Telka. Dead morraks, and even a horse, were being quickly recycled by the various scavengers of Dimar. Tara was glad to see that the horse wasn't Tzarina. The predators of Dimar may have made short work of the herd, but Tara still had hope of one day finding her horse. She promised herself she'd go for a ride again, if she survived the scan.

As if the Leader had been listening, he gently lifted her up with one paw and placed her on his back. "My apologies for the rough handling, Lady Tara."

"Thank you. It's nice to have something solid between myself and the ground." She winked, careful not to show any teeth as she smiled. His ears wiggled with amusement.

Tara was glad to be with at least one Leader with a sense of humor. Even with their shielding and her weak Psi, she could hear the arguing between other Leaders near them as they flew into the tiny single Ekal spire.

"Why are no E barryds, like Ekal, submitting for the scan?" Tara asked. She half knew the answer, but figured she should make some pleasant conversation.

"Before a Barryd chooses its art, it has the designation of E. Ekal is too young to have chosen one art, although they seem to heavily favor both Ela and Tel, Farming and Engineering. It will be interesting to see if they choose Ela. The Leader of Ekal is a most amenable fellow, not unlike yourself." The Elakolul Leader kept one eye on Tara, and one eye on where he was going.

Tara patted him on the neck, smiling at the compliment.

Their conversation was cut short by their arrival at their designated rooms. Residents of the upper levels of Ekal had offered their living space at the tiny Ekal Barryd to the Leaders for the time, to allow the Leaders more privacy and a proximity to the spire chamber where the scans would take place. The greeting songs echoed up the Spire, soothing Tara's nerves.

She was rooming with the large brown and white Elakolul, probably to make sure she didn't slip away in the night, but she didn't mind. Trust would be a long time in coming. She gave the Elakolul a little privacy by exploring the other rooms of the apartment, taking advantage of a Lita of Water they had left in one of the grooming chambers to repair her lacerated skin. She'd need to be in one piece to survive 30-odd Leader minds scanning her.

As the liquid did it's painful work, she enjoyed the apartment's finery. Paintings from as far as the Archipelago and statuary cut from solid stone decorated each room, leading Tara to assume that they were in a first acolyte's chambers, if not, possibly the chambers of Ekal himself. She could hear her roommate, perhaps warden was more appropriate, rustling about in the sleeping chamber, but didn't disturb him. She knew how hard it was being away from a Barryd when you were linked to it.

She slipped into the sleeping room and hopped into her hastily prepared cot. She could hear the big white and brown Dimar already snoring. She chuckled. The noise was soothing in a way. It quickly lulled her to sleep.

Chapter 31

Luuko shook himself out of the groggy stupor he had flown in all night. He was glad to see dawn breaking on the horizon. Riding in the sling carried by Olitar, even bolstered by the lift of his good wing, was uncomfortable. With light coming, they'd have to store the pod and rest a while, which might give him a chance to check his knitting shoulder. He heard Olitar bark commands out to the few Telkans and Mulkol guiding and encouraging the pod. He couldn't see the giant egg-like seed case or the golden winged parachute that billowed above it, but he could feel it. The attendants had been Watering it and singing to it as they drifted along.

"Keep it low to the treetops...we can't afford to be spotted. Lower! LOWER! You can do this!" Olitar was overseeing the guiding of the pod personally, but carrying Luuko was making it difficult for her to remain close. She, new to Pod launching herself, had to rely on a few young Telkans and rowdy Mulkol. To her credit, she wasn't rude to the Telkans, just efficient to a fault.

He shifted his weight in the sling, trying to give his good wing a little more area and slightly more lift. Olitar peered down to check on him, but didn't seem disturbed by his movement. She seemed as solid on the Wind as he was when he was healthy.

"How are you faring, Luuko? Can you handle a ridge landing?" Olitar tried to pry a bit into his mental condition to assess his injury, but Luuko blocked.

"If you need to, release me and I can glide down and reach

you on my own. The pod is what matters." Luuko answered flatly, shielding the fact that his shoulder had ached so badly that night that he had trouble staying conscious. The damage did extend to his wing flexors on the right side. He'd need more Water within the week to avoid a possible deadly infection or a mis-knitting, but he'd strike out on his own to find it. The Pod would need all the Water they'd brought with them to root successfully, especially if Tara and Telka had fallen to the angry swarm they had seen yesterday.

Luuko gathered his strength and reached out to Telka, and felt it, although significantly different from before. Tara was not there. Tara wasn't anywhere. Luuko thrashed his head from side to side trying to vent his fear without making noise that might call attention to the pod.

Olitar blocked his linking with Telka. "We're not supposed to make contact with anyone. Too risky. They'd be able to trace the Wind to the pod." She dropped her link with him to work with the pod, leaving Luuko to sulk at the rebuff.

With careful timing, they guided the pod in between two trees tall enough to prevent the casing from touching soil. The parachute tore along the front edge as a branch punctured it, and Olitar audibly swore. Luuko couldn't tell in the dim light of the morning how bad the damage was, but could feel that the pod still had quite a bit of lift it could generate. Swaying in-between the trees, the pod was eerily backlit by the rays of the rising sun. Luuko finally felt some hope. It was a beautiful pod, swirled green with gray, and even larger than Ekal's. It was eager to root–he could feel it growing, sensing the proximity to the ground.

Olitar hovered down, allowing him to touch down on three legs. She untied the sling, and it drifted down in billowy piles to either side of him. Shaky, Luuko lowered himself to the ground and nervously reached one of the other Telkans in the group. To his relief, it was Genar, the talented young student.

"Are we close enough to the ridge to allow the pod to use the valley for drop-lift, Genar?" Luuko couldn't see that far out in the dim light, but could hear her rustling around near the edge.

"Yes! There's both a normal wind and plenty of Wind coming up this ridge for it to lift tomorrow night. Olitar did a good job." Genar quietly returned, settling in next to Luuko's good side to help keep him warm.

"You did a good job. Olitar only barked out directions." Luuko snorted bitterly. He was resenting the Mulkol. Tara was gone, along with his ability to take Telka Leadership, all thanks to the Mulkol.

"No, Olitar cares. She'll see this project through even if she dies doing it. You should be kinder to her." Genar struck his neck with her nose in admonishment. "And, you talk in your sleep."

Luuko peered at her in the gathering light. "What does that mean, I talk in my sleep?" He hissed.

"You figure it out, morrak." Genar wiggled her ears and settled down to nap. Luuko wouldn't get much more out of her today. He tried to remember his dreams, but couldn't. Embarrassment washed over him; he wondered what he'd said. With the burning ache in his shoulder relieved somewhat from the rest, he settled down to sleep uneasily.

It seemed like only minutes had passed, but when he opened his eyes, light filtered down straight to the forest floor where they slept. Noises from behind him-brusque human voices, set his nerves on edge. Olitar was already awake, trembling with anticipation of the angry visitors. Her tail lashed side to side, and she licked her chops. "We were warned about some renegade people who'd settled this area. I didn't realize we had landed this close." Olitar padded silently into the woods as Luuko struggled to rise. His shoulder was considerably better-He could put his foreleg to the ground again and it would take some weight.

He padded after Olitar, snapping twigs as he went. He nearly roared a challenge as she poked her head out from behind a bush.

"Go back to the seed pod, Luuko. You need to be with it to guard it. I can handle this. I've scouted the area and I have a plan to lure these hunters off. They're only looking for food, I suspect." Olitar carefully nudged him back toward the camp.

"They're colonists. Promise me you won't kill them or eat them.

They're Tara's children, even if they've strayed!" Luuko growled at her, snapping his jaws in warning.

Olitar only laughed. "I'll only eat the babies. I'll hang up the adults on spikes, and make them watch me eat the babies feet first."

Luuko reared back, hissing. "No! No! No!"

"Luuko...is that what you really think of us Mulkol?" She shook her head, clucking. "Those people, mindless though they are, are hunters and warriors like me. I will enjoy their company over you fluffy Telkans. I will not kill them unless they threaten the pod." She snorted derisively and disappeared noiselessly into the dark forest understory.

Luuko didn't follow, but did climb up the tree, half hovering, half grappling with his strong legs and wing. He could see into the clearings from his vantage point while also surveying the damage to the pod-sail. A Mulkol attendant sprinkled the patched sail with Water. It was mostly mended but the thickened healing area would not generate as much lift. Luuko would need to try to fly today to allow Olitar's brute strength help the pod make up for the damage.

Movement caught his eye in a field. It was Olitar, about a half mile off, roaring and bugling. Somewhere, she had grabbed a tolu, a woodland leaf-eater, and had it pinned and bawling under one hindfoot. She was dragging her wing–it was twisted in an awkward position and looked damaged!

Luuko thought a moment about the humans and their rifles, and about Olitar... Should I send out the Mulkol with the Water to help her, or perhaps let the humans..? Slamming his head full against a tree, he couldn't believe what he was thinking! Of COURSE he should send out help. His antics got the attention of the Mulkol Watering the sail.

"Get out to Olitar, quickly! She's over there, in the field. She's hurt!" Luuko threw his head in the direction of Olitar's guttural cries.

The Mulkol swept up next to him, and screamed off down into the forest, straight toward Olitar. Humans emerged from the woods just as he broke into the air over Olitar, roaring a warning to the tiny mindless ones to stay back. The young Mulkol hadn't learned English, but his roars kept humans at a good distance.

Olitar swore, and broadcast something to the protective male hovering above her, trying to Water her wing. He sealed the Lita and flung it into the woods, and dropped into the field next to her. The bawling of the tolu mixed with the Mulkol's threatening cries. Luuko blinked. The Mulkol was growling at Olitar!

Slashing with her tail, she nearly struck the young male in the chest. He slumped, and fluttered away, sending the humans on the far side of the field running back into the woods. Luuko could see from his vantage point that the lad was unhurt, but he flew off with faltering half-wingbeats away from both the field and the pod, crashing into the forest some distance beyond.

"Olitar...Olitar...what the heck is going on?" Luuko reached out to her.

"Shhh! One of the no-minds has a spark...a tiny bit of psi. Use a covered channel." Olitar silenced him on a private bandwidth.

By this time, Genar and the others were scattered throughout the tree, watching with him in silence.

The humans emerged from the woods, brandishing their sidearms. Luuko knew that Olitar had no armor that could protect against the lava guns the humans used.

She hissed, slitting the throat of the unfortunate tolu. It's cries stopped. She picked at its throat, nipping off a bit of meat, pretending to ignore the humans. Three of them started to yell, waving his arms and walking toward her and one fired his gun into the air.

Olitar's scaly head whipped around, with an expression of shock. She bolted into the forest, half flying with the twisted wing. She moved off away from the field and the pod, off into the woods, crashing through the underbrush. With a sickening cry, the crashing stopped, and Luuko could hear no more.

Cheers went up from the three men in the field as they dragged off the dead animal. They patted each other on the back, making congratulatory noises Luuko couldn't hear from that distance.

The mood on the tree was frantic. Mulkol wanted to sweep down and crush the humans...the Telkans wanted to find their two missing party members and get on the move. Fighting broke out on shielded bandwidths between the two factions in the group.

Luuko just sank quietly into his branch, wondering what would become of the tiny pod, so eager to grow. This was supposed to be a joyous time full of hope and unity. This was not how he'd dreamed this day, he growled bitterly.

A tug on his tail got his attention, and he slowly turned his head down toward the forest floor where he had been sleeping. Olitar grinned up at him.

"Olitar! You're fine! Kalil! You're back too...what in seven spires was going on!?" Luuko couldn't believe his eyes. Olitar was sitting there, smugly watching the fighting crowd, now stunned silent. She wrapped her tail around her feet and rumbled with amusement.

"All I did was give the humans more excitement for one day than they could handle, plus a free meal. I'm hoping that once they've found their food, they won't have a reason to venture out this way again. I didn't want them choosing to explore around here, so Kalil and I pretended to die off the woods on the other side of the clearing. The humans will search over there for our carcasses to scavenge, and not here." Olitar arched her neck proudly and preened. She WAS clever. Luuko quietly vowed to himself that yes, indeed, he would keep a close eye on her.

"Humans don't eat Dimar, but you're right. That was a good ploy." Luuko clambered carefully down from his branch to rest on the warm soddy ground.

"Those humans would, if they got the chance. They really hate us 'invaders' from what I could hear." Olitar's scaly brow furrowed. "They crash on our home, and we're the invaders." She shrugged, and peered up at the pod.

"I wish there was a way we could shield the pod. It's singing its growth song more loudly now that it's near the soil. I could hear it from the field." She strode up underneath the swaying pod, nuzzling it lovingly. "It's got a nice quiet song, though. An inexperienced

Talent would mistake it for background noise from neighboring Barryds." Olitar dropped down on all fours and silently disappeared back into the forest to hunt. "We'll have fresh meat in an hour or two. Forage for now."

Luuko settled on the ground, nibbling some of the succulent plants that grew at the base of the trees to stave off his growing hunger. Genar continued her light napping with the other travelers, each taking shifts watering and singing to the impatient pod. Kalil, the young Mulkol male, settled in trees above the pod, unable to sleep from the excitement of his encounter with colonists. Luuko drifted off to sleep again before the pain in his shoulder could return in full.

A nudge on his shoulder awakened Luuko. "We've got company again." Mason was standing over him, listening. The others were already preparing the pod for the valley launch.

Familiar furry faces emerged from the woods, waving in a friendly manner. Luuko knew them from Telka–they were former Telkan residents now living at Keinsa Hive, not far from here. There was a mind among them, who reached out to him and Mason.

"You chose a dangerous spot to land in, friends. I'm Jasser, and this is Yira and Ellinara." The white and orange Arrallakeeni motioned to his friends. He turned to view the pod, now tinged with a golden glow from the setting sunlight. Luuko approved of the little Keeni. He could feel the reverence Jasser held for the pod. Jasser turned back, offering a warning. "Those three men you ran into are rotten to the core. They've been attacking our hunting parties, robbing us of our kills. Parasites. Very anti-anything that isn't human. You're practically on top of their valley camp."

Mason nodded, "I know one of them. He's not that bad, but he's impressionable, and he probably saw the gate close. He didn't know he wouldn't be going home from this trip." Luuko felt a pang of guilt ring through Mason's thoughts.

"Worse yet, they've got two females with them who are just as bad. They'll breed soon." The Arrallakeeni regarded his sidearm and growled.

"Why haven't you taken them out of the picture?" Mason made a slicing motion across his own neck, grinning slyly.

The Arrallakeeni blinked up at him, stunned. "Yeah, and weaken the human breeding population even further? I'd rather be living next to smart, mean humans than stupid, hairless toothless humans." He winked at Mason, who chuckled. "Next fire season, I have a feeling our human friends will warm up to the idea of getting 'alien' help. They haven't killed anyone yet. When they do, I'll take this conversation as active approval of any operation we undertake to rid our Hive region of their influence." Jasser bowed formally.

Mason deferred, "Better run it by Tara if you want an official call on that. We're going to be your northern neighbors quite soon. There will be plenty of chances to get together to discuss the less savory human element in these parts."

Luuko wondered if Mason honestly thought Tara was still with them. He detached himself from the conversation and tended to the pod to distract himself. His shoulder felt even better than before, with only a twinge of weakness. Genar smiled at him, as he experimentally pinned back a branch with his right foreleg.

"Almost as good as new!" Luuko wiggled his ears and whuffled pleasantly.

Genar nodded, continuing her own work to clear a path off the ridge for the pod. She was hiding something, but Luuko couldn't sense what it was.

Jasser and his companions watched from the ground as they launched for the final leg of their journey. He took up the launch song with the Dimar in attendance as the golden wing billowed with lift. The pod swayed back and forth gently, slowly rising through the trees and along the path they'd cut for it. Catching the rising air from the Valley wall, it lifted high, banking northward to remain along the ridge, taking advantage of its lift.

Inspired, Luuko spread both his wings, excited to find that the injured ligaments had almost fully knitted. His wing was going to be fine after all!

"That's some powerful Mulkai Water you have, Olitar. I'm

almost completely healed!" Luuko rose up next to her as she guided the pod along the ridge wind. He did a celebratory barrel roll to test his newfound strength.

Distracted, she nodded and gave him a friendly look. Luuko almost forgot his grudge against her as he took his position behind the floating pod and used his Wind generators to aid the package on its way to the bay in the north.

Chapter 32

Tara strode into the room ignoring the butterflies that were currently tickling her stomach. The piercing gaze of three dozen leaders and acolytes brought her hackles up. This wasn't going to be easy.

She took a seat, resting her back against a pillar situated in the middle of the vast spire chamber. Elakolul strode in after her, and looked down at her with a warm, friendly expression. With almost parental care, he wrapped her and the column in a silken blanket that would hold her upright if she slumped during the scan.

Holding out a crystal cup between two long, clawed fingers, Elakolul reassured her while instructing the crowd. "Each Leader will scan Lady Tara one at a time, overseen by me personally." He looked around the room sternly. "If you leave a suggestion, I will attack you, and you will then remove it. If you disrupt her normal functions in any way, I will kill you." Tara's hands were pinned to her sides by the silk blanket, so she carefully grabbed the lip of the cup of berry-wine with her mouth. She was careful not to spill any-she'd need all the protection the drug could provide.

Elakolul's dissertation of the rules droned on in her mind as the wine did its work. The stained glass ceiling of the room swirled like a kaleidoscope. Brilliant images of flying Dimar, lit by the dim gray light of the rainy season sky, swirled around her set in an opal sky. She smiled, and drifted off to sleep with the image of a snow white Dimar with a curious look figuring prominently in her dreams.

She awoke, blinking back against the all over ache that throbbed in every joint in her body. An acolyte was pouring Water over her carefully. Noises of discussions on private bandwidths reverberated through the room, but she couldn't catch anything of what was said.

Elakolul leaned over her, whuffling. "The scans are over. You may have your Academy."

She scanned the room, looking to see if anyone had tried anything that would have resulted in their deaths, but all the Leaders she could remember were there and talking in excited voices. Still aching, she managed to sit up.

"You have come a long way and achieved much in your life, Lady Tara." Freia strode up to her and bowed. "But your greatest achievements, I suspect, are yet to come."

"Amazing for one who, I hesitate to even speak the words aloud," Elakolul looked down sternly, "Failed Home Ec in the fifth grade of her Arts studies!" He shook his head in mock disappointment, ears twitching with amusement. Freia giggled a Dimar giggle, sneezing.

Tara laughed. "I knew that would haunt me for the rest of my life. My great failure. Home Economics." The aching in her head and shoulders dissipated as the Water dried from her clothes. "The Pod? Any news?" She looked for Karti, who would have best contact with the secretive Pod crew through his plant connections to the territory.

"It still flies and sings. However, Olitar and the others have been careful not to contact us. Many of the Leaders here need to return to their Barryds along the path you had chosen. We would be honored if we could take you to the Pod, and oversee its first roots." Elakolul helped her up, and placed her between his broad, marbled shoulders with the wine-stained silk blanket from her scan. Together, Freia, Karti and Elakolul marched out onto the room's prodigious balcony, singing a parting song. Tara realized just how late it was. The room behind them had been lit as bright as daylight by tiny pinpoints of blue and gold flames from the branch chandeliers. Outside it was dark, with a hint of light on the horizon signaling dawn.

Silks of every color fluttered on the breeze as the various

Leaders rose into the air around them. Some broke off to the south, others west, eager to return to their home cities. Despite the fatigue of being separated from their people, the majority joined in a V formation pointed northwest, toward the Pod.

Tara huddled in her wrap as the wet cold air soaked her. They flew forward at amazing speed, with Karti in the lead, bolstering them with barryd-augmented Wind.

Tawny bands of light streaked the sky as the sun through the heavy mist that marked what would be a light day in the raining season. In the distance, Tara spotted the shimmering pod-wing, glittering like a sheet of gold lace above the pod itself. The pod's green colors had deepened on the journey as it prepared to set down its first roots. Around her, the Leaders broke into a song she wasn't familiar with. A deep memory in her, a residual gift from her time at Telka and Mulkol, awakened, and she knew that this was a most ancient Barryd song reserved for only the most special occasions.

The nine pod attendants were visible as they moved in behind the drifting seed. Luuko and Olitar had the lead, oblivious to them as they guided the pod toward the clearing near the sea. Wind from the wings of so many Leaders caused the pod to drift upward, catching Olitar's attention first and drawing her out of her Pod guiding reverie.

She turned, and her surprise was audible. She broke from the guide group, flaring her wings defiantly, roaring out defensive challenges to anyone who might try to take the Pod. The Leaders just continued their songs, keeping a respectful distance from the Pod's guides.

Tara waved to her, "Olitar. We have approval! They are here to help the pod reach its rooting place."

"They're not going to tear us, and the pod, to shreds?" She dipped in the air as relief flooded through her. "Luuko will be very pleased to see you! He's a bit pre-occupied right now, encouraging the seed. I hope you understand."

"I do. I have some troubling news for you, though." Tara smiled as Olitar answered, hiding her trepidation at how the big gray might react to losing her Pod.

Olitar glided up next to her and Elakolul, who respectfully dipped his head and avoided listening to their exchange.

"You cannot take Leadership of the Pod. It has to be a non-Mulkol from now until the end of Academy days." Tara made it clear that there wasn't a discussion available in this.

Olitar sagged on her wings. "I was debating the position myself. There is one who wants it more than I. He's with it now." Olitar broadcast images of the pained Luuko, asleep on the ground, writhing and moaning with dreams of the pod. "In any case, as Leader, I would not be able to take to the Stars. I'd be stuck on the ground. There's no limit on us bonding with a ship, is there?"

Tara hadn't considered how the Dimar would consider piloting, and thought of her own first ship-a tiny fighter from the early Arrallin wars. Bonding was as good a term as any. "No, there will be no limit. In fact, Mulkol skills will be greatly needed as pilots for Starborn fighting. The first craft we make is yours."

Olitar looped in the air, broadcasting an image of a steel gray machine design that combined elements of the Mulkol crawlers and the Pride's lift engines. Shark like and elegant in design, it was chillingly beautiful, much like Olitar herself. Tara laughed! "You're getting a little ahead in the program, but that's a great design."

Olitar arched her neck proudly, "I have more where that one came from. We will build the engineering wing of the Academy first, I hope."

Tara grinned. "We'll have to ask the Leader what he thinks will be most appropriate. Should we tell him?"

"No. Let's let nature take its course." Olitar sneezed an impish Mulkol laugh, and flew back to her position beside Luuko.

Chapter 33

Luuko barely noticed Olitar as she left the formation. The seed was so eager to grow, it took all his concentration to keep it from sprouting right there in the air. He kept coaxing it to focus on flying, but it was like trying to argue with a newly hatched child. It didn't communicate in words, but what it wanted was clear.

Down Down Down Down

Up Up Up Up, Luuko would answer, keeping rhythm.

Down Food Down Food

Up Up Up Up, Luuko would answer in the traditional songs.

He grunted, swearing he'd never have any part in shelling children. He just didn't have the temperament for it.

He could see the landing site below, and thankfully, when Olitar returned, the Wind had picked up considerably. The giant pod drifted down on a strong course toward the rich soil in the clearing. It would take hours to completely bury the pod, allowing it to root, and after the long flight on a still tender wing, Luuko wondered how they'd manage.

Just over the site, Luuko changed his tune. The pod was ecstatic, leaving Luuko with a warm feeling inside.

Down Down Down Down Down

Yes. Down. Slowly Down. Food Down. Slowly Down he answered. Its relief and his were mingled. He wasn't sure who was happier.

Rich yellow light flooded the clearing. It was fully morning now. He couldn't hear Olitar or the others, but he could feel they were there helping him. He was in a kind of guide-stupor, so close to the energetic pod.

It hit the ground in the south part of the clearing, bouncing lightly as it released the sail. Crackling sparks emanated from it, as tender white shoots burst forth from the pod's underside, greedily churning the soil. Luuko scratched at his sides with his hind legs. They itched terribly, probably from the water treatment's final work.

He dug around the landing spot, instinctively knowing how to avoid damaging the ropy white shoots that the pod was putting down all around him. He took a moment to rest, enjoying the caress of the growing pod. Carefully, he slipped himself out of the pod's embrace and went back to work. Kicking up soil to cover the pod, he felt more rested and happy than he had the whole trip. It was finally happening! *This pod, my pod, my barryd, is finally safe in the ground.*

Happy. The pod answered. Or had he said it? Luuko wasn't sure.

Happy.

He felt the cold soil with a paw, wondering how the tiny pod would fare putting down this many roots so close to the freezing season. He'd be sure to cover it well, perhaps even grow a shelter seedling around it so it wouldn't be totally dormant during the cold season. They would be fine.

With the pod thoroughly coated with a hand's depth of soil, Luuko sat back on his dirt-encrusted haunches to survey his work and scan his new home.

The first face, and she was beaming from scaly ear to scaly ear, he saw as he became aware of his surroundings, was Olitar. She trilled a high approving tune.

Behind him, he could see Mason, Malik, Genar, Torula, Sebam, and the others in the guiding party. They were all excitedly talking between each other but they stopped and just trilled when he looked their way.

As the wind picked up, his eyes focused on something else quite amazing. Hanging from every tree where silks of various barryds. He padded toward one tree and sniffed experimentally. It emanated an unfamiliar scent. Olitar pointed toward the pod, but didn't approach it. He felt something bumping his pod! It registered as a tickle on his hindquarters, causing him to kick out his hind foot.

He galloped back to the pod, inspecting it's exterior. Silently, he crept along the base of the mound, stalking whatever it was that was thumping against the other side. Defensive rage welled inside of him.

"How dare you touch the growing barryd! It needs to root undisturbed." He had never felt this way about anything. Rounding the edge of the mound, he leapt forward, roaring, landing on all fours to face the invader.

Tara glared at him, arms crossed. "You might be the new Leader for this Barryd, bub, but I'm the headmaster. This is my seed too, and you darn well better welcome me in." She poked him in the nose, but couldn't keep up the angry bit for long.

"TARA! You're alive!" Joyously, he scooped her up in his muddy arms, spinning around on his tail.

"Uck!" was all Tara could manage. "Hey, don't get me all dirty. I've brought guests." She nodded over her shoulder.

Luuko dropped to his hind legs, and eyed those assembled.

He blinked, and gently set her down in the soil. A conglomeration of Leaders like he had never seen were arranged, silkless, around the seed. V's of Dimar, marked with different silks, streamed in from all directions bearing packages of gear, food, structures and all manner of supplies he had expected to go without.

"Thank you!" Luuko bowed to the large white Dimar he only knew from rumors and history lessons. It was Elakolul, one of the wisest and strongest of the farming Barryd leaders.

"We are here to help you, E...?" The white one tilted his head curiously. "What is your designation for this city?"

Luuko looked at Tara, and back at Olitar, who only shrugged. They'd been so busy planning, they had no time for a name. *Mahrmar. Everyone has forgotten her, but I have not. Her ways are part of this Barryd now.* Luuko whuffled wistfully. His mother's true name had been Sida. Sida had been a talented and fiery dancer and Tinar fighter in her youth. She'd passed her skills to him, showing him secrets of the Wind. Sida taught him the wonders of the Barryds and the Plan. She had prepared him well for this day, even if she never could have predicted it.

"Esida." Luuko sat up proudly. Tara nodded her approval, and patted him on a muddy shoulder. She tied the mud stained blanket of wine stained green and white that had been her wrap to one of his horns as an impromptu silk, and stood back to admire him.

"Leader Esida, of Barryd Esida. Please welcome your new charges." Elakolul motioned to the guide group.

Luuko tilted his head curiously as they came forward, and fell to all fours as the realization hit him. *I am Leader! I have to accept Olitar, Mason, and the others into the Barryd, or they'll be homeless. Freia and Karti have already released them from Mulkol and Telka to take residence with him! I am Esida first, the founding resident of the new Barryd.* He stared down at his muddy paws in disbelief. This was more than he'd hoped for even in his wildest dreams!

Olitar came forward, lowering her scaled head down to his forepaws. Gently, he touched the base of his chin to her forehead, chiming the traditional song to join her to the pod. He closed his eyes as her essence mingled with the pod, and him. When he opened his eyes she glowed with a blue light. Luuko's hatred for the Mulkol melted away as she became part of the Barryd. She was like Tara–resourceful, understanding, loving, altruistic. At the same time, she was fierce, competitive, proud. A powerful contradiction, but dedicated to her purpose.

One by one, the guide party mingled with the pod, welcomed by Luuko through the same ceremonious greeting, incorporating their skills, views and preferences into his own understanding.

Finally, he came to Tara. *Welcome Lady Tara! Child but not a Child you are. Come to me.* He chimed out the traditional bonding call.

But she declined, "I am a member of Esida Barryd, and it will know me over time. You know me well enough by now, Luuko." He could feel her relief at being free from a constant influx of Barryd feedback–free to be just a human again, and he nodded agreement.

Leaders, working in the mud like muck-room conscripts, assembled shelters and prepared food, dancing and singing long into the night. Reeling from the confusion and labor of his day, all Luuko could do was lie across the Pod mound and hum, watching his new home appear around him.

Happy. He thought, imagining the years to come. There was no more pod voice. It was only his. He was Esida, and his people would guard Dimar.

Happy.

Glossary, Index and Resources

ARRALLINS
Arrallin Species Profile

Arralla had 2 billion Arrallakeeni at Contact.

Arrallins left by the end of the Unwilling War: 50 million

These were split between 4,000 hives the size of San Francisco (Proper). Each hive has 50-100 breeding pairs, which produce approximately 100 kits per year. There are generally one or two breeding pairs per province in a Hive, but there are sometimes as many as 5 in a single province.

Approximately 250,000 Arrallakeeni are produced by each hive each generation (40 years).

Life span
   Alpha: 100 years
   Beta (Keeni): 80 years
Life span on Earth
   Alpha: 75 years
   Beta: 35 years

Physical statistics

Diminutive Terms used for Arrallins and Arrallakeeni on Earth:

Lupines, Felines, Fuzzies, Furries, Keeni (for only the non-Alphas)

Alphas
Height: 6'5" approximately (Both males and females)

Physical Features:
Canine in appearance, along the lines of a wolf. Two eyes, two pointed ears, with large lobes connecting down the sides of the head, one nose set on the end of a long muzzle. Generally walk on all fours, but do have a two-legged gait, and a five-legged gait that uses the tail. Tail is prehensile.

Hands:
They have opposable thumbs on both forepaws, and four toes that curl under (pads on knuckles.) Each finger or toe has a long claw (non retractable.)

Coat:
Alphas always have some kind of striking stripe pattern (black, dark gray or brown), a thick mane and a very long bushy tail that ends in a tuft. Their undercoat can range from dark charcoal gray to white, with all colors of tan, orange, brown, rust, or tawny golden. The stripes can vary in width from 5" to as thin as 1/4", giving some Alphas the appearance of being dark with light stripes. The mane may be a separate color from the coat, but the stripes are constant throughout the coat.

Eyes: Golden yellow or golden-green (Alphas only.)

Breeding:
Each Alpha has eight functioning mammary glands (both males and females.) Apart from that, males are males, and females are females. These glands do not store fat, like human breasts, so they generally lay flat under the coat unless the Alpha is raising kits at the time. Male Alphas carry fat stores on their backs for milk production. Females tend to have it more evenly distributed.

Females can produce 20-30 kits per litter three times a year.

Pairs mate for life, until the death of one member of the pair. They can then remate.

Arrallakeeni

Height: 5'3"
Physical Appearance:
Canine in appearance, along the lines of a wolf. Two eyes, two ears, one nose set on the end of a long muzzle. With Keeni, the muzzle can also be short. Generally, they walk on all fours, but do have a two legged gait, and a five legged gait that uses the tail.

Hands:
They have opposable thumbs on both forepaws, and four toes that curl under (pads on knuckles.) Each finger or toe has a long claw (non retractable.)

Coat:
Arrallakeeni have a wide variation in coats. They can have stripes, splotches, calico patterns, flea-bitten speckles, dapples, and any combination of these. Aggressive betas tend to have more striping than less aggressive ones, but this is not a rule.

Unlike Alphas, Arrallakeeni have even coats-no manes, and usually thinly coated tails (no tufts). One type of northern Arrallakeeni have long foxlike tails, but they don't have tail tufts at the end. Their undercoat can range from dark charcoal gray to white, with all colors of tan, orange, brown, rust, or tawny golden.

Eyes: Black, Brown, Tan, Blue, Blue Green, Dark Green, Gray, Violet, Hazel, Orange. Never yellow, golden or gold-green.

Breeding:
Arrallakeeni do not breed, but do parent young. Each has 2 functioning mammary glands which react to the presence of a kit

and an Alpha. A kit is usually given to a single Arrallakeeni or set of parenting Arrallakeeni a week or so after birth in an Introduction ceremony.

Details of the Introduction Ceremony

The Introduction Ceremony is a special day when Arrallin Alphas transfer kits (baby Arrallins/Arrallakeeni) to their new parents. It usually occurs when the kits are between 4 weeks and 8 weeks old. It's the equivalent of when wolves open their dens to let the pups out to play with the rest of the pack for the first time.

The families awaiting kits arrive a month or so before the Ceremony. This allows them to receive enough of the pheromone to begin lactating. Once they've received their new kits, they remain at the royal complex for another month or so. They are allowed to help with the den cleaning and babysitting duties under the watchful control of the court Keeni before the Introduction Ceremony. This also gives the Arrallins a chance to see how the parents are with the kits before they make the assignments and decide which kit goes with whom. The kits are too young to be aware or have any kind of a parental preference, and like humans, the Keeni parents-to-be are almost always so happy to be adopting that they don't have a preference for kits either.

The Arrallins have spent the last 6 weeks to 2 months cooped up in the den room of the Hive building. This room is usually in the basement, but can vary depending on the location of the hive. If it was in a swampy area prone to flooding, it might be the highest room in the building. It's always in the safest place — the heart of the hive complex.

The day before the ceremony, the great hall or meeting place of the royal complex is scrubbed down and festooned as you might imagine with banners of all the Arrallin and Arrallakeeni families' coats of arms, flowers, table cloths and runners, etc. The kits are washed up and wrapped in receiving blankets, and the Arrallins also get much-needed relaxing baths, as do all the court. The Arrallins dress in their court finery: chains of state, carrying traditional symbols of hive leadership-carved staves, etc. Alpha kits remain with the Arrallin royals to be trained to one day run a Hive of their own. Their receiving blanket is red, to set them apart from the other kits, who are usually swaddled in white or light pastel blankets.

The Arrallins process to the dias at the end of the hall, followed by two rows of courtiers carrying one kit each. If there is an Alpha kit, the female Arrallin carries him/her. Some speeches are made, and one by one, each family is called up to receive their new child. The name of the child (chosen by the Keeni parents) is announced by the Arrallins, and the kit is transferred to them.

After the introductions are made, the hive parties long into the night. The kits are snuggled away in cribs in the evening, and the parents may choose to stay with them, or go back to the festivities, leaving the kit under the watchful eye of a babysitter (usually another member of their immediate family). More rambunctious kits with daring parents are sometimes kept in front-carry pouches carried by their new parents if things aren't too rowdy.

Arrallin Gestation and Misc Baby Information

Gestation is about 4 Earth months long—usually between 100 and 130 days. (If food is good, the litter will come sooner.) Arrallin Alphas can have anywhere from 1 to 30 kits. If it's the Alpha female's first litter, it will probably be small, producing between 8 to 18 kits. Once she gets "up to speed", she'll regularly produce between 20 to 30 kits 3 times a year.

Child care is tough when there aren't a lot of Keeni in her royal court, because they are interim wet-nurses. Basically, the Alphas have 8 nipples each, and can easy nurse 16 kits. They can even handle as much as 20-25 themselves as a pair, but they won't be happy about it. Keeni have 2 nipples each, and immediately produce milk with the birth of the kits, since they're in closest contact with the Alphas. These Court Keeni generally don't adopt the kits permanently, but act as food source backup for the exhausted Alphas. A court usually consists of 5-12 Keeni who act as royal advisors as well as wet-nurse-aides to the Alphas.

Then, after eight or so weeks (depends on hive), non-court individuals or mated pairs of Keeni who have been living in the royal complex for the last few weeks to start milk production adopt the kits and take them to their own houses as their permanent children.

Child care for Arrallins is interesting. The young are born with spotted coats and downy fur, with eyes closed and deaf, and without teeth. It takes a month and half usually for all the kits' eyes to open and for them to develop hearing. It takes another five or so months for teeth to appear. I based the Arrallins a bit on cats—who have an interesting 'replacement' for diapers. Cats actually have to lick their babies to stimulate them to go to the bathroom, and then eat the results. However, I think this is a bit too gross—dealing with dirty diapers every day has made me rethink using this with Arrallins...I wouldn't want to role play that on a game. ;) So, instead, they do still have to stimulate the babies to get them to go, but have diapers for them, or some kind of receptacle for the waste. This is much easier than human babies, because you can always know when the baby's going to go, because you cause it. If an Arrallin parent waits to long to help the little guy go, though...It's explosively bad, and leads to a very fussy, and messy, kit! Arrallins and Keeni place the kits in a special tub and stimulate them to go to the bathroom with washcloths—probably 8-12 times a day for the first month, and then 6 times a day after that until about the age of 4-5 months when they're mobile, and can "use the litterbox".

Kits are mobile by about 4-5 months (crawling on all fours, or using a five legged gait involving the tail). They're like puppies-trying to eat everything. This is when the adults can start them on solid food. After 2-3 months of nursing and eating solids, the kits can generally wean (around 7-8 months old Earth time). They don't try their two-legged gait until they're around a year old, but they will be very handy (and mouthy) early on, experimenting with gripping and manipulating objects, just like a human baby, but faster developing.

The tail is prehensile, too, so they may start to try to climb or hang on it, or pick things up with it.

Arrallin Glossary

Alphas-The dominant breeding pairs of Arrallins are referred to on Earth as Alphas.

Arralla-The home world of the Arrallin species, found by Earth early in its Gate Program.

Arrallakeeni-The Beta members of the Arrallin species refer to themselves as Arrallakeeni. Keeni is a diminutive affectionate term.

Arrallins-Both Alpha and Beta members of the Arrallin species are referred to as Arrallins by humans, however the term Arrallin is only used to refer to Alphas in Arrallin society.

Furries, Fuzzies, Lupines-Derogatory term for Arrallins.

Ir'est-First Mate in Arrallin naval terms

Ir'kalan–First advisor to an Arrallin royal court. This is like a king or queen's right hand advisor, or a vice president.

Ir'mora-Chief engineer in Arrallin naval terms

Ir'tarku–First Warleader. This is the equivalent of a five star general in the Arrallin military.

Schnu-Arrallin expression, equivalent to 'Heh' or 'Yeah'. (It's more of a snort than a word)

Introduction Ceremony-This is a special day when Arrallin Alphas transfer kits (baby Arrallins/Arrallakeeni) to their new parents. It usually occurs when the kits are between 4 weeks and 8 weeks old. It's the equivalent of when wolves open their dens to let the pups out to play with the rest of the pack for the first time.

DIMAR
Dimar Species Profile

Dimar are divided into two main species groups: warbreed and peacebreed.

Physical Characteristics

All known Dimar are hexpedal (six-limbed), with two forelegs, two wings, and two hindlegs. The main body of a Dimar is very much like that of a dog or cat, with long forelegs, ending in graceful six-toed paws (four central fingers, and a thumb to either side.) The hind legs are well muscled, like a cat's, for leaping, and also have six toes: four central toes for propulsion, and two thumbtoes for hanging from vertical surfaces or branches.

All Dimar have a long graceful tail, and almost all Dimar tails end in a tail-blade or spade of some kind. All Dimar have fur, even if it's only a few tufts in the ears. All Dimar have long necks, very much like that of a heron or a python.

In both subspecies, the Dimar face consists of a long camel-like or reptilian snout with large eyes. These eyes are overshadowed by expressive, pliable muscular brows which provide shade, protection and expression for the Dimar. Extending from the rear of each brow are two horns. Horn configurations can vary widely from Dimar to Dimar, but the textures generally found are: striated (like tree-bark), smooth (like metal), spiral-texture (like a seashell or unicorn/narwhal horn), ridged, or bumpy. Below the horns are two fairly long ears, equine in shape. However, unlike horse ears, they do not stand upright, but tend to lay along the skull and neck of the Dimar for aerodynamics. A Dimar can flip his ears forward and up like a horse to get a better sound picture of an area, but most of the time this isn't necessary.

Dimar are warm-blooded animals. They regulate their own body temperature internally and do not require prolonged periods of exposure to heat or cold to moderate their internal processes. However, most members of the species do enjoy a long snooze in the sun, or a cool dip in a pool on a hot day.

Feeding

Dimar are omnivors, eating pretty much all animals native to Dimar (and a few that came from Earth) as well as many plants. Due to years of wars and genetic tinkering, they are impervious to most food-borne illnesses native to the planet. A large two-lobed liver provides a strong filter for poisons in the foods they eat as well. Despite the amazing ability to digest just about anything safely, Dimar are picky eaters, and have a tendency to be quite gourmet in their tastes. Just because they can eat something doesn't mean they like it.

They don't cook quite as much as humans do, but they do like to marinade their foods with various herbs and flavors to add variety. Warbreed Dimar are particularly fond of hunting, as it improves their war skills. Peacebreeds tend to slaughter their herds in an organized fashion to maximize the preservation of the freshness of the meat over time.

They do use cups for drinking, and plates or large round trough-pedestals for serving food. They also have knives and other utensils for serving food. However, these aren't always used–there is no taboo on Dimar for using your hands or your mouth to eat directly. An individual is allowed to use whatever works best for them, providing it doesn't inconvenience other diners. For instance, it would be bad form for a Dimar to bring a live morrak into a room and slaughter it on the table, as it would make a mess, noise and disturb other diners.

Breeding

All Dimar lay eggs. The usual clutch is 1 to 2 eggs. About 20% of fertile layings result in only 1 egg being produced, or the second egg not being viable. Many couples forgo mating in order to provide infertile eggs for the production of lita sacks used to carry Water to defend the barryd against fires.

All Dimar mate in a way very similar to mammals or birds on Earth. Courtship and pre-coital activity is long and complex, consiting of dances to impress a mate, and other dances and caresses to cement the bond. Dimar do not mate for life, and different partners in different breeding seasons is common. However, there are those pairs that are monogamous as well. A few warbreed families mate in flight, but most mate in the privacy of their homes or in other safe spaces. Dimar are as varied and versatile in their mating habits as humans. If it works, they'll use it.

Males

All male Dimar have the usual penis and testicles of male animals common to Earth. However, unlike Earth animals, Dimar do not urinate through this system. It is completely separate from the urinary tract, which actually empties into a cloaca pouch along with feces, to be discharged as a watery mass. The male sex organs are located in front of the tail vent (or anus/cloaca), in between the rear legs. Both male and female Dimar do not use urine to mark territory. Instead, the rub the sides of their faces or special glands on their eblows and heels on surfaces to mark them with scent.

Females

All female Dimar lay eggs via a duct under the tail in front of the tail vent. This mating tract is completely separate from the urinary-anal tract, and is tightly sealed closed by muscles to keep it free of any bacteria. The female must exert force to open the tract to accept a male, and must be conscious to do so. She also must be conscious and work hard to lay her eggs when they're ready for transfer to a nest or pouch. It is as difficult as human labor in some respects.

Eggs and Incubation

During times of peace, these eggs are usually incubated in an artificially warmed nest within the Barryd home of the Dimar for a period of five months. In the case of warbreed Dimar and peacebreed groups in cold climates, the eggs are cared for in a large crèche—a central protected room in the barryd where all parents bring their eggs to be warmed and guarded. They take shifts watching and turning the eggs. The eggs in this situation tend to synch up and hatch within 5 days of each other. Each parent knows which eggs are theirs, and which offspring, by smell, and immediately stow their children away in their pouches after they hatch. Dimar will adopt each others' children, but only if the original parents of the eggs have died.

The Dimar Pouch

However, for unsettled times or travel, Dimar have evolved a system for tending eggs and young hatchlings. Between the shoulderblades, on all Dimar, males and females, there is a pouch. This pouch is lined with downy fur, and is very strongly muscled to create a rigid casing around the passenger if protection is needed during a fall. Most of the time, the pouch will softly carry its contents with a gentle hold. The only 'live births' that occur are when an egg hatches when being carried inside a Dimar pouch.

Communication

All Dimar possess the ability to Mind-Speak. This is a telepathic mind-to-mind exchange of both words (symbolic communication) and images (exact visual communication). It's not actually 'telepathy', but explainable through science. It's very much like radio or magnetic waves. It is easier to broadcast words over a distance than pictures. All of an individual's mind-speaking has a particular flavor, voice or signature pattern that identifies the source of the message. Only a master mind-speaker can disguise their signature. Mind-to-mind communications, especially pictorial ones, are very specific and filtered by the experience of the broadcaster, which creates a very clear, almost indelible signature. Word communications are more easily disguised.

These mind-waves are broadcast and received not via the Dimar's ears, but actually via the horns, which act as antennae. Each horn encases thousands of broadcasting and receptive cells, tuned to the communications frequencies of the electromagnetic field of Dimar, referred to as the Wind. (The Wind is not like the magnetic field of Earth...it is another kind of field that we do not yet know how to detect.) It is excruciatingly painful to have a horn broken or altered. Changes or repairs to horns are always done with great care and under heavy painkillers and sedation, as this is the equivalent of brain surgery, but unlike the brain itself, Dimar horns have nerves below the thick protective covering.

Distinguishing Features between Warbreed and Peacebreed Dimar

The warbreed and peacebreed Dimar differ in several ways:

Horns

All warbreed Dimar have brachiated (branched) horns, with spikes emerging from the main horn at intervals. Some warbreed Dimar also have horns rising from their brows. These alterations were made during the Barryd Wars to allow the warbreed Dimar to directly interface with their warships. They drove their ships via psi broadcasts through their horns, and these additional spikes provided different sub-channels for controlling weapons systems, or even different divisions and other ships within their squadron.

Peacebreeds have the natural non-brachiated horns, which only allows them to interface with the most basic functions of a Dimar warship (unless they or the ship has been specially altered to fit them.) This ensured that the peacebreed, or slave Dimar, were unable to use the warbreed ships against their opressors.

Tail-blade

All warbreed Dimar have at least one tail blade, and have a thicker, stronger tail than peacebreed Dimar. It is used as a weapon in many territorial dances, mating dances or in battle.

Some peace breeds are lacking this chitinous protrusion entirely but most have a smaller, single tail-spade as is naturally found on the species.

Scales

All warbreed Dimar have scales year-round. Most warbreeds have a thick fur under their scales, but some do not, and use subcutaneous fat for warmth.

Peacebreed Dimar only have scales during the fire season, in order to protect their fur from the heat of the fires that annually ravage the mainland.

Eyes

Some warbreed Dimar naturally have cat-like eyes, rather than birdlike/human eyes. This gives them night vision, but the trade off is that they don't see color or detail quite as well.

All peacebreeds have human-like eyes (but with better long distance viewing), but they do not work well in the dark.

Alterations made with the Water can give any Dimar a hybrid eye structure that has the clarity of a hawk eye, the night vision of a cat eye, but the with color and detail reception of a human or bird eye. This is one of the most popular Water alterations Dimar will choose to have done to themselves.

Dimar Glossary

Acolytes-Acolytes are aids to the Great Mother or Father of a Barryd. They specialize in monitoring the Barryd plant-collective itself, and coordinating the efforts of the other arts in a barryd. They're essentially upper management, but they actually are effective (unlike most Earth upper management). See section on Acolytes below.

Arnas-These are the academies and universities where Arts and Crafts are taught. Everything from textiles to animal husbandry to music to trade and economics are taught in various Arnas. Every Barryd has several Arnas, but one particular Craft or Art
usually comes to the fore in older Barryds and becomes associated with it. For example, Calsida is the first planetary defense barryd (formerly Esida).

Barryd-A collection of plants and animals all working on concert to provide a stable self-sustaining ecosystem that supports all. Barryds tend to evolve into large cities over the course of thousands of years.

Barryd Types (Designations)
Not all are listed. More will be added to the website as Dimar evolves.

Ela-Farming study. Ela barryds focus on food production for trade, and often evolve as sub-barryds within a larger barryd of another type.

Cal-Planetary Defense. This is basically war arts, but with a focus on defending the planet as a whole from outside invaders. For political reasons, it was not given the designation Mul.

Mul-War arts. This is the study of ceremonial combats and combat dances through full scale Barryd warfare. It has Ela, Telkai and other divisions. (Multai is sub-class of Mul arts, a form of extreme wrestling, created by Ian Munro and described in his wonderful short story. Search for it on the Web–you'll be glad you did!)

Mir-Animal Breeding. Mir barryds focus on selective breeding of animals to produce new, stronger breeds, as well as maintaining large herds for sale or trade. They do work with Tel barryds on occasion, but prefer a 'back to basics' old style of animal husbandry to all that new fangled Water technology. The more extreme Mir barryds are equivalent to the Amish in America.

Olu-Arts and Crafts. These barryds focus on the creation of artwork, goods, performances and entertainment. They tend to be small, idyllic places, and are often chosen as retirement or vacation spots for Dimar who are not strongly connected with their central barryds. They also tend to be centers of wealth on Dimar because of their heavy Guild influence and surplus of tradeable goods.

Tel-Engineering Arts. Tel barryds focus on trying new technologies to tame the firestorms on Dimar in the dry season, as well as testing new configurations for the barryd plants for maximum efficiency. Tel artisans tend to enjoy cutting edge technologies. (See Telkai)

Tinar (Tin)-Firefighting Arts. Tinar skills also include precision flying using Wind lift, forcing back fires through Wind channeling and fire planning and control.

(and others...See Craft Conventions list below)

Dimar-The dragonlike species native to Dimar. Dimar is synonymous with 'earth' or 'truth' in the thinking of the Dimar.

Mul Dimar-Are a type of Dimar that evolved after years of Barryd wars. They believe they invented what they refer to as 'lesser

Dimar' (non-Mul) with Telkai engineering, but both are evolved from the most ancient Dimar, the Dimu, who are long since lost. A majority of Mul Barryds abandoned Dimar for star travel when the Barryd Wars resulted in the destabilization of the ecosystems and atmosphere of Dimar. The non-Mul Dimar at this time had been enslaved and used for production. They were left to die on the planet.

Firescales-Scaled plates that coat a Dimar during the Fire season. The scales are effective heat reflectors, as well as protecting the underfur of the Dimar while fighting fires.

Guilds-Each art has a guild associated if there is a sellable or tradable product produced through the study of the art. Guilds are like for-profit corporations, whereas the Arts tend to have a more religious feel to them. All guilds, regardless of the craft, have one mission: profit. The Arts are more academic in nature.

Leaders-Each Barryd has one Leader, who is the personification of the health of the Barryd-collective as a whole. They're like a thermometer for all the plants and animals that are linked to the Barryd.

Lita-A water carrying sack used by fire patrols for emergency healing of plants, animals or Dimar. It is made from the shells of infertile eggs laid by Dimar of a barryd. Resisting the urge to mate to create litas is considered an honorable sacrifice. Barryd members who do this are rewarded with gifts.

Miruls-Another species of Dimar meat-producing grazers. They're much smaller than morraks (the size of a whitetail deer or thereabouts, only shorter) and are easier to herd.

Morraks-Large ox-like animals with long rabbit ears and long tails that end in puffs. They lack horns, but have sharp three toed hooves. These massive creatures are relatively docile by Dimar standards, although their sheer size makes them dangerous to humans and earth animals in most cases. They were not given psi ability, as they are destined to be food. Oolars are used to move them.

Murrkila-Mainland. Mainland is the largest continent of the big 5 on Dimar. Dimar has 5 large landmasses and 11 sub-continental islands.

Nila-The monetary unit of non-Mul Dimar. They are large sheets of paper printed with a variety of symbols showing from which Barryd they originate, as well as their value and other features to make them harder to duplicate. Nila also come in a solid form–a sheet of wood or metal with the same impressions made as on the paper version. However, humans and Arrallins find these too difficult to work with.

Numu-tiny lemur-like tree dwellers.

Oolars-These creatures are Dimar pets. They are canine in appearance but are about the size of a large tiger and have a tiger-like tail. They have curving ram horns on their head, and tusks that emerge from the lower jaw. These features are remnants of when they were bred for war thousands of years earlier. They have mild psi abilities to make them easier to control.

War Oolars-This is the Mul version of an Oolar and are about the size of a large horse. They have protective scaling, much like firescales, and more pronounced horns and tusks. They are vicious fighters, adept climbers and have mild psi capabilities that make them easy to control. Some have wings, but most were bred for going into Barryds and slaying refugees hiding in the lower chambers, or for digging up the roots at the interior base of the Barryd to stun it or kill it.

Ranks-Each art or division of a barryd consists of many ranks. There is no set number. Lower ranks are lesser skilled, and are marked with higher numbers. The leaders are Rank 0, and First Rank are usually masters or peers of the leaders of the rank.

stripling-a term for a youngster. In the case of Dimar, approaching the age of its first flight. (around 4 cycles-8 years)

The Isle-The largest of 11 sub-continental islands on Dimar. It is considered Mul territory, and sacred ground, and non-Mul Dimar regard it as Hades.

Telkai-The great hero of Dimar's early Barryd Wars, as well as the study of genetic engineering and form improvement. It is considered an engineering and management branch of the healing arts.

Turaks-An early attempt at Telkai engineering that resulted in a species that failed and died out. Miruls were used as a base for these animals.

Water-A prized tool of all Barryds for growing and healing, the Water is a form of genetic altering material. In earth terms: It's a set of programmable viruses and cell-technology machines that can alter forms and give then a new genetic code, or can take the existing genetic plan and repair the object based on that blueprint. Dimar also has an abundance of regular water (H_2O). The Water is only found in Barryds or in special carrying sacks called Litas.

Wind-Wind is a form of magnetic field that envelops Dimar. It's very much like Earth's magnetic field, but magnitudes larger and stronger. As Earth hardly has any Wind, so our science was not evolved to sense it.

velvet-A protective, nutrient carrying membrane that covers a young Dimar during its infancy and adolescence. The velvet is lost in a fire-ritual to mark the transition to young-adulthood.

More Details on Dimar
(Special Thanks to the folks of DimarMOO for asking great questions that have helped me flesh out the world in much greater detail)

Dimar Acolyte System

Acolytes are sub-administrators of the Barryd. It's a bit like being in a Craft or an Art, but since Barryds are so important, it's almost more of a religious position, so it's given the term Acolyte. It has ranks, just like in the crafts, except they are ordered backwards from the crafts...where 1 is the lowest (apprentice) and it goes up to an arbitrary number based on the Arna's number of classes, specialties, etc. With Acolytes, being the Acolyte first is the highest you can be without being the 'Arch (Matriarch/Patriarch/Great Mother/Great Father/Leader) of the Barryd itself.

The number of sub ranks for Acolytes is arbitrary, but it's around 6 for a small barryd and 12 for a full barryd. There can be more than one acolyte per rank...and some ranks might be completely empty—a barryd may lack a second acolyte, for instance.

Generally, each rank in the Acolyte system corresponds to some administrative task of the barryd.

Acolyte firsts are the personal assistants to the Leader. They need to be just about as well tuned into all the activity of the barryd as the leader him/herself.

Acolyte Seconds deal with the barryd plant itself-overseeing engineering crews and construction, helping planning how the barryd will grow over time and deciding what the barryd can support. This takes a very complete understanding of how the barryd interacts with its local environment.

Acolyte third level deals with nutrition and trade, bringing materials to the barryd that the plant itself needs to grow.

Forth and Fifth deal with crops and farming to keep the animal populations of the barryd fed, and deciding which items can be used for trade or need to be stockpiled.

Sixth level deals with special features of the barryd-the records storage portion of the plant (where simulations are done, histories are kept...it's like the TV/Cable/Computer/Radio portion of the plant).

Seventh deals with Water, another special feature.

Eighth deals with firefighting and military border patrols (keeping the barryd safe)-It's kept low in the hierarchy just because the peacebreeds dislike war arts, but it's so necessary it's still above 12.

Ninth deals with internal barryd administration, helping assign existing rooms to various residents and working fair housing to meet the needs of residents. (Often, this just means overseeing a free market for the rooms, though. Only extremely crowded barryds, old barryds that have used up much of their lands, need to do room assignments to keep things fair.)

Tenth deals with the justice system, overseeing individual disputes in the Barryd.

Eleventh oversees the mechanics of trade-kind of like a Chamber of Commerce, since the Arts and Crafts themselves usually do much of the legwork for trade. This is just the official administrative branch that helps things along.

Twelfth acolytes are jacks of all trades. They're apprentices usually, learning about each level by acting as aides to other Acolytes in other levels.

This system is flexible, though, and can vary by Barryd. Barryds with serious fire problems might move that Rank to 4 or 5, moving down things like herd management and crops. Barryds near Mul barryds might separate War Arts from firefighting because they need serious full time soldiers to keep from losing territory.

Dimar Art and Craft System

(A snippet from a conversation with Leighton re: Crafts on Dimar)

There's a craft on Dimar for anything you can imagine people or Dimar needing, the same way there's a company to provide every good we need these days on Earth. The difference is that Dimar wouldn't call them by their human term...Dimar would have a word or term for each craft.

Just list off the crafts and I'll find the term the Dimar would use to describe it. I have some of them already designated, as Barryds themselves eventually associate themselves with a particular Art or Craft (Telka does Telkai, Mulkol does Mul, war arts) There's a list at the end.

The Crafts aren't organized quite like (some other roleplaying game) crafts, either...there's not a top master for the entire Craft type, although guilds and associations do exist within a particular craft—like individual corporations. This is the production side of a Craft. The guild masters run the equivalent of stores and factories to sell the goods to the Barryds. It's not medieval, where the crafts are required to provide the goods. It's capitalistic. They're really corporations. But, generally, in return for not paying taxes to a particular Barryd, a Guild of a craft located in a barryd will provide a certain amount of it's services to the barryd for low cost or free—so it does have that medieval 'if the town needs it, it gets it' feeling that the guilds had in medieval times.

The way a particular craft group is set up within a Barryd depends greatly on the individuals in it...every barryd is different... there are as many ways to work things out as you can imagine. Also, there can be more than one craft group of a particular type in each Barryd—competition is good for quality. :) It's not a rigid system...The Dimar are a very flexible species, much like humans.

Then, there's the 'Arts' part of a particular craft field. The Arnas are the learning halls for various crafts. Arnas are the equivalent of state colleges, usually sponsored by the Barryd in which they're located through the Dimar equivalent of Tax Dollars. :) A Tel Arna teaches Telkai. A Tinar Arna teaches firefighting. A Ewl Arna would teach weaving, a Naki Arna would teach music, etc. However, this is just my interpretation of how the Crafts on Dimar work. Dimar is a shared world. This means I'm not the final authority. If someone else has would like to define the crafts another way, they should do that. Dimar is an open book...designed for you to take liberties, so please do!

Craft Reference Conventions

A school dedicated to a particular Craft is an Arna. For example, a Tel Arna for biological engineering, or a Naki Arna for music. A master or ranking member of a craft (equivalent of a president or VP) is often referred to by the three or four letter prefix for his or her craft. Tel Kirra would be a master or ranking member of Telkai arts. It's like 'Dr.'

The Craft and City Designation List

Telkai (Tel) is animal/plant genetic engineering (Tel)

Tinar (Tinar) is firefighting subspecialty of Telkai

Mulkai (Mul) is war arts/combat/weaponsmaking

Multai (Mult) is a martial art wrestling subset of Mulkai (thanks to Ian Munro!)

Ekai (Eka) is healing arts

Elai (Ela) is farming

Mirrai (Mir) is animal breeding

Illai (Illa) is transport/trade

Oluai (Olu) is arts and crafts-not Arts and Crafts...just the production of decorative items (wall hangings, decorations, painting, sculpture-pure esthetic, non functional)

Ewlai (Ewl) is weaving

Nakai (Nak/Naka) is music

MAP OF DIMAR

The map is not yet complete. It's missing many mountain ranges and environmental features-especially on the continents that the first book didn't mention in detail. But, think of it this way-that's all the more room for you to make up your own Barryds, Hives and Towns! Please check at www.dreslough.com or www.Dimar.org for the latest map information on all variations of the world Dimar.

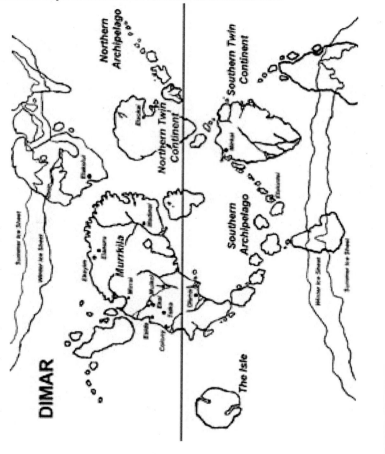

Other Illustrations

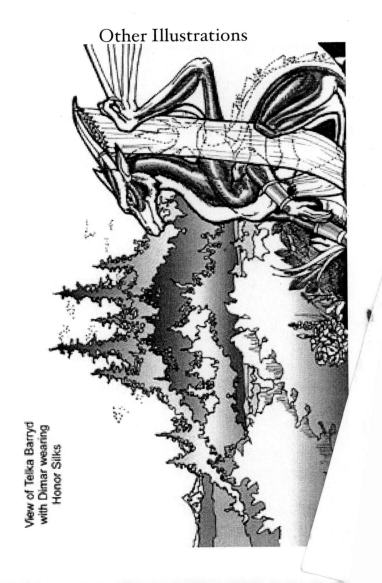

View of Telka Barryd with Dimar wearing Honor Silks

Arrallins

Alpha Male

Alpha Female

Beta Female
(Arrallakeeni)

Beta Male
(Arrallakeeni)

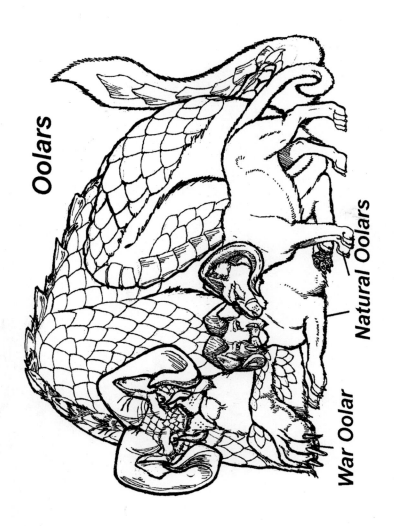

Oolars

Natural Oolars

War Oolar

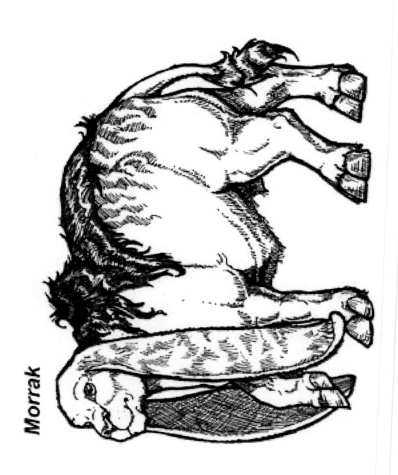

Morrak

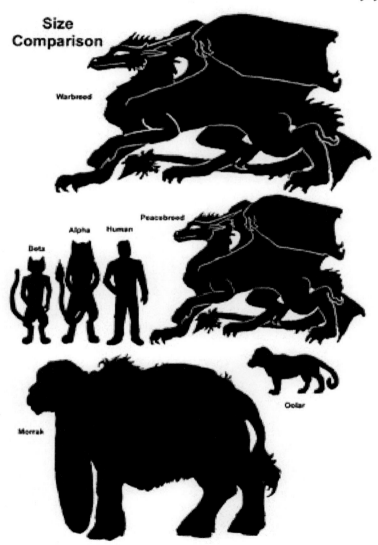

Size Comparison

Warbreed

Peacebreed

Beta

Alpha

Human

Oolar

Morrak

ABOUT THE AUTHOR

Dee Dreslough is 30-year-old fantasy and science fiction artist and web manager living in Massachusetts with her husband, Clay, her daughter Ellie, two cats and two goldfish. Artistically, she is best known for her dragons and Dimar, a species of fur-bearing dragons, as well as depictions of fantasy creatures. Currently she works mostly in digital but she does dabble with acrylics and black and white work. She is also working on a series of dragon and dimar sculptures to help young artists visualize and draw dragons themselves.

ABOUT GREATUNPUBLISHED.COM

greatunpublished.com is a website that exists to serve writers and readers, and remove some of the commercial barriers between them. When you purchase a greatunpublished.com title, whether you receive it in electronic form or in a paperback volume or as a signed copy of the author's manuscript, you can be assured that the author is receiving a majority of the post-production revenue. Writers who join greatunpublished.com support the site and its marketing efforts with a per-title fee, and a portion of the site's share of profits are channeled into literacy programs.

So by purchasing this title from greatunpublished.com, you are helping to revolutionize the publishing industry for the benefit of writers and readers.
And for this we thank you.